To Tricia
with warmest good
wishes for your health
and love from

[signature]

# 25 KILOS OF BUTTER

# 25 KILOS OF BUTTER

John Piper

Book Guild Publishing
Sussex, England

First published in Great Britain in 2012 by
The Book Guild Ltd
Pavilion View
19 New Road
Brighton, BN1 1UF

Typesetting in Baskerville by
Keyboard Services, Luton, Bedfordshire

Printed in Great Britain by
CPI Group (UK) Ltd, Croydon, CR0 4YY

A catalogue record for this book is available from
The British Library

ISBN 978 1 84624 675 3

*To Edith and Hans*

# Contents

# Cast of Characters

(In order of appearance in the narrative)
Clotilde Schultz – aged seven years in 1935
Fräulein Ulrike Müller – Schoolteacher to Clotilde
Eloise Hoffmann – best friend of Clotilde
Lisa Schmidt – classmate of Clotilde
Lilli Hahn – mischievous classmate
Millicent Lehman – teacher's pet
Greta Fischer – normally well-behaved schoolgirl
Kurt Zimmermann – aged seven in 1935
Marlena Zimmermann – aged ten in 1935 and sister of
  Kurt
Romhilde – maternal grandmother of Kurt
Fritz Fuchs – brownshirt
Bertina Schmidt – fellow train passenger
Wilhelmina – mother of Bertina
Genevieve, Karlie and Hermann – Bertina's children
Manfred Schultz – schoolteacher father of Clotilde
Suzanne Schultz – Clotilde's mother
Margit Schultz – older sister of Clotilde
Conrad Neumann – friend of Carl von Ossietzky
Lorelei Lang – maid to Romhilde
Lothar Meyer – fisherman
Maximillian Zimmermann – Kurt's father
Mitzi Zimmermann – Kurt's mother
Engelbert – first mate on Lothar's fishing boat

Johann Weber – police inspector on Rügen Island
Helga Köhler and Hans Krause – detective constables
Josef – son of bicycle supplier
Dr Julius Greenbaum – general practitioner to family
    Zimmermann
Dr Helga Greenbaum – née Steinberg
Nurse Greta Bauer
Joseph Steinberg – Professor of X-ray crystallography –
    with mother and father
Benjamin Klein – school science teacher – colleague of
    Manfred
Frau Esther Klein and daughter Rachel
Frau Rachel Getmann – neighbour of Schultz family
Gisela Richter – powerful passenger
Herr Fischer – geography teacher
Herr Schneider – junior mathematics teacher
Harald Quandt – stepson of Joseph and son of Magda
    Goebbels
Magda Goebbels – wife of the Minster of Propaganda
Joseph Schäfer – elderly Jew about to emigrate
Adolf Hitler – German leader
Spiridon Lewis – winner of the 1896 Olympic marathon
Jesse Owens – champion USA Olympic athlete
Conrad Braun – Maximillian's business partner
Gisela Braun – his wife
Jack Thornberry – trade attaché American Embassy,
    Berlin
Herr Meyer – teacher at Kurt's secondary school
Fritz Schäfer – headmaster at Manfred's School
Rudolph – gatekeeper at the Zimmermann factory
Nikolaus Koch – cook at the Zimmermann factory
Heinrich Schmidt – chemist at the Zimmermann factory
Sergeant Möller – regular German army
General Kurt 'Panzer' Meyer
Brigadeführer Oberon Krausse – SS

# CAST OF CHARACTERS

Heinrich Bauer – nephew of General Meyer

Maurice – butler in charge of pageboys at the Hôtel de Crillon, Paris

Madame Dimanche – watercress seller of Paris

Johann Lehman – German lawyer in Paris

Roland Freisler – Nazi judge

Marcel Petit – accused in Paris court

Bertina Hartman – junior leader of Marlena's German Girls League

Conrad Bauer – town hall official

Helmut Richter – air safety guard

Greta Lange – widow of a pharmacist

Wanda Schäfer – Suzanne's neighbour – with teenage sons Rudolph and Helmut in Hitler Youth

Two unmarried sisters –from Clotilde's apartment block

Trudie von Neumann – neighbour from apartment block

Oberst (Colonel) Engelbert König – aide-de-camp to General Meyer

Lieutenant Eloise Weber – secretary/typist in judicial party

Millicent Schmidt– secretary/typist in judicial party

Captain Conrad Lehman – lawyer in judicial party

Major Johann Jung – lawyer in judicial party

Oberleutnant Hans Köhler – Master of minesweeper KMS *Königstein*

Lisette de Lalujé – accused of harbouring an escaped slave

Marcel Mazarin – accused of listening to the BBC

Jutta Rüdinger – Reichsreferentin (Head of German League of Girls)

Josef Weber – Hitler Youth Leader

Ulrike Hofmann – school friend of Margit in Breslau

Opa – Grandfather of Clotilde – Suzanne's father

Oma – Grandmother of Clotilde – Suzanne's mother

Claude Girard – French farmer
Heinrich Schäfer – Former pupil of Manfred
Fritz Keller – Kurt's fellow anti-aircraft helper
Dr Jürgen Schmidt – elderly general practitioner
Wolfgang Braun – patient in doctor's waiting room
Wolfgang Wagner – Oberleutnant Commander Kurt's
    AA Unit Flack Tower II
Hans Weiss – AA Gunner with fractured femur
Dr Neumann – orthopaedic surgeon Flack Tower II
Lieutenant Schwarz – Group Commander of the
    Volkssturm
Gauleiter Krause – political leader of the Volkssturm
Doctor Maurice – emergency surgeon
American male nurse
Large American army sergeant
Werner Hoffman – AA colleague to Kurt at Stettin
Lord Haw Haw – William Joyce – Irish broadcaster in
    World War Two Germany
Captain Reginald Glanvill – British army medical officer
Wilhelm Weiss – former history teacher Fichte
    Gymnasium
Hermann Weiss – train driver – son of Wilhelm
Vladimir Orlov – Russian army colonel
Frau Bertina Schwartz – caretaker
Helga Schmidt – supervisor of 'Rubble Women'
Heidi Schmidt – woman in water queue
Eloise – raped woman
Dr Engelbert Richter – surgeon at the Gertrauden
    Krankenhaus
Hannah Peters – Nurse at the Gertrauden Krankenhaus
Gisela – raped twelve-year-old girl
Wolfgang – driver of donkey and cart
Farmer Bruhns
Frau Bruhns
Herr Fredericks – neighbour of Farmer Bruhns

CAST OF CHARACTERS

Nurse Captain June Cash – rehabilitation specialist
Greta Schneider – domestic assistant rehabilitation
  centre
Herr Walter Weber – headmaster of Kurt's secondary
  school
Helen Hoffmann – nurse
Günther S. (Schmidt) – former pupil of Manfred
Greta Khunsberg – leader of ski party
Klaus Schweitzer – member of ski party
Bertina Schröder – hostess at ski resort

# Acknowledgements

This book has been inspired by the lives of two German people and I have to thank them most profoundly for agreeing to be interviewed on a number of occasions in which they recalled details that could never have been found in any records or written accounts.

I wish to thank my wife Odete who has, as on previous occasions, tolerated me when my mind has drifted off to different times in different places.

I have had access to pamphlets and papers; there have been countless books written about the Second World War and some to them have been helpful to me but I have been most deeply moved by the war diary *A Woman in Berlin*. The author remains anonymous at her own request; after an initial unsuccessful German publication in 1959 she asked that it should not be republished until after her death, which took place in 2001.

I am also grateful to the family of the late Doctor Reginald Glanvill for information about their father and giving permission for his name to be included in the story.

I wish to thank Ms Diane Parkinson who has carefully read the draft, making constructive comments and suggestions. I am also grateful to my copy-editor, Robert Anderson, and Joanna Bentley, Janet Wrench and Carol Biss at Book Guild Publishing for all their help, useful advice and suggestions.

# Prologue

Berlin's most glamorous railway station, the Anhalter Bahnhof, linked the city to Europe's other great capitals and it was here that the tragic last act of the Weimar Republic was staged. Shortly after Hitler became Chancellor, Berlin's most gifted artists and intellectuals including Heinrich Mann, Bertolt Brecht, Kurt Weil, Georg Grosz and Albert Einstein gathered by the rail tracks with their bags packed for exile.

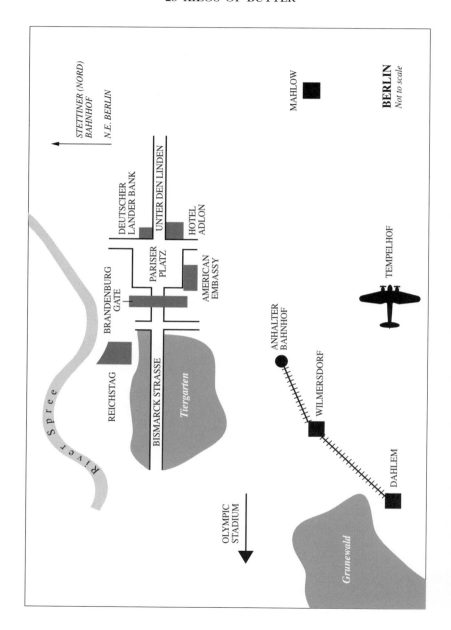

# 1

## *Clotilde – Berlin, June 1935*

Clotilde Schultz held tightly onto the left hand of the little girl walking beside her in the crocodile of smartly dressed schoolchildren following their teacher on a pleasantly warm summer morning in the great German capital city. She concentrated on the head and shoulders of Fräulein Ulrike Müller leading her pupils to the campground where she took them once a month in the fine weather to enjoy the open air.

The seven-year-old girl wore a gingham pink-and-white short-sleeved dress, white knee-length cotton socks and her fair hair, parted down the centre of her head, was tied in two plaits with pink ribbons. It was only three weeks since her birthday and she was wearing the shiny black shoes given to her by her grandmother of which she was immensely proud.

Clotilde and her companion were the third pair out of twelve following Fräulein Müller and when the teacher raised her right hand they all came to a halt as if they were one. They had come to the edge of the wide pavement on the opposite side of the main road where the bus would stop to take them to the campground at the edge of a lake in one of the forested areas outside Berlin.

'What do we say, girls, before each of us cross the road?'

'Look left, look right, look left again and if all is clear we proceed across to the other side,' the little voices piped up enthusiastically and in unison.

1

Ulrike Müller waited until the last pair of girls had set off across the apparently clear wide street and then followed behind; as she neared the bus stop she heard the approaching wailing siren that she knew belonged to one of the vehicles of the new government. Ulrike thought of it as new, although the Nazi Party had now been in power for over two years. Perhaps it was because it was so different. By the time she was on the pavement she turned her head with its short black hair and saw a lorry with an open back, crammed full of miserable-looking men, clasping bags and battered suitcases. Standing at each corner in the transport were four well-built men wearing smart full-length black leather coats and dark-grey wide-brimmed trilby hats; their expressions set in unsympathetic disregard for their forlorn charges.

Clotilde also turned her head to watch the vehicle that had so loudly drawn attention to itself pass by and she saw that there were no children among the occupants. While they were getting back into formation she raised her hand and looked at her teacher.

'Yes, Clotilde.'

'Fräulein Müller, it's such a beautiful day – why did those people in that lorry look so very unhappy?'

The schoolteacher had expected such difficult questions for some time. It was inevitable those young enquiring minds should notice what was going on around them. 'They are poor people being taken to a better home.' In truth she suspected that they were being taken to one of the concentration camps that Germany was beginning to hear of for the first time.

'Then they should look happy if they are going to a lovely new house or apartment,' Clotilde persisted.

The logic of a child can be quite disconcerting for an adult in certain circumstances and the truth was that even Ulrike did not really know what was happening to these people or many others like them in Germany. 'I'm sure there is a very good reason for what you've seen.'

The schoolteacher felt a tinge of uneasiness as she answered her pupil.

'Yes, Fräulein Muller.'

At that moment a single-deck yellow bus drew up beside the school party and the class of seven-year-old girls climbed on board followed by their teacher. Having earlier already walked the two kilometres from her home in the Dahlem district of south-west Berlin to her school, Clotilde's little legs were tired and she was grateful to sit down next to her best friend, Eloise Hoffmann. 'Are your sandwiches in there? ' She pointed to the little brown leather case on Eloise's lap.

'Yes, my mother made them with ham; I also have an apple and a bottle of orange juice.'

Eloise smiled back at her friend. She wore a bright green-and-white striped dress and her dark-brown hair had a similar style of plaits to Clotilde with matching green ribbons. 'What have you got?'

'My mother is the best cook in the world and has made cheese and brown bread sandwiches and I have an orange for afterwards.' She was very proud of her lovely mother.

Eloise giggled. 'My mother must be the second best cook in the world then.' She gave her pal a playful pinch on the arm. 'They can't *both* be the best.' They laughed loudly.

'Girls, a little decorum, if you please.'

'Sorry, Fräulein Müller.' The voices were subdued.

Just before the bus came to the Hauptstrasse it passed some tall buildings with three massive red banners flowing down from the roofs to a metre above street level. Midway down the bright-scarlet material was a large white circular spot on which was a black cross, rotated at 45 degrees, with its equal-length arms bent, facing right, at 90 degrees.

'Fräulein Müller, why are those pretty flags on those

3

houses?' Clotilde was, like so many young people, observant and had an insatiable thirst for knowledge.

Once more Ulrike Müller was faced with a question she would prefer not to answer. 'Young lady, you know we like order in our school, which means raising your hand and waiting to be asked by me before asking your question.' The schoolteacher was playing for time.

'Yes, Fräulein Müller.' The schoolgirl's right hand shot up.

'What did you wish to ask, Clotilde?'

'Why are those houses covered by large red banners with a funny cross on them?' While asking the question the inquisitive girl pointed out of the back window across the road at the fluttering drapes.

'We have had a new German government since you were five years old... What year was that, young lady?' Ulrike might not be comfortable with the direction of the questioning but felt she should try and make it as useful as possible.

There was a slight pause. '1933, Fräulein.'

'Excellent, Clotilde, and the design that you can see is called a swastika; it's the emblem chosen by Germany's new leader.' The schoolteacher was grateful that there were no more questions on the subject; she did not think politics was a suitable subject for seven-year-old girls.

The bus had now crossed the Hauptstrasse, and trees and bushes with numerous criss-crossing footpaths could be seen out of the vehicle's windows. 'We're now entering the Grunewald and as we pass through I want you to write down the names of any of the trees that you recognize.'

There was a rustling as paper and pencils were searched for in pockets and schoolbags. 'There are some very old trees in this beautiful Greenwood.' Ulrike was relieved to have diverted her charges' attention away from the rapidly changing affairs of the German state.

'I can see an oak tree!' a voice piped up at the front of the bus.

'Very good, Lisa; write it down.'

The bus was now passing along the edge of the forest and after about three kilometres it turned right along a wide pathway, crossed another horse-riding track, and continued three more kilometres until the glistening waters of the Schlachtensee came into view. There were gasps of excitement from the occupants of the bus.

'We are near our destination, girls.'

The bus gently pulled up to a halt close to a wooden table with bench seats on either side–long enough to accommodate the whole school party and Fräulein Müller, who with her own collapsible green chair, would be seated at one end.

Before the driver could reach the door to open it and let the children out into the fresh air, there was a crashing sound. One end of the heavy table rose up, a bench seat went flying through the air and a light-brown furry animal with a massive body, short stout legs and tusks near its snout shot out from underneath and headed rapidly towards the woods. There were squeals and exclamations from the alarmed pupils.

'What was that giant animal, Fräulein?'

'Will it hurt us?'

'Shouldn't we stay in the bus?'

'Keep calm, girls.' The schoolteacher was much happier dealing with this emergency rather than answering the inevitable questions about disturbing events that even young children were noticing and commenting on. 'What is the name of that animal that has just given us such a fright?'

'Hermann, Fräulein Müller.' The mischievous author of this particular answer was Lilli Hahn who had already established herself as a troublemaker in the mind of the schoolteacher.

'Lilli!' the Fräulein's voice was stern in tone. 'Your name

5

is that of a flower which is a symbol of innocence, purity and beauty…' There was a pause and a sharp intake of breath. 'Would it be too much to ask that you live up to your lovely name just a little bit?'

'No, Fräulein.' The spirited young lady was temporarily subdued.

'Now, girls, can we have a sensible answer, please?'

'It was a wild boar, Fräulein Müller.' Millicent Lehmann was not especially popular with her classmates and frequently brought a present, like a packet of chocolate biscuits, for her schoolmistress, which she placed on her desk at the front for everyone to see.

'Quite right, Millicent dear.'

'Teacher's pet,' came a voice from near the back of the bus.

'Who said that?' Ulrike was angry. No one answered. 'We're not getting off this bus until I know who made that uncalled-for remark.'

There was silence for a few moments then the voice spoke again. 'It was me.' It was much quieter this time and came from Greta Fischer, a normally well-behaved seven-year-old.

It was not such a great crime and Ulrike did have some sympathy with her; Millicent really was an irritating sycophantic child; but she could not ignore the mis-demeanour completely.

'Greta, you will remain on the bus for ten minutes after everyone else has got off and is enjoying themselves.' The poor girl looked miserable.

'Driver, would you please open the door so the rest of us can go out into this lovely summer's day.' She approached him and said quietly, 'Is this your turn-around point?'

'Yes Madam, I set off back in twenty minutes.'

Ulrike whispered to him, 'Please open the door for Greta in ten minutes.'

6

The driver smiled, 'Certainly … as you know there is a bus every hour for your return.'

'What about the wild boar, Fräulein?' Clotilde sounded anxious.

'We will be quite safe if we stay together and don't make any sudden movements.' Fräulein Müller reassured her. 'Since we have seen one we will talk about the wild boar when we have our first break.'

All but the miscreant trooped outside followed by their teacher who shut the door after her. The pupil left behind could hear her classmates squealing with delight as they chased after each other and played with a large beach ball. But Ulrike Müller was as good as her word and ten minutes later the door of the bus opened and Greta bounded out.

'Come on, little lady.' There was a friendly affectionate tone to her voice. 'Bring your lunchbox and put it on the picnic table with the others.'

Once the rest of the class saw their teacher and Greta sitting down together they ran and joined them.

'Are you going to tell us about the wild boar, Fräulein?'

'Most certainly.' She looked to see that everyone was present and performed a quick head count, and when she was satisfied that all were present she gave a rare smile and began. 'Who can tell me the difference in the appearance of the face between the mother and father boar?'

'The tusks!' Greta was anxious to get back into favour after her earlier blunder.

'Very good. Tell us some more.'

'It's the father boar who slashes upwards with his tusks when he charges; he can injure humans if he feels that he or his family are under attack.'

There were 'oohs and arrhs' of admiration from her fellow pupils.

'Greta is quite right, girls. The tusks are really two big teeth.' Ulrike was warming to her subject. 'There's something very funny about the name wild boar because boar is also what we call its domestic cousin, the man pig that is kept on the farm...' The unexpected appearance of the animal on their arrival at the campground had provided a wonderful subject for teaching her charges about the natural world.

'Does anyone know what they eat?'

'My father says they dig for roots and tubers at night.' Millicent was trying to redeem herself in the eyes of her fellow pupils but was greeted with silence.

'That's true. Sometimes they eat frogs and other small animals... Well, girls, I think we've had enough about creatures that live in the forest; it's now time for the egg and spoon race to give you an appetite for your lunches.'

Each girl took an egg and a spoon from a box at the end of the table and they went and stood in a line about fifty metres from the table and benches where Fräulein Müller stood to judge the winner.

'Remember, girls, if your egg falls onto the grass you have to go back to the starting line, replace the egg and run as fast as you can to catch up!'

Just before the race began Clotilde noticed a man wearing a black leather coat, brown trilby hat and horn-rimmed spectacles standing partly concealed behind a bush on the edge of the forest. Although she did not like the look of the person she did not say anything.

'Ready, steady and go!'

The girls set off balancing the eggs on the spoon with difficulty and quite soon a few of them were running back to start all over again. The race was won by Greta Fischer with Millicent Lehman coming in a close second, who then proceeded to glower at her for the remainder of the outing.

After everyone had finished they all sat down to discover what was in their lunch packages. Clotilde exchanged one of her cheese sandwiches for one of Eloise's ham delicacies and similar trading went on between other members of the class.

'Not too many hands on the lunch items please, girls; we don't want to spread nasty germs.'

'Or Nazi germs!' This time it was the mischievous Lilli Hahn who was responsible for the witticism.

'You're treading on very thin ice, young lady, any more of your wisecracks and a letter will be on its way to your mother.' The schoolteacher tried to hide her own amusement though her effort was not very successful – she knew that both the remark and her half-hidden smile might well be dangerous in the current political climate.

'Yes, Fräulein,' Lilli looked suitably chastened; she was clearly a very good actress.

Ulrike turned to the other girls. 'Now while our lunch settles down we will see what you all wrote down about the trees you've seen in the Grunewald.'

Clotilde stole a glance in the direction of the bush where she had seen the mysterious man, but he was no longer there.

The pupils all started talking at the same time and waving their pieces of paper and urging their teacher to look at their individual efforts. 'Girls, girls, one at a time if you please; give me your papers and I will see what is what.' They all handed in their results and the teacher sat down to read them. 'Oak and beech ... those are the oldest trees here...' She continued to leaf through the pages. 'Pine, birch, acacia and poplar...' Ulrike looked up and smiled 'You've been very observant, young ladies. Now that you've had time for your food to settle inside you I think it's time for our sack race.' She looked around her and put on her sweetest voice. 'May I have a volunteer to run and fetch the sacks which are under the oak tree over there?' Two hands shot up – Millicent's and Eloise's.

'Eloise, how very nice of you. Come back as quick as

you can.' As her pupil raced off towards the tree, Fräulein shot Millicent Lehman an icy look. 'You, young madam, have contributed enough to today's outing.'

Eloise, meanwhile, had reached the pile of sacks and saw something on the grass gleaming in the sunlight. She stooped down to pick it up and held it in her hand. It was a silver-coloured pin with a wreath made of a similar metal mounted at the top and within it was what she now knew to be a swastika and standing above it was a miniature eagle with its head and curved beak turned to its left. She imagined it to be the sort of pin that men and women wore in the lapels of their jackets; Eloise thought it would look smart on her new yellow dress and it easily pierced the light cotton just below her collar. She picked up the sacks and carried them back towards her fellow pupils and set them down on the ground keeping the one uppermost for herself.

'Thank you, Eloise...' the teacher's voice tailed off and her face paled as her gaze fixed on the decorative pin on the schoolgirl's dress. 'Where did that come from?' Ulrike knew perfectly well that she was looking at the emblem of the Nazi Party.

'It was on the grass over by the oak tree. Isn't it pretty?' The words were spoken with the endearing innocence of extreme youth.

Fräulein Müller felt she was in deep water. 'Eloise even though you think it looks good on your lovely yellow dress, I must ask you to give it to me.'

'Why, Fräulein?'

'Please do as I ask.' There was something in the tone of voice that Eloise could not contradict.

The little girl unpinned the emblem from her dress and handed it to her schoolteacher. 'Here you are, Fräulein.' She then climbed into her sack.

'Right, girls, everybody take a sack, form a straight line

10

and wait for my signal... The winner is the first to reach that beautiful tall poplar tree over there. ' She pointed at a magnificent specimen with its leaves shimmering in the light breeze and sunshine. 'Now hurry into your sacks.'

Greta Fischer put one foot into her sack and fell over as soon as she lifted her other foot. The schoolteacher hastened over to her and dusted the little girl down. 'No cuts and bruises, nothing broken...' she smiled. 'It's very difficult to stand without at least one foot on the ground!' With that she helped the little girl up onto her feet, wiped her eyes with her own clean handkerchief, and helped her to the starting line for the race.

'Thank you, Fräulein.' Greta's sombre face brightened.

After a little bit of friendly jostling for position, Ulrike's clear voice sang out, 'Ready, steady, go!'

The girls held the tops of their sacks up against their chests and, with a peal of giggles, started to jump up and down to propel themselves towards the tall poplar tree. Some fell, while others found themselves facing the wrong way, but eventually all righted their mistakes and were heading towards the winning post.

'My knickers are falling down!' the mischievous Lilli Hahn yelled.

'You'll still be respectable in your sack,' Fräulein Müller reassured her. 'Come on, girls! I do believe Greta is going to win.'

Indeed she was right and the previously unhappy girl was first to touch the trunk of the tree.

'I've won, I've won!'

'Quite right but hug your friends and tell them how well *they* did.'

As they all touched the tree and recovered their breath, Lilli Hahn could be seen doing some remarkable contortions inside her sack. 'When your legs are free, fold up your sacks neatly and bring them back to the table where we'll

11

finish our drinks before catching the bus. You will have seen a public toilet close by which you may wish to use before we set off.'

All was done as instructed and Clotilde set off towards the public convenience; she felt she was near to bursting. The building was single-storey and very clean, with separate entrances for ladies and gentlemen. This fine facility had only been in place for a little less than a year, one of many buildings that had arisen under the aegis of the new regime. The seven-year-old girl entered one of the cubicles and closed the door only to be faced with what she now knew to be a swastika crudely painted in black on the back of the door. Below the emblem she slowly read out, 'Heil Hitler', though she really did not understand what it meant. When she had finished and was walking back to rejoin her group she resolved not to tell Fräulein Müller about the mysterious picture in the public toilet. A few of the other girls were also returning from the building including Clotilde's best friend, Eloise Hofmann.

'I'm thirsty after all that sack racing. My mother packed a bottle of home-made apple juice. I will give you a sip of it if I can have a taste of your orange juice.'

'Of course you can. Did your mother really make it at home?'

'Oh yes, she makes lots of things.' Clotilde spoke with pride.

Soon they were repacking their lunchboxes with the empty bottles and were ready for the bus to take them back to the school.

'I've got a secret!' Clotilde whispered. 'I'll tell you on the bus.'

'It won't be a secret then.' Eloise giggled.

'Follow me, girls. It's time to go home. We've all had a lovely day!' Fräulein Müller set off briskly towards the place where she knew the bus would pick them up. Within a few minutes it arrived and shortly afterwards drew away from the campground with the two friends sitting side by side.

Clotilde gave Eloise a playful gentle pinch on her arm and whispered in her right ear. 'Did you see the painting on the door?'

'What door?'

'In the toilet'

'No.'

'What do you mean "no"; there was a swastika and the words "Heil Hitler" written on the inside of the toilet door.' All these exchanges were conducted in very loud whispers.

'I didn't use the same toilet as you, Clotilde.'

At that moment Fräulein Müller caught the word 'toilet' coming from the pair. 'Clotilde and Eloise, I hope your whisperings aren't rude.' There was an immediate cessation of all sound from the direction of the two girls.

The bus proceeded through the Grunewald towards Dahlem and in the middle of the afternoon twenty-four tired little schoolgirls stepped down from the yellow vehicle, thanked Ulrike Müller for a lovely outing and set off for their respective homes.

The two friends went together knowing that a large part of their two-kilometre journey would lie in the same direction. As soon as they thought they could no longer be heard Clotilde could not contain herself a moment longer. 'It was there on the back of the door in black paint, some of which had dripped down towards the floor.'

'I believe you.' Eloise thought for a moment. 'What do you think it means?'

'May be nothing at all.' There was a tinge of doubt in her voice but there was a bounce in her step as she seemed to put it out of her mind. 'Where are you going for your holidays?'

'To the seaside with all that lovely sand and ice cream.' They both laughed.

They had now reached the turning where their paths separated. They waved to each other and hurried to their respective homes.

That night Clotilde was pleased to get to bed but took a long time to go off to sleep. The truck full of sad people, the mysterious pin that Eloise had found and the ugly painting on the back of the cubicle door all stayed vividly in her mind until at last, exhaustion overtook the little girl and sleep engulfed her.

# 2

## *Kurt – Usedom Island, August 1935*

At eight-thirty on the morning of August 3rd, 1935 seven-year-old Kurt Zimmermann and his sister Marlena, who was three years older, ran to keep up with their grandmother, Romhilde, who strode briskly alongside the great steam train and carriages standing at the Stettiner Bahnhof in central Berlin which served the north of Germany.

'Come along, children, we must find coach seven.' She consulted the tickets to make sure she was correct.

After passing one more coach they boarded the right part of the train and found their seats. Kurt was quite breathless due to the long walk from the bus that had brought them into the middle of Berlin after they had left their house in the south-eastern suburb of Mahlow.

'Here at last, Grandmamma.'

'Yes and thank you for looking after us ladies, young man.' Romhilde had a twinkle in her eye. 'Now you can sit down and rest.' Kurt flopped down onto one of the seats and was followed by Marlena beside him.

Their grandmother sat down opposite the two excited young people, there were shouts, a whistle blew and there was a slight jolt.

'We are on our way to the seaside, children.'

The train slowly gathered speed as it headed north out of Berlin. Romhilde looked across at her granddaughter

15

who appeared pale with sweat on her face. 'Are you all right, Marlena dear?'

'I'm very thirsty Grandmamma.'

The older lady opened the bag in which she was carrying items required for the journey and pulled out a large glass bottle of water, a cup and a red napkin; she poured out a cupful and handed it to the young girl. 'There you are, my dear, it's getting very warm today.'

The ill-looking girl eagerly and gratefully took the cup of water from her grandmother and drank it down as quickly but in as ladylike a fashion as possible. 'Thank you, Grandmamma.' She took another gulp of water. 'Do you think it's going to be a very hot month?'

'Your father tells me that his beloved radio has told him that the weather forecasters are saying that it will be a very warm August with lots of lovely sunshine.' She smiled at her two grandchildren. 'Do you feel better now, Marlena?'

The colour had returned to the delicate features of the ten-year-old girl. 'Oh much better, Grandmamma, and I'm really looking forward to seeing the sea and the sand dunes.' With that note of excited anticipation, she and Kurt turned their attention to what they could see passing outside the train window. The streets and buildings were gradually getting smaller as they passed into the northern suburb of Pankow where the train passed through without slowing but gave a blast on its siren to warn suburban travellers to stand away from the edge of the platform. Soon they were passing through farmland and eventually the locomotive drew to a halt at Eberswalde and a tall, overweight gentleman came into their compartment; he was wearing a light-brown shirt with a peaked hat of a similar colour, his tie was dark brown as were his trousers, which were baggy and tucked into black knee-length leather boots and held up by dark-brown belt; on his left upper arm he wore a deep-red band with a black swastika set in a white circle on it. He carried a long flagpole with a small silver-coloured spear shaped tip; the flag was furled up around the pole but was also deep red. The previously serene countenance of the grandmother changed at the sight of the new arrival.

'Good morning,' the large man beamed as he took his seat. 'It's a very fine day, isn't it?'

'Yes, sir,' responded Romhilde in a quiet voice. The sensitive ear of Kurt picked up the note of fear.

'Every day is a good day now that we have the great leader Adolf Hitler to make our futures happy and prosperous.' He leaned forward and patted Kurt on the head. 'Eh, young man?'

'Yes, sir,' the seven-year-old boy dutifully replied.

'I'm going to a rally in Neubrandenburg and my name is Fritz Fuchs.' Although his uniform and bulk made him intimidating, he was trying to be friendly.

The children turned their attention back to what could be seen out of the window and were pleased to see that they were leaving the town; now the houses were replaced by fields with cows and sheep in them.

However, Romhilde's upbringing had taught her not to ignore anyone even if they were distasteful. 'That is very interesting, Herr Fuchs. When is the gathering?'

'On Saturday, madam.'

'But today is Monday!'

'I'm one of the people who have to make the preparations; there's a lot to be done.'

His chest swelled with pride. 'It will be a great day – fifty thousand of my colleagues will be present and we will be addressed by that great orator, Dr Joseph Goebbels.'

The children's grandmother definitely did not like the direction in which the conversation was proceeding; she held her own opinion about the aforementioned Minister of Propaganda; she had been told by a lady friend who

17

worked in a government department that she once overheard him say that 'If you tell a big enough lie and repeat it enough it will be believed by the masses.'

'I don't know anything about politics. I look after my grandchildren for my son and his wife who are very busy with their business; we're going to the seaside for the summer holidays.'

'All good Germans have to be interested in politics now.' The man in the brown uniform suddenly did not sound so friendly.

'Sir...' The tall slim elegant lady stood up and glared directly into the eyes of the fat man in his official clothes. 'You're speaking in front of children – stop this talk immediately!'

This was a man, so used to his own bullying tactics, was completely taken aback and lost for words. He turned away, snatched up his banner and left the compartment.

Marlena, who had witnessed the amazing performance of her beloved grandmother, rushed forward and flung her arms around Romhilde's neck. 'Grandmamma, you were fantastic; he was such a horrid man!'

Kurt joined in the hug. 'I hated it when he touched me on the top of my head; I think you're wonderful making him go like that.'

The heroine of the moment could not take the weight of both children and collapsed back on to her seat.

'I'm very grateful to you for your approval; I have to admit that I was frightened.' This statement was followed by extra hugs. 'I ask you both to forget about this incident and please don't talk about it to anyone.'

Kurt smiled. 'Not even God?'

The proud grandmother laughed. 'Oh yes you may tell him and thank him for bringing us safely through our frightening encounter with Herr Brown Shirt.'

The two children laughed with her.

'Look out of the window, children! We're approaching a town.'

Kurt and Marlena followed Romhilde's gaze and saw some red-brick houses and shortly after that a high wall then white cottages with black wooden beams in their walls. 'Ah we're arriving at Prenzlau; it's a very old town.'

The railway train gradually drew to a halt and a loudspeaker confirmed the name of the town; a short while later Fritz Fuchs could be seen striding along the platform, radiating self-importance as he headed towards the exit.

'There's that nasty man, Grandmamma. Do you think we should stand back from the window so that he can't see us?' Kurt was apprehensive.

'No I don't think so. We're very unimportant people to him; he is obviously a top man in the Party.' Her sarcasm was probably lost on her listeners.

'Why did his rally need a doctor?' Marlena sounded mystified.

'There are doctors who do other things apart from looking after you when you're ill.'

'What sort of things and how do they become doctors?'

'They've already been to university...' Romhilde had not been to university herself but was an avid reader of newspapers and spent many hours in public libraries.

At that moment there were shouts, a whistle blew and there was the sound of doors closing; again with a slight jolt the locomotive moved forward taking the passengers further on towards the Baltic Sea.

'Off again! I think our next stop will be Anklam where the train takes the branch line to Usedom Island and Seebad Ahlbeck.'

'Why do they become doctors when they're not doctors who make you better when you're ill?' Kurt persisted.

'Well, when some people have finished their university studies they can apply to do what is called research into

19

a chosen subject that greatly interests them and if the university accepts their proposal they can then investigate it and after some years that person produces a thesis on the subject; if it's good they are given the title "Doctor of Philosophy"; now no more on the matter please.'

'Can I ask just one more question please, Grandmamma?'

'All right and that will be the end about doctors who are not doctors.'

'What did Dr Goebbels research?' Marlena sounded as though she really did want to know the answer.

'I think it was Romantic drama at Heidelberg University.'

'Gosh,' there was a hint of wonderment in Marlena's response.

'Is that the Baltic Sea, Grandmamma?'

'Not yet, Kurt, that's Lake Unterucker... Now how about something to eat and drink?'

Romhilde stood up and took down a picnic basket from the luggage rack.

'Oh yes, I'm really thirsty, Grandmamma.' The ten-year-old girl was quite tall for her age but very – too – slim. 'I have been like that for some months.'

'Like what, my dear?'

'Drinking lots of water.'

'I expect it's all a part of growing up.' The elderly lady was reassuring but she had misgivings. 'We also have hard-boiled eggs, bratwurst in brown-bread sandwiches and orange juice,' she smiled sweetly at her granddaughter.

'Now I *am* hungry!' Kurt cried. 'I would like a sandwich, please.'

'Here you are, young man.' His grandmother handed him a cloth-wrapped package. 'What about you, Marlena?'

'May I have a boiled egg and a piece of brown bread?'

'Of course, my darling child.' Romhilde put an arm around the girl's shoulders and was surprised to find how easily she could feel the shoulder blades through her blue-

and-white striped dress; she reached into her basket once more, produced the hard-boiled egg, a piece of bread and poured out the drink.

'Thank you, Grandmamma. I hope you're going to have some refreshments as well.' Marlena loved her Grandmamma dearly.

'Of course I am.' A broad smile appeared on her face. 'Though I see Kurt has already finished his large sandwich.' She dipped her right hand into her apparently bottomless picnic basket and produced two more wrapped parcels. 'There you are, young man.' She handed him one of them and started to unwrap the other for herself.

Kurt's chest swelled with pride at being called young man, although he was dressed in a red-and-white check short-sleeved shirt and smart short grey flannel trousers with knee-length navy-blue socks and black lace-up shoes. 'Thank you very much, Grandmamma.' A smile crossed his face and there was a twinkle in his blue eyes. 'I'm glad you've saved one for you. I wouldn't want you to starve.'

'I should hope not.' Romhilde sat down, bit into her sandwich and looked out of the carriage window. 'I think we should be talking about our holiday and in particular where we're going.'

'Are you going to ask us to solve a riddle?' Kurt knew the way his grandmother's mind worked. 'Is it geography or history?' His enquiring mind loved her way of making him and his sister think really hard to work out the answer.

'Geography.' Romhilde was pleased to have diverted the children's minds away from brownshirts and politics.

'What is the question, Grandmamma?' Marlena was just as excited by this game.

'What is the difference between the North Sea and the Baltic?'

The children looked blank.

21

'I will give you a clue: what can you do on the beach of the North Sea that you can't do on the Baltic?'

Marlena started to bounce up and down on her train seat. 'I know, I know!' she was bubbling with excitement.

'Do you know the answer, Kurt?' Romhilde was always fair in not wishing to favour one grandchild over another.

'No, Grandmamma.' He was a little downcast and then suddenly he smiled. 'Rock pools!'

'And catching crabs!' Marlena was giggling. 'They tickle my toes.'

'And what makes the rock pools?'

'The tides! That's the difference; there's no tide in the Baltic and no rock pools!' Kurt was really pleased with himself for having solved his lovely grandmother's puzzle. 'When do we turn off towards Usedom Island?'

'Oh not for another seventy kilometres, after we arrive at Anklam Station.' The train was gathering speed as it headed north.

'I expect we'll be joined there by some "hooray for the holidays" passengers from other parts of Germany.' Romhilde spoke from a long experience of vacations on the Baltic coast.

Sure enough within an hour they had come to a halt at Anklam station and some adults with even more children appeared on the platform outside the carriage windows and noisily boarded the train; the grandmother noticed with a shudder of distaste one family of four with a boy and a girl wearing red swastika armbands on their upper arms. The man in the party carried a copy of *Der Stürmer*, '*The Stormer*', the Nazi Party newspaper, under his arm.

Three children and two women came into the Zimmermanns' compartment. 'Good afternoon,' the younger woman greeted them.

She replied with a courteous and smiling 'Good afternoon'

and then introduced Marlena and Kurt. 'We're going to Seebad Ahlbeck; may I ask where you're holidaying?'

The lady exclaimed, 'What a coincidence – so are we!' She turned to the older lady beside her. 'this is my mother, Frau Brandt, and I'm Bertina Schmidt. These are my children, Genevieve, Karlie and Hermann.' They all shook hands, sat down and shortly afterwards the train was on the move again.

'Is this your first holiday on Usedom Island?' Romhilde enquired in a kindly tone.

For the first time Frau Brandt spoke. 'Oh no, I came here many years ago but it's the first time for my daughter and her children. ' She gained confidence as she continued. 'We live in Munich, so we've had a very long journey, though we've just stayed overnight with my other daughter in Anklam.'

'You must be tired...' Marlena spoke with feeling. 'We've only come from Berlin and I'm feeling quite weary already.' She managed a smile at the other children.

Genevieve sympathized. 'I don't feel particularly tired; we went to bed rather early last night.' She moved across the compartment and sat beside Marlena. 'I expect you had to get up really early this morning.'

'Yes we did. We had to catch the bus from Mahlow where we live.' She was pleased to have found a new friend. 'I'm sure I will feel better once we get onto the lovely sandy beach.'

Marlena looked out of the window. 'Look, Genevieve, those houses over there must be on the edge of Wolgast.'

'That's right. My mother's brother used to live there.' A sad expression appeared on the girl's face. 'He's not there now.'

'What happened to him?'

'He's a really nice man – tall, fair-haired, good-looking and we loved him especially when he brought presents to us in Munich.' Genevieve stole a glance in the direction of her mother. 'He was always friendly and Karlie, Hermann and I often wondered why he wasn't married; he didn't even have a girlfriend, though he did have a special friend called Hans; Mother doesn't like us talking about him.'

Marlena's curiosity was aroused. 'What's his name?'

'Friedrich,' the words were whispered, 'he disappeared last summer.'

'Didn't you try and find him?'

'We were told he had had gone to a special hospital for treatment...' Genevieve looked over at her mother who already had a frown on her brow. 'I mustn't say any more; it only upsets Mother.'

Marlena was left intrigued but did not say anything more about the mysterious relative. 'I do hope we're staying near each other and close to the beach.' She felt she had made a good friend and her spirits rose.

Kurt's face was close to the window and there was a curve in the railway line. 'I can see the bridge onto Usedom Island; come and look, Grandmamma.'

His excitement was infectious. Romhilde rose from her seat and stood behind her grandson resting her hands on his shoulders. 'Oh yes, it's the Peenemünde Bridge – it's been lowered for our train...' Her face showed her pleasure. 'It's lovely to be back here again, I can hear the sand singing already.'

Kurt looked up at her over his shoulder. 'Is that true, Grandmamma?'

'Would I tell you a lie, Kurt?'

'I'm sure you would never do that, so the sand does sing.'

'Absolutely, this beautiful symphony takes place on Usedom beach; when the wind conditions are quite right the rubbing together of the fine white grains of sand sets off a chorus of little squeaks like music from a tiny orchestra of invisible violins.'

24

Kurt felt a warm glow in the sunshine of Romhilde's smile. 'I must listen carefully when we get to the beach.'

'I promise you the sand of Usedom has a magic all of its own!' She looked out of the train window. 'We're on the bridge already. Look, Marlena!' They dutifully looked down at the blue-green water of the Peene River as it flowed from the Oder estuary towards the sea.

'I really feel I'm on holiday now, Grandmamma,' Marlena exclaimed.

As if it had heard her the railway train accelerated along the white sandy coastline towards Usedom Island. At last it stopped at the little resort of Zempin where the calm sea and white sand were now on the left of the passengers. Kurt noticed the family with swastika armbands walking past on the platform. Just as they were disappearing from his view, the man's newspaper, which had been clamped under his arm, fell to the ground; he appeared not to have noticed.

Kurt opened the carriage door, jumped out and ran to pick up the discarded newspaper.

'Sir, sir, your paper!' shouted Kurt at the top of his voice. The man with the swastika armband walked briskly on down the platform to the exit and showed no sign of having heard him.

Romhilde looked with alarm at her young grandson standing on the station platform vigorously waving a newspaper above his head. 'Kurt, Kurt, please get back on the train.' She reached out through the door, extending an anxious hand to help him back. 'Your mother would have been horrified to see you outside the train just as we were going to leave the station.' She closed the carriage door just as the whistle blew announcing the continuation of their journey to Seebad Ahlbeck.

'You aren't going to tell her, are you?' Kurt had a worried look on his face.

Romhilde laughed. Of course not. I know my grandson was, as always, just being helpful to everyone who crosses his path; I'm sure your mother would be proud of you.' She took the newspaper from him and placed it on the seat beside her without giving it a glance.

'Are we nearly there, Grandmamma?' Marlena asked a quarter of an hour later. She looked exhausted.

Romhilde tried to cover her anxiety about her granddaughter's health by being light-hearted.

'The eternal question of children going on holiday all over the world.' She smiled at the girl and noticed her pale complexion; she was not reassured and looked down at the newspaper on the seat beside her as though she was seeking inspiration. She read the title, *Der Stürmer*, and saw the crude cartoon on the front page: a grotesque hook-nosed hunchback clasping what appeared to be a sack of gold and looking down on apparently healthy fully clothed girls wading through a river beside a semi-naked blonde woman. She read the caption with increasing horror and incredulity:

Ignorant, lured by gold,
They stand disgraced in Judah's fold.
Souls poisoned, blood infected,
Disaster broods in their wombs.

She carefully picked up the hugely offensive, anti-Semitic journal and folded it up into a small enough package to fit into her travelling bag.

'Is there something you've read that has upset you?' Kurt read his grandmother's expression and correctly interpreted her distress.

'There are some very bad people in this world, Kurt, and I pray they will not influence your lives.'

The train chugged on down the coast to Kolinsee and

26

as they approached the little town there was a much better view of the sand and sea. 'There now, isn't that a beautiful sight, everybody?'

From the train they could see people on the beach, some throwing large balls, some making sandcastles and others going into the placid lapping sea. The engine gently drew to a halt and a number of passengers excitedly descended onto the platform.

'Next stop Heringsdorf and then Seebad Ahlbeck; imagine the Emperor Friedrich the Third strolling along these promenades in all his finery in 1888.'

'What was he like, Grandmamma?' Marlena was brightening up as they approached their holiday destination.

'He would walk along the seafront in the current fashions with all his friends; sometimes they changed their clothes three times a day.' Romhilde smiled as she related one of her favourite pieces of history.

'Why did they change their clothes such a lot of times?' Marlena was intrigued.

'Partly because they were as proud as peacocks and wanted to display as many outfits as possible and partly because they were taking the spa treatments, bathing in the health giving-waters.'

'What about Emperor Friedrich, did he do the same?'

'Oh yes, my dear, but it didn't help him.'

'Why was that?' Now Kurt was really interested.

'He had to wait until 1888 for his father to die at the age of ninety and then Emperor Friedrich died himself after only ninety-nine days on the throne.'

'Poor man, no wonder he had been so keen on health spas.' It was Marlena's new friend Genevieve, who had been carefully following the history lesson, that expressed her sympathies for the late Emperor, just as they all arrived at Heningsdorf.

Kurt pointed out of the window to the beach. 'Look,

Grandmamma, at those funny chairs.' He was right, scattered across the broad stretch of sand were numerous elaborate white wicker chairs with sunshades and foot rests, each with a different number on the back.

Romhilde gave a broad smile. 'Now I *know* we've arrived at Seebad Ahlbeck.'

# 3

## *Rügen Island – August 1935*

Manfred Schultz welcomed August 1935 with a prolonged sigh of relief. Life in the boys' school where he taught German, French and English was becoming increasingly uncomfortable; he could feel his own institution and country changing.

'You look lost in deep thought this morning, my dear.' Suzanne Schultz came and put an arm around her husband's right shoulder as he sat at the empty breakfast table where they had eaten toast and honey washed down with coffee. 'We go on holiday tomorrow and you've six whole weeks away from those demanding boys.'

'I like teaching the boys, although some of them do need a little discipline for their high spirits.' He smiled as he looked up at Suzanne. 'I know it's holiday time but I feel that I need it more this year than in previous times; there's a change at the school.'

'My darling Manfred, we know, the school knows and above all the boys know that you're a fair, strict but very good teacher.' She squeezed his right arm reassuringly. 'Now I have to be sure that Clotilde and Margit are packing their cases for the trip.' Suzanne left her husband in the unusual position of not having to go to work on a weekday.

He strolled into the entrance hall of the apartment and picked up his copy of the *Deutsche Allgemeine Zeitung*, dated August 1st, 1935, and noticed a report on the upcoming

29

Nuremberg Rally predicting Herr Hitler would make a dramatic and far-reaching announcement about some new laws on the final day, September 15th. 'Probably more new regulations making my job more difficult.' He spoke out aloud to what he thought was an empty room.

'Father, the whole family knows that whatever the difficulty you have in your profession you will overcome it.' His ten-year-old daughter, Margit, had quietly come into the entrance hall to stand beside her father.

He put his arm around his daughter's shoulder. 'I appreciate your confidence. Margit, but I have a terrible feeling something awful is happening in our country.'

'These are gloomy thoughts the day before we go on our summer holidays.' Suzanne had joined her husband and elder daughter.

'You're quite correct but I have to tell you that one of my colleagues, the senior mathematics teacher, confided in me that he will not be returning for the autumn term.'

'My friend Eloise's brother goes to your school and he said that the maths schoolmaster is leaving for another country.' This came from Clotilde, who now lowered her voice almost to a whisper. 'He's Jewish, isn't he?'

'Hello, my little one.' Manfred's voice was solemn. 'You're right but I have to ask you all not to talk about this matter to anyone, even your best friend, Eloise.'

'We will all be discretion itself,' Suzanne assured him.

The remainder of the day passed off uneventfully. Clotilde went to say *au revoir* to Eloise whom she would not be seeing for six weeks. They hugged each other and swore to be best friends for ever. The remainder of the household meanwhile completed their preparations for the following day and everybody had an early night's sleep.

August 2nd was a beautiful day and started off without a cloud in the sky. The family Schultz travelled by bus in high spirits from their Dahlem apartment to the Stettiner Bahnhof and boarded the train that was about to take them to the Baltic Sea. The ever-observant Clotilde sitting by the window saw two large posters on the station wall outside her carriage. One depicted a fair-haired young woman in a green dress, holding a baby with a caption saying 'Support the assistance programme for mothers and children,' while alongside was another showing a brown-shirted Stormtrooper with a peaked cap and beside him a helmeted soldier; its caption read: 'The guarantee of German military strength.' The little girl pointed at the hugely contrasting pictures.

'Father, will you look like that in uniform?'

Manfred felt a shudder pass through his body. 'I hope I won't have to.'

'Mother, did you look like that after I was born?'

'Well, not exactly; I don't like green dresses.' Everyone laughed, a whistle blew and they felt the train move as it started its journey north to the seaside.

The railway journey was smooth and uneventful for the two hours that it took from Berlin to the ancient fortress town of Anklam; Suzanne stood up and took down her picnic basket from the luggage rack. 'Who's hungry?'

They all raised their hands in good schoolroom fashion and chorused, 'Me!'

'I have bratwurst and sauerkraut with some chocolate cake to follow.' The announcement was greeted with enthusiastic 'oohs' and 'yes pleases', and Frau Schultz duly handed round the delicious-smelling lunch. They started eating while the train was still standing in the station. Their enjoyment was interrupted by a sound of jeering and sneering from just outside the carriage window. The diners could hear such words as 'idiot', 'lunatic', 'crazy' and 'insane'; this was followed by '... doesn't deserve to live in the new Germany.' The family looked out and saw a poorly dressed woman with a green headscarf, short in stature and apparently poorly nourished clasping a mongol boy protectively to her chest. Presiding over this dreadful scene, as if giving it a seal of approval, was a picture plastered onto the railway station wall portraying a doctor wearing a white coat with his hands resting on the shoulders of a grotesque caricature of a mentally subnormal man; the caption underneath read: 'This genetically ill person will cost our people's community 60,000 marks during his lifetime. Citizens, that is your money!'

The woman's and boy's faces betrayed the terror they felt from the abuse of the baying travellers.

Manfred stood up and put his lunch plate on the seat and headed to the carriage door. 'This is outrageous and can't be tolerated!' He placed his hand on the door handle of the carriage but at that moment a whistle blew and the train started to move out of Anklam station.

They travelled on but their mood was now sombre. For a full minute no one spoke.

'What is happening to our country?' Manfred's words were spoken softly but with genuine anguish.

Suzanne reached across and wordlessly rested her hand on her husband's forearm.

Manfred smiled at his wife and daughters. 'Thank you for your sympathy, darling. I'm not sure what I would have done if I had been able to confront that mob.'

'Oh I'm sure you would have said something devastatingly eloquent and the pack of wolves would have fled in terror.' Suzanne's humour lifted the spirits of the whole Schultz family and there was much laughter.

The train was now passing through farmland with some grazing cattle and small lakes; eventually the locomotive passed through the agricultural town of Züssow. Afterwards they came to the larger historic town of Griefswald then on to the big holiday town of Stralsund where they came to a halt and some passengers alighted and others boarded for the journey to Rügen Island.

While their carriage remained stationary they observed the town's ancient, well-maintained buildings; some of red brick; some plastered and painted white and supported by gables.

'My teacher says these lovely houses are an inheritance from the times when Sweden occupied this part of Germany.' Margit had been very quiet throughout the journey but now she was animated by the beauty of the architecture in Stralsund; 'I really like this part of the country, it's such a contrast to our apartment in Dahlem. Germany is a really beautiful country, isn't it, Father?'

'It's very good to love your country and it's also very good to say that you love what your country has to show the world.' Manfred's face became clouded by a tinge of sadness.

Once more, Suzanne felt that she had to lift her husband's spirits. 'We're going to have a lovely long holiday on this wonderful island and afterwards things will all look so different.'

'Oh yes, they will!' the girls chorused.

Their father cheered up immediately. 'You're all quite right, of course.'

At that moment there were the sounds of the train starting to move again, as it left the platform. Manfred looked out of the left side of the carriage and saw the single span of the blue bascule bridge descending. 'The bridge is being lowered for us; we'll soon be on the island.'

There was a much more serene atmosphere in the carriage as they approached and then started to cross this wonderful piece of civil engineering; there were a number of other examples of these single-span bascule bridges including the crossing on to Usedom Island.

'Look, there are a lot of boats here, Father; that one over there's really beautiful.' Margit pointed at a sleek three-masted sailing boat with a white hull and varnished

33

wooden masts and spars. 'It makes those grey ships on the mainland side of the water look ugly and menacing.'

'They are warships, Margit!' Manfred tried to keep the sense of alarm out of his voice.

The family's attention was diverted as the locomotive neared the island side of the bridge and Clotilde became very excited.

'I can see the white cliffs gleaming in the sunlight; they make me feel I'm really on my summer holidays.'

Suzanne hugged her daughter. 'Of course you are, my darling Clotilde, and now we're going to the other side of the island where the sand is white and feels lovely underfoot.'

'How far is it to Baabe, Mother?' Margit asked.

'It's about fifty kilometres; for the last bit after Potbus we transfer to a bus and so, if we're lucky with the connection, we'll arrive at our holiday house in about two hours.'

Margit looked at her new Eterna Minx watch given to her by her parents to mark her tenth birthday; it had an elegant square face with a black dial and encased in stainless steel of Swiss make. Clotilde was a little envious when it had been presented to her sister but knew her father and mother were scrupulously fair and she would be given a similar gift when she reached her tenth birthday.

'You're amazing, Mother,' her elder daughter commented later as she consulted her watch again when their bus came to a stop in Baabe at the top of Strandstrasse. 'After crossing the whole of Rügen it's half past twelve exactly; we've taken precisely two hours to get here.' The two girls and their father gave Suzanne an enthusiastic round of applause.

When the party had descended from the bus with their suitcases in one hand and their coats folded over their opposite arms they set off towards the seaside and the rented holiday home facing the sea.

Manfred was wearing a long-sleeved white shirt and tie

34

with a check pattern in blue with yellow and long fawn-coloured trousers; his wife was equally formally dressed in a pale-blue short-sleeved dress extending to mid-calf and her fair hair was swept back at the sides.

'Are we here at last?' Clotilde was weary after the journey. 'What a lovely house! I wonder which will be my bedroom.' She gazed up at the two-storey white building with a red roof and a balcony on the first floor. 'I think it's that one.' She pointed to one of the windows leading out onto the balcony.

'We'll see but first I have to collect the front-door key from the next door neighbour, Frau Meyer.' Suzanne walked towards the adjacent house while the rest of the family set down their luggage in the street.

While she was gone a tall man in his fifties wearing a short-sleeved blue shirt and the khaki shorts of a holiday-maker walked passed and then stopped and looked carefully at Manfred.

'Excuse me, it's Herr Schultz, isn't it?'

Recognition appeared on the girls' father's face. 'Well I never, it's Herr Conrad Neumann, is it not?'

'It is indeed. I joined your school ten years ago for a brief period when one of your colleagues was ill.' They shook hands and he introduced the newcomer to his daughters who also shook hands with Herr Neumann and favoured him with little curtsies.

'We've only just arrived here at the beginning of our summer holidays; my wife has gone to our neighbour to collect the key.'

At that moment Suzanne returned waving a key above her head. She was also introduced to her husband's former colleague.

'Although we've our unpacking to do you would be very welcome to come in for some refreshment.' Suzanne felt that in ordinary circumstances most people in the same situation would have sensed that this was not a good time to intrude and would have excused themselves for another time. Herr Neumann's reply therefore came as a complete surprise.

'I knew you were coming here today and I'm very anxious to speak to your husband in a place where we can't be seen or overheard.' He saw the amazement on the woman's face. 'I have to talk to him; he is the only person whom I know I can trust.'

The pair of them had moved a few paces away from the rest of the family. Suzanne turned towards her husband and saw that he had not heard the stranger's request to speak in private. She reluctantly addressed her husband, 'Herr Neumann wishes to speak with you in confidence.'

The schoolteacher was equally puzzled but his courteous nature prevailed. 'Please come in.'

He led the way and once inside he removed a sheet that was covering a well-upholstered green armchair. 'Kindly take a seat.'

Meanwhile Suzanne, ably assisted by her daughters, flitted around the furniture lifting off the sheets at amazing speed. 'Come on, girls, we'll put out a piece of the chocolate cake for our guest and pour out a glass of that lovely refreshing apple juice ... I'm sorry, Herr Neuberg, I can only offer you apple juice at present; I haven't had the chance to go the shops.' She could not quite entirely disguise her irritation with the unexpected guest.

'Here you are gentlemen,' she said a little later, returning from the kitchen. 'I hope this facilitates your deliberations.' She laid the plates with the cake on it and the glasses of apple juice on the table between the two seated teachers.

'You'll excuse me, I hope, while I go shopping.' She turned to Clotilde and Margit. 'Let's go and spend some of your father's money.' Giggles could be heard as the front door closed behind them.

'Now, my former colleague – and I hope my friend – what is it that distresses you so much that you have come to us here at our holiday home.' Manfred tried to keep the irritation and exasperation that his holiday had started so badly out of his tone of voice.

'I most profoundly apologize for seeking you out here on Rügen Island.' Neumann had taken off his fawn-coloured peaked cap and was folding and unfolding it furiously.

'I have received a telegram from Stockholm; it concerns my long-time friend Carl von Ossietzky; you may remember my mentioning him when I joined you for a period at your school.' He looked anxiously at Manfred. 'Perhaps if I remind you he was a pacifist, the leader of the peace movement after the First World War and editor of the anti-militarist newspaper *Die Weltbühne*.'

'I do remember your speaking about him, but you use the words "he was"; does this have significance?' The language teacher was an enthusiastic linguist and felt every word spoken should carry the full weight of its meaning.

'He was imprisoned in 1932 for exposing German rearmament and one year later was transferred to a concentration camp when the Nazis came to power.'

'I am sorry; I didn't know.'

'There's no reason why you should.' Conrad's voice was sombre. 'The newspaper was closed down on March 1933. Carl is suffering from worsening lung tuberculosis.'

'I'm so sorry,' Manfred deplored all human suffering but was especially distressed in this case because the poor journalist's pain and humiliation was being inflicted by the state. 'I'm horrified by the news you bring but why are you telling me this and what was in the telegram from Stockholm?'

'Carl von Ossietzky has been awarded the Nobel Prize for Peace!' For a few moments Conrad allowed a beaming smile of pride in his friend's achievement to linger on his

37

troubled face. 'The tragedy is that he won't be allowed to go to Oslo to receive it.' There was a sudden noise and he looked over his shoulder furtively. 'I'm sure I wasn't followed here from Berlin; I took great precautions to leave undetected.'

'How did you do that?'

'I simply bought a Stormtrooper's uniform and wore it under my working suit, walked into a public toilet with my small holiday suitcase, went into one of the cubicles, took off my jacket, shirt and trousers, put one of those ridiculous caps on my head and there I was – a different person.' Conrad, for the first time since they had met, radiated some sense of achievement.

'What about the boots?'

'Ah the boots!'

'Yes the boots, all those Nazi thugs wear highly polished knee-length boots.'

'You're right, Manfred; may I address you by your first name?'

'Of course ... Those boots are a key part of their damned uniform, a symbol of the terror they spread in the streets.' The schoolteacher was immediately unhappy with himself; he had shown his true feelings to someone whom he had really only met half an hour ago, even though he had worked with him ten long years before.

Conrad hastened to reassure him. 'I share your feelings, my friend, although they are dangerous views to hold in Germany in 1935.' He paused to think for a moment. 'Let me tell you the final part of how I came here and then I will explain why I wished to confide in you.'

At that moment three happy shoppers came in through the front door and the two young girls threw their arms around their father's neck.

'We have ice cream, Father,' announced Clotilde.

'And frankfurter sausages and sauerkraut and eggs and

a chicken...' an excited Margit added; her voice faded away when she saw that her father still had his visitor. 'Oh I'm sorry.'

Manfred laughed. 'It's quite all right, my little angel; I'm pleased that you've had such a successful trip.'

Suzanne followed her daughters into the room. 'Come along, girls, let's leave your father and his guest to their discussions; we'll go into the kitchen and attend to the shopping.' They quietly left the room.

'May I continue?' Conrad's eyes followed them as they departed. 'You've a lovely family.'

Manfred was becoming irritated; he wanted to be with his family and could not see how he was relevant to the new Nobel Peace Prize Laureate. 'Please proceed.'

'I *was* concerned about not having the appropriate boots but relied on the fact that the people who might be following me were great in brute force but poor in the intellect department.' He smiled weakly.

'And so they wouldn't notice your missing jackboots– not a very reliable theory.'

'You're quite correct but I was lucky and arrived here safely two days ago, found some accommodation and waited for you.'

'Well, now that you've found me, what is it I can do that others can't?' Manfred's tone was becoming frosty and suspicious.

'First I must tell you that all Germans have been forbidden from accepting any Nobel Prize...' He hesitated for a moment. 'I think that any contravention of this would lead to arrest, incarceration in a concentration camp and almost certain death one way or another.'

'I don't think that I want to hear any more of this,' Manfred suddenly exploded. 'My priorities are my family and then my job as a teacher.'

'Please hear me out, I beg of you!'

39

'Very well, but we're near the end of this interview.'

'I will come to the point of why I'm here,' Conrad took a deep breath; 'The award of this prestigious prize to Carl von Ossietzky is a great event in German history and I believe it's about to be buried so deep by the Nazi administration that it will never again see the light of day.' He took another deep breath. 'I wish to entrust you with all the information I have about the life and work of this great German.'

'But why me?'

'Because you're the only person I know with the integrity required to carry this considerable burden.' Conrad hesitated a further moment. 'I believe my life is in danger; I was working on Carl's periodical up until March when it was closed down.'

'And you think I can hold onto the story of injustice and oppression and when things have changed I can resurrect this man of peace?'

'Yes I do and I have all you need in this small briefcase.' He handed it to Manfred.

Suzanne came in to the room carrying a tray of cucumber sandwiches and some ice cream.

'Teatime!' she announced.

Conrad stood up as a matter of courtesy; a shot rang out and there was a shattering of glass; the courteous visitor fell to the floor, the back half of his head splattered over the furniture, walls and ceiling.

Suzanne and her daughters stood in shock with their hands stifling the screams that all tried to force their way out. The tea-tray fell, scattering broken dishes and food in amongst the gore.

Manfred quietly commented. 'Well, they did notice the missing jackboots after all.'

# 4

## *Seebad Ahlbeck*

Lorelei Lang stood on the platform of Seebad Ahlbeck railway station. A warm wind from the Baltic ruffled her yellow headscarf and full green-and-red floral patterned cotton skirt. The white sandy beach could easily be seen stretching out towards the grey-blue sea. She had arrived two days earlier having been sent by her mistress, Romhilde, with instructions to seek out the most economical accommodation she could find with an adequate kitchen.

The train had crossed onto Usedom Island a little to the north and had then followed a gentle curve around and along the Baltic coast eventually coming to a halt at Seebad Ahlbeck. As the carriage doors opened Lorelei scanned up and down the train until she saw Romhilde's tall elegant figure stepping down onto the platform and she immediately walked the few paces to join her.

'Welcome to the seaside, madam.' She took her employer's suitcase with one hand and helped her down with the other.

The elderly woman smiled, 'Thank you, Lorelei. Please help the children and especially Marlena, who is a little unwell.'

The maid from Berlin, having ensured that Romhilde and her luggage were safely on the wooden planks of the platform, turned towards Marlena, who almost fell into her arms covered by the sleeves of her white cotton blouse.

41

'Lorelei, how lovely to see you!' The young girl clung onto her tightly. 'Have you found us somewhere exciting to stay?'

'I have indeed, Marlena; we're going to stay in a fisherman's house right across the road from the beach.' She gently lowered Marlena down onto her feet but was surprised by how light she felt.

Kurt followed close behind and proclaimed to her a very grown-up 'Good morning, Lorelei! It's good to see you again,' and then shook her hand. It had been a full two and a half days since they last been together. 'May I introduce you to our new friends. This is Genevieve, Karlie and their brother Hermann.'

Lorelei shook hands with the three children in a friendly manner. 'It is really nice to meet you all and I hope we'll see a lot of you during your holiday here on Usedom Island.' She looked beyond them. 'Is that your mother and grandmother?'

'Oh yes it is.' Kurt was taking very seriously his assumed role as master of introductions, 'Our new friends' mother is Frau Schmidt and her mother is Frau Brandt.'

'Has your search for rooms with a large kitchen been successful, Lorelei?' Romhilde quizzed. She knew that her friend and employee always found somewhere for the family to stay that was excellent value for money but she always asked the same question.

'Madam, I think you will be very satisfied; we're living in a part of a large house of a fisherman who not only catches the fish but smokes them himself.' She had good reason to be pleased with her arrangements; she had secured four full-sized bedrooms, a well-equipped kitchen and a dining room with a table extended by two extra leaves. There had been a little haggling about the price but the fisherman whose name was Lothar fell for the twinkle in Lorelei's eye.

'Has he any family living with him?' The ever-practical Romhilde didn't want a large bunch of riffraff running about the house getting under her feet and making a lot of noise.

'Oh no!' the maid hastened to reassure her; 'he lives entirely by himself.'

'How many bedrooms are there?' Kurt and Marlena's grandmother was making allocations in her mind even before they had left the railway station.

'The house has six bedrooms, madam; four in the portion where we'll be staying.'

'Does that mean I can have a room all to myself?' Kurt's face lit up immediately.

'We have to remember, young man, that your mother and father will join us here at the weekends.'

Marlena's expression was a picture of happiness, which shone through her tiredness.

'Do we have far to walk, Lorelei?'

'Oh no, it's just at the top of the beach over there, next to the railway line. Look, it's the second house on the left.' Romhilde's maid picked up her mistress' suitcase and led the party along the platform.

After saying their goodbyes to the family Schmidt and promising to see them again soon Marlena and Kurt followed their grandmother and her treasured housemaid into Seebad Ahlbeck; after a very short walk they entered the front gate of a white three-storey house with a grey slate roof.

Kurt took in the elegant building at a glance. 'Fantastic! To think we'll be staying here for six whole weeks.' He looked up at the gabled roof surmounted by a parapet with ornamental pineapple-shaped concrete moulds along the top.

'I love the front garden with all these flowers and trees.' Marlena was looking at pink and yellow roses, two young beech trees and a small fir. 'What is this over in the corner by the front wall.' She pointed at a square brick structure with a soot-stained metal grille on the top.

'That's where Lothar, our fisherman, smokes his fish.' Lorelei smiled sweetly. 'He'll be preparing a lot of the fish he has caught for us during the next six weeks.' She produced a set of keys and led the way towards the varnished pinewood front door and opened the house to the holiday party.

'This is a beautiful house, Lorelei. Are we going to have to pay a lot of rent?' Romhilde had a reputation for being careful with money.

'Oh no, madam; Herr Lothar is a very reasonable man.' She handed her employer a piece of paper with neat handwriting on it. 'This is our agreement for a tenancy lasting six weeks; I thought it was so inexpensive that I signed it on your behalf; I hope that was satisfactory.'

The youthful grandmother sat down on a comfortably upholstered dark-blue sofa, took off her maroon felt hat, laid it on the seat beside her and smoothed out her white-and-red floral-patterned cotton summer dress. She carefully read the agreement. 'This is a very satisfactory arrangement, twelve marks and ten pfennigs for the whole six weeks!'

'May I respectfully remind you that they are Reichsmarks and Reichspfennigs,' Lorelei blushed as she attempted to prevent her mistress from getting into trouble with the authorities.

'Oh thank you, my dear!'

'Can we go and explore?' Kurt's enthusiastic voice brought everybody back to the new house.

'I would like to know which room I'm going to have.' Marlena's voice sounded a little weak. 'I would like to lie down for a while after our journey.'

Romhilde stood up and put an arm around the girl's shoulders. 'Of course, Marlena, let's start by looking at those two rooms at the top of the house; they must have a wonderful view of the beach.'

She led the way up the broad staircase and they came to the first-floor landing with polished pine floorboards, five surrounding oak doors and a narrow staircase leading to the two rooms on the top floor; they carried on to the upper part of the house and found themselves on a small platform with a window at the back overlooking the railway track. A door at one side was revealed by the eager Kurt to open onto a tiny bathroom, with a shower, hand basin and a toilet, all in white and spotlessly clean.

'Everything I've seen so far is in very good order, Lorelei.' The grandmother smiled and opened the door to the first of the two bedrooms facing the sea. It contained two single beds either side of the entrance, each with a small bedside table on which was placed an upended glass and water jug.

'How lovely!' Marlena walked over to the projecting bay window framed by red-and-blue flowered curtains and looked out. 'What a marvellous view of the sea and sandy beach. I can see as far as Finland ... well nearly!' They all laughed. She took a deep breath and exclaimed 'What a beautiful smell there is in this room; what is it, Grandmamma?'

'Lavender, my sweet.' Romhilde went over to the windows which she easily opened and almost immediately the lavender fragrance was mixed with the salty fresh air.

'Who is that coming in through the front gate, Lorelei?'

'That's Lothar, madam.'

'We must go down to meet him.' She turned towards the door. 'Meanwhile I think this room will do very well for you and Marlena.' She looked at the two of them. 'You don't mind sharing, do you, girls?'

'I will be very pleased to share with Lorelei but may I stay here and have a rest while you all go down to meet fisherman Lothar.'

'Of course, my dear.' A feeling that all wasn't well with her granddaughter again crossed Romhilde's mind. 'Lorelei, would you be good enough to come straight back up to this young lady after you've introduced us to Lothar?'

'Of course, madam.' She followed her employer and Kurt as they descended the narrow staircase down to the first floor landing where they found Lothar Meyer stepping up from the top stair onto the polished landing.

'Good afternoon, madam.' He held out his hand towards the advancing grandmother.

She shook his hand and found herself looking into the clear, pale-blue eyes of a tall, handsome, broad-shouldered man in is early forties with wavy blond hair. He was wearing a navy-blue open-necked shirt and similarly coloured thick cotton trousers held up by broad canvas braces. There was a strong odour of fish about him.

'Good afternoon, Herr Meyer.'

'Good afternoon. I trust you've had a very pleasant journey.'

Herr Meyer seemed to Romhilde to be almost over-polite but she dismissed it as her being sensitive due to tiredness and worry concerning Marlena. 'Do you think we could have a look in the rooms on this floor,' she smiled sweetly; 'we've seen one of the rooms on the top floor, which is lovely – my granddaughter is resting there at the moment – but we've not yet seen the other one yet.'

'It's similar but smaller and only has one bed,' Lothar explained; 'these two doors at the back of this floor lead into my bedroom and a room in which I store all my personal belongings.' He indicated the two light oak doors opening off the back of the landing. 'I would be very grateful if you asked the children not to go in there. I have some precious instruments I would rather not have disturbed.'

'Of course, Herr Meyer.' Romhilde thought his insistence on that matter a little odd, but decided to dismiss it from her mind. There was clearly more to this Herr Meyer than met the eye.

'Here is the bathroom...' The owner opened a door at one side opposite the top of the stairs. 'As you can see it's a bath, bidet, toilet and a washbasin.'

Romhilde looked inside and nodded her approval at the spotless white bathroom furniture.

'Excellent, Herr Meyer; now may we see the two front bedrooms?'

At that moment Kurt took the opportunity to hurtle up the narrow staircase and disappeared from view.

'I apologize, Herr Meyer; we seem to have lost my grandson.'

Lothar opened the door to the front double bedroom, which was spacious and tastefully decorated.

'This will do very nicely for my daughter and her husband who will be arriving at the weekend.' Together they went into the other front bedroom watched by Lorelei who remained behind. This room was smaller with a single bed, was equally well appointed and had a fine view of the beach.

'I hope this all meets with your approval,' Lothar remarked.

'Most certainly, Herr Meyer, and the rental is very agreeable; all we've to do now is to look at the last room upstairs where, I think, we'll find Kurt.'

The owner and Lorelei followed the energetic grandmother up the narrow stairs again and found Kurt proudly ushering them into his comfortable little bedroom wallpapered with a pattern depicting sailing and motorboats.

'Welcome to my new room with a view!' he grinned. 'I shall be able to see everything that is going on in Seebad Ahlbeck.'

Lorelei and Romhilde laughed but Lothar Meyer's face was carefully expressionless.

'If you will excuse me I'm going to see if Marlena is feeling better.' Lorelei left the room and could be heard knocking on the door of the adjacent room.

47

She found Marlena still on the bed fully clothed but looking much better with some colour in her cheeks; she stretched her arms above her head as though she had been asleep.

'Hello, Lorelei! I already feel much better after that snooze!' She was smiling and her voice sounded much stronger. 'I would really like to come downstairs and help you and Grandmamma prepare supper.'

Lorelei gently placed an arm around the back of Marlena's shoulders.

'Marlena, you're a lovely girl, always thinking of other people and how you can help them; you will make some lucky man a wonderful wife one day.' The young woman stretched out her right hand and the young girl took it and with its assistance bounded onto her feet. 'Quite athletic as well!'

At that moment Kurt ran past the open bedroom door and hurtled down the narrow staircase; Lothar the fisherman followed at a more modest pace and the third member of that party came in to join her granddaughter and maid.

'Who was the man who just walked past the doorway?'

'My word, Marlena, you do look much better after your rest.' Romhilde came into the room and embraced her granddaughter. 'That was our landlord for the next six weeks and he has just solved our supper problem; he's gone to fetch two plaice and some Baltic sprats all freshly caught today.'

'How wonderful, madam, but I think we'll need some potatoes and sauerkraut, too. I took the liberty of buying some this morning.' She smiled at the grandmother who now had her arm around Marlena's slim shoulders.

'We're all set then, let's go and explore the kitchen.'

When they reached the ground floor the front door was open and Kurt's back could be seen as he followed Lothar through the front gate. Romhilde was horrified. 'Kurrrt!' she commanded. 'Come back here *immediately*.'

The boy stopped in his tracks as if he had walked into a brick wall, slowly turned around and, with his eyes downcast, dawdled back into the house. He came to a halt in front of his grandmother; meanwhile the fisherman continued on down to the beach without a glance over his shoulder. The elderly woman laid an affectionate hand on the dispirited boy's head. 'My dear, who is captain of this ship?'

'You are, Grandmamma.'

'Whose permission do you have to have before you go out alone?'

'Yours, Grandmamma.'

'And where were you off to?'

'The fishing boats on the beach, Grandmamma.'

'And what were you going to do there?'

'Well, I was going to have a look at Lothar's boat and then help him carry the fish back here.'

'Kurt, would I be correct in thinking that you also had a tiny little hope that there might have been an opportunity to climb onto one of the boats and have a look around?' Romhilde was smiling and so were Lorelei and Marlena who had both come down the stairs to join them.

A sheepish grin appeared on Kurt's face. A very soft 'Yes, Grandmamma' emerged from his lips.

Everyone laughed.

'It was a good plan,' Kurt added.

'Of that I have no doubt, young man, but it lacked one essential ingredient.'

Kurt looked up at his beloved grandmother. 'Your permission, Grandmamma?'

'Exactly, Kurt, and I would have been happy to give it if I had been able to speak to Herr Meyer before you left.'

'Is that my name I hear being mentioned.' The man in question's tall frame cast a long shadow across the hallway.

'Here you are, take these.' He handed Kurt two beautiful fresh plaice tied together with a piece of string and with his other hand he gave a wet wriggling newspaper parcel to Romhilde.

'Oh!' she exclaimed. 'Thank you, my dear.' Lorelei rescued her mistress by taking the squirming parcel from her hands and disappeared into the kitchen at the back of the house.

'Baltic sprats, gnädige Frau; I will see you tomorrow.' He turned and walked towards the front door. 'With so little tide I have to have a team of men to help me launch my boat and they will be waiting for me now.' He departed into the dusk.

'I would so like to have gone on his boat, Grandmamma.'

'It's early days, Kurt my dear!' She smiled at both her grandchildren. 'Now let's go and help Lorelei in the kitchen prepare those lovely fresh plaice for supper.'

Two hours later Marlena, Kurt and Lorelei with Romhilde presiding were sitting around the large polished pine kitchen table; through the large back window there was darkness with a few lights twinkling and before them were the skeletal remains of their sumptuous fish supper.

'Well, Kurt and Marlena, wasn't that a delicious meal?'

'It certainly was, Grandmamma.' Kurt's reply was enthusiastic and Marlena nodded in agreement, although she hadn't eaten as much as the others.

'I think it's time for bed.' She noticed that Marlena could hardly keep her eyes open. 'Upstairs, please.'

The two tired young people got up from their chairs and came round to their grandmother and both gave her a hug and Marlena added a kiss on the cheek.

'Thank you, Grandmamma, for bringing us.' Kurt spoke for both of them. 'I'm so pleased to be here on holiday, and thank you, Lorelei, for finding this lovely house! Tomorrow we'll go to the beach.' With that parting shot the irrepressible boy bounded up the stairs after his sister.

The next day was bright and sunny with occasional white fluffy clouds slowly crossing the clear blue sky. Romhilde was sitting in one of the wicker beach chairs, with the number nine on the back; Lorelei was sitting on a towel on the sand reading the *Collected Poems of Kurt Tucholsky*.

'Would you mind keeping an eye on the children, my dear, while I have a nap?'

'Yes, madam.' Lorelei put her open book face down on the towel. 'You relax and I will keep watch.' She looked back up into the basket chair shielding its occupant from any sudden gust of wind; the occupant's eyes were already closed. 'Have a nice rest, madam,' she almost whispered, 'Yesterday was a long day.'

She turned her gaze towards the sea and quickly picked out Marlena in a bright-blue costume splashing around with two other girls of about the same age, whom she recognized as Genevieve and Karlie Schmidt

Kurt in a smart light blue swimming costume that revealed his wiry frame was carrying a bucket of water with the help of another boy. She thought he was probably Hermann and she watched them proceed towards a partially built sandcastle. She guessed that they had built their architectural masterpiece near the water's edge because the fine-grained sand didn't bind together very well without plenty of moisture.

Down at the water's edge, the two boys were chatting away. 'Hermann, I think this is going to be the most superest sandcastle ever,' Kurt looked at his new friend, who nodded his agreement. 'I have got something really fantastic to put on the top.'

'What is it Kurt?' Hermann had a mischievous look in his eyes. 'Is it a model of a fat Stormtrooper?' There was a lot of giggling.

Kurt walked over to where he had put his shirt and trousers in a neatly folded pile and took a cylindrical little parcel out of his trouser pocket. 'Close your eyes for a minute and I will tell you when to open them.' Kurt unfurled a small paper flag that he had copied from one of his father's encyclopaedias and stuck it in the tallest tower of the sandcastle. 'Open your eyes now, Hermann.'

'Wow, Kurt that's really smashing.' There was true admiration in his voice as he fixed his gaze on the horizontal black, white and red stripes on top of which was a black Maltese cross. 'That is really amazing, Kurt...' He hesitated a moment before he began again. '...But I don't recognize it.'

'That's not surprising, my friend; it's the Imperial German Flag that represented our country from 1903 to 1919 when it was abandoned.' He was kneeling down patting the sand around his piece of art to secure it from the light breeze when a shadow obscured the sun from the castle.

'Now it's ready to show, Grandmamma!' Kurt said joyfully.

'No, it's not! Heil Hitler!' Two harsh voices spoke in unison.

The startled boys looked back over their shoulders and saw the boy and girl from the train whose father's newspaper Kurt had rescued and tried to return to him; the girl was about eleven years old and wore the uniform of the Jungmadelbund, or League of Young Girls – white shirt, black skirt and a brown tie; on her right upper arm there was a swastika. 'That's not a Nazi flag!' she screamed at the boys.

Kurt and Hermann stood up in amazement and turned around to face the perpetrators of the onslaught; they saw the children's right arms raised in the Nazi salute; the boy was dressed similarly to the girl but with black shorts, showing him to be a member of the Deutsches Jungvolk, or German Young People. He was probably ten years old and had his fair hair combed across his forehead, beneath which was an expression of fury.

'How dare you place any other flag than that of the Nazi Party on your sandcastle,' he yelled.

'But it's a German flag!' Hermann leapt to his friend's defence. 'An historic flag.'

'It's got to be a swastika.' The girl who had her blonde hair tied in plaits with black ribbons had an expression of hatred on her face. 'Like this!' She produced a red paper flag with a central black swastika in a white circle. She then grabbed Kurt's flag and tore it up, while the obnoxious boy kicked down Hermann and Kurt's carefully crafted structure. Finally the girl stuck her Nazi flag in the ruins. The two younger and shorter friends watched with tears rolling silently down their cheeks. Lorelei witnessed the whole business and hurried down the beach towards the distraught boys, but when she was halfway there the two swastika children ran off.

When she arrived at the ruined castle with its Nazi flag obscenely flutteringly in the light breeze Kurt rushed towards her followed by Hermann; she put a comforting arm around both.

'I saw it all; it was shameful what those two monsters did!' She looked over the boys' heads and saw a man in a brown shirt standing with his feet astride and hands on his hips and a broad smile on his face. Beside him stood a blonde-haired woman wearing a white blouse and full black skirt; in front were two children who turned around and raised their right arms. Mercifully at that moment a gust of wind made the sand sing, drowning out the screamed words.

Lorelei noted Marlena who was already walking towards the group.

'Hermann, we can meet again tomorrow. Let me dry those lovely blue eyes; all right now?'

'Yes, thank you, Fräulein Lorelei.'

'Your sisters are just coming up from the sea; can you go and join them?'

The little boy trotted off towards Genevieve and Karlie in their maroon swimming costumes. A few moments later Lorelei had taken the paper Nazi flag from the sand castle ruins and folded it up and put it in her dress pocket.

Marlena arrived and saw Kurt bravely fighting off more tears. 'What's happened?'

'Our brave soldier here had to defend his castle from the marauding Visigoths!'

'Is that really what happened Kurt?' Marlena was impressed.

Lorelei's strategy worked like magic. Kurt's head was up, his chest puffed out and his normal chirpiness restored. 'Well, they did attack in large numbers but my men beat them off and as a reward they will all have ice cream for lunch.'

'What a good idea, Kurt; they will be pleased.'

'Shall we go back to Grandmamma now. I really have enjoyed the sea but I would like a rest.'

'Of course, my dear.' Lorelei thought this was rather strange statement from a ten-year-old girl, an adult way of expressing her thoughts; at her age the young woman remembered that she had kept going all day with boundless energy, until eventually she welcomed bedtime. 'Can you two tell me the number of your grandmother's wickerwork beach chair?'

'I know, I know!' Lorelei was pleased to see Kurt was back to his usual self.

'It's number nine and I can see it now.'

True enough Romhilde had turned her chair around to shield herself from the 'singing sand' – a warm wind was whipping up the fine white grains. The children bounded up and found their beloved and bespectacled grandmother reading Lorelei's book of poems. Marlena was first to come face to face with her. 'Grandmamma, the sea is lovely and warm; you should come and try it.'

'Is it, my dear? Perhaps I will do some paddling tomorrow.' At that moment Kurt peered around the corner of the wickerwork. 'And what have *you* been doing on the beach?'

'You're not going to believe this, Grandmamma.'

'Try me.'

'Well, Hermann and I built the biggest sandcastle ever...' He stretched his arms apart to show how big it was. '... And placed the Imperial German flag on the tallest tower, but in spite of our men putting up a great defence it was overrun by Visigoth hoards.'

'How terrible! What are you going to do about it?'

'I have awarded all our men an Italian ice cream cornet for lunch.'

'Isn't that a bit expensive? I hope we can afford it.'

'I'm sure you will, Grandmamma.'

'Come on, Marlena, I'm ready for lunch.' Romhilde said. 'You run on ahead.'

She followed behind the children with her maid.

'I did enjoy dipping into your Kurt Tucholsky book, my dear; I read the little piece "The Embryo Speaks" and it's really so true.'

'I know, madam! It's so sad; he died a few months back at the age of forty-five and perhaps his early death was nature's way of protecting him. He was a German Jew you know.'

'I know what you're saying, my dear.' She looked at her grandchildren and then at her maid. 'I fear for their future, I fear for your future, Lorelei, and I fear for Germany's future.'

Kurt suddenly rushed back down the beach towards them.

'Grandmamma, what time does the train bringing Mother and Father here arrive on Friday?'

'We'll be waiting on the station at six thirty in the afternoon.' Romhilde thought it was a curious question. 'We only arrived yesterday, my dear.'

'Well,' said Kurt, 'that means there are seventy-seven and a half hours before they arrive.' He then changed the subject without explanation. 'Can we go to the pier tomorrow?'

'Of course, have you had enough of the beach already?'

'I would like to talk to Father before going back to the beach.' He sounded unusually serious. He ran back up to join Marlena as she walked up the beach towards the house.

Lorelei laid a hand on her mistress's arm. 'May we just delay a moment before we catch up with the children.'

The older woman stopped in her tracks and looked at her maid in alarm. 'What has happened?'

The younger woman reached into her dress pocket and produced the Nazi paper flag and then told Romhilde the real story behind the marauding Visigoths.

'Oh poor boy! Thank you Lorelei for thinking up that story to help him save face; no wonder he doesn't want to return to the beach. I don't know what the world is coming to.'

The two women caught up with the two children and the lovely grandmother put a hand on both their shoulders. 'I'm so proud of you both.'

As they all approached the road that separated the beach from the houses a wonderful smell reached all their nostrils.

'Madam, that fantastic aroma is coming from our front garden.'

Romhilde took a deep breath in. 'That, everybody, is the unmistakable whiff of smoked herring. I asked Herr Meyer if we could have some for lunch.'

At that moment Lothar Meyer's blond hair bobbed up above the top of the front garden hedge.

Romhilde pushed open the front gate and walked over to where the fisherman was tending the smoking of his catch. 'Herr Meyer, I have another request to make.' The remainder of this conversation was in hushed tones with Lothar smiling and nodding his head in agreement.

The smoked herring lunch was enjoyed by all including Lothar who also joined them at the table. Even Marlena seemed to enjoy the food.

'May I have another herring, Grandmamma?'

'Of course, my dear! ... Congratulations, Herr Meyer, you are a very gifted cook; no one else recently has been able to tempt Marlena to ask for more.'

'Please, call me Lothar. None of this Herr Meyer! I dislike such formalities.'

'The fish is really delicious, Lothar,' Marlena lifted up her hand and blew him an imaginary kiss, which he deftly caught

'Thank you, young lady. When we go fishing on Thursday I will catch some more for you.'

Kurt's face lit up. 'You said "we" – does that mean I'm coming fishing too on Thursday?'

'It certainly does. A good captain needs a good crew and I shall be depending on you.' Lothar could see the swelling chest of the young boy. 'We set sail at seven o'clock.'

'Aye-aye, Captain.' Kurt saluted as Lothar rose from the table and gently shook Romhilde's outstretched hand before he left.

All the talk was now of Kurt's fishing trip on Thursday. 'Grandmamma, do you think Hermann could come with me?'

The following day, Frau and Herr Zimmermann arrived, repeating the visit every weekend during the six-week holiday. Marlena did not gain any weight, in spite of eating well, and on return to Mahlow Mitzi made an appointment for her daughter with their family practitioner.

# 5

## *Holiday Horror – Aftermath*

Conrad Neumann's assassination would stay engraved on the minds of the family Schultz for eternity. By the time the police, ambulance and doctor had arrived the enormity of the crime had completely erased all memory of the small briefcase the dead man had been carrying. Although the Nazi police force under Reichsführer Himmler was penetrating every facet of Adolf Hitler's Germany, the process wasn't yet complete and the rural gendarmerie was still in place on Rügen Island.

It was therefore the rather old-fashioned and humane Polizeikommissar Johann Weber who arrived at the holiday cottage of the distraught family. He introduced his colleagues, a tall fair-haired woman and a youngish, rather thickset man, beside him. 'This is Detective Constable Polizistin Helga Köhler and Polizist Hans Krause.' Both wore civilian clothes as did their chief; uniformed men were already stationed at the doors and in the street outside. There were formal handshakes and bows following which there was an awkward silence.

'May I?' Helga moved over to the two young girls.

'Of course.' Suzanne was relieved that a sympathetic and authoritative woman was going to comfort her two devastated daughters. The policewoman put an arm around each of the girls' shoulders.

'So what are your names?'

'I'm Margit and this is my younger sister, Clotilde.'

'It's a pleasure to meet you both.' It was a delicate situation that Helga was handling with real expertise. 'Would you like to come outside with me into the fresh air?'

'That would be lovely.' Clotilde's voice was a little stronger than that of her sister.

'Come with me, my dears.' She took a small hand in each of hers and they edged past the body of Conrad Neumann, which was now covered by a sheet, although it was becoming increasingly blood-stained in the region of the mutilated head.

Johann Weber breathed a sigh of relief as Hans Krause closed the door behind them. 'Your daughters are in good and trustworthy hands Herr Schultz.' He indicated the soft chairs and sofa. 'Please, Herr and Frau Schultz, be seated.'

After Suzanne had sat down Manfred joined her and held her hand.

'Polizist Krause, kindly supervise the removal of this poor unfortunate man's body.'

'Certainly, Inspector.' Everything was done with efficiency, decorum and respect for the dead man; afterwards they listened to the sound of the ambulance driving away.

The senior policeman sat down opposite the still-trembling parents. 'Do you know this man?'

There was a warning note in the tone of voice that Suzanne and Manfred quickly picked up. They glanced at each other. 'No, we don't know this man' Suzanne spoke for them both with conviction.

'My report will say precisely that.' There were a few more questions and at length he stood up and shook hands with the schoolteacher and his wife. 'I will submit my report, but it will probably not be read and you will probably not see me again'. He saw the puzzled expressions on Manfred and Suzanne's face. 'There's a terrible change sweeping through Germany and I fear it's going to sweep me off Rügen Island.'

'You paint a very grim picture of our country, Inspector.'

'You're a very well-educated man Herr Schultz; may I ask what subjects you teach?'

'French and English,' Manfred paused, 'to secondary school boys.'

'You're a valuable member of society, sir; I hope you have a peaceful and restful holiday, although it's going to be difficult for your two lovely daughters to forget what they have seen.'

'I shall have to speak with them very carefully,' Suzanne replied, 'but I assure you my girls will have a happy holiday, Inspector.'

The courteous Inspector gave a formal bow to Suzanne and Manfred Schultz. He paused before turning to leave. 'Nothing is worth more than this day; no one is worth more than your two delightful daughters.'

The Polizeikommissar walked out of their lives towards the perils of the unknown, and the children ran back to the house into the arms of their mother and father.

Suzanne was the first to speak. 'Goethe from a policeman! With a little extra for our girls.'

Her husband was equally amazed. 'This has been an unbelievable start to our holiday. I want us to put it behind us, but we've got to be very careful what we say to anyone and not breathe a word about what has happened in this room.'

Suzanne, with the help of her two daughters, prepared a light meal of salami and cheese sandwiches while Manfred searched the *Deutsche Allgemeine Zeitung* for any mention of the Nobel Prize winner, but he found nothing . He also cast around for any sign of the small brief case that the late Conrad Neumann had brought with him; he could find none and assumed that it had been removed with the corpse.

The following morning Suzanne rose early and went into

town. She returned at eight o'clock with four bicycles and a fifteen-year-old boy.

'Let me introduce Josef whose father hires out bicycles.' The boy smiled a little awkwardly at the girls but his handshake was friendly. 'He will instantly repair anything that goes wrong with the machines. We'll be ready in an hour,' she told him and the boy turned on his heels and vanished.

Margit could already balance well on her bicycle at home but Clotilde was only just starting her cycling career and already had a few scraped knees and one bump on the head. 'I think I'm getting better on my bicycle every day, Mother.'

'Especially now you have your father around to make sure you don't fall off.'

Margit had a generous spirit and was only too pleased that Clotilde was going to have some special bicycling tuition from her father.

'May we cycle down the Strandstrasse to the beach after breakfast, Mother?'

'Of course, my love.' Suzanne was suitably dressed in a deep-mauve blouse with a full light-blue cotton skirt and girls were wearing loose-fitting yellow shorts with white blouses. 'It will help take our minds off yesterday's awful events.'

Manfred, in a white short-sleeved cotton shirt and khaki slacks joined them at the dining room table.

'Did I hear those bicycles have arrived?'

'Not by themselves!' Clotilde giggled.

'Your wit is only matched by your beauty, young lady.' He placed his hands on both his daughters' shoulders. 'You've been wonderful after what you've seen here.'

The two concerned parents filled up that six weeks' summer holiday on Rügen Island with activity every day: trips to the sandy beaches, chalk cliffs, beech woods carpeted

61

with anemones and ancient megalithic graves dating back thousands of years.

'I think I could ride my bicycle all round Rügen Island,' Clotilde enthused. 'I like Father to be close by but I can ride much better than when we came on holiday.'

The four of them were sitting on a blanket on the fine white sand of Baabe beach enjoying a picnic lunch of brown bread, jam, honey and boiled eggs. 'Can we take the bicycles on the bus to the chalk cliffs again tomorrow?' The previous trip a week earlier had been a great success. 'I loved riding along the tracks between the tall beech trees.'

'Can you remember the name of the highest cliffs?' Manfred had always taken an interest in nature's wonderful work in his own country and wished to share this with his daughters.

'I can, I can!' Margit was just as enthusiastic as Clotilde to join in her father's passion.

'Very well, my clever daughter; so what is the answer?'

'The Königstuhl, or King's Chair, and its one hundred and sixty-one metres high.'

'Exactly right, my darling daughter.'

'And so it's back to those wonderful white cliffs tomorrow.' Susanne was helping her husband keeping the girls so busy that when it came to bedtime and they put their heads on the pillow sleep engulfed them immediately; there was no time to think about the tragic and terrible event that had occurred within hours of their arrival on Rügen Island.

The following day the family Schultz travelled on a bus to the beautiful beech woods above the white chalk cliffs at the north-east corner of Rügen Island. They unloaded their bicycles and set off along one of the tracks that criss-crossed the area; Clotilde who was by now highly confident in the cycling department almost rode straight into one of the water-filled dells that were scattered throughout the woods.

'Oops!' she cried as she applied the brakes just in time to prevent a very wet experience. 'How do these water-filled hollows come to be here, Father, even though it's summer and there's little rain?'

'They are relics of the development of our planet many, many years ago when this part of Earth was frozen. They are sometimes known as dead ice holes; for reasons I have not understood they never drain away'

Margit stooped at the edge of the hollow, parted the grass and leaf mould to reveal a beautiful purple flower. 'Look, everyone, I have found an orchid.' She smiled up at the rest of the family.

Suzanne came close. 'You're right, Margit; now you've a big decision to make.'

'What's that, Mother?'

'Either you leave it here in all its glory or you pick it from lower down its stem and take it home to put it in a vase of water.' Suzanne then added: 'Or you could do both.'

Margit looked back at her mother in astonishment and then understanding dawned on her lovely face. She went to where she had placed her bicycle leaning against a tree, opened her saddlebag and took out her pencil case containing coloured crayons and a notebook. Now, full of enthusiasm, she drew a fine picture of the pale-purple flower with a yellow centre.

'What do you think of this, Clotilde?'

'Oh it's lovely, Margit. The colours are just right.' Both girls turned their heads towards a scuffling sound that came from the cycle leaning against one of the beech trees. 'What was that?'

'I can't see anything but I certainly *heard* something.' Suzanne had joined the girls again. 'Perhaps it was a bird that flew over to admire your drawing, Margit?' They all laughed.

Margit threw her pencil case and crayons into her large saddlebag and fastened it shut.

The family started their ride back towards the cliff top where they would catch the bus back to Baabe. They could see house martins flying in and out of their nests in the chalk face; dusk seemed to come early on the east coast of the island. The journey to their holiday home took an hour and a half, and they were all very tired. They left their bicycles in the hall just inside the front door and they wearily went into the kitchen. Suzanne removed the muslin covering a loaf of bread, a block of butter, a pot of honey and a jug of orange juice and brought them out of the larder; they all helped themselves.

'It's been a wonderful day, Mother.' Clotilde was still her bubbly self, although Suzanne could see that a lot of effort was being put into propping her eyelids open. Clotilde kissed her mother, father and sister goodnight. 'Thank you, everyone!', then the exhausted little girl left the kitchen and her tired little legs took her up towards her bedroom. The kitchen door was closed and no member of the Schultz family noticed a black-and-white cat with a little pink nose jump out of Margit's saddlebag and noiselessly follow Clotilde up the stairs.

A short while later Margit, her mother and father all retired to bed; they walked quietly past Clotilde's partially closed bedroom door. 'We'll see you in the morning, Margit,' Suzanne whispered to her elder daughter.

There was no sound throughout the night and the sun was already peeping between the slats of the louvered window shutters when Clotilde was roused by something soft and gentle patting her left cheek. She opened her eyes and was surprised to see a black-and-white cat by her head. 'Hello, pussycat, where did you spring from?'

As though the animal was answering the little girl's question it pulled on her left plait of hair until she got out of bed and followed her new friend down the stairs to the entrance hall which also served as a sitting room; the cat jumped up onto the green sofa and pulled at the corner of a small brown briefcase that lay behind one of the matching cushions. 'Oh you are a clever pussycat though I don't know if you're a lady or a gentleman pussy.' That problem was instantly solved by Clotilde's feline friend bounding off the sofa, walking elegantly to the corner of the room, spreading its hind legs and leaving behind a little puddle on the polished pinewood floor.

'Ah you are a lady pussycat.'

A ladylike meow acknowledged her correct deduction.

'Clotilde, you sound like you're having a conversation with someone whom I have yet to meet.' Suzanne's voice heralded her descent down the stairs. 'Whom have you got down there, my dear?'

The little girl really didn't want to remind her mother of that terrible first day of the family holiday, so she took the paper contents out of the briefcase and slipped them inside her pyjama jacket; she then returned the briefcase to its hiding place behind the green cushion.

'I have a new friend, Mother. Let me introduce you to Fräulein Müller.' She picked up the friendly black-and-white purring cat.

'Is that what you think of your schoolteacher?'

'She is very cuddly and I'm sure she will teach us a lot, if only we can take her home.' Clotilde gave her mother a hug and kissed her cheek.

'We'll have to see if your father agrees.' Suzanne knew that this was a battle that she never had a chance of winning. 'You will have to feed her, make sure of her toilet arrangements and rescue her if she is stranded up a tree.'

'What is all this discussion about?' Manfred Schultz trotted down the last few stairs.

Clotilde lost no time in telling her father about 'Fräulein

Muller' and he could not resist his daughter's request. 'Very well then!' He stroked the purring animal's head.

At the end of six weeks the family Schultz and pussycat returned to Berlin. The small briefcase remained wedged down the back of the green sofa while its contents travelled in the bottom of Clotilde's little red suitcase.

# 6

## September Shocks – 1935

Dr Julius Greenbaum was a kind, gentle man who had trained at the Vienna General Hospital, qualifying as a medical doctor in 1926, and following this with a two-year course in internal medicine. During this time he became close to fellow postgraduate student Helga Steinberg from Berlin and towards the end of their joint internship they were married in the synagogue in the Steinbergs' home suburb of Mahlow. They completed their studies in 1928 and decided to set up in practice together near Helga's family home.

'Good morning, Frau Zimmermann.' Dr Julius stood up to greet his first patient of the day as Mitzi and Marlena were ushered into his smart but not opulent office by Nurse Greta Bauer. 'How can I help you?'

Mitzi shook the outstretched hand and was pleased to see Marlena follow her without any sign of trepidation. 'Good morning, Dr Greenbaum.'

'Pleased be seated.' His tone was courteous and friendly. 'Which one of you is the patient?'

'I am.' Marlena was keen to speak for herself.

'What is the main thing you have noticed to be wrong, young lady?' Mitzi was going to intervene when Marlena spoke up again.

'It's a little bit difficult to explain, Dr Greenbaum, but I'm always hungry, even when I have had the same or more to eat than Kurt...' The girl thought for a moment. 'I thought I needed extra food because I was starting to grow very quickly like some of the other girls at school.'

'Have you noticed anything else, my dear?' His softly spoken words were reassuring to Marlena.

'I seem to be very thirsty.'

Mitzi Zimmermann felt it appropriate to speak. 'What Marlena says is very true; her grandmother has also noticed how often she has to get out of bed at night to pass urine.'

'Oh Mother!' Marlena was embarrassed to have her visits to the toilet discussed in this way. 'I'm sorry, Dr Julius.'

'Never you mind, young lady. It could be a clue. Do you mind if I measure how tall you are and then we see how many kilograms you weigh?'

'Of course not!' Nurse Greta Bauer appeared without being summoned and guided Marlena to the scales, weighed her, and measured her height; then she took the girl to the examination couch and helped her up onto it. She gave her patient a reassuring pat on the shoulder, covered her with a light blanket and pulled a screen to separate the supine girl from the rest of the office.

While Marlena adjusted her navy-blue-and-white dress after being examined, Dr Julius returned to his swivel chair. 'Frau Zimmermann, your daughter shows signs of recent weight loss when at her stage in life she should be gaining kilograms; in addition her thirst and frequent passage of urine at night suggest that she is not at all well; do you mind if I ask Nurse Bauer to get Marlena to provide a specimen of urine?'

Greta Bauer had taken one step from behind the screen and stood in her smart white uniform with large white buttons down the front and a crisp white hat on her dark-brown hair.

'That will be perfectly in order, Doctor.'

'If you please, Greta.'

'Certainly, Dr Julius.' She disappeared behind the screen and returned a short while later holding a glass flask covered with a white cloth and handed it to the physician. 'Here you are, Doctor.'

A few moments later Marlena emerged from behind the screen and sat down beside her mother; she was composed but there was evidence of worry in her facial expression.

Julius Greenbaum took the flask to the workbench between the door and the window overlooking the street outside; he poured a small quantity of the flask's contents into a test tube. 'I'm now going to add Benedict's solution.' He showed them the clear Prussian blue liquid in a chemical reagent bottle. 'If there's sugar in your urine it will turn yellow or red.' He poured it in and almost immediately the fluid turned a rich brownish red. He poured away the contents down the sink in the workbench and repeated the process with the same result.

'Without any doubt a positive test.'

'What does this mean, Doctor?' There was some alarm in Frau Zimmermann's voice.

Dr Julius Greenbaum washed his hands and returned to the seat behind his desk. 'It means that your daughter is suffering from diabetes.' Marlena put her hands to her mouth but made no sound apart from the sudden intake of breath.

'But she's only a child!' Mitzi sounded a note of disbelief.

Julius laid a hand on the distraught mother's gloved hands that were now clasped together. 'So she is, but even children develop diabetes.'

'What are we going to do?' She knew that until comparatively recently diabetes had been both serious and fatal.

'It does mean a big change in your life, Marlena, but you're living in a progressive age.' He smiled at his patient. 'We'll need to give you a diet that ensures that you don't have too much sugar for your body to deal with and you will have to learn how to give yourself an injection once a day.'

Marlena's response was a surprise both for her mother and her doctor. 'Oh I'm so pleased; thank you very much, Dr Greenbaum.'

Mitzi Zimmermann put an arm around the girl's shoulders. 'I'm very proud of my daughter; you're so brave, my darling.' She was lost in thought for a few moments; it seemed odd that her daughter was pleased to be told that she had a serious illness.

'Marlena are you really pleased to know what Dr Julius has told you or are you in some way relieved?'

'Yes, I'm relieved, Mother.'

'Why, what were you worrying about?'

Since the doctor could see that his patient was finding it difficult to answer her mother, he decided on a change of tactic. 'We've only known about the cause and treatment of diabetes for thirteen years. Before 1922 the doctor was helpless and patients didn't do well.'

Frau Zimmermann was astonished, she had heard of the disease but didn't know any sufferers. 'That's amazing, Doctor; such a short time.'

'Then I am very fortunate!' Marlena brightened up considerably. Dr Julius had reassured her sufficiently for her to volunteer her previous fears. 'I had thought that people would think I was imagining feeling weak and that I wasn't trying to get better.'

'Oh I'm so sorry you felt that way.' The distraught mother took a handkerchief from her hand bag and dabbed a tear that had started to roll down Marlena's left cheek.

'Now, young lady, we must get down to practicalities.' Dr Greenbaum had a reputation for being an excellent diagnostician, a pragmatic therapist and a caring human being who followed his patients' cases meticulously. 'The medicine you are going to inject into your arm or leg is called insulin.' He got up from his chair and picked up a glass syringe with a fine needle attached. 'Nurse Bauer will show you how to inject it just underneath your skin, Marlena.'

'Oh!' There was alarm on her face. 'Do I really have to do it every day?'

'I'm afraid so, but you can see the needle is very thin and you will hardly feel it at all.'

'And is it really safe to inject?' Mitzi Zimmermann was apprehensive about this alarming treatment.

'In the early years there were some abscesses at the injection site but the recent refinements have largely resolved that problem. I shall want to see Marlena once a week for a while to check that all is well and she should visit Nurse Bauer twice weekly to be weighed and have her injection sites checked.' He turned back to Marlena. 'You will have other questions and we can answer those when you come back in a week's time; now will you go with Nurse Bauer, please?'

The still-shocked mother sat and waited for her daughter in the doctor's anteroom and thought how much this illness of diabetes was going to affect her family's lives. Nonetheless she was enormously thankful for the medical discoveries that had been made; there were compensations for being alive in Germany in 1935. Her thoughts were interrupted by her daughter joining her.

'Come, my lovely girl; we'll call in at the pharmacy on the way home.'

They emerged onto the street smiling and hand in hand and barely noticed the two men standing in a doorway on the opposite side of the street; it was still summer although the evenings in Berlin were becoming cooler. Nevertheless they were wearing light raincoats and trilby hats; they appeared not to notice Marlena and her mother as they hurried off down the street.

71

'I really liked Dr Greenbaum, Mother, and I already feel so much stronger after he explained why I was ill.' By now there was a spring in her step.

As they left the pharmacy, Mitzi noticed a newspaper boy selling the *Völkischer Beobachter*. Beside him was a flyer pasted onto a board declaring 'New Laws at Nuremberg Last Night'.

As they neared their house Marlena excitedly exclaimed. 'Father is home early; there's his new motorcar.'

True enough the large elegant black Buick with chrome attachments, wide running boards and white-walled tyres was parked outside their house. Business in the family battery factory had recently flourished mainly through the hard work of its staff; they had even established a subsidiary company in Slough in England. It was for this reason that Maximillian Zimmerman had recently been able to buy this fine American motor car.

'Of course! Your father told me last night that he would be back in time to listen to the broadcast about the Nuremberg Rally.' Mitzi looked down at her daughter and forced a smile to cross her face. 'I was so worried about our visit to Dr Julius that I had completely forgotten about it.'

They went into the modest detached house and could hear the newsreader speaking in a loud excited voice. In the far corner of the comfortably furnished sitting room they found Maximillian dressed in a smart blue business suit and red tie leaning forward in an armchair next to the radio which was placed on a low table; it was a modern piece of electronic equipment with a two-toned veneered casing.

Marlena's father looked up as they came into the room and smiled. 'Hello, little lady, how did the visit to Dr Julius go?'

'He was very nice to her. Have you finished listening to the radio; it must have been important for you to come home from work especially to listen to it.' She gave him a kiss on the left cheek.

'Yes, it was both very interesting and very worrying.' His expression was grim; he switched the radio off.

'Well, we've some very good news about Marlena. Although she has an illness, it can be treated.' Mitzi felt she should break the cause of Marlena's problem slowly to her husband. 'Would you like to tell us about the broadcast now and then we can talk about Marlena?'

'I think that would be best, before Kurt comes home from school.' Maximillian was subdued. 'I have been listening to the speech that Herr Hitler made at the rally in Nuremberg last night.'

'Will this mean a lot of changes?' Marlena was interested and her parents had agreed that she was old enough to hear what was happening in her own country.

'Certainly for Jewish people, but for all of us. Do you know the man made the outrageous comment they are polluting the racial purity of the Aryan race.'

Mitzi's face registered horror. 'That is a vile thing to say; the Jews are among our most distinguished citizens: they are leaders in the professions and the civil service.' She put an arm around Marlena's shoulders. 'Dr Greenbaum, who has been so wonderful with our daughter today, is Jewish.'

'He also spoke of the Aryan race being the true Germany!' Maximillian sat back in his armchair beside his much-loved radio which had, only a short while before, delivered such devastating news. 'I have read about it in some newspaper article; it all seemed to me like a lot of pseudo-scientific mumbo-jumbo.'

'What did it say, my dear?' Mitzi regarded her husband as an intelligent and observant man who was unlikely to be misled by anything that lacked logic and truth.

'The piece was about the original speakers of Indo-European languages being the true ancestors of the German people but it didn't mention any real facts.' He spread his hands and shrugged his shoulders. 'These are the genuine Aryan race and those who don't belong don't have a place in Nazi Germany.'

'It's disgraceful!' Mitzi turned to her daughter. 'Remember, darling, don't mention these matters outside our house ... Now I am going to make us all some lunch while Marlena tells you about her consultation with Dr Greenbaum.'

'No extra sugar for me, Mother, please.' The young girl reminded her mother as she left the room. 'It's part of my new diet, Father. I have a condition called diabetes which means I have too much sugar in my blood because I don't produce enough of a chemical called insulin.'

Maximillian, though shocked, was impressed with his daughter's understanding of her illness. 'I think you must have listened to your doctor very carefully, darling.'

'I was very pleased to hear what he said even though it means giving myself injections of insulin.' She smiled happily at her father. 'You see, I thought people would think that I was pretending to be ill so that I wouldn't have to go to school.'

'Do you dislike the teachers, Marlena?'

'Fräulein Fischer, the games mistress, was always saying that I didn't run as fast as I should because I wasn't trying hard enough.' A tear trickled down the distressed girl's right cheek. 'It was so upsetting to be accused of not making any effort.'

Maximillian had no idea that this bullying by a teacher had been taking place. 'Marlena, I know that it's just not in your nature for you to avoid doing your very best at everything you do; I'm so sorry that you were anxious in this horrible way. Now you know what is wrong and that it's going to be treated, I'm sure Fräulein Fischer will be astonished to see you fly past the other girls.' He gave her a kiss on the forehead.

'I shall look forward to seeing Marlena fly!' Kurt bounded into the sitting room with his satchel containing his schoolbooks still on his back. 'It sounds as though a miracle took place at the doctor's office.' The exuberant young boy had a wide grin on his face.

'You're home early from school, young man?' said Mitzi, entering the room carrying a plate of roast goose sandwiches. 'Are your teachers on strike?' She smiled at her son.

'No, Mother, we were given a half-day holiday by Herr Braun, the headmaster, who told us that an emergency had arisen and that he needed to hold a special staff meeting with all the teachers.' He smiled happily while his mother and father exchanged perplexed glances. 'But anyway, what happened at the doctor's Marlena?' His voice showed his genuine concern.

The little boy was told about Marlena's illness and what Nurse Bauer had taught her about preparing the syringe and insulin for her daily injection.

'Can I give Marlena an injection.'

'That, young man, is taking helpfulness and enthusiasm to excess!' Mitzi smiled at her irrepressible son.

'I'm sorry, Mother.' Kurt was a little downcast but he brightened up when he saw his favourite goose and sauerkraut sandwiches. 'Can I help myself?'

Marlena giggled; she knew what her father would say.

'You can help yourself, Kurt,' Maximillian smiled, 'but the question you should be asking your mother is *may* you help yourself.'

'All right, Kurt, please take one.' Mitzi joined in the general good humour. 'I think your father has finished his schoolteacher role for today.' She returned to the kitchen and came back with a smaller plate of biscuits, boiled ham, half a grapefruit and a small glass of milk. 'There we are, Marlena. I hope you find it appetizing even without sugar!'

The rest of the day passed very quickly and eventually

the two young people's eyes could hardly stay open and there was little protest when their mother ushered them upstairs with the promise of some warm milk once they were in bed.

Once all was quiet Mitzi came and sat beside her husband. 'Was the speech in Nuremberg as serious as you had expected?' She didn't try to cover up her anxiety now.

'It was certainly that! In fact sinister describes it best.' He took in a deep breath and let out a sigh. 'Although the Jews are the Nazis' main target, I think other unfortunate people are being caught up in this orgy of loathsome prejudice ... the mentally ill, gypsies, homosexuals ... Sometimes I think none of us will be spared in the end!'

'What do you think will happen next?

'Very little. The Nazis will have to keep a semblance of respectability because of the Olympic Games next year; the eyes of the world will be on Germany.'

'Do you think this will put us even more under the spotlight?'

Maximillian embraced his wife and kissed her on the forehead. 'Yes I do, my love; yes I do. That is my hope...'

# 7

## *Towards the Olympic Games*

After the family Schultz had arrived back at their apartment in Dahlem, Clotilde rapidly unpacked her suitcase; she left the document from the Rügen briefcase inside and put it on top of her bedroom cupboard. Then she turned her attention to Fräulein Müller, the new addition to the household, the black-and-white cat that had joined them on their island holiday.

Manfred collected the large amount of newspapers and mail that had accumulated during their absence and sat down at his roll-topped desk that stood against the wall opposite the large bay window in the living room of the family's apartment. The piece of furniture had belonged to his grandfather and he had known it all his life. On the top of the pile was the September 16th edition of the *Deutsche Allgemeine Zeitung*; the headline announced in large letters 'Draconian Laws Declared at Nuremburg Rally'.

The schoolmaster was alarmed by what he read and called to his wife who was unpacking in their bedroom. 'Suzanne, my love, can you come here?'

'I will be with you in one moment.'

While he was waiting Manfred noticed an article on one of the inside pages: 'Revenge for Versailles Humiliation of Germany'. Underneath it continued: 'We remind our readers that the 1919 treaty forced our country to accept sole responsibility for the world war, insisted that we disarm to an army of less than one hundred thousand men, make territorial concessions and pay reparations of 132 billion marks. This newspaper regarded the so-called treaty as grossly unfair and it is, therefore, not surprising that military conscription was reintroduced on March 16th earlier this year...'

He had just finished reading the article when Suzanne came into the room. 'You sound upset, my dear.'

'Look at what the Führer declared at Nuremberg last night. New so-called laws to prevent the German Jewish population from polluting the racial purity of the Aryan race in this country.'

'That not only sounds terrible; it's also ridiculous.' Suzanne was outraged. 'Why would anyone fall for such nonsense?' Suzanne could not believe what was happening in her own country.

'I'm no psychologist but I think this is mass hysteria. That man is neither handsome in appearance nor beautiful in his thoughts.' He spread his hands in despair. 'He has charisma but more importantly he has that evil little propaganda monster Dr Joseph Goebbels who tells him what to say.' He paused for a moment. 'I think we should be even more careful about what *we* say.'

Suzanne called out to her daughters, and Margit and Clotilde came and joined their parents.

'Girls, we live in dangerous times, and what we say here in the house, let it stay inside the house when we go outside into the wide world.' She looked at her children. 'It's a lot to ask of you at your ages but your father and I are so very worried by what is happening in Germany.'

'We won't breathe a word, Mother.' Clotilde sounded amazingly mature for her seven years. She didn't mention that the two sisters had already discussed some of the unhappy sights they had already witnessed.

The parents went on to tell their daughters about the

new laws and the programme of militarization that was underway.

'Will we be affected by all this?' Margit asked.

'Well, I hope that I won't be conscripted into the army, although I think I'm too old for that at the moment. I think what we'll really notice are Jewish people losing their jobs as professionals and in local government.'

Suzanne looked horrified. 'What you're saying is that all Jewish people in public life – your colleagues, doctors, lawyers and architects – will be dismissed.'

Her daughters looked up at their mother but remained silent.

'You know I'm not naturally pessimistic...' A smile crossed his face. '...Except where the prospects of some of my pupils passing their final grades in French and English are concerned.'

The girls both giggled and their mother smiled. 'I do think we'll notice immediate changes in our lives but the worst will be held off until after the Olympic Games.' His tone was grim and foreboding.

'Why will the athletics have an effect on politics?' Margit asked.

Manfred looked towards his children. 'The eyes of the world will be on Germany! We'll be in newsreels, newspaper reports, radio and innumerable magazines across the world. The economy of our country is still fragile and the new government doesn't want to upset any trade agreements or other arrangements that affect the financial prosperity of our people.'

'And the Games will bring in money for the Government, too, remember!' Suzanne commented. 'The authorities will use the profits for their own particular projects which I fear will be militaristic.' Suzanne tone was grave.

'What *are* the Olympic Games mother?' Clotilde's intervention broke the tension that was developing.

'You will have to ask your father.' Suzanne smiled at her diplomatic young daughter.

'I teach English, French and German,' Manfred grinned. 'It will have to be your mother that gives the history lesson.'

'Oh please, Mother, do tell us the history of the Olympic Games!' Margit cried.

'It looks as though your father is excused, but you will have to give me a day or two to do my homework.' She paused a moment. 'You've the rest of the week to put all your energies into school and I will have everything ready for the Olympic history lesson on Saturday.'

'I'm sorry if we've given you a lot of work mother.' Margit beamed at Suzanne. 'Though I can hardly wait until Saturday.'

'Neither can I!' Clotilde joined in.

At that moment the cat that had been irreverently named Fräulein Müller strolled into the sitting room and her owner picked up the affectionate animal.

'That young lady is hungry, Clotilde. You remember what we agreed: if she came home with us you would look after her.'

'Yes, Mother. Come with me, Fräulein Müller, we'll go and find those delicious fish heads I saved for you, my lovely pussycat.' Clotilde was rewarded with loud purring.

Manfred put an arm around his wife's shoulders. 'You must admit, my dear, our daughter is keeping her promise.'

The week passed by – both girls' minds were occupied by so many things at school that Saturday breakfast time arrived almost without warning.

'Boiled eggs, toast and honey ... my favourite! Thank you, Mother.' Margit was ravenous and attacked her first egg with vigour.

'I'm pleased it meets with your approval. Clotilde has an appetite this morning, too!' Susanne was pleased to see her daughters eating well. 'I hope you also have an equal hunger for the great Olympic history lesson?'

'Oh yes, oh yes!' the two sisters chimed in together.

When the breakfast table had been cleared Suzanne sat down opposite her daughters and produced her notes which she spread out in front of her.

'The first Games were held in Greece 776 years before Christ was born,' she began.

'That's BC, isn't it, Mother?'

'Absolutely, Margit. In legend they had been started even long before that by a very strong man called Hercules in the valley of Olympia in the south-west of the country; it was a beautiful place with many statues and temples...'

'What are temples, Mother?' Clotilde was paying great attention to the lesson.

'They are similar to churches but existed long before the start of Christianity.'

'Do you think Adolf Hitler is a Christian, Mother?'

'I really don't know, Margit, but I do know that has nothing to do with the ancient Olympic Games.' Her tone was a little severe, though she had asked herself the same question occasionally.

'I'm sorry, Mother. Please continue.'

'One of the statues was made of ivory and gold; it represented Zeus, the king of the gods and was a great bearded figure carrying a thunderbolt; this amazing creation was one of the Seven Wonders of the World...'

'I wish I could go and see Olympia, Mother.' Clotilde was loving her mother's story.

'The valley is still there but all that remains of the former structures erected to honour the gods are a few broken columns and some of the stone amphitheatre seats for the spectators of the Games.'

'Does anything happen at Olympia nowadays, Mother?'

'Oh yes, my darling Clotilde, that is where the ceremony

81

of lighting the Olympic torch takes place and then it's carried by athletes, changing over at intervals; until it's brought into the Olympic Stadium where the Games are due to take place ... and this time it's Berlin that is hosting the event, four years after the previous games in Los Angeles.'

'Was there anything else at Olympia in the beginning?' Clotilde was paying full attention.

Suzanne consulted her notes. 'A king named Iphitus was told by the oracle at Delphi to command Hercules to plant an olive tree at Olympia so that the leaves could be used to make the wreath which was put on the head of the athlete who won a race or other event.'

'Where is Delphi and what is an oracle?' Margit was trying to redeem herself.

'Delphi is a little further north of Olympia, in the central part of Greece ... The oracle was a humble woman of good character chosen to be the voice of Apollo, the son of Zeus; people great and ordinary came to ask her advice.'

'What a lovely story, Mother,' Clotilde said with a mischievous smile. 'If she's still there we could go and ask her if she could make Fräulein Müller nice to everyone at school.'

'She's not there now, it was a long time ago, and anyway I think that's a silly idea.'

'It was, Mother. I'm sorry!' At that moment the other Fräulein Müller jumped up onto the young girl's lap. 'You're telling the story very well; can we go on?'

'Of course but no more silliness! At the first Games there was only one event – the two-hundred metre dash called a stadium.' The storyteller looked down at her papers. 'The next Games were four years later, also at Olympia, but there were now two events – the one stadium and the two stadia races.' Suzanne now had her audience's full attention. 'In 720 BC the twenty-four stadia race was added; after another four years came the pentathlon consisting of five events – running, wrestling, leaping, discus and javelin throwing.'

'Were all five competitions won by the same athlete?'

'Exactly, Margit. The winner was the man whose overall performance was the best ... Anyway, that's how the Games remained for the next six hundred years and during that time the four-year intervals became the basis of the Greek calendar.'

'That is amazing. What happened next mother?' The older daughter was now keen on the lesson.

'The Romans occupied Greece and then General Sulla moved the Olympic Games to Rome and there they continued every four years until AD 393 when the Christian Emperor Theodosius the First abolished the Games; they had taken place at four-yearly intervals without interruption for 1,170 years.'

'That wasn't a very Christian thing to do.' Clotilde was quite angry.

'What wasn't?' Her sister was puzzled.

'Abolishing the Olympic Games.'

'I have to say I agree.' Suzanne nodded approval at her younger daughter. 'People in this world want to ban things when they feel threatened by them.'

'Do you think the Romans wanted to watch the Games rather than go to church, Mother?'

'I expect that was the explanation, my dear.' The self-appointed tutor on the history of the Olympics looked down and consulted her notes. 'Well, now we come to the modern Games which were the idea of Baron Pierre de Coubertin who campaigned for them to be re-introduced. And so the first modern Games were held in Athens on March 24th, 1896 ... That's it, girls. My lecture is complete.'

Both girls clapped their hands enthusiastically. 'What a wonderful lesson, Mother, you must have worked very hard.'

'Thank you, Margit. I hope you remember a little bit of it at least. Do you have any questions?'

'Where is Athens, Mother?'

'It's the capital city of Greece, Clotilde.' Suzanne felt quite tired after her marathon lesson. 'It seemed only right to hold the first new Games in the country where they had originated.'

At that moment Manfred came into the room clapping his hands together. 'I have one more question.' All the ladies' heads turned towards him. 'Who won the first race?'

'I can answer that...' The great Olympic Games teacher consulted the last page of her notes. 'The winner was James Conolly, a student.'

The whole family laughed, cheered and hugged each other.

# 8

## *Mahlow – March 1936*

Mitzi Zimmermann was a follower of fashion but not extravagantly so; she only bought new clothes when it was necessary and always carefully selected her purchase. Today she wore a slim-line, long navy-blue skirt with a white polka dot pattern together with a wide-collared white silk blouse and a matching navy-blue jacket; her fair hair was cut short at the back with waves passing down in front of each ear.

She greeted her eleven-year-old daughter Marlena at the front door of the family house in Mahlow; the girl was returning from a routine follow-up visit to Dr Julius Greenbaum at his surgery two streets away in Weisestrasse.

'Did everything go well with the doctor, my dear?' She had great confidence in their Jewish physician's professional ability.

'Oh yes, mother. Dr Julius was very kind; he weighed me, measured how tall I was and tested my urine and told me everything is fine. I've grown three centimetres and put on two and a half kilograms since we came back from our summer holidays in Seebad Ahlbeck.' The girl looked healthy, happy and full of energy; her fresh-complexioned face was lit by an enchanting smile. She was a striking contrast to the weak, emaciated and semi-comatose creature that had returned from the Baltic seven months earlier.

'There was one thing that was different at Dr Julius's surgery today.' A puzzled expression puckered her forehead.

'What was that?' Her mother was suddenly struck by her daughter's emerging beauty.

'There were no other patients. On my previous visits there were always five or six more people in the waiting room.'

'Did Nurse Bauer make any comment?'

'No, Mother; she was her usual super-efficient self.'

'I expect it was just a quiet day,' Mitzi heard herself reassuring Marlena but felt uneasy. She walked towards the kitchen. 'Would orange juice and a snack be all right, my dear?'

'I don't think I should have a chocolate biscuit until later but I would like a plain one with the drink.' She was getting to know her body and understand her illness very well and her family were both pleased and proud of her.

'Very well.' Marlena's mother had already poured out their drinks before she noticed a neatly written note on lined schoolbook paper on the table. 'There's a letter here from Kurt.' She brought it into the sitting room on the tray with the snack. She placed it on the table and read out what Kurt had written. ' "I will be a little late home from school as I'm meeting Lothar." '

'Does Father allow him to go off by himself after school?'

'Not usually, my dear; he has only just had his eighth birthday...' She frowned. 'Your father likes to keep an eye on Kurt's activities although I think he finds it a bit of a full-time job especially when he dreams up a new scheme to save the world.'

Marlena giggled. 'Like last week when he had this brilliant idea of saving the dodo from extinction; he really thought he had succeeded.'

The children's mother smiled. 'I just wish he had not used that delicious goose out of the icebox and your father's beautiful new umbrella with a beech-wood handle as his magic wand.'

'What do I hear about my umbrella?' Maximillian Zimmermann had quietly entered the room and now walked over to the sofa, sat next to his wife, put one arm around her shoulders and stretched out his opposite hand to his daughter who ran over and took it.

'Kurt used it as a magic wand to conjure the dodo back from extinction!' The young mother spread her hands and shrugged her shoulders.

'Ah, I do remember ... not a scintillating success,' he said with a smile. 'In fact I think we could reasonably say it was an abject failure.'

'Did our imaginative young son mention anything to you about what he was going to do after school?' Mitzi sounded and looked anxious.

'Just as I was going out of the door this morning on the way to the factory Kurt briefly asked me if it was in order for him to speak to Lothar ... I couldn't remember who he was to start with, then I recalled that very polite man with fair hair from whom we rented the holiday house on Usedom Island and who took Kurt fishing.'

'He has gone to *meet* him, not just speak with the man.'

'At least we know what he is doing even if we don't know where he is doing it.' Maximillian didn't seem to share his wife's concern.

'Max, he is only just eight years old and this is Berlin!' Mitzi's use of her husband's shorter name betrayed her anxiety. 'Were you going to your rowing practice on the River Spree? If so...'

Marlena interrupted to break the tension. 'You know, I think Father secretly thinks he is going to take part in the Olympic Games in August.'

Meanwhile, a couple of kilometres away the entrance to Kurt's school was suddenly filling up with excited young boys and girls all speaking at the same time as they exited into the playground and headed towards the gates. Among the waiting parents was the tall blond-haired Lothar Meyer. The eight-year-old fair-complexioned schoolboy spotted the fisherman immediately.

'Hello, *mein Kapitän*. *Gut dass ich sie wider siehe!*' He vigorously shook Lothar's hand. 'I found your letter in my satchel but I don't know how it got there.'

'You didn't see me on the bus when it brought everyone to school yesterday. I was sitting right behind you and slipped it in quite easily.'

'Amazing, *mein Kapitän*; I felt nothing. Anyway how can I help you?' Kurt had only just finished shaking Lothar's right hand. 'It's months since I last saw you but I'm available if you need crew for the boat.' There was enthusiasm and hope in his voice.

'You're about thirty-three jumps ahead of me, young man.' The seasoned sailor laughed as he took in the boy in his navy-blue shorts, a grey shirt and black shoes and socks; he had grown noticeably since they were together during the previous summer. 'Do you remember Engelbert who was with us when we went fishing together?'

'I certainly do! He was super friendly; me and Hermann really liked him; I hope nothing bad has happened to him.'

'Oh no,' the man hesitated. 'Well, he has been conscripted into the army and is now undergoing training to be a fighting soldier.'

Lothar's look of concern alarmed Kurt. 'I don't know what "conscripted" means.'

'It's a new law; he has been made to join the military.'

'Why was it just Engelbert; why not you as well?'

'He is twenty-two years old, I'm forty-seven; they wouldn't want old bones like mine.'

'Very good fisherman bones, my friend.' A broad smile lit up Kurt's face.

'I trust you're correct about that, sailor, but I have to tell you something else about Engelbert; he had another job in addition to working on the boat; a very important and difficult mission.'

'What was that, Lothar?'

'He found out that there were some people in serious danger.' The man bent his head and spoke to Kurt in hushed tones. 'He discovered a family of five from Berlin hiding in a boatshed on the beach outside Seebad Ahlbeck and we took them into my house where they stayed in the bedroom at the back beside mine.' While this conversation was taking place Lothar had been gently guiding the boy along the street away from the school. 'The father of the family told us that he was a member of the Communist Party and that he feared for his family's life.'

'When was that, my old friend?' The young boy was fascinated.

'Not so much of the "old" if you don't mind.' They both laughed and then Lothar's expression changed to one of seriousness. 'Didn't you hear them? They were in the house at the same time as you and your family?'

Kurt hesitated. 'I think something woke me at about two o'clock one morning and I looked out of the window and saw you and three other people together with two children walking onto the beach.'

'How did you know it was me?'

'It was a full moon that night!' The excited boy thought for a moment, recalling that night in August; it seemed a long time ago now since he had leaned out of that top floor bedroom window. 'You were lit up very well and no one else is as tall as *mein Kapitän*.'

Lothar smiled. 'We thought nobody had seen us!' He put a strong hand on Kurt's left shoulder. 'We obviously didn't allow for my eagle-eyed shipmate here.' They both burst out laughing and carried on walking along the street towards Kurt's bus stop.

'Actually, this is a serious matter my friend.'

'I know, *mein Kapitän*.'

'How is that, my sailor-man?'

'I saw the expression on your face when you told me Engelbert had found a family hiding in a boathouse ... Was there something ... unusual about them?'

He was clearly a very astute boy for his eight years and Lothar felt he should not hide the truth from him. 'They were an unwanted German family.'

His young friend didn't miss a trick. 'I know that Gypsies, Jews and Communists are having a very bad time at the moment. Somehow they have become different kinds of Germans.'

'You're quite right; we were all Germans until last September in Nuremberg; now there's us and them.' Lothar's tone betrayed great sadness. 'And it's *them* I mean to help. We've been taking them by boat over to Bornholm, the Danish island you can see from Rügen.'

They came to a halt and Lothar turned and looked Kurt straight in his bright blue eyes. 'Kurt, I need your help to help these people.'

'Yes, *mein Kapitän*; ' Kurt's gaze back didn't waver. He felt very proud to be part of Lothar's rescue plan. 'I think you're a great man, *mein Kapitän*. I will do whatever you ask of me.' The boy put his small but perfectly formed right hand into the roughened palm of the tall fisherman.

'I have thought about your part in this enterprise, my friend, and I'm going to ask you and Lorelei to meet a Jewish family and bring them to me at Stettiner Bahnhof.' He paused and saw that Kurt was listening intently. 'It will look less conspicuous and with your fair complexion the party will blend into the crowd at the station.'

'Lorelei?!' The boy's astonishment was made clear by the one-word question.

'Yes, I found her very helpful when your family was

staying in my house for your holidays last August ... Lorelei was wonderful to them, keeping their spirits high and feeding them.'

'It's wonderful that you and Lorelei have been doing these things.' The schoolboy drew himself up to his full height, 'I had my eighth birthday last month and I think I'm old enough to be the crew on your boat.'

'Kurt, my sailor-man, I can't possibly take you on the boat to Bornholm; there's your family and school to think of; it would be terrible if I took you away from them.'

Just as the boy opened his mouth to protest the bus approached.

'Have a safe journey home; we'll meet again outside your school tomorrow.' He gave a helping hand to his young friend and the bus moved off on its way.

Lothar turned to walk away towards his lodgings. As he progressed along the wide pavement he stroked the stubble on his unshaven chin. 'It might just be possible,' he mused.

At the Zimmermann home Maximillian had changed from his business suit into his red rowing tracksuit and now came down the stairs to where Marlena was sitting at the hall table doing her school homework.

'Kurt not home yet?'

'No, Father.' She turned her attention back to the rivers and mountains of Europe.

Mitzi appeared from the kitchen, looking worried. She saw her husband in his rowing clothes.

'Max, Kurt is still out. You can't possibly be thinking of going rowing!'

'Lothar was a very pleasant man,' her husband protested. 'He could not possibly get Kurt into any trouble.'

At that moment the boy came in through the front door. 'Me get in any trouble? Impossible!' There was a broad grin on his face, 'I'm always safe with *mein Kapitän.*'

'Now that we're sure Kurt has come home in one piece,

91

I will go to my rowing training.' Maximillian started to walk towards the front door. 'I will see you all for supper.'

'Before you leave, Father, may I ask a question?

'Of course, Kurt! Ask away.'

'May I go and stay with Hermann in the school holidays which start next week?'

'But he lives in Munich; that's more than six hundred kilometres away.' Mitzi was alarmed.

'I can go on the train; Hermann's father will meet me at the station.'

Maximillian resolutely walked towards the main entrance. 'Kurt, I think you should discuss this with your mother; I will support whatever she decides.' He patted his son on the right shoulder and departed.

'Kurt come into the kitchen and have some orange juice and biscuits, it's been a long time since your school lunch.'

'Yes, Mother.' He followed her from the room.

Once the drink and chocolate biscuits were on the table Mitzi brought up the subject of the Munich visit again.

'I didn't know you had kept in touch with Hermann.'

'Oh yes mother, we've been exchanging letters every week.'

'Every week, Kurt?'

'Yes, Mother'

'Kurt, I have never heard so many "yes, Mothers" from you or anyone else.' Frau Zimmermann's voice rose slightly. 'Will you tell me exactly what is going on?' She sat down at the kitchen table and tried to look into her son's eyes which were firmly focused on his plate of chocolate biscuits. 'And please don't say "yes, Mother".'

'No, Mother.'

'Kurrrrt!'

The eight-year old realized he was crossing the line and his lovely mother was becoming angry. 'Me and Hermann want to get together.'

'Why is that, young man?'

'We're friends.' At that moment Kurt thought he had an inspired idea. 'We'll be able to compare each other's schoolwork, especially geometry.' The accompanying smile was broad.

'Kurt, you know that I know that when two young schoolboys get together in the school holidays the last thing their thoughts turn to is geometry; it's much more likely they will be planning which river bank they will bicycle to in order to try out their new fishing rods!' Mitzi articulated the last words very firmly.

'Yes, Mother.' Kurt wasn't making the same mistake twice. 'You're quite right, we're going fishing and I'm really looking forward to it.' The smile that followed this little white lie was truly angelic – the eight-year-old boy reasoned it was in a good cause, a very good cause.

'Why didn't you say so to begin with?' Mitzi came over and embraced her son. 'Of course you can go and see Hermann in Munich. Why don't you go to your father's office and telephone him now? The Schmidts' number is in the little book.' Mitzi's face had an expression of relief and as he departed he heard her give a big sigh: 'That's all right then!'

Kurt entered the small oak-panelled office, shut the door behind him and sat down behind the desk. He lifted up the receiver, waited a few moments and then asked the operator to be put through to the Munich number. Fortunately it was his friend who answered. 'Hermann, my old friend, good to hear your voice; how are you?'

'Kurt, is that you up in Berlin?'

'It is indeed, my fellow fisherman. The Easter holidays are here; would you like to come up to the capital city and we'll arrange some fishing trips?'

'I would like that very much, my friend; I will go and ask my mother if it will be in order; can you hang on a moment or two?'

'Of course, Hermann.' He could hear his friend speaking to Frau Bertina Schmidt but didn't catch the exact words that were being exchanged.

A few moments later he heard, 'Kurt are you still there?'

'Yes, can you come?'

'Mother says it will be fine if I don't mind travelling alone on the train.'

'Fantastic, it's our last day of school tomorrow so I will meet you off the first train from Munich in two days' time. Is that all right?'

'Sure, see you then. Bye.'

'Great! Bye.' Kurt put the telephone down quietly.

The following day Lothar waited outside Kurt's school and watched as his young friend came hurtling out of the school. He really didn't like his studies, mainly because of one particular teacher who seemed to think that knowledge could be imparted into his pupils by hurting their delicate young hands with a thin whippy cane.

'Hello there, sailor-man, you were quick to escape the seat of learning.' He paused while the schoolboy regained his normal breathing.; 'I have bad news, Kurt. I'd found a crewman for our Bornholm trip but he's pulled out; he fell from a mast he was climbing to unsnag some wires and broke his leg...'

'No problem, *mein Kapitän*.' The smile was huge.

'It's a *big* problem; I can't manage to sail my boat all by myself.' Lothar spread his hands hopelessly. 'We'll have to postpone the exodus of the Jewish family we had planned for tomorrow.'

Kurt drew in his breath sharply; things could not have worked out better. '*Mein Kapitän*, I think I have the solution to your crewing problem.'

'I value your support, my friend, but I cannot see how you can possibly solve this problem.'

'It's simple, Hermann and I together add up to one

94

sailor...' He wanted to press home his surprise announcement. 'We can easily be your crew.'

At that moment a smartly but inconspicuously dressed woman in her mid-thirties walked along the street and joined them. Kurt took her unexpected appearance all in his stride. 'Good to see you again, Lorelei. How is Grandmamma?'

Romhilde's maid wore a slim-fitting high-waisted dark-green skirt, matching jacket and a white cotton blouse. 'She's well, thank you, Kurt.' She turned towards Lothar and gave him a saucy wink. 'Are you two arranging another fishing trip?'

'No, Lorelei, it's much more important than that.' The schoolboy drew himself up to his full height. 'My friend Hermann and I are going to make up our Captain's crew on his next rescue mission.'

The surprised woman's mouth opened but no sound came out and she covered it with her left hand. She rapidly recovered her composure. 'Is this true, Lothar? It could be very dangerous: there are the risks on the boat and not least the ever-present new secret police. And in any case his family will never agree!'

'It's the first I've heard of it too,' Lothar protested. 'I haven't agreed to this young sailor's brave suggestion.'

'You will take us, *mein Kapitän*, won't you?' Kurt then thought he should play his master card. 'Surely it's very dangerous for the family you've arranged to take to Bornholm Island to stay here in Germany?'

'It is indeed, my sailor-man.'

'I went to see them in their house in Charlottenstrasse close to where it crosses Unter den Linden this morning and Professor Joseph Steinberg is becoming very agitated; he's now fearful for his family's lives.' Lorelei's anxiety for the Jewish academic was clear in her voice. The two adults looked at each other as if silently asking what they should do.

'Kurt, this man's name is a very big secret; please don't mention it to anyone.'

Lothar put his hands on both of the young schoolboy's shoulders. 'I know I can trust you, my sailor-man.'

'Not a word, *mein Kapitän*. Does this mean I can come?'

Lothar hesitated and then seemed suddenly to decide. 'Yes, Kurt. Be at the Stettiner Bahnhof at six o'clock tomorrow afternoon, where Lorelei, the family Steinberg and I will be waiting for you to catch the night train to Seebad Ahlbeck.'

# 9

## Anxious Times at Dahlem

The sun shone on the Berlin suburb on March 7th, 1936 and there was a strong cold wind from the north-east; most of the winter snow had now melted but there was still some present on the lower branches of the taller trees in the Grunewald. Into this scene skipped a happy Clotilde on her way home from school for the Easter holidays; she wore a navy-blue woollen coat and a light-blue knitted scarf with white horizontal stripes.

'Hooray for holidays!' she sang to nobody in particular. She didn't dislike her school and teachers but nonetheless mused out loud, 'Anyone could have too much of Fräulein Ulrike Müller.'

She thought about how earlier that day the good schoolteacher had spoken to Clotilde's class about Adolf Hitler's many new laws.

'One of them concerns all of you.' The eight-year-old school girl remembered the buzz of excitement that greeted the announcement. 'Those of you that have worked hard will stay in this school three years instead of the usual four and move into the senior grammar school twelve months before you had expected.' Afterwards the astonished girls had spoken of nothing else all day.

Clotilde was now approaching the Schultz family apartment building. 'I *will* be one of those who go to the senior school a year early.' There was quiet determination in her

97

voice as she addressed the front door. She let herself in and found Margit in the entrance hall with her finger pressed to her lips.

'Shush, Father came home early and is now telling mother about something terrible that happened at his school today.' She cupped her ear to try and hear what was being said on the other side of the closed sitting room door.

'... His face was white, his lips were trembling and his hands shaking when he returned to the staff common room ... Herr Benjamin Klein has been a wonderful science teacher at our school for twenty-two years; the examination results for the boys he teaches have been better than anywhere else in the city; he was loved by the pupils and enormously respected by his colleagues...'

Margit knocked on the sitting-room door and it was opened by their mother, Suzanne. 'Come in, girls. Your father has come home for the school holidays with some very upsetting news about his good friend the science teacher.'

The two Schultz girls followed their mother into the sitting room and saw their father with a dejected look on his face. He was slumped in one of the light blue-and-white upholstered armchairs.

'Manfred, my dearest, our daughters are both home from school and looking forward to the Easter holidays.' Suzanne sat on the arm of her husband's chair and put her right arm around his shoulders.

'I know how deeply you feel about Herr Klein losing his job, darling, and the danger he and his family are facing but I may just have an idea where we may help them.'

The devoted teacher of German, French and English visibly brightened. 'What is it?'

'Just wait and see!' Suzanne smiled, tapping a finger against her nose.

'Come here, girls' Manfred said. 'We've got a surprise.'

The two children approached their parents and joined in a collective family hug.

'Your mother and I were planning a trip to Potsdamer Platz tomorrow; we'll go by steam train and eat at the Wertheim Restaurant.'

'How wonderful, Father!' Margit hugged him even harder. 'I think these Easter holidays are going to be really special.' She kissed her father on the forehead.

Clotilde, who by now was firmly grasped in this family knot and having a little bit of difficulty in breathing, croaked, 'It will be thrilling.'

Suzanne immediately recognized the problem and disentangled herself from the group and headed for the sitting-room door. In the hall she took her thick dark-green raincoat off the clothes hook and tied a yellow-and-blue headscarf covering her long fair hair.

'I'm going out for a few minutes. There's some lemonade and biscuits in the kitchen; it will help you to plan the trip.' The front door closed.

'Where has she gone, Father?' Clotilde's curiosity was insatiable.

'I really don't know, my darling daughter.' Manfred took both daughters by the hand and led them into the kitchen. 'The first things we need are pencils and a notebook.'

'Surely, Father, the first things we need are lemonade and biscuits.' Margit sported a mischievous grin.

'You're quite right, young lady,' he smiled. 'I usually find that my pupils' minds work better if their stomachs are full.' He poured lemonade from a jug into three glasses and they all helped themselves to thick yeast and buttermilk biscuits.

'Now to work, young ladies.' Manfred opened the notebook. 'What time do we need to set off to Dahlem railway station to be in good time for the train to get us to Potsdamer Platz by ten o'clock?'

'Why do we have to be there so early, Father?'

'Because there's lots to see before we have lunch at the Wertheim Restaurant in the Jewish Warehouse.'

Suzanne had slipped back into the apartment unheard by the rest of the family.

'You got back quickly and your smile tells me that you've had a successful expedition. Are you going to tell us about it?'

'Later, we have to complete our plans for tomorrow morning.' She picked up the notebook. 'Not much progress here.' She read out: 'Time of arrival at the station ... nothing!'

'You were only out for a few minutes!' Margit was a little hurt, Eventually, however, the plans were made, allowing time for a light breakfast and a fifteen-minute walk to the railway station.

Later that evening after the girls had gone to their bedrooms Manfred asked. 'What was your mysterious trip all about?'

'After you went to school this morning I had a visit from Frau Getmann who has the apartment immediately below ours,' Suzanne smiled. 'I just wanted to be quite sure that I had correctly understood what she had said to me.'

'And what was that?' Manfred sounded only mildly curious.

'Rachel, her husband Nathan, their two daughters and her mother are planning on leaving Germany . . .' She paused for a moment. 'Permanently!'

'But why? Things aren't so bad yet for the Jews!'

'I think they're already bad. They've been getting abusive remarks in the streets. Someone they knew was even assaulted.'

'Poor Benjamin Klein said that the headmaster had been told that if he didn't dismiss him he would be sent to a concentration camp to learn about Nazi principles. They'd send round the Brownshirts to intimidate him.'

'I think your colleague Benjamin Klein and his family may be in real danger.'

'Why especially him?'

'He's a well-respected intellectual who is Jewish; they see him as a threat.'

'Do you think I should warn him. I wonder what he would do.'

They discussed the grim news and suddenly Suzanne shone some light into the gloom. 'We can't foretell the future; our focus tonight should be giving our two lovely daughters a wonderful first day to their school holidays.'

Manfred brightened up immediately. 'As always, you're seeing things more clearly than I do, my darling,'

He rose from his armchair and went over to his wife and kissed her forehead. 'It's been an eventful day; I'm ready for bed.' They both slept fitfully that night, tossing and turning; their sleep disturbed by anxiety about the science teacher.

The following morning, after a light breakfast of ham rolls and tea, the family set off on foot for the railway station; Suzanne wore her dark-green raincoat over her grey calf-length woollen skirt with a light-blue jumper on top. Her daughters were dressed similarly to their mother but with short grey socks and black lace-up shoes. Their father was a remarkable sight on this dry but windy March day: he sported a very smart pair of light brown plus-four trousers, long fawn socks, a yellow shirt and a dark-brown tweed jacket.

'I hope you're proud of your father's new outfit; I certainly am.' Suzanne linked her arm through that of her husband. She thought she detected giggling from in front of her. 'Girls!' Her tone was firm and the silence was immediate, interrupted only by the family's footsteps.

Manfred was oblivious. 'They certainly have noticed my plus-fours; I expect I look ten years younger.'

101

'I'm sure that's the case, dear!'

'Oh yes, Father,' Clotilde said, anxious to repair any possible damage. 'You can be my boyfriend if you like.'

'I'm afraid you can't have him, my darling daughter; he's already *my* boyfriend,' Suzanne laughed. Then she leaned down and hugged Clotilde and whispered, 'I got there first.'

At nine o'clock precisely Manfred was buying their tickets at the station office.

'Two and two halves return to Anhalter Bahnhof, if you please.'

'Certainly, sir. The railway train is due at 0914 hours.'

At the appointed time the modern wonder of steam and engineering with fourteen gleaming wheels, a maroon red boiler and a great deal of highly polished brass pulled serenely to a halt at its last stop on the way from Dresden to central Berlin.

Manfred checked his wristwatch as he held open a carriage door for his wife and daughters.

'Exactly on time! Dependable as ever!' His chest swelled momentarily with pride; there remained some good things that Germany had to show the world.

A whistle blew, there was a puff of steam and with a barely perceptible jolt the great steel beast moved off towards central Berlin; the two girls had secured window seats owing to the kindness of a young couple and they looked out in wonder as the railway train gathered speed.

'Margit, there's the Grunewald with all the trees mentioned by Fräulein Müller,' Clotilde cried enthusiastically. 'I think I can see the first bright-green buds of the new leaves on the beech trees.'

Her sister followed her pointing finger. 'Yes! You are a clever girl. I can see them too.'

A short while later they left the greenery behind as it was replaced by a few houses and then by much taller buildings.

The ever-observant Clotilde noticed that the long red drapes with swastikas in white circles were not hanging from the tall buildings they were now passing. 'Look, Father, the long red flags are missing from the high houses; why's that?'

'I think, Clotilde...' Manfred paused. 'This is only my opinion and I don't wish to speak loudly.'

The nine-year-old girl crossed the carriage and placed her left ear close to her father's lips. 'I think the new government doesn't want the rest of the world's newspaper reporters and photographers to see the Nazi symbols.'

Clotilde put her lips to her father's right ear. 'Why, Father?'

'Because the eyes of the whole world will be on this new Germany in a few months at the Olympic Games and they don't want anything that might be thought to be bad to be seen.'

'I quite understand, Father,' she whispered back though she was still puzzled; she returned to her seat seeing many tall buildings and then she saw a fine church standing in among some trees and grassland. 'What is that called, mother?'

'That, my love, is the Matthäus-Kirche.'

Margit was keen to show her knowledge. 'We're in the Schöneberg area of Berlin.'

'Quite correct, Margit.' Suzanne wished to encourage the girls equally.

Margit smiled at this acknowledgement of her efforts. 'So I think we're halfway there.'

After a further ten minutes the train started to slow.

'I think we're coming into the Anhalter Bahnhof.' Clotilde pointed out of the carriage window towards the steel girders of a bridge underneath which flowed the sluggish waters of the Landwehrkanal.

Sure enough a few minutes later the train slowly passed

beneath the elegant wrought-iron arches of the station roof and finally came to a halt. The family Schultz stepped from the train onto the platform with Manfred giving a guiding and steadying hand where necessary. Once they had alighted they all stood still and looked around in wonder; they were standing on one of the platforms of the largest, most glamorous and awe-inspiring railway stations in continental Europe.

Margit looked up at the huge iron-and-glass roof whose centre was far above her. 'It's amazing, Father, how is such a roof built?'

'Very carefully!' he smiled. 'I'm a language teacher, my darling daughter, not an engineer but I should imagine that the design of the curve is very important to the stability and strength of the structure.' His smile broadened. 'That is why we study mathematics.'

The family walked along the platform toward the spacious booking hall.

'There are so many people here, Mother.' Clotilde had never seen such a multitude. 'Are they all going on a train?'

'Oh no, my dear. Some are meeting friends or family; some are working here; some have just arrived like us and some are about to leave.'

They now were passing through the central of three arches that lead onto Stresemannstrasse with its wide, tree-lined pavements.

After they had walked a few metres from the entrance, Manfred put one hand on each of his daughters' shoulders. 'Turn around and look at the station now.'

The family Schultz stopped and whirled round as one.

'It's amazing, pheeeew!' Margit sucked in her breath as she gazed at the neo-Renaissance façade of Berlin's most famous international railway train station.

Suzanne knew the building well but had seldom looked at it in bright spring morning sunlight. She stood there in awe. 'It makes me proud to be German when I look at this impressive building – it's more like a concert hall than a railway station.'

'Follow me, family Schultz,' Manfred ordered. 'I think it's better if we all hold hands in this crowd of people.' So saying he led his crocodile along the broad façade of Anhalter Bahnhof with the bustling Askanischer Platz opposite and onto Stresemannstrasse. Once in the wide street it was easier for them to walk as a group as they headed up towards Potsdamer Platz. Clotilde was now definitely of the opinion that adults walked too fast.

'Can we walk a little more slowly, Mother?'

'Of course! Manfred not quite so athletic if you don't mind.'

'I'm so sorry. I'm just anxious to get to that special restaurant in the Jewish Warehouse.' The party continued at a more sedate pace.

'What is special about this place, Mother?' Clotilde was less breathless.

'At the Wertheim you can eat as much as you like for the same cost.' Suzanne smiled. 'I hope that makes you feel hungry; it makes me feel full already!'

'It certainly does,' Margit didn't hesitate.

As she spoke they came into Potsdamer Platz and stopped to take in the profusion of cafés, bars, cinemas and, of course, people.

Manfred bent a little and whispered in his wife's left ear. 'Do you have the feeling that we're being followed?'

Suzanne glanced over her left shoulder. 'I don't see anyone I recognize.'

'It must be my imagination. I think the events at school have made me paranoid.'

'What does that mean, Father?' Clotilde was always curious about new words.

'I have a very big imagination, little lady.' Manfred laughed and hugged his younger daughter. 'I'm sure that there's nothing to worry any of us.' He very much hoped that he was correct.

'Manfred my dear, which way is the Jewish Warehouse?' Suzanne was getting their plan for lunch back into everyone's minds.

'It's that tall red-brick building at the far left side of the square.'

The family slowly made their way through the throng of people, past bars and cinemas, which the curious girls peered into, and eventually entered an imposing building which housed shops, stalls and restaurants including the Wertheim. Manfred held the door open. 'In we go, ladies!'

They were greeted by a wonderful assortment of smells including pea soup, sizzling pork and freshly baked rolls. The family Schultz soon found a table for four, took off their coats and sat down.

'It's self-service here, girls,' Suzanne informed them.

This was a whole new experience for Clotilde – she liked filling her bowl with pea soup and then returning for some slices of pork with sauerkraut. 'This is fantastic, Mother.'

Margit was also enjoying herself. 'Yes it is. Thank you for bringing us here, Father.'

At that moment a shadow fell across their table.

Manfred looked up at the man in astonishment. 'Herr Klein! Have you been following us?' His anger gave way to sympathy when he saw the anxiety on his colleague's face.

'Yes I have followed you here!' He was wringing his hands as though he was squeezing the water out of a sheet. 'After I left school yesterday I went home and there were three large men in the house with my wife and daughter, who were clearly petrified and weeping; when they saw me they pushed past me and left.'

Manfred was horrified. 'What were they saying, Benjamin?'

'They'd already told my family that I had been dismissed from the school and that we were not wanted in the new Germany.' His misery could easily be detected in his voice.

'Sit down my friend. Margit, will you fetch another chair and then bring Herr Klein a plate of soup and two fresh bread rolls?'

When the poor man had sat down and was clearly enjoying his lunch, Manfred felt that he could enquire further his fellow teacher's situation. 'What else did they say?'

'That we had forty-eight hours to leave the house or be sent to a concentration camp.'

Suzanne then unexpectedly joined in. 'I thought something like this might happen; you must leave the country as soon as possible.'

'I know, but how?'

'At eight o'clock in the morning pack as little luggage as possible. Clotilde and I will come and collect you with your family; from there we'll all go to the Stettiner Bahnhof by bus.'

Benjamin rose from his chair and put an extra bread roll in his pocket. 'We'll be ready.' He embraced Manfred, shook hands with the remainder of the family Schultz and walked briskly out of the Wertheim Restaurant.

'I will come with you, Mother, if we can help Herr Klein, but I had promised my furry Fräulein that I would spend the day with her.'

'I think that your pussycat will very much approve of your helping Father's friend, Clotilde,'

Manfred was amazed at his wife's arrangements.

'Suzanne how did you know what to do?' Then he thought a little more. 'I don't even know what is it you *are* going to do?'

'Do you remember that I slipped out of the apartment for a few minutes last night?'

107

'Yes but it was only for a short while.'

'I told you I went to see Rachel Getmann downstairs...' She stopped and looked around her in the crowded restaurant. 'Look, I will tell you the rest on the train.'

They were soon on their way out of Potsdamer Platz and walking back to the Anhalter Bahnhof.

'So who are you going to meet at Stettiner Bahnhof with Benjamin and his family?' Manfred asked his wife as soon as they had sat down in a carriage all of their own.

'A fisherman. He is going to take both them and the Getmanns to Seebad Ahlbeck and then sail to the Danish island of Bornholm...'

Manfred gasped and Suzanne smiled at her husband.

# 10

## *Bornholm Bound*

At three o'clock on the afternoon of March 25th, 1936 two eight-year-old boys holding small suitcases were talking excitedly to one another at the main entrance to the Stettiner Bahnhof.

'Are you sure Lothar said this was the place for us to wait for him, Kurt?'

'Absolutely, Hermann; are you sure you're happy about our little expedition?'

Kurt too would have admitted to being a little bit nervous about the plan, especially about going behind his parents' back.

At that moment Lorelei appeared accompanied by a worried-looking man with grey hair, wearing a fawn raincoat and carrying a heavy brown suitcase that caused him to lean over to one side; he was panting heavily.

'Hello, Kurt?'

'Lorelei!' Hermann came forward and stood beside Kurt. 'You remember my friend?'

'Aha, another of Lothar's replacement crew.'

'Exactly, may we be introduced to your friend?'

'Of course! Meet Professor Joseph Steinberg.' Kurt stretched out his hand and took the larger hand in his, finding the grip gentle but firm. While they shook hands a white-haired elderly lady and gentleman drew near and paused to draw breath.

'These two people are the Professor's parents and will need your help on the journey, boys.'

Lorelei gently urged them forward and the two friends shook the frail hands.

Hermann was first to speak. 'We'll do all we can to make your passage to the island as easy as possible.'

Kurt went over to Joseph Steinberg and helped to lower the suitcase to the ground.

'Thank you, Kurt. Would you take my mother and father to that wooden bench seat over there under the entrance arch?'

'Of course, Professor.' Kurt guided the couple over to the seat and they gratefully sat down.

At that same moment Lothar appeared holding the hand of a fair-haired girl of about the same age as Kurt.

'Hello, sailor-man.'

'*Mein Kapitän!* Good to see you; Hermann is here with me.'

'Excellent, let me introduce you to Clotilde. Her mother will be here shortly with a science teacher, his wife and daughter.' The two children shook hands and their eyes met for a magic moment.

'Good to meet you, Clotilde.'

'And you. We'll be leaving straight away but I hope we meet again one day, Kurt.'

Suzanne Schultz now hurried up, followed by Benjamin Klein, his wife Esther and their daughter Rachel. Clotilde ran back to her mother, flung her arms around Suzanne's waist and they soon melted away into the early evening throng of people.

There were no more introductions. Lothar, Lorelei, Kurt and Hermann helped the two Jewish families and their luggage onto the northbound railway train.

'There are remarkably few Brownshirts around the station.'

'I know, Lorelei. I think it's because we're so near to the Olympic Games and there are many overseas visitors here in Germany.'

Lothar closed the door leading into the carriage. 'Lorelei, would you mind finding us some soup for our guests from the station restaurant. Kurt, have a look into some of the other compartments and see if any of them are empty or only have one or two passengers in them. We'll probably need two or three.'

'Very well, *mein Kapitän*. Hermann can scout down the corridor in the opposite direction.'

Lothar nodded his approval and the two boys separated to explore the remainder of the carriage. Only a small number of people seemed to be travelling to the Baltic holiday resorts and quickly ran back to rejoined the party.

'*Mein Kapitän*, there are plenty. Would you like me to conduct Professor Joseph and his parents to their own compartment?'

'Please do that, sailor-man, and look after them. Hermann, your job is to stay with the Kleins.'

'You know that you can trust me, *mein Kapitän* ... both of us!' Kurt who was rapidly maturing beyond his years, led the way for the scientist and his elderly parents along the corridor and into a compartment. There was just one other passenger – a portly middle-aged lady whose dyed blonde hair was partially concealed by a red headscarf tied loosely under her chin. She sat clutching a large wickerwork basket on her lap.

She smiled at the new arrivals. 'Come in, my dears,' she said, standing up to assist Frau and Herr Steinberg to their seats. She then lent a hand to Kurt who was struggling with both hands to drag a heavy leather suitcase with a broad strap around its centre into the compartment.

'What on earth have we here, young man?'

'A very heavy case!' Kurt grimaced.

111

'Then let me help you put it up on the luggage rack.' The middle-aged lady swung the suitcase up onto the rack with amazing ease.

'You're very strong. Frau...?' The boy's cherubic face looked up at her enquiringly.

'...Richter.' Her warm smile broadened. 'Gisela Richter. I have been shopping in Berlin and have bought some beautiful silk to make into new curtains for my sitting room.'

'Very pleased to meet you, Frau Richter.' He shook her hand vigorously. 'May I introduce my Uncle Joseph – he's teaching me how to play the violin! And these nice people are Grandma and Grandpa...'

She offered 'Uncle Joseph' her hand and Professor Steinberg took the gloved hand in his and brushed his lips across the backs of the fingers. 'Delighted I'm sure, Frau Richter, Kurt is making great strides with his oboe playing.' The absent-minded professor was not too good at role-playing.

Gisela burst into peals of laughter, startling the Professor who nervously pushed a hand through his grey wavy hair. 'Did I say something amusing?' He looked over at the boy who was now furiously miming playing a violin.

'Of course! How silly of me. I meant the violin. I *used* to teach you the oboe, but you were hopeless.'

'Thank you, Uncle,' Kurt replied with a smile.

Lorelei now came in carrying a tray with four steaming bowls of spinach and potato soup, 'Kurt, would you go and serve our other guests.' The young man scampered out and up the corridor.

'What a wonderful smell!' Steinberg looked over at his mother and father and was pleased to see their eyes light up. 'How considerate of you.'

Lorelei handed out a bowl and spoon to the three refugees. 'Can I offer you any, madam? There's a spare bowl.'

The smiling Frau Richter introduced herself as she took the bowl and spoon from the tray. 'Frau Gisela Richter, seamstress of Seebad Ahlbeck at your service, Fräulein.'

'Enjoy the soup, Frau Richter.' Lorelei hurried off after Kurt and found him telling Lothar all about their new travelling acquaintance.

'She is a very strong!' The ever-inventive young man flexed his biceps muscle and then gave a very fine impression of a weight lifter.

Lothar put a protective arm around Kurt's shoulders. 'Well, as long as you didn't reveal his real name?'

'Oh no, *mein Kapitän*, she thinks the Professor is my uncle and violin teacher.'

'Very inventive, though you'll have to be doubly careful not to make any slip-ups. We can't really trust anyone any more'

'OK. What shall I do now, *mein Kapitän*?'

'You can go and see if Hermann is all right looking after the Kleins. Tell him to come back here and have some soup ... Oh yes, while I think of it, put these in your pocket.' Lothar handed him some train tickets. 'There's a set for the Kleins and another for the Steinbergs ... And here's their tray of soup.'

Lothar held the compartment door open. At that moment a whistle blew and the locomotive slowly started its journey north to the Baltic coast. Kurt steadied himself against the carriage window as he passed along the corridor. He found the science teacher together with his wife and daughter and Hermann in the next compartment but one. The younger woman jumped up from her seat and opened the sliding door.

'Hello, I'm Rachel. Come in.' She held the door in its open position while the new arrival carried in the hot soup. 'I think you're the one whom Lothar calls his sailor-man.'

'Lothar wants you, Hermann ... Yes, that's me,' he

113

continued once Hermann had slipped away. The soup carrier felt an overwhelming sense of pride. 'Let me offer this magnificent concoction of potato and spinach from the Stettiner Bahnhof's finest restaurant.'

As he served the Klein family the locomotive gathered speed. Herr Klein consulted a beautiful gold pocket watch which he slipped out of the pocket of his best three-piece navy blue pinstripe suit.

'Eighteen twenty-nine ... departure one minute early; I'm reassured, my dear.' He patted his wife affectionately on her arm and she looked up at him and smiled; there was an audible sigh of relief.

At that moment a ticket inspector appeared at the carriage door and Kurt immediately sat down on the vacant seat next to the science teacher as the door was slid back.

'*Guten Abend, Herren und Damen*. Tickets please.'

The fat man squeezed his large frame into the small space. Herr Benjamin looked worried.

'Don't worry, Father. I've got the tickets. You know you always give them to me.'

Kurt produced the tickets from his pocket, at the same time as a piece of sandpaper, which he carefully placed on the seat beside him.

The Inspector punched a hole in all four simultaneously and handed them back to Kurt; as he did so he leaned forward and peered more closely at the boy: 'You're a pretty one then, aren't you?' The eight-year old instinctively recoiled from the fat bespectacled official. 'You look much more German than the rest of your family,' he added in an undertone.

The object of the fat official's scrutiny didn't blush but his hands became sweaty. The obnoxious man patted the boy's head and left the compartment. There was a collective very quiet cheer.

'Hoorah, well done, Kurt; you're my hero!' Rachel gave

him a kiss on the cheek. 'But what's that?' The young woman pointed to the abrasive.

'Ah that's sandpaper. Lothar advised me to carry it for use in an emergency; the Nazis are frightened of scarlet fever. If they become threatening all I have to do is to vigorously rub my face with it and as soon a Nazi sees me he will run away screaming.

Rachel burst out laughing. 'But that's ridiculous!'

The remarkable young man flashed his angelic smile around the compartment. 'You wait and see. He thinks of everything does *mein Kapitän*.'

The night train to the Baltic coast continued its progress, stopping at the same stations as it did in the summer but with far fewer passengers joining or leaving it; the two Jewish families and their escorts had long since allowed sleep to engulf their tired minds and bodies by the time it reached and drew to a gentle halt at Seebad Ahlbeck. Lothar stirred with the familiar jolt, opened his eyes and looked out of the window beside him.

'We're here, everyone.' Lorelei's head was resting on his shoulder and he gently touched her cheek with right hand.

She stirred; stretched out her arms and opened her deep-blue eyes.

'I was having such a wonderful dream; I was at a ball given by Friedrich the Third when he was a young dashing prince. I was in his strong arms wearing a beautiful light-blue flowing silk dress and we were whirling around the ballroom to the strains of the "Blue Danube"; now I find myself in Seebad Ahlbeck!'

Lothar laughed. 'Sorry to disappoint you! ... Come, my girl, let me whisk you away from your Austrian reverie so that we can get our passengers onto our ship and over the Baltic to the safety of Bornholm Island.'

He slid open the door to his compartment, popped his head out of it and saw that Kurt was already hauling the

115

family Klein's solitary suitcase into the corridor. 'Do you need any help with that heavy case, sailor-man?'

'No thank you, *mein Kapitän*. I'll manage.'

Meanwhile Hermann was doing his chivalrous best to assist Professor Steinberg's elderly mother and father to alight from the carriage. 'Lean on my shoulder, Frau Steinberg...'

'You're very kind, Hermann.' It was the first time Lothar had heard the lady speak and he was struck by her beautiful musical tone of voice.

Once she was off the train the considerate young man stooped down to tie one of her shoelaces that had come undone. She looked down on Hermann with a warm smile playing around her lips. 'You remind me of my childhood when we imagined we were beautiful princesses with handsome princes wooing us. I wonder if those days will ever return...'

'Of course they will, Frau Steinberg, I'm sure one day you will return to your beautiful palace in Berlin with your prince by your side.'

The royal personage in question followed them onto the platform after handing down their brown leather suitcase with the strap around it. Hermann had correctly interpreted the elderly lady's feelings about leaving her home in the capital.

Finally the Professor joined them and they started the walk along the wooden platform towards the exit to Seebad Ahlbeck. As they drew near to the final part of the walkway their path was blocked by five large men standing in a row with their hands on their hips; in the centre of the group was the fat ticket collector, who now wore a red armband with a white circle and black swastika on it.

The party, led by Hermann, slowed down and finally came to a halt. Lothar and Lorelei did the same but Kurt suddenly stopped walking and ducked down behind Rachel; Hermann faced up to the menacing, scowling thugs.

'Why won't you let us pass?'

'It's not you we want.' The grin on the ticket collector's face sent a shiver down Professor Steinberg's spine. 'It's your cheeky playmate we're after.' The great bully pushed Hermann to one side, brushed past the family Steinberg as though they didn't exist and amazingly treated the impressively athletic Lothar in the same way before confronting the family Klein.

'Where is he, Jew?'

The gentle Benjamin was outraged at the language. 'I am a respected German science teacher.' He suddenly realized his precarious position and his resistance crumbled. 'How can I help you, sir?'

'That fair-haired boy, the *German*-looking one who claimed you're all part of the same family; I'm sure he was lying. If so, you'll all be in a lot of trouble!'

Astonishment registered on Benjamin's face, which became even greater when Kurt emerged from behind Rachel with bright-red cheeks and emitting an agonized groan.

'Oh I feel so unwell. I told you, Father, I shouldn't have played with those children with scarlet fever.'

'*Mein Gott, Scharlachrot!*' The five bully boys turned on their heels and fled the scene in blind panic scattering passengers, luggage, pets and railway staff in all directions. Apart from Lothar, Rachel, Benjamin and Esther were the only ones to know about the sandpaper trick and burst out laughing. Rachel gave Kurt a huge hug while Lothar set about helping his fellow passengers back onto their feet and reuniting them with their cases, poodles and umbrellas.

There were no more unwelcome surprises; the escape party spent a comfortable night before boarding Lothar's boat and enjoying a smooth passage to Bornholm Island. The crew members performed well and Kurt returned to

117

the house in Mahlow after three days away with no one suspecting where he had been, although Mitzi thought she saw a line of salt on her son's shoes.

# 11

## *Fichte Gymnasium, Berlin – May 1936*

Johann Gottlieb Fichte was a renowned eighteenth-century German philosopher who, among other things, gave his name to the *Gymnasium*, or grammar school, on Karlsruher Strasse in south-west Berlin. At 0800 hours precisely on the morning of May 2nd, 1936, Manfred Schultz entered the three-storey building. His mood was sad and he barely noticed one of his pupils arriving at the same time. 'Good morning, sir' was the cheerful greeting, but all he could manage on this sunny morning was a simple ' hello' without using the boy's name – this from a man who prided himself on knowing all his pupils by both first and family names.

He walked with a heavy heart towards the staff common room on the first floor where he and his colleagues met between lessons, used a row of hooks for their coats, hats and scarves, and took coffee; he scarcely noticed two of his colleagues talking in hushed tones by the window which overlooked the busy suburban street. Manfred gave Herr Fischer, an excellent, teacher of geography, and Herr Schneider, the junior mathematics master, a curt 'Good morning'.

The pair of younger men seemed startled by the interruption and hastily replied in unison:

'Good morning, Herr Schultz.'

Schneider enthusiastically pointed to a letter lying unopened on the coffee table. 'That is addressed to you,

Herr Schultz.' The tone was both curious and deferential. Manfred picked up the buff-coloured envelope, saw his name and recognized Benjamin Klein's neat, precise handwriting.

'We think it's from the Jewish science teacher.'

'Herr Klein is a first-class science teacher who has served this school in a dedicated and expert fashion for many years, he has had wonderful examination results and many of his pupils have had distinguished university careers.' Manfred paused and took in a large breath of air. 'None of this, I repeat, none of this, has anything to do with Benjamin Klein being Jewish.'

The two younger men hung their heads in shame. Herr Fischer spoke for them both. 'Of course, you're quite right, Herr Schultz, we apologize! But as you must be aware there are increasing anti-Jewish feelings both inside and outside the school...'

'I'm a schoolteacher; I regard it as part of my job to notice what is going on around me. But vulgar anti-Semitic prejudice is not something I choose to indulge in!' He turned away to read the letter.

The geography master hesitated a moment. 'Is there anything in Benjamin Klein's letter that we should know about?'

'I will read it out to you if you wish?'

'Please do!' It was Schneider who spoke.

'It simply says *au revoir*.'

'But that's French.'

'Yes, I noticed that, too. I am a modern languages teacher...' Manfred's patience was wearing a little thin.

'But Herr Klein teaches ... taught ... science.'

'Herr Schneider, I know that but scientists are not prohibited from foreign languages, are they. Or is that a new rule, too?'

'What do you think the letter means, Herr Schultz?'

'It means *au revoir*. He won't be coming back.'

Manfred left the room abruptly, trying not to slam the door behind him but doing so nonetheless.

Later that day Manfred breathed a sigh of relief when his last class of the day finally came to an end and he was able to hurry down to the staff room and collect his brown trilby hat, grey woollen scarf and long blue double-breasted winter coat; to his dismay Herr Schneider bounded into the room after him.

'Off to earn the really big money, eh Herr Schultz? I expect your employer will be able to get you a seat at the Olympic Games.'

Manfred was putting on his coat. 'I'm not interested in going; I expect it will be used simply to glorify the government.'

'Well, you would know more about that than me.'

'I *really* don't know what you mean.' With that he turned and left the room, but as he walked down the stairs to the ground floor and out through the main entrance into Karlsruher Strasse, he wondered how the extra tutoring work he was doing had become common knowledge at the school. He comforted himself by visualizing the beautiful piano he planned to purchase with the extra money he would earn from the extra work.

He took a train to Unter den Linden, crossed Pariser Platz to the newly named Hermann Göring Strasse and came to a halt outside number twenty; he rang the bell.

'Good afternoon, Herr Schultz.' The English accent of his young pupil, Harald Quandt, was near perfect.

'And a very good afternoon to you, Harald, I'm pleased to hear you've been working hard on your English vowels; I find your pronunciation much improved.'

'Please come in, sir!' The fifteen-year-old boy was fast rising in Manfred's estimation. 'We do go in the usual room.'

Manfred followed his pupil up the broad staircase to the first floor and could hear the squeals and laughter of young children coming from the floor above. 'I think we're going to have to correct that last little bit of English a little, but I commend you for the effort Harald. I can hear your family enjoying themselves. I trust their happy sounds don't distract you from your studies?'

'Oh no, sir; it's very nice for me to hear my mother Magda playing with my new sisters, Helga and Hildegard, and brother, Helmut.' The young man hesitated for a moment.

'I'm very pleased to hear that you're happy here, Harald.'

They reached the small room that had been set aside for the tutorials and sat down at a small table. 'now what should you have said earlier?'

There was a pause. 'We ... *are going* to our usual room?'

'Excellent, Harald!' Manfred was encouraged by the young man and the class continued with good progress for a further one and a half hours; they were just closing their books when there was a knock on the door.

'Come in!' The schoolmaster's tone was friendly.

The door opened and a smartly dressed maid wearing a short-sleeved black dress with a starched white apron came in; she gave a barely noticeable curtsey and announced, 'Frau Magda Goebbels to see you, gentlemen.'

A tall blonde-haired handsome woman wearing a smart calf-length navy-blue cotton dress with a white ribbon border made her elegant way towards Manfred and handed him an envelope.

'Herr Schultz, I trust that you're satisfied with Harald's progress.' Magda Goebbels was a charismatic and commanding presence with a Wagnerian beauty that was said to appeal to Adolf Hitler.

'Frau Goebbels, I'm pleased with your son's energetic application to his studies, but he has now reached the stage where he should be thinking in French and English as well as just speaking them.' Manfred felt that, although he loathed the people who were paying him for these private tutorials, he should maintain the integrity of his teaching; in fact he had the forlorn hope that somehow he was saving the mind of Goebbels' young stepson.

'That is all very well, Herr Schultz, but our main objective is the school leaving examination!' There was both menace and coldness in her voice.

A shiver went down Manfred's spine. 'Of course, Frau Goebbels.' He gave a slight but formal bow, turned and started to walk away.

'Herr Schultz.' The two words were spat out venomously. 'You're not a Jew, are you?'

Manfred stopped in his tracks and turned around; he knew he was betraying his countrymen and himself when he replied, 'Certainly not, Frau Goebbels.'

'Good afternoon to you and please remember our target for Harald.' The tone was softer and she came over to the schoolmaster and shook his hand.

'Good afternoon, Frau Goebbels. I shall remember.' Once again he turned, and this time he walked away uninterrupted.

He left the building and crossed the Pariser Platz but instead of walking into the Unter den Linden railway station he carried on past into Wilhelmstrasse until he came to a handsome shop with a wonderful display of musical instruments; dusk was now falling but lights had already been switched on inside and a spotlight picked out a beautiful black Blüthner grand piano.

'You're beautiful,' Manfred spoke out loud through the window. 'One day I know you'll bring wonderful sounds into my family's house.'

As he gazed into the shop window a passer-by stopped, looked around and a puzzled expression appeared on his face; he saw a lone figure in a dark blue double-breasted suit, carrying a briefcase and apparently talking to a piano. 'Are you all right, sir?' The enquiry was kindly and concerned.

Manfred saw the reflection of the new arrival in the glass. It was an elderly man with a slight stoop, who in spite of the warm May evening wore a grey overcoat and a black Homburg hat from underneath of which peeped strands of silver hair.

'I'm very well, thank you.' The languages teacher was embarrassed to be found indulging his secret passion for the musical instrument. 'I was admiring that beautiful piano and imagining the sounds that would come out of it.'

'Aha, the Blüthner, truly a work of art,' the old man smiled. 'My uncle was a piano tuner in Julius Blüthner's factory in Leipzig.' He shook Manfred's outstretched hand. 'My name is Joseph Schäfer. Uncle Heine used to tell me stories of the craftsmen that came to work with Julius in 1853; by 1900, you know, they were making five thousand instruments every year.'

'That's amazing! I'm very pleased to make your acquaintance; my name is Manfred Schultz and I'm a teacher of modern languages.'

They began to walk together back towards Pariser Platz. 'I would be interested to hear those stories, Herr Schäfer. Perhaps I can buy you a cup of coffee?'

'It will be my pleasure.'

They sat down at a pavement café and a waiter wearing a white apron, white shirt and black bow tie, took their order for coffee with cream; when it arrived Manfred poured out two cupfuls and gave one to his new friend Joseph Schäfer.

'You're Jewish, I think.' Manfred was cautious in his approach.

'I'm indeed, sir; I was taking a last look around this city

of my birth before taking the train from the Anhalter Bahnhof tomorrow morning at ten o'clock; I regret to say that it's no longer safe for me and my wife here any more.'

'I'm truly sorry to hear that, Herr Schäfer. What has happened to make you take such a big step?'

There were tears in the eyes of the elderly gentleman and they started to roll down both cheeks. 'I came back from Munich three weeks ago; I have been in Dachau concentration camp for three months.' He sipped his coffee but the tears continued to flow. 'They just came one day and took me away; they said that I was lucky to live and soon all Jews would be killed. They never told my wife where I was.'

Manfred had suspected such things were going on but this was the first time he had faced the realities of such persecution. 'I apologize to you on behalf of Germany!'

'Perhaps you now understand why we feel our only option is to leave this city and the country of our birth.'

'Where will you go?' Manfred tried to imagine what he would do in such a situation.

'The Olympic Games have helped us in an unexpected way.' The old man had regained his composure and took a more enthusiastic gulp of his coffee.

'How exactly?' The schoolmaster was very curious.

'Well, my friend although the press and the athletes have not yet arrived here in Berlin, the businessmen are here already. Among them are some old business contacts and I've been able to make discreet enquiries about our best option.'

'And what was your conclusions, Herr Schäfer?'

'We will leave Europe altogether! We set sail for the United States of America tomorrow evening. I fear I will never see my beloved home country again.'

Manfred once again expressed his dismay and sympathy. He called the waiter and paid their bill. 'It's been a pleasure meeting you, Herr Schäfer, and I wish you a safe journey and a happy future.' The pair shook hands and went their separate ways.

# 12

## *Kurt's Olympic Games – Berlin, August 1936*

Saturday, August 1st, 1936 was cloudy and cool with intermittent showers – not at all the fine sunny 'Führer weather' that usually favoured great Nazi events. However, this didn't dampen the enthusiasm and excitement of Kurt and Marlena as they waited for their father to come downstairs for breakfast.

'Good morning, everybody!' Maximillian was equally cheerful. 'What will you do while we're working hard at the Games, my love?'

Mitzi came into the dining room carrying a steaming-hot pot of coffee. 'My mother will be here at ten o'clock and we're going shopping.' She went back to the kitchen and collected brown rolls, butter and apricot jam. 'She is going to stay with us tonight.'

'I hope you don't make her too tired.' Marlena was always anxious about Romhilde's welfare.

'She's very good for her sixty-two years; I have no worries about her health; though it's very kind of you to show such concern.' She sat down and turned to face her husband. 'I presume you've filled up the car with petrol, checked the oil, water and polished the headlamps?'

Maximillian beamed back at her. 'You know I think of everything.'

'Then I expect that you've also prepared lunch with drinks and that it's all packed and waiting for you in the back of the car.' Mitzi fixed her gaze on her husband, who stopped smiling; he didn't notice his daughter's grinning face or Kurt trying to suppress his laughter.

'It's a good thing that you've a family to look after you, otherwise you would starve!'

Maximillian stared back at his wife open-mouthed.

'Your long-suffering children will let you into a secret,' Mitzi continued mercilessly.

Kurt and Marlena burst into peals of laughter.

The children each took one of their father's hands and led him out through the entrance hall and front door to where the Buick stood with a few drops of rain on its otherwise gleaming surface. Kurt opened one of the rear passenger doors and with a flourish of an arm, like a magician, declared: 'Behold – refreshments for the whole day!'

The boy's father looked onto the back seat and saw a large picnic basket that he had completely failed to spot when preparing the car.

'Your mother has been very good to us!' He smiled at his son and daughter.

'Not just mother,' said Marlena. 'We helped as well.'

'I cut the bread for the sandwiches,' Kurt proudly announced.

'And I made the bratwurst with sauerkraut filling,' the twelve-year-old girl smiled. 'With a little help from mother.'

Maximillian had now recovered from his 'humiliation' and was able to conclude: 'Then we've all made our contributions to a wonderful day.'

Mitzi came out to join them. She put her arms around her husband and gazed admiringly at the fine-looking motor vehicle. 'You've certainly done a good job on those white walls of the tyres; they give our beautiful Buick a distinctive appearance.'

She handed Marlena a small, flat stainless-steel box. 'Here's your insulin equipment in case you're away from home longer than we expect. I've popped in two lumps of sugar for emergencies'

'Motherrr...' The word carried a note of irritation. 'I can do all that.'

Her mother knew better than to say anything further. She kissed each member of her family; Kurt climbed into the front passenger seat beside his father, Marlena sat in the back next to the picnic basket and her mother handed two umbrellas into the car. 'Have a safe journey and enjoy this historic day.' She was always apprehensive when her dear family were away from home but particularly now, with so much uncertainty in the air. She waved as the Buick drew out of the small front driveway, heading towards the newly built Olympic Stadium, seven kilometres south-west of the Berlin suburbs.

'Father, what time is the opening ceremony due to start?' Kurt was becoming excited.

'Four o'clock in the afternoon; we've got plenty of time, don't worry.'

But before long vast numbers of buses, cars and other forms of transport were converging on the Olympic site and the pace of the Zimmermann family car slowed noticeably.

'Kurt, there's a programme in the glove compartment with the tickets for our seats. Read us some of what it says'

Kurt began to read the illustrated brochure. 'Listen to this! "The Games will be watched by one hundred and ten thousand seated spectators with five thousand athletes taking part..."'

Marlena was kneeling on the back seat looking out of the rear window at all the vehicles packed with people that were going to the event.

'Father, the cars and buses behind us are stopping to let a runner carrying a flaming torch pass by.'

Maximillian immediately pulled over onto the grass verge and, sure enough, a beautifully built, fair-haired man wearing white shorts and singlet swept past the Buick and its amazed occupants; Marlena put her hand out through the open car window and it brushed the right shoulder of the young man as he jogged past.

'I touched him, I touched him!' Her excitement was infectious.

'I'm very happy for you, my dear. Now, Kurt, what else have you found out?'

'"Fifty-one countries will be represented, marching in alphabetical order led by Greece and with Germany, the host country, bringing up the rear."'

The motor car started to move slowly forward again. 'It's a good thing we left with plenty of time to spare, Father; there are lots and lots of people on their way to the Stadium.'

Progress was slow but eventually they arrived at the huge parking area specially created for the event. Maximillian took some time to find a suitable place to leave the Buick, and as he did so he thought about how throughout the journey he had been pleasantly surprised by the absence of 'Jews Not Welcome' signs outside hotels and restaurants.

Marlena was first to step out of the vehicle and immediately spotted something unusual. 'Look! Oh look, Father, Kurt'

As they emerged from the car the two glanced up to where the girl was pointing.

'It's huge!' was Kurt's first impression as he looked up at the giant zeppelin the *Hindenberg* circling above the Olympic Stadium. For a few minutes all three of the Zimmermann family and those around them stared at the silver-coloured cigar-shaped colossus of the skies trailing the Olympic flag as it moved slowly around the venue.

'I wonder what the future can be for such an extravagant form of travel!' Maximillian exclaimed. As an engineer, too, he worried about its safety, especially with regard to the hydrogen which was used for buoyancy.

'Kurt, will you bring the picnic basket out off the back seat?' His son did as he was asked, Maximillian took it by its handle and the three of them set off on the longish walk to their places in the Stadium.

The Zimmermann party arrived at their seats just before three o'clock and when they had settled Kurt produced the event brochure which included a plan of the Stadium. He pointed to a place on the plan and then towards a structure almost opposite them across the athletics field. 'That's the Bell Tower and beside it is a platform with a great bowl on it where the Olympic Flame will be lit.'

Father and daughter followed to where he was pointing and could see a massive tripod with steps passing up the left-hand side.

'Look at all the people, Father; there must be thousands and thousands.' Marlena was right; the rows of seats were filling up quickly and there was a buzz of excitement echoing around the vast amphitheatre. Maximillian sat down at her side with the picnic basket on his knees and Kurt sat on his left; he opened the lid and his daughter sniffed the air.

'How delicious my sandwiches smell!'

Maximilian let the children help themselves to sandwiches and poured out some apple juice for both of them and a cup of tea for himself. Meanwhile, things were beginning to happen in the Stadium.

'Look, soldiers!' Marlena pointed to where a parade was forming in front of the Bell Tower.

Kurt consulted his programme. 'They're the Honour Battalion of the National Army.'

'So what happens next, Kurt?' The father was only too happy to let his son play 'master of ceremonies'.

131

'We're expecting the Führer...'

'Herr Hitler, Kurt.' Maximillian was emphatic. 'We call him Herr Hitler.'

'But it says here...'

'I don't care what it says there; *we* call him Herr Hitler.' The boy's father had second thoughts and adopted a gentler tone. 'I know what is written there. Kurt, but I'd rather we didn't use it.'

'Right you are, Father!' The boy took it all in his stride. 'Herr Hitler will enter the arena at five minutes before four o'clock accompanied by the Presidents of the International Olympic and the Organizing Committees.'

Marlena looked at her watch. 'It's nearly that now.'

Just then the noise in the Stadium was silenced by a shrill loud sound from the direction of the entrance to the great amphitheatre.

'Heil Hitler!'

The Hitler Youth were greeting the Head of State.

'There he is and it's exactly four o'clock,' cried Marlena, bursting with excitement.

A large orchestra played martial music as Herr Hitler, who was wearing a brown uniform with jackboots, and his party approached the reviewing stand.

'What is that music, Kurt?'

'It's the "March of Allegiance" by Richard Wagner, Father.'

'I've not heard it before.' There followed the more familiar strains of the Deutschland Über Alles, or Germany over all; the national Anthem. 'We should stand for this,' he added as all the Stadium's occupants rose to their feet and one hundred thousand German voices sang as one. This was followed by the 'Horst Wessel Song', which had become something of a Nazi anthem.

'What happens next, Kurt?' Marlena asked.

'At twelve minutes past four the German Naval Corps will raise the flags of all the participating nations' he replied and, sure enough, exactly on time the array of colours ascended their flagpoles in perfect unison and one minute later the massive Olympic Bell rang.

This was the signal for the first of the participating teams to enter the arena. A German placard bearer held up the name of Greece as the famous words of Baron de Coubertin came over the loudspeaker: 'The important thing in the Olympic Games is not winning, but taking part.'

The Zimmermann family watched enthralled as the huge number of athletes passed the reviewing stand. They noted there was no uniformity in the saluting; some, such as the Austrians, gave an enthusiastic Nazi salute, while others including Great Britain merely gave the military-style 'eyes right'.

'Look at those funny people marching past the reviewing stand now.' Marlena pointed towards the Bulgarians who were performing a very peculiar goosestep.

The march-past of athletes continued. Most of the flag bearers dipped their flags as they passed the dignitaries but Marlena, ever observant, noted that the United States of America didn't follow this example. 'Why didn't the standard bearer dip the Stars and Stripes, Father?'

'I think it's in their constitution, my darling daughter; they only dip their flag to their President.'

The Games organizer gave a short speech and was followed to the rostrum by Adolf Hitler:

'I proclaim the Games of Berlin, celebrating the eleventh Olympiad of the modern era, to be open.' He said nothing further on that inaugural day.

This was followed by the hoisting of the Olympic Flag, salutes fired by the artillery squad and the release of a flock of carrier pigeons.

Kurt was once again ready with information. 'There are thirty thousand of those birds; in a moment trumpeters will play a fanfare introducing the Olympic Hymn with music composed and conducted by Richard Strauss, which was selected by the public from three thousand entries.'

The family listened, together with thousands of others, to the wonderful music and while this happened the last torch relay runner entered the Stadium carrying the flame that had come all the way from Olympia. He paraded it once around the athletics track and then used it to light the fire in the giant bowl next to the Bell Tower.

A middle-aged, slightly built gentleman stepped forward and presented a circle of woven leaves to the German leader. 'That's Spiridon Lewis, the winner of the marathon in 1896 presenting the winner's laurel wreath. Kurt took hold of Marlena's wrist and looked at her watch. 'It's now a quarter past five and in three minutes we'll have the Olympic Oath.'

Sure enough the German flag bearer, accompanied by one of the athletes, raised his right hand, grasped the German flag with his left and spoke from the platform by the tower. 'We swear that we will take part in the Olympic Games in loyal competition, respecting the regulations which govern them, and desirous of participating in them in true spirit of sportsmanship, for the honour of our country and for the glory of sport.'

'That's it,' said Kurt. 'It's all over now until tomorrow.' The reviewing stand rapidly emptied and the competitors were leaving in the order that they had arrived.

The Zimmermann party slowly moved down the rows of seats and towards the exit. Maximillian took the opportunity to obtain a programme of the track and field events during the coming week; it didn't surprise him when Kurt asked if he could come again the following day.

'I would really like to see Jesse Owens; my friends at school have all heard about him.'

'You can study the programme when we've found our way back to the Buick.'

They were still surrounded by vast numbers of people and finding their car was difficult. 'Aha, there it is.'

They walked around the end of yet another row of vehicles and were nearly alongside the sleek black car when Maximillian clutched his forehead. 'Oh no, it hasn't got white-walled tyres.'

There was a look of profound disappointment on Marlena's face. 'Then it's not our car?' She was looking pale and tired. 'Can we have a rest for a few minutes?'

'Of course we can have a rest,' Maximillian said, alarmed. 'I am so sorry that you needed to ask, my darling.' He placed the picnic basket on the ground, opened it, took out a bottle of water with the last of the sandwiches; closed the basket and placed it on its end for Marlena to sit down on top.

'Thank you, Father.' She gratefully sat on the basket and accepted the food and drink. 'I don't feel in need of sugar but I do think I should take my insulin.'

Maximillian looked at his wristwatch. 'It's seven thirty; I didn't realize how much the crowds would slow us down.'

He and Kurt watched as Marlena took out her silver box and administered her usual evening dose of the life-saving medication.

'You tell us when you're ready to move on back to our faithful Buick.'

The patient started to laugh. 'Father, you are funny.'

'Why, my dear?'

'How can a car be faithful?' She stood up and the returning colour was highlighted in her cheeks by the late-afternoon sunshine that had made a belated appearance after the earlier persistent light rain. 'I feel much better now; let's go and find our devoted automobile.' Her father picked up the picnic basket and they all walked to the next row of parked cars. Kurt had run on ahead and amazingly spotted the car with the white-walled tyres almost immediately.

'It's here, it's here, Father!' The excited boy pointed to the Buick and they all piled in with sighs of relief. 'That was a worry I thought someone may have stolen our beautiful car.' Kurt joined in the praise and personalization of the American motorcar.

The family Zimmermann now started to make slow progress away from the crowds of people. Kurt started to study the programme for the rest of the Games.

'Father, as I told you I really want to see Jesse Owens running and I think the one hundred metres final is the race to watch.'

'So which day would that be?'

'Err ... Wednesday. So does that mean we can go?' A broad grin appeared on Kurt's face.

'Yes, I suppose it will be exciting. How are you feeling, Marlena?' Max briefly looked back at his daughter sitting on the back seat.

'Very much better, thank you, Father.' Her characteristic smile was back on her face. 'I don't think I'll come with you on Wednesday; I have enjoyed today immensely, especially all the flags and the music, but I did get a little tired. Thank you, Father, for bringing me to this wonderful occasion; I'll never forget it!'

The faithful Buick eventually delivered them safely home to Mahlow. The following Wednesday Kurt was thrilled to see Jesse Owens win the one hundred metres and set a new world record.

Adolf Hitler was nowhere to be seen.

# 13

## The Autumn of Peace

Clotilde was pleased to return to school for the last term of 1936 after the long summer holidays. There had been another holiday in Rügen and during the packing of her little red suitcase she had been astonished to find the Nobel Peace Prize certificate of Carl von Ossietzky still at the bottom of it. Only then did she remember the events of the previous August and a shudder passed through her little frame. She decided to leave it where it was.

At the moment she entered the school she was greeted by a familiar voice. 'Clotilde my dear, welcome back after the long break. I have some good news for you.'

'Good morning, Fräulein Müller.' The schoolteacher had never been a favourite with Clotilde but her enthusiasm for academic glory now took precedence. 'How wonderful! I can't guess what it is.'

'The headmistress and governors have had a meeting...'

'Yes, Fräulein.'

Ulrike Müller could not keep the note of smug self-satisfaction out of her voice. 'They have decided that each class should keep the same teacher as they pass right through the school. Isn't that wonderful?'

'Oh ... that will be wonderful' was the slightly hesitant reply.

'Good morning, Fräulein Müller.' Eloise Hoffmann had joined them wearing a blue-and-white check cotton dress; a grey wool cardigan and navy-blue socks with black shoes.

'Good morning and welcome back, young lady.' The schoolteacher looked at her with an encouraging smile. 'Clotilde, will tell you the news while I get along to prepare some schoolwork.'

'Eloise, you've grown!' Clotilde flung her arms around her best friend. 'Did you have super summer holidays?'

'Oh yes and you've grown too!' The best friend stood back and looked the other girl up and down. Her gaze followed the retreating figure of their schoolteacher. 'I'm surprised Madame Perfect didn't notice how tall you are.' Eloise stuck her tongue out at the back of Fräulein Müller.

'Eloise, that's rude!' Clotilde took hold of her friend's right hand with both of hers. 'I think I have bad news. She is going to be our teacher for the whole time we're at this school.'

The expression on the schoolgirl's face was a mixture of surprise and horror. 'Goodness gracious; thank the Lord she didn't turn around.' Then she lowered her voice. 'I have not been her number one pupil.' She turned to face her friend. 'I remember what she said and I really want to make that leap into the *Gymnasium* with you.'

'We're both going to have to work hard and, although you're my best friend, I do think you will have to be careful what you say to Fräulein Müller and not repeat what you did just now.'

Eloise gave a mischievous smile. 'You mean that I have got to take up tongue control?'

'Exactly, my friend!'

And from that moment the two girls concentrated both at home and at school on their studies; they avoided distractions such as outings to parks that were not part of their education and parties except for birthdays of their close friends.

Later that evening Clotilde was in her bedroom reading and memorizing her geography homework which was about the oceans of planet Earth; she could overhear her mother and father talking together.

'...And now the Jewish children are being penalized! Three Jewish boys in my class have not returned to school...'

In the sitting room Suzanne came over to the armchair where her husband was sitting, perched herself on one arm and placed her hand on his shoulder. 'You can't take on the problems of the whole world, my love; we shall have to wait and see if the boys come back.'

'I don't think we'll see them again.' Manfred's tone was gloomy. 'We're already seeing signs that the temporary clean-up for visitors to the Olympic Games is over and as the "Jews not wanted" signs are returning to the streets. There's more Brownshirts around and there was a rumour in the staff common room today that many Gypsies are being arrested and sent to concentration camps.'

'Are they terrible places, my darling?'

'We just don't know. The difficulty is that the people who really know are either the political police or those inmates who are lucky enough to have been released. Neither groups say anything; the authorities because of secrecy and the ex-prisoners from fear of reprisals.'

Clotilde overheard nothing further that night and both she and Eloise applied themselves to their schoolwork with such energy, dedication and diligence that sometimes their parents thought that their daughters were letting the world pass them by. One evening as Christmas was approaching Suzanne knocked on Clotilde's bedroom door and received a cheery 'Come in!'

On entering the room she was struck by the tidiness and organization of her daughter's books, school things and clothes.

'All work and no play makes Jack a dull boy.'

'What a strange saying, Mother; I've never heard that before.' Clotilde had a puzzled expression on her face. 'I suppose it's because I'm neither Jack nor a boy.' She ran over to her mother and hugged her tight. 'I do love you, Mother, and didn't intend to be rude but Fräulein Müller told us something that has made me work harder.'

'It sounds important, my darling. Please continue.'

'Well, Mother,' Clotilde was anxious not to appear overconfident. 'Remember I told you that some of us would only stay in the junior school for three years and pass up into the secondary school a year early. I really want to do this and am trying hard for the honour.'

'Oh darling, of course, but I didn't realize that was the reason you spend so much time alone in your bedroom.'

'Not quite alone, Mother. Fräulein Müller with four paws has been very good company and I can talk to her ... I'm sure she understands me.'

'I'm glad your lovely little pussycat is looking after you well.' Suzanne felt Fräulein Müller brushing against her leg and then vibrating as she began to purr. 'Your father will be very pleased to hear of your hard work and enthusiasm but neither of us want you to become exhausted or lose interest in your hobbies.'

'Mother, I assure you and Father that as soon as I feel tired I will tell you immediately.'

Clotilde sounded as though she was growing up very fast. Suzanne kissed her daughter on the forehead and wished her a good night's sleep and quietly left the room to rejoin her husband and tell him what she had just learned from her daughter.

'Manfred, you know about this new system for primary school children of course?'

'Oh yes, we were told but none of the affected children have come through yet and Margit's too old to have been included in the scheme.'

'Well, I think I've solved the mystery about Clotilde.'

Manfred appeared to be lost in thought. 'Yes, of course! Hers will be the first school year to be affected; our Clotilde has the chance prove herself a very clever girl.'

Germany marched confidently into the New Year knowing that for six months a civil war had been raging in Spain – a war in which she was openly supporting the fascist rebels. One evening Clotilde's father came home a little earlier than usual from his school. After he had embraced Suzanne and kissed his daughters he turned back to his wife with a smile.

'I've heard some cheerful news today.'

'I think we need some of that,' she smiled back. 'What is it?'

'Dr Hjalmar Schacht, the Minister of Economics, has spoken out against putting money into the military and colonization; he says it will lower the standard of living in Germany.'

Manfred's voice struck an optimistic note. It was to prove a false dawn, however. There was to be little good news through the last years of the decade. Manfred still struggled to protect his Jewish pupils, of course, but lost that particular battle on November 15th, 1938 when a law was passed sending Jewish children to segregated schools. This was only five days after the monumentally destructive Kristallnacht during which the Stormtroopers had carried out a near-systematic attack on Jewish businesses and institutions. The schoolteacher had thought it an ominous sign when Hjalmar Schacht was demoted in November 1937 and wasn't surprised when Schacht was dismissed two years later.

The bright star that lit up the sky of the family Schultz was when Clotilde's hard work paid off and she passed the examination that enabled her to transfer, at the age of ten, to her secondary school one year early.

When the news arrived of her success Suzanne flung her arms around her daughter's shoulders.

'My clever clever girl. How wonderful! I'm so proud of you.'

Clotilde was remarkably composed. 'Thank you, Mother. I'm very pleased. May I telephone Eloise?'

'Of course, my love.'

Her younger daughter sped off in the direction of the telephone.

# 14

## The Buick Becomes a Soldier

For Kurt, the excitement of the Olympic Games seemed to make the rest of 1936 pass quickly and in September he commenced his final year in his mixed primary school. His father Maximillian's dry batteries business was doing well. Together with his partner he had had a factory in Berlin since 1919 employing 250 people and a branch in the province of Thüringen, 250 kilometres south-west of the capital, where a further 150 people worked; in addition to this the overseas factory in Slough to the west of London was also progressing well.

Kurt was always keen to accompany his father on visits in the Buick to the branch factory and he was able to do so on a school holiday at the beginning of October. On the return journey Maximillian enjoyed talking about many different subjects to his son.

'One day soon, young man, there will be pictures on the radio.'

'That will be amazing, Father, but how will it be possible?' Kurt had his father's interest in all matters of a technological nature.

'Radio waves through the atmosphere! In time all sorts of things will be transmitted in that way.' He thought for a moment. 'All sorts of scientific advances are being made and in all sorts of different areas. For example some dogs are being trained to lead blind people and keep them out of danger.'

'That's amazing, Father!' He was truly impressed by this piece of information. 'Do you mean that the dogs will be the eyes of the blind person?'

'Exactly, Kurt, and the best results have been with our very own German shepherd.' The driver paused for a moment. 'They are strong, intelligent and obedient.'

'I really think that is wonderful, Father...' A thoughtful frown appeared on Kurt's face. 'Perhaps I could help in their training?'

'I'm proud of your enthusiasm for humanity and affection for animals but you still have your secondary education at the *Gymnasium* and your time there will probably shape your life.'

They drove on back towards Berlin. 'These are important formative years for you, young man.'

'Yes, Father.'


The new year – 1937 – started quietly for Kurt but, one day, during the first school holidays in the spring he found himself in the Buick on the way to the Olympic Stadium where his father was going to take part in a gymnastics competition.

'Father, can you explain to me exactly how this competition takes place?' The nine-year-old boy looked up at his father both inquiringly and admiringly watching him drive.

'Well, Kurt, there are a number of pieces of apparatus in the athletic gymnasium...' Herr Zimmermann was now driving in the countryside near the Stadium and it was noticeable how few people there were on the roads, not nearly as big a crowd as when they had come to the Olympic Games.

'There's the beam which requires balance and agility; the rings which demand enormous strength in the forearms and shoulders; the high and low horizontal bars on which the athlete performs spectacular feats; the parallel bars and finally my specialty, the horse with pommels.'

'What are pommels, Father?'

'They are two loops attached to the top of the gymnastic horse for the hands to grip on to it. You will see all of them in action at the competition.' Maximillian drove into the car park of the Stadium which still had a sparkling new appearance.

Kurt was enthralled by the spectacle of the gymnasts and greatly admired their skills though he wasn't sure that it was his 'cup of tea' After the event was over and they were walking back to the car he felt he should say something about his father's achievement. 'Congratulations on your bronze medal, Father, but I think the judges should have made you the winner.'

They found the Buick much more easily than in the previous August and set off towards home in Mahlow. 'I'm grateful for your views, young man, and know that I can always count on your support.'

Kurt returned to school for his last term before starting at his boys-only *Gymnasium*. However, on May 6th a rumour circulated throughout the school about a German disaster that had occurred and at the end of the day the headmaster toured the classrooms to inform the pupils that there would be no school the following morning to enable the pupils to listen to the radio news; for those pupils whose parents had no radio he would provide one in the school.

When Kurt arrived home he was met by his father.

'Kurt, do you remember the *Hindenburg* airship that we saw circling over the Olympic Games?'

'It was an amazing sight, Father; I could never forget it.' Then a look of horror crossed his face. 'Has something awful happened to it?'

'That is what I've been hearing on the telephone from our factory in Slough. They have heard a live eyewitness commentary by a British journalist and I believe that a German translation is to be broadcast tomorrow morning.'

Sure enough at eleven o'clock the following day the family Zimmermann were gathered around the radio in the sitting room.

'This is the German Air Ministry. We have to report that the great passenger airship *Hindenburg* burst into flames as it tried to dock in Lakehurst, New Jersey, in the United States of America at seven twenty-five this morning. The British journalist Herbert Morrison recorded an eyewitness account for WLS Chicago and a German translation follows this announcement...'

There was a short interval before a different voice started to speak, describing the landing and then the horror as the catastrophe unfolded:

'... The back motors of the ship are holding it just enough to keep it from ... IT'S BURST INTO FLAMES! It burst into flames and it's falling, it's crashing! Watch it! Watch it! Get out of the way! Get out of the way! Get this Charlie! It's falling on the mooring mast, and all the folks agree that this is terrible; this is one of the worst catastrophes in the world. All the passengers screaming around here. I told you, I can't even talk to the people, their friends are out there! It's just lying there, a mass of smoking wreckage...'

At last, much to the family's relief, the announcer's voice came back onto the radio. 'That was the report. We don't know the cause of this disaster, although there has been speculation about sabotage, a static spark, lightning, incendiary paint and a fuel leak. The casualties are as follows: there were thirty-six passengers on board of whom thirteen died; sixty-one crew of whom twenty-two died, and there was one of the ground crew killed. That is the end of this special broadcast.'

No one spoke until the transmission was finished. Maximillian stood up and went and switched off the set.

146

'That is an appalling tragedy but you know that I've always been worried by these gas-filled zeppelins.'

'I presume there will be an investigation?' Mitzi remarked, still horrified by what she had witnessed.

'Oh I'm sure there will but I've a feeling that it will remain a mystery.'

'Why do you say that, Father.' Marlena had followed the report and discussion carefully.

'Well, my dear, the heat must have been so intense that it will have destroyed all the evidence that could help establish the cause of the disaster.'

Kurt had been lost in thought. 'Father, do you think this terrible accident will have an effect on the future of airships carrying passengers?'

'I'm sure it will, Kurt. I think airplanes will take over very quickly.' He put his arms around his family. 'Let's think of other more cheerful things...'

In August Maximillian drove the family to Usedom Island for a wonderful summer holiday. On the return journey at the end of the month he said to Kurt, 'How would you like to see the State Visit of Mussolini on September 28th just before you start at your new school?'

'That sounds fantastic, Father. Where will we be able to see the parade?'

'From the balcony of the American Embassy.' There was a smile on the face of the boy's father who was very pleased with his son's boundless enthusiasm.

'That is going to be truly amazing, Father.'

The boy's excitement grew as the big day drew near and eventually Kurt found himself being driven by his father into central Berlin. The crowds of people in and around the Unter den Linden were so great that they had to approach the American Embassy from the rear. After they had parked the car they entered the Embassy and found a group of people talking excitedly together. A tall fair-haired slightly balding man wearing a light-grey suit stepped away from his colleagues and extended his right hand.

'Maximillian, good to see you and is this young man your son you've told me about?'

The two men shook hands. 'Yes he is. Kurt, let me introduce you to Jack Thornberry who works here and has helped me with my business.'

'Hello, sir. I'm very pleased to meet you; were you the gentleman who gave father the Buick?'

'How do you do Kurt,' they shook hands formally; 'I didn't *give* it to your father exactly because I'm the trade attaché here and therefore quite naturally I did a trade with your father.'

'I understand, sir.' Though actually Kurt didn't quite understand but didn't want to upset either his father or this very nice new friend. 'Are we going up to the balcony?'

'Yes, Kurt.' Mr Thornberry turned to lead the way towards the elegant staircase and Maximillian followed together with his son.

When they arrived on the first floor Jack led them across a gilt and mirrored room to a long set of French windows. The trio stepped outside and surveyed the scene.

Crowds of people moved like an ocean as far as the eye could see.

'Well, what do you think of the view?' the trade attaché asked.

'Phew, it's amazing!' It was a bright sunny day and Kurt saw immediately on his left the six great pillars of the Brandenburg Gate topped by its great sculpture of Victory riding a chariot drawn by four horses.

'Father, just look at all those people.'

His voice was incredulous as he pointed at the Pariser Platz, packed with cheering spectators extending back to the Bank Deutscher Lander at the far right corner.

'It's a fantastic sight, Kurt.'

Maximillian could not resist giving the occasion at least some educational value. He indicated the Brandenburg Gate. 'Do you know when that was built?'

'No, Father.'

'It was 1789, the same year as the French Revolution.' He smiled down at his son's upturned head. 'Have you learned about it at school in your history lessons?'

'Not yet, Father.' The impatience of youth could not be restrained. 'When will the procession arrive, Mr Thornberry?'

The slightly surprised trade attaché looked at his wristwatch. 'It's now two o'clock; we're not scheduled to see Hitler and Mussolini for another half-hour.'

In some strange way Kurt's voice sounded hungry and Jack picked up on this immediately. 'Come with me, Kurt.'

Kurt followed him over to the east corner of the balcony in the shadow of the Hotel Adlon, its neighbour on the Unter den Linden. He lifted a cloth that was covering a table to reveal an array of biscuits, cakes and fruit juices. 'Help yourself, young man.'

'That's a wonderful spread,' Maximillian said, joining them just as his son sank his teeth into a large piece of chocolate cake filled with cream. 'Oh hello there!' He extended his right hand to some more people emerging from the huge French windows.

The new arrivals passed down to the other end of the balcony.

'Jack, it would be best if Kurt stood at the front of the balcony; I think we should go back there now.'

'Oh, yes please!' The excited boy led the two men back into the warm afternoon sunshine at the balcony railings.

A moment or two later a sound could be heard coming from the other side of the Brandenburg Gate; it gradually grew in intensity and loudness.

'Can you hear that, Kurt?'

'Yes, sir.' He leaned forward with his hands on the stone rail of the balcony. 'I think it's cheering crowds but I can't see anything yet.'

Mr Thornberry took another look at his watch. 'Two twenty-four; the convoy is just passing the Reichstag and after that it will turn left to pass through the central arch of the Brandenburg Gate over there...'

Sure enough at two-thirty a massive roar came up from the vast crowds of people in Pariser Platz when they saw the open-topped gleaming black Mercedes-Benz limousine with chromium headlights and trimmings appear in the central arch of the Gate. As the beautiful great motor car seemed to float beneath them Kurt waved at the two figures standing side by side in the back of the vehicle.

'I think that they saw me, Father.'

Kurt took in the stern unsmiling figure of Adolf Hitler. He wore a brown uniform and peaked hat and was striking an imperious pose with his left hand resting on his leather belt, drawing attention to the swastika armband which matched the pennant on the front of the car. There was a simple Iron Cross on his breast pocket and he wore a white shirt and brown tie. The only elaborate part of his outfit was his hat: it had a shiny black peak; above the gold braid an insignia topped by the Nazi swastika in the claws of an eagle.

Only then did he notice the flamboyant fleshy figure of the Italian dictator standing to the right of the German leader. Benito Mussolini wore a light-grey uniform, black shirt and tie as well as a massive cluster of medals on his left breast pocket; and on top of all this was a sky-blue sash crossing from under his right epaulette to the left side of his waist. A broad black stripe ran down the sides of his trousers and he wore shiny black jackboots. This stunning peacock had on his head an ornate black cap with a massive gold eagle badge on the front and a black tassel nonchalantly hanging forward beside it.

'They are very different, aren't they, Father?'

Maximillian put his hand on his son's shoulder. 'You're quite right, young man.'

'I think he looks as though he has just stepped out of a shop window.' A few people standing close by roared with laughter.

Mussolini gave a Nazi salute with his right arm and on his left sleeve there was a black triangle with a gold eagle embroidered on it. Above the adulation of the crowd Kurt heard a voice behind him saying, 'I heard that he used to receive one hundred pounds each week from the British secret intelligence service...'

The entourage passed slowly eastwards at slightly more than walking pace and Kurt's eyes followed it as far as the huge numbers of people allowed.

'Thank you, Father, for bringing me here; I shall never forget this day.' The excited schoolboy slipped away for a moment and when he returned he carried two pieces of chocolate cake and handed one to his father. 'They were the last pieces left!'

Maximillian laughed as he took his son's offering. 'That is very thoughtful of you, Kurt.'

Two days later Kurt started at the *Gymnasium* and from the moment he entered the doors of the all-boys school he felt comfortable to be there. Each of the new boys was greeted individually by one of the teachers and it was really nice when he heard the words, 'Welcome, Kurt, I hope you will be happy here; if you have any problems please come and talk to me. My name is Herr Meyer.'

On December 11th he returned home to find his father listening intently to the radio. 'What's happening, Father?' His voice was cheerful and enthusiastic.

'Italy has withdrawn from the League of Nations.' There was a note of foreboding in the answer.

'Is that bad, Father?'

151

'I think so. Italy doesn't want peace.'

'I'm not surprised after seeing Mussolini; he looked like a man who wanted a war.'

'You're right, young man. He's already occupied Abyssinia and doesn't want anyone to interfere as he builds himself an empire in Africa,'

Christmas came and went and the world entered 1938. Shortly after the beginning of the new term, Mitzi told Marlena, now almost a teenager and growing fast as well as beautiful, that she would no longer be being treated by Dr Greenbaum.

Mitzi noticed a tear trickle down her daughter's left cheek. 'Don't be alarmed, my love, I've already arranged your future medical care.'

'You know it's not that, Mother. I am worried for *him* not me!'

The year passed on. Kurt celebrated his tenth birthday with some of his new school friends on February 9th and on March 13th, Maximilian, who had been listening to the radio, announced to his family that Austria was now a part of Germany; he seemed to think this was bad news. However, the whole family enjoyed driving up to Rügen Island to visit Marlena who was staying in a house owned by her school for a short holiday and in August they drove to the North Sea coast for their summer holidays. Both Marlena and Kurt enjoyed the rock pools teaming with sea creatures and thought back to the holiday on the Baltic with their grandmother which seemed like a long time before.

Maximillian spent increasing amounts of time listening to the radio and on September 30th he called Mitzi to join him.

'Chamberlain, the British Prime Minister, and Hitler have signed an agreement in Munich; our country will have the Sudetenland of Czechoslovakia as *Lebensraum* in exchange for no war with England.'

'That has got to be good!' Mitzi sounded cheerful and embraced both her children as they bounded into the room.

'I'm very pleased; it makes war less likely.' Maximillian smiled at his family. 'I've telephoned the factory in Slough and they tell me they're pleased. They've seen a newsreel showing Neville Chamberlain waving a copy of the agreement and saying "Peace in our time".'

There were sighs of relief in the Zimmermann household. However, when Kurt was at school on November 11th he heard other boys talking in hushed voices about the broken glass of shop windows, the burning of synagogues and other anti-Semitic activities. This was Kristallnacht, the extreme violence against the Jewish population and institutions, but there were few German Jews in Mahlow and therefore Kurt and his friends had seen little of the carnage of the previous night.

Christmas and New Year were quietly celebrated by Kurt's family and as they moved into 1939 Maximillian spent even more time listening to his radio and reported back to his family. On March 15th he said to Mitzi, 'The Munich Pact has been abandoned; I'm sure this will lead to war.'

'Will you be conscripted into the military?'

'I don't think so. I'm forty-nine years old and I think there will be a big demand for batteries both from the government and the general public.'

A few days later there was a very unwelcome radio announcement. Maximillian was horrified as he heard that the German national flag that had proudly displayed its black, white and red horizontal stripes above his house for years had been declared illegal by the government and must be replaced immediately by the new red national flag with its central black swastika in a white circle.

'That is outrageous,' he roared at the radio. Mitzi heard him from the kitchen and came rushing in to see what had upset her husband and he told her what he had just heard.

'You're quite right! It is outrageous but we must get on and do as we're told – for the children's sake, darling.'

Her husband calmed down. 'I agree, my love; you're always the wise one. I will go and get the new flag and put it in place.'

Mitzi kissed his cheek and left the room.

On September 3rd the radio told the family Zimmermann their country was at war and that very day two men in military uniform came to the house. When Maximillian opened the front door one of the soldiers smiled broadly and pointed at the Buick parked outside. 'We've come for that.'

Without a word Max reached into his trouser pocket, produced the keys and handed them over. He watched them drive away in his beloved car and a tear rolled down his cheek.

'Oh well, petrol is rationed anyway,' he said out loud, trying to console himself.

# 15

## *Conscription*

Suzanne Schultz wore a smart costume of olive-green velvet that matched her brownish-green eyes and set off her long dark-brown hair fashioned into a neat bun at the back of her head. On the afternoon of March 31st, 1939, she walked into the sitting room of their apartment to find her husband sitting beside the radio; a notebook in one hand and a ballpoint pen in the other.

'Hello, my love. I see you're putting my Christmas present to good use.' She was speaking of the pen, a new invention the previous year by Lazlo Biro in Hungary.

'Ah you mean my "Biro", as the boys call it. Everybody is very envious; I don't know how you managed to buy one.' He smiled briefly at his wife and then the expression changed as he glanced down at his notebook. 'There has been so much happening to our country lately that I have decided to make notes of all the events.'

'You spend so much time in here listening to the radio that it worries me.' She went over to his armchair and stood behind it, placing both her hands on his shoulders. 'What's your entry for today?' she asked, massaging his trapezius muscles.

'"The British Government has issued a statement supporting Poland."' He looked up at his wife. 'You look very chic, my darling; did you really make that matching jacket and skirt yourself?'

155

'I did indeed.'

'You're incredibly professional in your needlework; I'm extremely proud of you.'

She smiled down at him. 'Thank you, kind sir.'

Her husband stood up and she joined him in front of the chair, her medium height contrasting with his tall frame as she rested her head against his chest. 'So what is your notebook telling you?'

'It's partly for my benefit but also for the boys at the school – one by one this terrible and violent government's actions are leading Germany into a second world war.' He looked down into his wife's eyes. 'I've thought about this carefully and I'm sure this is the way things are going.'

'I do hope you've not expressed your views to your pupils or colleagues!' There was alarm in her voice and on her face.

'You're the only person I've spoken to about these matters, however I think my so-called colleagues have a good idea where my sympathies lie, although no one has said anything to me. I'm more or less being ignored.' He sounded forlorn.

'I'm so sorry for you, my darling husband; it must be very lonely for you at work.'

She took the ballpoint pen from his hand. 'You're still the one who has the Biro; your colleagues are just jealous.' She put her hand in his.

'I wish that were the case but there's one person who makes me feel it's more serious.'

'Who is that?'

'That poisonous little junior mathematics teacher Schneider.'

'Manfred, I've never heard you refer to another schoolmaster in such a way.' Suzanne's eyebrows had shot up and there were deep furrows across her forehead. 'What has he done?'

'I think he has been put into our school by the Nazis to inform on me and other people who share my distaste for our new leader and his obnoxious cronies.'

'Manfred, please don't say these things.' She held his hand tightly with both of hers; 'What if one of the girls should hear you and repeat it outside the house?' She could see that her husband's treatment by his colleagues was having a devastating effect on his psychological well-being.

He squeezed her hand. 'You're quite right, my angel!'

'Please be careful.'

On April 7th another piece of news was announced on the radio and entered into Manfred's notebook:

*Italy has invaded Albania; it took only one week to overrun the country.*

Suzanne joined her husband who was, once again, sitting close to the radio. 'I've another item for you to enter into your records.' She twirled around. 'My creation for the coming summer; do you like it?' As if expecting a positive answer she leaned forward and kissed him on the forehead.

Her husband studied the smart, beautifully tailored dress with its blue, red and green flowered pattern on a white background; the sleeves were short with shoulder pads and there was black tape tied at her neck in a bow. While he was admiring the outfit she went to the table, picked up a broad-brimmed white hat, and placed it on her head at a jaunty angle; finally she picked up a small black leather handbag.

'Did you make everything?'

'Yes, including the hat and the handbag.'

'It's amazing.' He was smiling and Suzanne had not seen him so happy for months.

She gave him another twirl and as she did so Clotilde

157

and Margit entered the sitting room. Both clapped their hands.

'Mother, that is a really lovely dress!' Margit embraced her mother.

'I think we've the most talented mother in the world...' Clotilde had a mischievous expression on her face. 'Did you make the shoes as well?'

'You know I didn't,' Suzanne laughed and started to chase her younger daughter around the sitting-room coffee table but eventually gave up, feigning being out of breath. 'You've a wicked sense of humour! Come with me into the kitchen for your evening meal before you do your homework.'

The children followed their mother towards the delicious aroma of bratwurst.

Later that evening as the two girls lay in bed they could hear their mother and father talking in soft tones though they couldn't hear what was being said. However, they were reassured by the glorious sounds of their mother playing the new Blüthner piano and then her beautifully trained soprano voice singing from her favorite opera, Mozart's *The Marriage of Figaro*:

> *O säume länger nicht geliebte Seele!*
> *Sehnsuchtsvoll harret deiner hier die Freundin.*
> 'Oh tarry no longer, beloved soul!
> Your ardent lover awaits here,'

Such cheerful sounds had not been heard in the Schultz house for some months and with a smile Clotilde allowed peaceful refreshing sleep to engulf her.

On the morning of July 22nd, two days before the end of the school term Manfred was taking a senior class in French literature – on this occasion they were discussing the historical significance of Victor Hugo's *Les Misérables*– when there was knock on the schoolroom door.

'Come in.' The school-teacher's tone was friendly.

The door opened and a pupil who had finished his end-of-school exams came in and handed Manfred a sealed white envelope; he didn't say a word but turned on his heel and left. The insult was calculated and didn't go unnoticed by the class, some of whom were grinning.

'That will be all for today, boys.' Manfred had never, ever lost his temper at school and wasn't about to do so now.

When he was alone, although he could still hear the boys chattering; he opened the letter and read: 'Herr Shultz, would you kindly come and see me in my study after classes today.' It was signed by Fritz Schäfer, the headmaster. Manfred had no idea what this request was about but he had a feeling that it wasn't going to be good news; however, it wasn't in his nature to put off difficult confrontations. He gathered up his books, papers, pens and pencils, packed them into his briefcase, put on his light-grey jacket and set off to see his headteacher.

'Come in!' was the response to his single knock.

Manfred opened the door and stepped into the modest office with its armchair and matching sofa covered in soft light-brown leather. In addition there was a large flat-topped patterned gold-and-red leather-covered desk, behind which was sitting Herr Schäfer.

'Good afternoon, Herr Schultz.' The tone was non-committal but definitely not friendly.

'Good afternoon, Headmaster.'

The foreign language teacher held out his right hand but there was no response; Fritz Schäfer remained seated in his high-backed mahogany chair. He surveyed Manfred over the top of his half-moon glasses, there was no smile and no clue to the cause of this uncomfortable interview.

'I've asked you to come here because I've been requested by the state authorities to recommend certain teachers for exemption from military service on account of their special status as teachers of the sons of Germany. In the cases of all your colleagues I've been pleased to supply such commendations; however, in your case Herr Schultz I've not been able to do so.'

The headteacher drew back in his chair as though expecting a tirade from his fellow teacher and colleague of many years' standing; it was surprising that he didn't know the man even after their long association.

'Thank you, Headmaster; good afternoon.' Manfred turned and strode purposefully out of the room.

Schäfer's shouted words followed him along the corridor. 'It's because of you helping the Jews; you shouldn't have done it.'

The foreign languages teacher dejectedly made his way home but didn't mention anything about his interview with the headmaster; in Manfred's view Fritz had sold his soul to the devil. He was fearful that Suzanne might have gone to the school and confronted the poor specimen of humanity who had done him such a grievous wrong.

The following day was the last one before the summer holidays and Manfred Schultz strode purposefully into the school premises. The first person he met was the junior mathematics teacher.

'I didn't think you would come here today, Jew lover, if there's a war I hope you're the first soldier killed.'

'Schneider, listen to me very carefully; if you had one scintilla of intelligence you would have worked out that there will be a war and at the end of it I've little doubt you will be in the front line of the Nazis receiving retribution for the outrages our country is committing.'

Manfred didn't prolong the conversation and walked briskly towards his classroom. Later that morning, his last class of the day joined him and sat at their desks. 'As you know only too well the school summer holidays start tomorrow...' The statement was greeted by 'hurrahs' and hand clapping but their teacher thought the response was a little more subdued than in previous years. 'We'll have this final English lesson and then join the rest of the school for the end-of-term assembly.'

Manfred now spoke in English and the pupils enthusiastically took up the various characters in Shakespeare's *Julius Caesar*. On this final day they had just reached the plains of Philippi before a battle where Cassius parts from his friend saying:

> *For ever, and for ever, farewell Brutus!*
> *If we do meet again we'll smile indeed;*
> *If not, 'tis true this parting was well made.*

Manfred could not help himself from almost enjoying the irony.

At that moment the school bell rang summoning the pupils and staff to the assembly and the boys left the classroom in as orderly manner as could be expected on the day before the summer holidays. Manfred didn't follow them but decided that he had heard enough of the headmaster to last a lifetime and made a solitary figure as he walked out of the main entrance. As he set off home carrying his briefcase he murmured to himself the following lines adapted from his beloved Shakespeare:

> For ever, and for ever farewell Fichte-Gymnasium
> I don't think we'll meet again.

A few passers-by looked at him and sadly shook their heads; they thought he was mad. And indeed he felt a kind of crazy joy that he had not allowed his integrity to be damaged by the Nazi Party.

On arrival home he was greeted by a series of hugs and kisses from his family.

'To what do I owe this wonderful welcome?'

Suzanne, who still had her arms around her husband's neck, answered, 'Because we love you.' She smiled. 'We know about the school. The headmaster announced it in assembly and was greeted with jeers and catcalls, and our telephone hasn't stopped ringing with outraged parents on the line.'

Manfred's daughters both laughed and embraced him over their mother's arms. Margit spoke for all of them. 'We don't mind that we're not having a summer holiday by the sea this year.'

'We can go to the Grunewald and other places near here instead.' Clotilde knew perfectly well that her father was deeply disappointed three weeks earlier when he announced there would be no seaside holiday this year. In fact, Manfred had overheard Schneider boasting how the Nazis had built a huge holiday resort on the beach at Rügen Island, which they were going to use to indoctrinate the German population. It was definitely no longer a place to take children.

'I'm very proud of you all adapting to difficult times; we'll have a nice summer holidays in our own home.'

'Hooray for stay-at-home holidays,' Clotilde cried, dancing around the sitting room.

Her father really did stay at home; to be more precise he stayed at home beside the radio. On August 23rd he entered into his notebook:

*Non-aggression pact with Russia (I would not trust either of them!).*

Then on the first of September came the news that Germany had invaded Poland, although Hitler tried to persuade listeners that his army was merely responding to being attacked.

At eleven o'clock on the morning of September 3rd, 1939, Manfred Schultz called his family to come and join him beside the radio. Suzanne sat on the arm of his chair and the two girls sat on the carpet at his feet and heard the announcer:

'Great Britain and France have declared war on Germany because they object to our defending our country against the inhuman aggression by the Polish Military.'

'And so we go to war on a lie,' the schoolteacher spoke passionately. 'The Poles fight on horseback against German tanks.'

Clotilde anxiously looked up at her father. 'Is it serious?'

'It's *very* serious, my darling daughter, and we don't know to what it will lead.' His sad eyes followed the family as they left the room.

The late-summer days passed and on September 17th Russia invaded eastern Poland followed by Finland on the thirtieth of that month – both events were gloomily entered into his journal.

On October 1st Manfred's papers commanding him to join the military arrived by post. Suzanne's comments about Fritz Schäfer used words that Manfred had never heard his wife use before.

# 16

## *Bombs on Berlin*

The family Zimmermann quickly recovered after the change of flag on top of the house and the commandeering of the Buick. Instead of driving, Maximillian took to travelling by train to the factory in the central Berlin district of Neuköln. In mid-September Kurt was still on his school holidays and loved to accompany his father to work whenever it was convenient.

'Do you think they will call you for military service, Father?' The eleven-year-old boy was walking beside his father on a warm morning; they were halfway along the short distance between the railway station and the factory.

'I don't think so. I'm forty-nine years old and not so fast on my legs as I used to be.' Max rested his hand affectionately on his son's shoulder. 'There's another reason – the factory! There will be a huge increase in demand for batteries.'

'But you're still a great gymnast, Father! It was only two years ago that you performed on the horse in the Olympic Stadium.' Kurt smiled up at his father. 'Anyway, why will people want more batteries?'

'Bombing, that's the reason.'

'But surely we're safe here in Berlin, Father.' Kurt simply could not believe that any attack on the capital city was possible. 'There are no more *Hindenburg*-type airships and it's a long way for an aeroplane to travel from England or

France!' He thought a moment longer. 'But why would bombing mean that people would need batteries?'

'Germany and other countries have been developing warplanes on a massive scale over the past two years and much of this war is going to be fought from the air. The Nazi government has been preparing for an air war for even longer; our civil airline Lufthansa has been training pilots to fly fighters and bombers.'

'Is that bad, Father?'

'It's against international law as laid down in the Treaty of Versailles...' They were entering the factory gates. 'Good morning, Rudolph; you remember my son, Kurt?'

'I certainly do, sir.' The white-haired gatekeeper shook Kurt's hand. 'You're growing fast, young man; it's very nice to see you again.'

'Thank you, Rudolph, sir.' Kurt followed his father to his office. 'Can you tell me about the Versailles Treaty, Father?'

Maximillian laughed, 'I'm here to work, Kurt, not teach you! Come on, today is my inspection day; let's do the tour.' He placed his briefcase on his desk and they set off to look over each department starting in the casing area, moving into the chemical laboratory and finishing with the packaging room.

'It's good to see everything running smoothly.' He smiled. 'We'll go and have some fruit juice in the staff canteen.'

Father and son made their way to a large room near the entrance to the factory and pushed open the swing door with a small window in it. Only one of the five wooden-topped tables was occupied.

'Good morning, Nikolaus.'

The grey-haired older man sprang to his feet. 'Good morning, Herr Zimmermann.'

'Kurt, this is Herr Nikolaus Koch, our esteemed chef.' They all shook hands. 'He has been serving up bratwurst, chocolate cake and coffee since the day we opened the factory.'

'Good to meet you, Kurt; your father has told me a lot about you!' There was a sparkle in the man's blue eyes that the eleven-year old really liked. 'It's true – I've been working here at your father's battery factory since he opened it in 1919; it was a godsend to people like me, fresh out of the army with no sign of work...'

'It was a bad time for Germany and its battered soldiers, Kurt.' Maximillian rested his right hand on the chef's shoulder.

'Your father was my saviour. So many of my comrades ended up either beggars, thieves or thugs.'

Maximillian waved generally in the direction of the factory. 'We started, Kurt, in a wooden shed with a corrugated-iron roof and I had one unpaid assistant who had studied chemistry at Heidelberg University before being drafted into the army and the trenches.' Kurt's father paused for a moment as he recollected events buried deep in the past. 'It was the two of us and Nikolaus roasted frankfurter sausages over an open wood fire in an old oil drum with holes punched in the side; now we've more than one hundred and fifty workers in this factory alone.'

Kurt and his father went to sit down at one of the tables, while Nikolaus fetched them some juice. 'What happened to the chemistry graduate?'

'He came back from the foul water-sodden trenches already coughing up blood; nevertheless he worked day and night to establish the technical side of the business.' The father of Kurt and Marlena was momentarily overcome by sadness. 'Within eighteen months he was dead as a result of tuberculosis of the lungs. His knowledge and expertise were essential for our success and I shall always be grateful to Heinrich Schmidt.'

Kurt finished drinking his apple juice then followed his father out of the canteen.

'Well, young man, you got a good history of the factory Zimmermann this morning.' They walked out onto the street. 'Next stop the bank to collect the wages we pay our workers.'

Kurt looked up at his father with an enquiring expression on his face but said nothing.

'I know, son, the Treaty of Versailles; we'll talk about it on the way home.'

'Oh thank you, Father, I really do want to know about the history of my own country.'

Later that day the train journey home started in silence as Maximillian gathered his thoughts and memories together.

'The Great War ended at the eleventh hour on the eleventh day of the eleventh month nineteen hundred and eighteen; the guns large and small became silent; there was massive relief all over the world but mainly in Europe, where the destruction had been unprecedented. I can't tell you what we endured in the trenches, Kurt. The appalling conditions of mud, rotting horses, dead soldiers and, of course, a terrifyingly high risk of being killed or wounded.'

'It must have been awful.' Kurt's imagination was vivid and emotional. 'I expect that even when the men were really tired they could not get any real sleep.'

'You're quite right, Kurt, mind you it was the same for both sides; the British and French suffered just as much as the Germans. The only people who didn't suffer were the generals on both sides who didn't seem to care how many soldiers died while they were trying to achieve their petty military objectives.'

'That's criminal, Father, weren't these generals punished?'

'No, Kurt, it was Germany that was made to suffer by being forced to accept the Treaty of Versailles.'

'Couldn't our country have refused to agree to the Treaty?'

'I'm afraid not. Our men were exhausted and had few supplies. America had come into the war; if we had refused we would have been decimated.'

'What did the Treaty do, Father?'

'I think there were four parts to it, Kurt. First Germany had to accept sole responsibility for causing the Great War; this was called the "war guilt clause"'.

'That's not fair, Father; it wasn't totally Germany's fault, was it?' It was rare to hear anger in the young man's voice and Maximilian was quite gratified by the passion shown by his son.

'You're quite right but we were in no position to argue. The second condition was that our country had to disarm; then we had to make enormous territorial concessions both in Europe and in Africa, giving away our African colonies.' As he reeled off what had been demanded from Germany twenty years before even the normally level-headed Maximillian realized that the Treaty had been outrageous. 'Finally Germany had to agree to pay reparations of 132 billion marks!'

'That is an unbelievable amount of money, Father.'

'You're quite right, young man; many economists said that it would take seventy years to pay off that amount of money, leaving our country impoverished. But that has all been changed by our new government, Kurt.' Maximillian and Kurt walked from the small station towards their house.

'How has it all changed, Father?'

'Because our new leader has broken every clause in the Treaty and, no doubt to his delight, found that the rest of the world took no action apart from diplomatic niceties.'

'Surely the German people are pleased by this?'

'Well, rearmament has certainly provided employment and money but unfortunately they have marched the country into war, let alone the other costs we are paying.'

When they arrived Mitzi was in the hall to meet them. 'There has been some good news on the radio. President Roosevelt has asked both sides to restrict bombing to strategic targets.'

'Does that mean we'll be safe, Father?' Marlena came down the stairs and threw her arms around his neck.

'I hope so, my darling daughter.' Maximillian looked out of the sitting-room window into the beautiful large garden. 'Though I don't trust the bunch of hooligans who have taken over this country.'

'Please, listen to me, Kurt and Marlena...' Mitzi put an arm around each of her children's shoulders. '*Never* repeat what your father has just said either inside or outside these four walls.'

The anguished mother looked at her husband questioningly.

Maximillian joined the group and his arms stretched around them all. 'Your mother is quite correct; I've just expressed my true feelings but we live in dangerous times in a dangerous country and we could all be in serious trouble if my indiscreet words are repeated.'

Some days later some of the workers from the factory arrived to clear out the cellar of the house, and install reinforced concrete pillars and crossbeams and a ceiling of steel meshwork.

During a coffee break, the foreman chatted to Mitzi. 'Your house will be bombproof, gnädige Frau. You'll be perfectly safe now. Your husband has taken similar precautions at the factory though I don't think it will ever be necessary myself.'

'I hope not, but thank you just the same.' Mitzi said but adding to herself, 'Knowing my husband these precautions will be absolutely necessary.'

Kurt enjoyed his new school and found that a boys-only

institution suited his temperament at that stage of his life. Meanwhile another doctor had taken over the care of Marlena's diabetes and, although the illness was stable, she still would have preferred her dear Dr Greenbaum to have been looking after her.

Apart from the triumphalist broadcasts on the radio by Doctor Goebbels the war was not affecting life in Berlin at the end of 1939; the war in Poland was apparently going well but seemed somehow very far away.

Kurt could not avoid hearing the radio and what the other boys were talking about at school.

'What is *Blitzkrieg*, Father?' Maximillian had just come in the front door after a railway trip to the subsidiary factory he had established in Thüringen 220 kilometres south-west of Berlin. He had, of course, lost his factory in Slough at the outbreak of war back in September but it was his nature to accept such events and just move on. Now it was April 1940 and business was booming. The blackout, long in place; had caused a surge in demand for torch batteries.

'What a greeting, young man, after my long journey.'

'I'm sorry, Father, but all the boys are talking about it at school.'

'At least let your father come in through the front door, Kurt.' The boy stood aside and took his father's brown woollen winter coat and hung it up in the hallway; Maximillian sat down in one of the armchairs in the sitting room.

'*Blitzkrieg*, young man, is an intense military campaign intended to bring about a swift victory in war, as quick as lightning so to speak; it's come to mean very heavy gunfire and bombing from the air followed immediately by a rapid advance by the army with tanks and machine guns, it's been very effective in Poland.'

'Poland attacked Germany, didn't it, Father?'

'That is what we've been told, Kurt.' Maximillian took

170

in a deep breath. 'Please please don't repeat what I'm going to say.'

'I promise, Father.'

'I don't for one moment think that Poland attacked Germany. For goodness' sake their cavalry was still on horseback! ... They were sitting ducks for our highly trained tanks!'

'So our armies are not the heroes we're being told they are on the radio?' Kurt had a look of astonishment on his face; he was now two months past his twelfth birthday maturing in mind and body. His judgement was that he preferred to believe his father rather than anything he heard on the radio or at school.

His father shook his head.

'The rumour among the boys is that the military are preparing a Blitzkrieg against France, Belgium and Holland, Father.'

'Do you think that's true my love?' said Mitzi, coming into the room with a small glass of whisky for her husband.

'I can believe anything of that lunatic Adolf Hitler.' Maximillian suddenly realized what he had said but Kurt rushed to his rescue.

'Father I didn't hear a word.'

'I said we'll have to listen to the radio carefully. I think we must always have one of us tuned into each news broadcast.'

Marlena, who had just come into the room and who liked diagrams and charts, became enthusiastic. 'I will draw up a duty roster and then we'll all know what is happening.'

And so the family Zimmermann began to follow events of the developing war.

On the afternoon of May 10th Mitzi was listening to the news shortly before the children came home from school when her attention was caught by the newsreader saying, 'A military operation has been taking place since dawn this morning; its codename is Operation Yellow. German armoured forces have speedily penetrated the Ardennes Forest, cutting off the French, British and Belgian soldiers who are rapidly retreating towards the French port of Dunkirk; heavy casualties have been inflicted on the enemy with thousands killed, wounded or taken prisoner.'

Mitzi related this to Maximillian when he arrived home while Marlena and Kurt listened in silence. Her husband heaved a big sigh. 'It could be worse.'

'What do you mean, my dear?' Mitzi was as puzzled as her children's expressions showed they were.

'Well, so far there has been no massive attack on civilians although we really don't know what is going on in Poland.' He put his arm around Mitzi's shoulders. 'Providing there's no so-called area bombing we're safe here in Berlin.'

The family continued to rely on the radio to learn how things were going but Maximillian continued to read the *Berliner Local Anzeiger* which he found a reliable newspaper and on May 15th a headline caught his eye:

## MASSIVE AREA BOMBING OF ROTTERDAM.

He read on how the port had been immobilized by the aerial attack but there was no mention of civilian loss of life or injuries. 'Oh my God, how could the government have been so stupid?'

The answer to his question was reported a few days later when Britain's Royal Air Force dropped bombs on the industrial Ruhr. The blast furnaces were like self-illuminating targets but the damage wasn't very great.

On June 5th there were further radio reports which Marlena heard and wrote down. The German forces, in an operation codenamed Operation Red had outflanked the main French defence strategy called the Maginot Line; Paris was occupied on June 14th and on the seventeenth

Marshal Pétain asked for an armistice which was signed on the twenty-second. Over half of the country was occupied by the German military and its associated political police, the Gestapo, while a small area in the south remained nominally under French administration with its capital at Vichy.

On August 25th the Royal Air Force dispatched ninety-five aircraft to bomb Tempelhof Airport. Not all the planes reached their destination but eighty-one dropped their bombs, and there were five more raids in the next two weeks. No great damage was done but the bombing of Berlin had begun, the Blitz on Germany.

# 17

## Paris – June 1940

The German victory parade in Paris following the fall of France took place along the majestic avenue des Champs-Elysées on June 22nd, 1940. The massive army in steel helmets both on foot and on horseback was followed by horse-drawn heavy guns and was watched by the stunned people of Paris, their sad faces reflecting how incomprehensible the events of the past few days had been to the French citizens.

The huge army had assembled to the west of the Arc de Triomphe. Marching in rows eight abreast the grey columns of men wheeled around the south side of the massive arch, thus avoiding passing over the flame on the shrine of the Unknown Soldier that had been lit in 1923; then carried on eastwards down the Champs-Elysées towards the place de la Concorde.

The vast majority of the conquering army was young, stern-faced, self-assured and proud to be where they were. Soldat or Private Manfred Schultz wasn't such a person. Conscripted as a result of a malicious act by his headmaster as revenge for his kindnesses to his Jewish pupils and colleagues, at forty-two years of age he was twenty years older than most of those among whom he marched along Paris's grandest thoroughfare on that early-summer day. He didn't share the triumphalism of his fellow helmeted and uniformed colleagues and whispered under his breath in French, 'Oh Paris, city of beauty and culture, please don't follow my beloved Berlin along the path of the barbarians.'

The men gradually disassembled in the Jardin des Tuileries and Manfred started to walk towards the stables to attend to the horse that pulled his bakery cart. After basic training he had been assigned to delivering bread to the military units; it was mind-numbingly boring but he had decided not to complain or do anything to attract attention to himself.

Suddenly he heard his name.

'Private Schultz, stop where you are.'

Manfred stopped in his tracks and turned to face Unterfeldwebel or Sergeant Möller, a stocky powerful figure.

'May I help you, sir?'

'This is not an afternoon tea party, Private.'

'No, sir.' Manfred saluted.

'You're different from the others who came into my platoon.'

'Yes, sir.' Manfred saluted again.

'Is that all you can say?' The Sergeant's voice was raised and there was spittle at the corners of his mouth. 'Are you trying to be insolent?'

Manfred had years of experience of the human male at boiling point and realized that he had to defuse the situation. 'Sergeant, I admire you as a professional soldier; it's something I could never do, although as a schoolteacher I've taught many young men whom it was my judgement that they were right to choose the military as a career and have made a great success of their chosen field; as indeed I am sure you're doing, sir.'

'Thank you, Private Schultz. I've a request here for you to report to the adjutant to General Meyer at the reception desk of the hôtel de Crillon at number ten in the place de la Concorde; I don't know for what reason you're summoned but I suspect it will make better use of your talents.' He handed Manfred his written orders, he offered his hand, which Manfred took. 'I wish you good fortune schoolteacher'

'Thank you, sir.' Manfred turned and walked away. Birds were singing in the chestnut and mulberry trees.

'Isn't it wonderful to be in Paris.' The speaker was a soldier similarly dressed to Manfred in a grey–green wool uniform with a Wehrmachtsadler, or armed forces eagle, above his right breast pocket and a plain grey-green shoulder insignia with a silver border; he had taken off his helmet and it was slung over his left shoulder. He was a fair-haired young man of about twenty years of age and apparently not bothered by being the lowest rank in the military. 'I've never been out of Germany; it's very exciting and I'm grateful to the Führer for being part of the greatest nation in the world.'

'It's a beautiful city, enjoy the moment while it lasts and please treat the Parisians with respect.'

'Of course, of course!' They shook hands and Manfred hurried on towards the *hôtel* on the north side of the famous square. The schoolteacher wasn't keen to fraternize with the younger soldiers and he could not help but wonder what the future had in store for these enthusiastic, fit but belligerently indoctrinated young men; in addition he wasn't pleased to have been picked out from the crowd after such a short time in military service.

He entered the majestic *hôtel* which had been built in 1758 by Louis XV and was awestruck by the magnificent luxury of the tapestries, chandeliers and gilt-brocade upholstered furniture. Despite the mêlée of high-ranking officers he had no difficulty in spotting General Kurt 'Panzer' Meyer. It was typical of the man to meet the individual he had sent for personally rather than sending an adjutant, even though he was famous for his dramatic success in the invasion of Poland; he had now been transferred to oversee the occupation of France. He advanced towards the only Private in the room with his hand outstretched. 'You must be Private Manfred Schultz?'

The schoolteacher, as he still preferred to think of himself, liked the firm handshake of the senior officer, He took in at a glance the fine grey gabardine tunic with a gold thread embroidered eagle and swastika above his right breast pocket and his shoulder straps of woven gold on red surmounted by a silver lozenge indicating his rank of *Generalleutnant* or Major General.

'We'll ask le questions...' a short thin balding little man wearing huge horn-rimmed spectacles interrupted. 'You're le schoolteacher of le French, le English and le German?'

It was immensely difficult for Manfred to avoid laughing at the garbled language of this grotesque caricature of a man dressed in the black gabardine uniform of an SS Brigade führer

'Let's not be too hasty, Oberon.' General Meyer tried to hide his irritation at the intrusion of the SS officer. 'I need to get to know our linguistics expert, Brigadier Krause.'

'Of course, Herr General.'

Manfred sensed a tension between the two men and it wasn't surprising bearing in mind that even he knew the reputation of the General and was amazed that he had been given this clown to be in charge of security. 'I was merely trying to...'

'So stop trying, Krause!' The SS man looked as if he could cheerfully murder his superior officer.

'Let's walk outside into this beautiful June evening.' Manfred followed the charismatic soldier out through the main entrance of the stunningly beautiful *hôtel*. 'I shall not be needing you anymore this evening Brigadier.'

'But, Herr General, this man has been brought here for my department's work against any possible resistance by the French.'

Oberon Krause looked as though he was about to explode

but clearly thought better of it. Manfred was aware of four large regular Wehrmacht, or Defence Force, men walking with them at a discreet distance. When they were what, Manfred judged to be, out of earshot of 'Orrible Oberon' the General stopped and put a firm but gentle hand on his left forearm. 'Private Schultz, I sent for you because I know you're a first-rate language teacher with a poorly disguised loathing of our Nazi masters.'

'I'm amazed at your knowing these things, sir, or should I call you General?'

'Protocol demands "General" and I think we had better stick to that to maintain a proper distance between us for the benefit of any observers...' He paused. 'Do you remember one of your pupils having difficulty in reciting the verses of Shakespeare's eighteenth sonnet "Shall I compare thee to a summer's day"?'

'I do, Herr General, that would be about two years ago; the young man just could not memorize the text and I showed him a method using numbers and colours to solve the problem.' Manfred smiled warmly at the senior soldier.

'That young man is eternally grateful to you; his name is Heinrich Bauer; his English teacher is his hero and he is my nephew.' Kurt Meyer smiled momentarily and then a frown creased his forehead. 'This may be my only opportunity to speak to you without that fool Krause interfering and making things worse rather than run smoothly here in France.'

'Yes, Herr General; may I ask what it's exactly you wish me to do?'

'I want you to balance out the crimes against France that the evil little monster Oberon Krause has planned, very few of us Germans speak the language and we need your help to ensure that there's no miscarriage of justice in the military courts we're establishing to deal with any insurgency against the occupying German forces.'

'I'm not a willing participant in this war, General, but if I can do anything that will help justice and the alleviation of suffering I will do my duty.'

'I'm delighted to hear that, Private. If there's anything you wish to convey to me without the knowledge of Brigade führer Oberon Krause, don't approach me directly but communicate through Heinrich Bauer, who is standing over there under the horse chestnut tree as part of the quartet of my bodyguard.'

'Yes. Herr General, are there any cases pending of which I should be aware?'

'There's one, which is why I'm speaking to you this evening and it's one in which Krause wishes to make a huge example of the accused; it concerns a man who openly listened on his radio to the speech made by General de Gaulle from the BBC in London three days ago.'

'May I ask when this case is being heard, Herr General?'

'I think it's better that we finish our meeting now. Anything further should be through Private Bauer; he will be your shadow but it's equally important that neither of you attract attention.'

General Kurt 'Panzer' Meyer saluted and with a soft 'Good night, Private' he turned and returned to the *hôtel*.

'Private Schultz!' Manfred turned his head in the direction from which the voice had been softly spoken; 'Follow me!' The schoolmaster walked towards the beckoning finger of Heinrich Bauer who led him around the west side of the elegant eighteenth-century façade and near the back of the building. The General's nephew and bodyguard took him down some steps and into the basement which was in darkness.

'It's good to see you again, sir!' They shook hands. 'It's a privilege to be your liaison with the General but these are dangerous times and I ask you to be careful.'

'I thought we Germans were all on the same side.'

179

'We are but the secret police, the Gestapo, favour a more aggressive and cruel approach to the population of the occupied country than the Wehrmacht or regular army and there's fierce rivalry between the two.'

'It seems to me that I'm going to be in between these two military groups.' Manfred didn't sound enthusiastic.

'You're quite right, sir,' Heinrich still felt as though this was his hero schoolmaster and still addressed him as such; they remained comfortable with the terms. 'But it's the Gestapo that everybody has to watch out for.'

'Heinrich, where will this trial of the Frenchman take place?'

'It will be at number eleven, rue des Saussaies, the former building of the French Secret Police; it will take place in the people's court and start at ten o'clock.' He reached for the door handle. 'I will be here while you fetch your kit; meanwhile I will tell your unit sergeant that you've been seconded to the General's staff; I will also make sure you've not been followed and when you get back I will show you to your new room.'

Manfred slept well in his basement bedroom which was really comfortable and in the morning he joined the *hôtel* staff for an excellent breakfast of croissants, butter, jam and coffee; an elderly gentleman in a butler's uniform had heard the unwilling soldier thanking one of his colleagues for passing the butter.

'You speak excellent French, young man.'

Manfred was hugely amused by being addressed as 'young man' and had not been consciously aware that he had started to speak French in the hotel staff kitchen; it had just happened naturally.

The schoolmaster smiled as the Frenchman sat down next to him. 'I've an advantage, Monsieur; I teach the language and its literature in Germany.'

The butler, who told Manfred that he was in charge of

the pageboys in reception, took a seat next to his new found friend, 'I'm very pleased to meet you, Monsieur; my name is Maurice.'

'I'm pleased to make your acquaintance. I'm Manfred and as I expect you can easily guess I am here to translate, though I can't say any more than that.'

'Of course not.'

'I can't help but notice the pageboys under your command are somewhat mature.'

'Paris is a bad place for young men at the moment; many people have travelled south.' He shook his head sadly.

Manfred thought of asking him directions to the court but then thought much better of it. He took his leave of Maurice, left the basement area and proceeded north from the place de la Concorde into rue Boissy where he selected an elderly lady wearing a mauve woollen shawl and selling water cress. He saluted her and wished her good morning and asked if she knew where he could find the rue des Saussaies.

She looked him up and down and then spat onto the street near his boots. 'I would not go there if Casanova himself asked me.' There was something about this German soldier that puzzled the watercress seller of Paris. 'You're old to be a Private; you must have done something to upset your Führer.'

'My name, Madame, is Manfred and ten months ago I was a teacher of French, English and German; my colleagues thought I wasn't sympathetic to the new Germany.' His words lit up the face of his new acquaintance. 'May I ask your name, Madame?'

'I'm Madame Dimanche and the women of my family have sold watercress here in the rue Boissy for over two hundred years. The next turning on the left is rue Faubourg Saint-Honoré and that takes you into rue des Saussaies, but, I warn you, it's a dangerous place to be at the moment.'

'So I understand. Thank you, Madame Dimanche, for your friendliness and help; I wish you well in these difficult times.' He had nothing to give her but warmly shook her hand. On reaching the end of rue Boissy he turned into rue Faubourg Saint-Honoré from there it was easy to spot the dreaded number eleven with two SS guards wearing grey uniforms, black collars and shoulder straps standing impassively outside the main entrance.

Positioned between the two intimidating heavily armed men was a Gendarme Sergeant wearing the easily recognizable navy-blue uniform and characteristic-flat topped brimless hat of the French police. He was holding a clipboard and looked up when Manfred approached. 'Can I be of assistance, sir?'

Manfred was surprised to find a French Policeman working alongside the army of occupation. 'I am here to act as an interpreter in the People's Court.'

'Tell him to address you by your rank of "Private" and not to call you "sir".' It was one of the SS guards speaking.

'Did you understand what he said, Sergeant?'

'No, sir.'

'He wants you to call me "Private" and not "sir".'

'Yes, sir ... I beg your pardon ... Private; may I have your name, please?'

'Private Manfred Schultz.'

'Ah yes, People's Court Number Six.' The two men saluted one another and the newly appointed translator followed the appropriate signposts and was ushered into the court. He was led to a seat at one side, just below the dais on top of which three tables overlooked a lower table with a single uncushioned chair facing the raised part of the court. Manfred saw a large group of people at the back of the court and as far as he could tell they were excitedly speaking French. A man in a white bow tie and stiff wing collar came and sat beside Manfred and said quietly in

German. 'I'm the lawyer presenting the case; my name is Johann Lehman.'

No sooner had they shaken hands than the onlookers at the back of the court became silent and a short balding man in a bright-red gown with a gold Nazi insignia entered; he was followed by two assistant judges in black suits with white shirts, wing collars and white bow ties; the red-clad gentleman indicated everyone to be seated.

'I'm Judge Roland Freisler...' The voice was strident, unfriendly and intimidating. 'Bring in the prisoner.'

A side door opened and a Gestapo soldier entered. He was roughly grasping the wrist of a frightened-looking man in his mid-fifties with grey thinning hair and bruises on his face; he led him to stand behind the chair and desk in front of the judge. The prisoner wore no tie and his blue-and-white striped shirt was buttoned up to the neck. The escort pulled out the chair and sat on it; the accused individual remained standing.

'What is your name?'

'Marcel Petit.'

Judge Freisler screamed, 'The accused will address me as Reich Richter.'

Manfred explained this to the French prisoner and went over to the table in front of Marcel Petit and started to write the correct form of address on a piece of paper.

'If the accused shows any more disrespect to the court he will go to prison until I return from Berlin.'

Manfred translated, explaining *Richter* meant 'judge' and Marcel said 'Yes, sir' to the teacher.

'Herr Lehman, present the case.' The tone was surly.

'This is a simple matter for the court.'

'I will decide what is simple, Herr Lehman.'

The young lawyer looked downcast.

'On the evening of June 18th, 1940, the accused was seen listening to General de Gaulle broadcasting seditious statements against the Third Reich from the BBC in London on his radio.'

Manfred translated this for Marcel Petit who unhesitatingly answered. 'Impossible!'

When the court heard this in German, the judge, who seemed unable to control his violent temper; screamed, 'How can it be impossible? He is here in my people's court?'

Johann Lehman was nonplussed. 'Of course the court is correct.' He turned towards the accused. 'Please explain your statement.'

'I was sitting outside the café de Marigny taking an absinthe and a rest on my way to the shop of Monsieur Girard to get a new valve fitted to my radio which is rather heavy.'

Manfred explained and the lawyer responded. 'We have a witness who says that your radio was plugged into the electricity supply in the café and saw you listening to it.'

Again the interpreter, who was playing a much larger part in the proceedings than he had expected, did his job. 'Impossible!'

Monsieur Petit saw the look on the judge's face and realized that although he didn't speak French he wasn't stupid and quickly added, 'The electric cable had come unwound while I was carrying the radio and the absinthe out to the table.'

After Manfred had explained the situation to the court he saw Judge Freisler open his mouth to utter an expletive but clearly changed his mind. 'Why did the prisoner want the radio repaired when he knew they were going to be made illegal by the occupying forces?'

The interpreter saw the danger. 'Listen to me very carefully, Marcel...' He took a deep breath. 'Did you want your radio repaired to hear the instructions to Parisians by the occupying forces?'

'Oh yes, sir.'

Manfred didn't think it safe to let the Frenchman say anything else and cut him off smartly. 'The radio repair was to enable the accused to hear the proclamations to the people of Paris.'

The lawyer started to speak. 'Would the People's Court like to inspect the radio?' He was going to continue about how helpful this would be when he noticed Judge Freisler gathering up his papers; he had a thunderous expression on his face.

'No!' he screamed and rose to his feet, scowling at the interpreter before leaving the court.

The lawyer turned to Manfred. 'It's over and the prisoner is both free and very lucky!' He paused for a few moments and then continued. 'I've worked in the People's Court for the past four years with Judge Roland and felt sure Marcel Petit was going to hang today.'

The unwilling interpreter was horrified by what he heard. 'I hope I never have to work in that monster's court again!' he murmured and felt a desperate need to speak with his beloved Suzanne on the phone, although he realized he would not be allowed to tell her the shocking details about this case. He left the building to look for a telephone.

# 18

## *Berlin – November 1940*

Maximillian Zimmermann was sitting by his radio early on the evening of November 9th, 1940; the announcer's voice was strident. '...Last night the criminal Royal Air Force bombed the historic centre of Munich.'

Marlena, who had just arrived home, came and sat beside her father; she seemed a little tired as she rested her head on his left thigh.

'Has something serious happened, Father?'

'Munich has been bombed, my little angel, and dropping bombs on civilians is serious, or as we say now, blitzed.'

The radio came to life again. 'We've just been handed the details of the damage in Munich; it includes the New City Hall with its famous Glockenspiel that used to perform a miniature tournament several times a day. It was much loved by our glorious Führer; there was also severe damage to the open-air loggia which has been such a wonderful rallying point for the Nazi Party.' There was a short pause. 'That great friend of the Third Reich Herr William Joyce will now address the British people on this day of infamy.'

An Englishman began to speak in an exaggeratedly posh accent and the two Zimmermanns, father and daughters, found it hard to follow.

'This is "jairmany" calling ... I speak to England on behalf of the Third Reich: the unprovoked attack on Munich has deeply upset the German people and their Führer; there will be retribution.'

'Who is that man with a head cold?' Kurt came into the room. 'He has a very peculiar voice. I can't believe anyone likes him.'

'In England he's called "Lord Haw Haw" but he is a political friend of the Nazi Party and has now taken German nationality. I don't trust him and if the British ever capture him they would certainly execute him.'

'Does that mean he would die just for what he said, Father.' Marlena had a horrified look on her face. 'Isn't that terrible for saying what you think?'

Maximillian felt that his children should have a clear understanding of the seriousness of the situation. 'In time of war any action taken by a person against his own country which assists the enemy of the day is committing what is called high treason and usually carries the death penalty.'

'Father, before I came home today I was called to a meeting at Mahlow Town Hall.'

Kurt sounded very 'matter of fact' as he changed the subject from the terrifying thought of treason and its consequences.

Maximillian was alarmed. 'I think any such interview should have had the approval of me and your mother.'

'These people said it wasn't necessary.' Kurt was completely casual about the matter.

'Had any other boys been interviewed?'

'Oh yes but they didn't talk about it afterwards.'

'How were they dressed, Kurt?'

'They were two men wearing the same sort of business suits, one dark blue and the other black; they were smart like you when you go to work.'

'What did they ask you?'

'What would I do if one boy couldn't afford to buy the Hitler Youth uniform?'

'What did you say?'

Kurt sounded very philosophical. 'Well, I *thought* to myself, "My father could pay but why should he?" therefore I didn't say anything.'

'What happened afterwards, Kurt?' Maximillian was troubled.

'What are we talking about?' Mitzi came into the room and there was also anxiety in her voice. 'Has something terrible happened to you, my darling son?'

'No, Mother. I just had a short interview with the Hitler Youth people; I stayed silent after a question and they told me that I had not been selected.' He smiled sweetly at his mother.

'Maximillian my dear, this is ridiculous. Kurt is only twelve years old and the authorities have clearly said that boys have to be fourteen to be admitted to the Hitler Youth; it's the same age for girls to be taken on by the League of German Girls.'

'I agree and I'm really proud of Kurt's response to these busybodies; they may be very good at turning young boys into soldiers but it's not a good business.' The head of the household suddenly changed the subject. 'After that raid on Munich I think we had best look to our own defences.'

The whole family followed him down into the cellar. He flicked the switch down but there was no light. 'We'll have to make use of our own Zimmerman batteries.' He switched on a powerful torch that he had brought with him and swept it around the cellar.

'Dear oh dear, dust accumulates so quickly. It was less than a year ago that your workers from the factory strengthened the cellar against bomb damage.' She sighed.

'I think that before I make a start here, you should pay a visit to the Mahlow Town Hall to see what they recommend about air raid protection and whether they feel we should stay at home or use the local shelters.' She put her arms around her husband, kissed his cheek and patted his shoulder to send him on his way.

When he had left Marlena turned to her mother. 'Will we have Grandmamma to stay while Berlin is being bombed?'

'I will telephone Romhilde when we've made a good start on the list of provisions we must get in for the siege.'

'We must remember my insulin and the syringes together with swabs, disinfectant, test tubes and Benedict's solution.' Marlena was now fifteen years old and the maturing fair-haired girl had already been attending the afternoon meetings of the League of German Girls for a whole year. 'Maybe I won't need to go to be with those awful girls and their so-called leaders while we're using the cellar as an air raid shelter.'

'I know that you've been ridiculed and made to feel inferior because you have diabetes, my darling daughter, and all they think about is silly physical exercises and daft songs.' She gave her daughter a big hug. Secretly Mitzi was fuming over the way her lovely Marlena had been treated and she thought there was also bias against the girl because she was learning how to play the violin; it had been her own choice and she was beginning to show some talent for the instrument.

'I think those women who organize the League meetings are philistines where the arts and intellectual pursuits are concerned. I will never forgive them for the type of society they represent'

Marlena had never heard her dear gentle mother speak so vehemently about a group of people. Nevertheless she was grateful to her for the support. 'Thank you, Mother. I really appreciate what you've said; I just wish I could see an end to all this marching and shouting.'

'I quite agree with you, my dear.' Mitzi looked around her and spread her hands. 'This is what all that aggressiveness has achieved – forcing us down into our own cellar!'

'Where shall we start, Mother. I think we should begin by sweeping up all the sand left by the workers and putting it in sacks.' Marlena started to sweep. 'It's a good thing we made the bonfire using my dolls' house last year on the day before the men from Father's factory arrived.'

Mitzi laughed. 'I love your enthusiasm, my darling, but a bonfire would soon have one of those Air Safety Guards knocking on our front door and threatening all sorts of dreadful things for providing a guiding light to British bombers.'

'I remember hearing about illegal bonfires on the radio.' She looked up at the ceiling for a moment. 'I'm not sure what the security police would do but I've a feeling the first thing would be to disband us as a family.'

'That would be terrible, Marlena. I've forgotten about bonfires already; we won't do anything that could separate our lovely united family.' She picked up one of the now filled sacks. 'Where do you want these love?'

'I think they could be really useful if we put them around the bottoms of the walls of our house to protect us from the shockwaves of exploding bombs.'

'That's a wonderful idea, Marlena; is it your own?'

'Not really, Mother. I have to admit we've been discussing it at the meetings of the League; our junior leader, Fräulein Bertina Hartmann, told us how best we can help protect our homes against the bombing.'

'No more training to be domestic goddesses then?'

'No, now we're preparing for such activities as nursing, providing entertainment and working at train stations. There's training as office staff, signals auxiliaries, searchlight operators and even talk of being flak helpers.'

'I don't know what "flak" is.'

'It's an abbreviation, Mother, of the word *Flugzeugabwehrkanone*, or Aircraft Defence Gun. I learned that at the meetings, too!'

190

'That is amazing. So girls are becoming part of the civil defence?'

'Exactly, Mother.' Marlena flung her arms around Mitzi. 'It's our country as well.'

'Who is claiming it's their country?' Kurt came down the cellar steps with his father. 'We've had a good time at the Town Hall.' He jumped down the last three stairs.

Maximillian followed his son down into the cellar and looked at the cleanly swept floor and the last of the sandbags. 'What do we have here?'

'Marlena thought we could use them to protect us from some of the bomb blast around the base of the walls of the house. It's going to mean a lot of hard work.'

'I agree, though I've been very encouraged by Herr Conrad Bauer at the Town Hall who thought, by my description, that it would be best for us to stay in the house during the air raids. However, he is putting us on a list for him to inspect and make suggestions how the Department of Public Works can assist us. He said he'll come in the next two or three days, so we'll need to get cracking.'

'Herr Conrad was very nice and encouraging.' Kurt's enthusiasm and excitement was infectious. 'He said that all this is only a precaution because of the great distance that the Royal Air Force has to fly at night with no navigational landmarks. He says we almost certainly won't have much bomb damage here in Berlin.'

'I hope that's true.' Mitzi had the protective tone in her voice that all mothers would have when there was talk of bombs falling on their homes. 'Although I'm sure what we're told by the authorities is meant to cheer us up. I've not forgotten the air raid near Tempelhof Airport back in August.'

'It didn't do much damage, Mother,' Marlena tried to reassure Mitzi.

191

'I've a feeling that as a nation we've embarked on a terrible and strange journey.' Mitzi was opening her heart in a way that her family had never heard before. 'In all these aggressive words that we hear on the radio and read in the newspapers from the Nazi Party I hear none of the thoughts of Goethe and the beautiful music of Brahms and Beethoven...'

'I agree, my love.' Maximillian put an arm around his wife's shoulders. 'We're in a place of our making but not in a time of our making and we've to do our best with where we find ourselves and with the resources that we have.'

Two days later Herr Conrad Bauer arrived at the Zimmermann house accompanied by two junior Town Hall officials.

'Good morning, Herr Zimmermann.' The tone was respectful and friendly and the whole party was dressed in smart navy-blue overalls. 'Shall we start with the cellar, sir?'

'We've already made a start on clearing the underground part of the house and given some thought to defence against shock waves from the bombing,' remarked Maximillian as he led the way down the steps. 'I would prefer that we take refuge in our own house rather than use the air raid shelters.'

In the cellar they found Mitzi with a headscarf covering her hair and smothered in yellow and grey dust.

'Hello, Herr Bauer welcome to our humble cellar; my husband has told me how helpful you've been.'

'I'm very pleased to meet you, Frau Zimmermann.' They shook hands. 'We're placing a high priority on your family battery business here in Mahlow.'

'I see that you've more or less cleared out the room and it probably seems much larger than you thought it was?'

'It certainly is and I think we'll be able to have all that

we need in here if there are any more bombing raids.' There was a note of alarm in her voice.

'I think you're more apprehensive than most Berliners about our situation, Frau Zimmermann. I will try and reassure you concerning your safety.' He produced a large tape measure from a beautiful leather case and marked out two points down the centre of the rectangular cellar. 'Herr Zimmermann, will you now conduct me around the rest of the house, if you please?'

Kurt had remained remarkably silent up until that moment. 'I will show you around, sir.'

'Lead on then, young man.' Conrad Bauer had a really nice manner with children; the whole family followed the tour conducted by Kurt who led them into every room in the house. Finally the party finished up back in the underground cellar.

'I think this house is very suitable for use in time of air raids; we'll install a crossbeam down the length of the room and two supporting pillars; we've been well prepared for this eventuality and have plenty of stout wooden beams already cut.'

'When will you be able to do the work?' Maximillian asked.

Herr Bauer took his notebook out of the breast pocket of his overalls. 'I think we can do this the day after tomorrow.' He shook hands with the whole family; he and his team then left in a dark-green vehicle with 'Mahlow Rathaus' written in large white letters on each side.

The following day was November 15th and at six o'clock the Zimmermann family gathered around the radio to listen to the news. 'Last night,' the announcer's voice struck a serious note, '515 aircraft of the Luftwaffe attacked the English city of Coventry in the heart of the industrial Midlands, a region which manufactures aircraft, tanks and many other items crucial to Britain's war machine; the raid was codenamed "Operation Mondscheinsonate" or "Moonlight Sonata". It was led by a group of thirteen Heinkel 111s modified with a special "X-Gerät" navigational device which dropped marker flares. Then the bombers dropped high explosive on the water and electricity utilities, thereby hampering the fire-fighters. The raid inflicted massive damage...'

The Zimmermanns felt a curious mixture of both horror and relief.

# 19

## *Dahlem – November 1940*

Clotilde slowly opened the front door of the Schultz apartment. As she cautiously peeped around the edge of the door, Fräulein Müller – her pet cat not her former teacher – also peered at the caller and expressed her disapproval at what she saw with a plaintive 'meow'. The twelve-year-old girl's growth was accelerating and she was really quite tall for her age; this autumn Saturday morning she was wearing a thick light-blue woollen jumper, a grey woollen skirt with long navy-blue socks and black shoes.

'Good morning, how can I be of help?' The greeting was mature and polite; before the caller could reply Clotilde stooped and picked up Fräulein Müller whose arched back was an indication of hostility.

'Are you the lady of the house?' The speaker was short and stocky and wore a dark-grey suit; the badge of the Nazi Party was pinned onto the left lapel of the jacket. Clotilde recognized it immediately and loud alarm bells rang in her head as she remembered the school outing with Fräulein Müller five years previously.

Clotilde, although alarmed by the Nazi Party member, was nevertheless amused by the term 'lady of the house' and continued the formal exchange. 'May I enquire who wishes to know?'

'My name is Helmut Richter. I'm the Luftschutzwart for

this block of apartments.' He peered more closely at Clotilde. 'You're too young to be the head of the family; where is she?' The twelve-year-old noticed an unpleasant change in the tone of the caller's voice, it was more abrupt, less friendly and certainly threatening.

Clotilde unwillingly opened the front door sufficiently to allow the official's admission. He pushed past her rudely, at which point Fräulein Müller took the opportunity to jump up at him and drag the claws of her right paw across the back of his left hand. The 'air safety guard' squealed: 'Get off, you little monster!' The cat gave a triumphant loud 'meow', and scuttled away towards the kitchen.

'Clotilde, what is all this noise?' Suzanne came out of the kitchen only to see the decidedly unappealing sight of Helmut Richter dripping blood onto her beautifully polished parquet floor in the entrance hall.

'Whoever you are would you kindly stop dripping your blood on my floor; it's taken a lot of time and a lot of elbow grease to get that beautiful sheen on it.'

'If that is your cat, you ought to have it shot!' There was venom in his voice.

'It's not my cat.'

'Then your husband should have it exterminated painfully.' He wrapped his hand in a handkerchief.

'My husband has been conscripted into the military and is presently with the German Forces in France.' She looked him up and down. 'Shouldn't you be fighting for your country?'

'I'm in a reserved occupation in the Nazi Party but at night I'm designated the air safety guard for this block of apartments.' He looked and sounded pompous. 'I need to inspect your cellar to advise on structural alterations.'

'I would have to obtain the permission of the other occupants.' Suzanne was both defensive and resentful at this intrusion.

'That will not be necessary, Frau...?' His smile seemed to Suzanne to be insincere.

'Schultz.'

'I've a pass that gives me access to all parts of this building.'

'Clotilde, find your sister Margit and tell as many of our neighbours as possible to join us in the cellar.' Her younger daughter left in search of her sister.

'Lead on, Frau Schultz.' Helmut Richter left through the main door in front of a far from reassured Suzanne.

Approximately thirty people gathered in an underground room of the apartment block. They were mostly women and children since it was Sunday morning and the schools were closed. The group included Greta Lange, the widow of the pharmacist in the Hauptstrasse, who had died of cancer of the bladder nine months previously; Wanda Schäfer with her two teenage sons both wearing brown shirts with swastika armbands (her husband, as she repeatedly told her neighbours, had recently been conscripted to the Waffen SS and held a very high rank); and two unmarried sisters, Lotte and Helga Herder, in their mid-fifties, both of whom had had fiancées killed in the Great War, one at Ypres and the other at Passchendaele leaving them permanently lovelorn and unable to cope with the male of the human species. There were others there whom Suzanne did not know well but she had a feeling that she was going to get to know them better if the bombing continued.

They were crowded together in one of the numerous walled-off cellars allocated to each apartment. Helmut held up his right hand and quite inappropriately said, 'Heil Hitler! Tomorrow these little cellars will be converted into a single air raid shelter with the ceiling and apartments supported by concrete pillars and wooden beams. I instruct you to give every assistance to my team of workers.'

'Oh you instruct us, do you?' The speaker was a tall

elegant lady dressed in a smart navy-blue woollen suit and with long grey hair.

'Who are you?' Helmut Richter rudely demanded.

'I'm Trudi von Neumann.'

'Think you're too posh to obey orders, do you?' The sneer was unmistakable.

'No I don't, but I don't think your disparaging attitude is necessary either.'

Suzanne with her arms around the shoulders of both her daughters listened to this impressive woman whom she had previously only met in passing. She felt that she should say something. However, she waited a few moments for someone else to speak up; no one did.

'Herr Richter, it's my understanding that you're here to help protect the residents of this block of apartments from the expected air raid assault. Don't you think it would be appropriate to discontinue your verbal bombardment?'

The Nazi Party representative was, for the first time that day, lost for words. 'Listen to me, Frau...'

'I've already told you once, Herr Richter. It's Frau Schultz! I would be grateful if you would, in future – and unfortunately it looks like being a long future – remember to address me so.'

'Very well, *Frau Schultz*.' There was no attempt to hide the sarcasm in his voice. 'My men will start tomorrow by knocking down the walls between the individual cellars allotted to each apartment.' The petty official now became businesslike but still had the offensive sneer in his tone of voice. 'My department has studied the architectural archives in the Rathaus and this apartment block is well supported by pillars and cross beams and we know where we have to put in extra pillars to resist the bombing that may take place.' Helmut's face exhibited what he thought was a smile but in fact was a rather hideous parody made worse by some appalling dentistry. 'Any questions?'

'May we remove our possessions before the walls are demolished?' It was Wanda Schäfer who spoke up.

Given the clearly declared allegiance of the Schäfer family on the arms of the two boys, no one was surprised at Helmut's sudden change of attitude. 'Of course, my dear, and if I can be of any personal help I am at your service.' The obsequiousness was in stark contrast to his earlier remarks.

The remainder of the residents gave a collective sigh, realizing that no one else was going to be offered Helmut Richter's dubious personal assistance; they returned to their apartments as quickly as possible to collect boxes and brooms to preserve whatever might be valuable or useful in their cellars. Clotilde, Margit and their mother were as keen as the other residents in the apartment block to salvage what they could from their own individual underground storeroom and they soon returned to get to work.

'There's an awful lot of dust here, Mother.' Margit was the first with the broom and quite soon was clearing a pile of logs in one corner. 'Look, it's Clotilde's little red cardboard suitcase that she used to take on holiday to Rügen Island all those years ago.'

'It's only two or three years ago, darling! And we did go again last summer holidays, not long before your father was conscripted.'

Fräulein Müller came bounding into the room and immediately began to scratch the battered red cardboard case vigorously as if she wished to open it. 'You're very interested in that old thing, pussy. Perhaps you think there's something inside it.'

Suzanne picked it up. 'Let's see what it contains, if anything.'

Clotilde's memories suddenly came flooding back to that terrible day in Baabe. 'Mother, there *is* something in that red case.'

199

'Oh is there, my darling? I think I threw it down here in our cellar a couple of years ago when I saw it falling into pieces and collecting dust. I hope it wasn't something special.' Suzanne handed it Clotilde. 'Here you open it.'

'You may be angry, Mother.' Clotilde seemed resigned to whatever effect the contents might have when revealed. She opened the case and removed a dusty but clearly gold-embossed fine vellum parchment and handed it to her mother. 'Here you are, Mother.'

Suzanne took it and as she started to read it her eyebrows became more and more raised. Margit saw the expression on her mother's face. 'Please read it to us.'

'At the top it says this is a copy in German of the original in Swedish,' she replied. 'There's a gold embossed emblem and then it reads:

CERTIFICATE OF NOBEL PRIZE
K. KAROLINSKA
MEDIKOKIRURGISKA INSTITUTET
November 27th, 1935
ALFRED NOBEL
TO
CARL VON OSSIETZKY
FOR CONTRIBUTIONS TO PEACE STOCKHOLM
OCTOBER 25th, 1935

'Then there's a lot of signatures.'

'It looks and sounds beautiful, Mother, but what is it all about?' Clotilde was excited.

'It's a document stating that a very great prize was awarded to a very wonderful German man.' She quickly and quietly read it again. 'How did this get into your case, my darling?'

'It was at the time of the shooting in Baabe; there was so much confusion with many people coming and going

200

into the house...' she paused as if she could hardly get the words out. 'There was that white sheet over the body with all that bright-red blood seeping through.'

Suzanne encouraged her daughter. 'Take your time; there's no danger in here.'

'I saw the leather briefcase lying on the sofa with part of the document protruding from it and I thought it was something that could make trouble for you and father.' The twelve-year-old girl was apprehensive as to whether she had done anything wrong but was determined to tell the whole story. 'I took the piece of paper out; put it under my cardigan and put the leather case behind one of the cushions on the sofa, and a little later I slipped upstairs and put the document in my little red holiday case and then I forgot all about it.' Clotilde could not look her mother directly in the eyes. 'Did I do a very bad thing, Mother?'

'Of course not, my darling, and you've nothing to worry about.' Suzanne smiled. 'It does show how little housework I did on that holiday; otherwise I would have seen that leather case.'

The three of them had a family cuddle with the absence of the fourth member being felt but not mentioned, as cuddles go this was a long and heartfelt one and when they separated the mother spoke with a serious but not sad note in her voice. 'In the present Germany we must hide this document until one day; in happier times, we'll know what to do with it.'

'Mother, I know just where to hide it.' Clotilde was excited.

'Well, you put it somewhere secure, my darling, and don't tell me or Margit.'

'Yes, Mother!' She took the vellum parchment and tucked it inside her blouse.

At that moment the two boys with swastikas on their

arms sauntered arrogantly into the Schultz cellar with their hands in their pockets.

'Wasting your time chattering! You women should be getting on clearing up this mess.' It was the taller fair-haired boy who spoke and without any further comment he picked the old battered red case and threw it against the wall in the corner of the room.

'Our cellar is spotlessly clean; our mother is very well organized,' Margit protested.

In the absence of her husband, Suzanne's emotions were tighter than a violin string and the insulting language of this thug was the last straw that broke the camel's back. The normally calm, gentle, sweet and loving lady exploded and turned her wrath on the sneering youth.

'I do not know your name nor do I wish to; your offensive remarks and loutish attitude are a disgrace to the human race; leave this room immediately.' Her voice was raised more than either of her daughters had ever heard.

The boys showed no sign of moving. The smaller one put his face close to Margit's face, 'I rather like it here. I think I'm going to stay.'

Clotilde was incensed at the way these two horrible boys were treating her mother and sister. She picked up a broom and holding the brush end wielded the handle with as much force as she could muster and brought it down across the younger boy's thinly clad buttocks.

'Owweeeeee! Mummy, help!' And with that pathetic plea for his mother's assistance he fled the scene closely followed by his brother.

Mother and daughters were so relieved that they indulged in another communal huddle. 'Clotilde, you were wonderful!' Suzanne kissed her daughter on the forehead.

'Do you think they heard us talking about the Nobel Prize Certificate?' Margit was alarmed. 'They could tell the authorities; I wouldn't put it past them. What should we do?'

202

Suzanne remained silent for a full two minutes. 'I don't think we should do anything; I'm sure those two monsters have no idea about our discovery today but we should keep it that way and never discuss it again for the foreseeable future.'

'What about my hitting Rudolph on the bum with a broom handle?' Clotilde could hardly conceal her giggles.

'I don't think a proud member of the Hitler Youth would want to tell anybody that he had been hit on his bottom with a broom handle by a girl much younger than himself and run away to his mother!'

That, at least, was what Suzanne fervently hoped.

# 20

## *Paris – Late 1940*

Manfred had not been able to make many telephone calls to Berlin to speak to his beloved Suzanne and gorgeous daughters all of whom he had sorely missed since his arrival in Paris in June. His life had been made very much easier by the friendship that he had established with Maurice the Butler who supervised the pageboys at the Hôtel de Crillon; once more he enlisted the assistance of the distinguished-looking gentleman to place a call to Suzanne in Berlin.

The telephone itself was in the basement quarters and the separated couple had agreed to use a mixture of German, English and French to confuse any eavesdroppers in either Paris or Berlin; Manfred would greet his wife in English and she would reply in German and so on. They had also managed to establish codenames for themselves and many of the other people in their lives: for example Manfred was Mickey (Mouse), Suzanne was Minnie (Mouse) and Donald (Duck) was General Meyer. Snow White was Clotilde and Margit had laughingly agreed to be Olive Oil in these communications.

'Hello, my love.' Manfred at last was speaking to Suzanne.

'How are you, darling?'

'Missing you and the girls but I'm in good health, well fed; in fact because I'm part of Donald's entourage I'm embarrassingly well nourished. How is the food situation with you?'

'The pink ration cards give us just enough, as you can imagine, darling, but some of the items are not always in the shops.'

Manfred was alarmed to hear such news. 'Bugs Bunny' (the name they had agreed to use for the great leader, Adolf Hitler) 'assured us that going to war wouldn't cause shortages. I wish I were there to look after you all!'

'Well, it's not a problem at the moment. We've had a visit by an obnoxious official from the Town Hall … Let's call him Dopey! Dopey's converted our cellar into an air raid shelter and knocked down the partition walls so that the whole apartment block has one big area to use when the bombs start falling…'

'Well, I hope Dopey has put in some more supporting pillars…' Manfred was very much aware that they were using up valuable telephone time with wartime matters and not what he really wished to hear about. 'Anyway how are Olive Oil and Snow White?'

'They are well and both growing fast, they don't go hungry and, yes, we've got concrete-reinforced pillars. We may not like Dopey very much but he and his men have, in my judgement, done a pretty good job.'

'I'm very pleased to hear it!' The schoolteacher in uniform knew that he was coming to the end of his allocated telephone time. 'I think Donald's unit's about to move out of Paris, so I'll be going with him. I love you, Minnie, *au revoir*…'

'There is one more thing; we found that postcard from Baabe in Snow White's little red case. Lots of love from us all. Take care, Mickey, bye…'

The line went dead and Manfred put the receiver down and left the telephone room. The following day he received a handwritten note instructing him to attend a Staff meeting of General Meyer's group on December 30th in the General's conference room on the first floor of the Hôtel de Crillon.

Manfred thought to himself. 'Now I have two things to puzzle over...' He continued to walk towards his quarters. 'One, what is the subject of the General's Staff meeting and, two, which is much more curious, what on earth is the postcard from Baabe?'

Manfred was treated very well in the hotel over Christmas both by his German superiors and by the aging French staff but it wasn't nearly the same as being at home with his darling Suzanne and two beautiful daughters, Clotilde and Margit.

December 30th was cold in Paris but no snow had begun to fall. However, the chill had penetrated the corridors and the German military did not take off their greatcoats as they sat down in the Conference Room; no one seemed to know any details about the meeting with General Meyer, who arrived exactly on time.

'Good morning, everyone.'

There were good-natured murmurings of response from around the room.

'As you know, our work here in the field of counter-espionage in the greater Paris region has for the time being come to an end and the unit will be moving into other areas of northern France. We now have our new orders. We'll be transported to Dinard on the north-west coast and then cross by ship to Guernsey, which we've occupied together with the rest of the Channel Islands. When our business is done there we'll work our way through Brittany and Normandy before finally returning to Paris.'

And so, on the morning of January 2nd, 1941, General Kurt Meyer's party left Paris by train. Manfred, who sitting in the same carriage as the senior officers, which he presumed was due to his linguistic expertise. He listened to the conversation with interest but didn't utter a word.

'I'm sorry to be leaving the Hôtel de Crillon, sir.' The speaker was Oberst, or Colonel, Engelbert König, Meyer's aide-de-camp.

The General smiled. 'We're all sorry to be leaving, Colonel.' His facial expression saddened. 'I don't think we'll have such luxurious accommodation and food until after this war is well over.'

They travelled on in silence, both deep in thought; eventually the General broke the silence. 'Does this locomotive take us all the way to Dinard, Colonel König?'

'Yes, sir, we've two short stops – at Le Mans and Rennes.'

'Aha, Le Mans ... the twenty-four hour motor car race!' General Meyer became more animated. 'I was a spectator at the 1932 event when the wonderful red Alfa Romeo of Sommer and Chinetti swept past the pits with Bertelli and Driscoll's green Aston Martin still being attended by the mechanics!' Nostalgia was a powerful emotion in the high-ranking Panzer Corps officer. 'It was an amazing sight.'

'Did you follow motor racing closely, General?'

'My passion has been for the motorcycle. I was delighted when I received the command of the Leibstandarte SS Adolf Hitler Motorcycle division for the invasion of France.' The General had a broad smile on his face. 'It was a nice change from the static anti-tank command that I had in Poland in 1939.'

After approximately two and a half hours of travelling through the French countryside – during which time the schoolmaster and reluctant soldier saw some villages and farms virtually undamaged but others quite clearly devastated by war – the locomotive started to slow.

'We're approaching Le Mans, sir,' Colonel König announced.

'Excellent, have you arranged for lunch to be brought onto the train, Engelbert?'

'Yes, it will be here shortly after we arrive.' The other members of the party looked enquiringly at the Colonel; apart from Manfred there were Lieutenants Eloise Weber and Millicent Schmitt, who were very efficient secretaries-

207

come-typists in SS uniforms, together with Captain Conrad Lehman and Major Johann Jung, who were lawyers in SS uniforms.

König acknowledged their quizzical looks. 'Don't worry! There's enough for all of us, including our interpreter.'

That last-mentioned person quietly remarked to himself: 'There are a few compensations.'

The train drew to a halt at Le Mans railway station. 'There hasn't been a twenty-four-hour race here for eighteen months,' the General said to no one in particular.

'For a motor-cycle enthusiast you've a remarkable knowledge of this event, sir.' Major Jung's tone was full of admiration.

'I've been following the race for years.' Meyer was flattered by the lawyer's observation; 'the 1939 meeting was the last one.' He shrugged his shoulders. 'Goodness knows when the next one will take place.'

'Do you know who won that last race, sir?' This was the voice of Lieutenant Millicent Schmitt.

Manfred could not help but detect the note of sycophancy in his colleagues' remarks; Meyer, in short, was being buttered up.

'I do indeed!' The smile was broad showing well-cared-for teeth. 'It was Jean-Pierre Wimilie and Pierre Veyron driving their supercharged Bugatti – they covered 248 laps which was thirteen more than the runners-up...'

There was a faint rattling of plates cutlery and glasses coming from the corridor outside the General's compartment which gradually grew louder. '*S'il vous plaît, s'il vous plaît!*'; An employee of the French railways system dressed in a white shirt and black bow tie with a white apron tied around his waist pushed his trolley into the compartment.

'*Bonjour, mesdames et messieurs – sept Steaks Diane.*'

He then laid white linen tablecloths on the fixed small

tables in the well-appointed train compartment and served the delicious-smelling meal.

'Bon appetit!'

And with that he wheeled out his trolley. A few minutes later, with a whistle and a noisy puff of black smoke, the locomotive started to draw out of Le Mans and the French waiter could be seen standing on the platform by his trolley smiling and waving cheerfully; Manfred returned his wave but no one else followed his gesture, although they were clearly enjoying his meal.

'I congratulate you, Colonel König; you've arranged an excellent lunch.' Meyer smiled all round the compartment and received dutiful smiles in return. 'How long is it before we arrive in Rennes?'

'It's about one hundred and fifty kilometres. After we stop there the train will branch north to Dinard.' The Colonel was clearly pleased with himself. 'From there a minesweeper will take us to Guernsey.'

Manfred saw that his own countrymen displayed their usual efficiency in France.

'I shall want you to stay in Dinard, Colonel, to save us trouble when we return from Guernsey.'

'Yes, Herr General.'

When the train stopped at Rennes, Manfred for the first time dared to voice an opinion. 'There seems to have been a massive amount of bomb damage here.'

Colonel Engelbert König, of course, was the soldier with the knowledge. 'There was an extraordinary event last June: three bombers hit a French ammunition train in a siding and beside it there was a stationary troop train; over one thousand people were killed and many buildings were demolished.'

There was neither triumphalism nor sympathy in his voice. This was the schoolteacher's first sight of the devastation of war.

Eventually, an otherwise unremarkable journey brought the train and General Kurt Meyer's party to the docks at the port of Dinard on the north Brittany coast. Night had fallen when they left the carriage and boarded light motor vehicles that took them to the gangway leading onto the three-year-old minesweeper KMS, or Kriegsmarine Schiff, *Königstein*. The captain, an Oberleutnant, or Full Lieutenant, Hans Köhler, saluted the party. 'Good evening, General Meyer; we won't be doing any minesweeping on our way to Guernsey, so therefore we're not a full crew, which has made space for you and your party.'

Manfred could only see the silhouette of the ship as he followed the others on board; it was quite small lying low in the water with a single funnel next to a small superstructure; there were two masts and the remainder was open deck and it reminded Manfred of trawlers he had seen on the Baltic Sea when on holiday at Rügen Island, which now seemed to have disappeared into the dim and distant past. He was ushered into a tiny cabin with two sets of bunks. The upper ones were occupied by the two lawyers leaving him no option but to lie on one of the lower ones and he could feel the throb of the idling ship's engine.

There were some shouted orders on deck. Manfred could not hear the actual words but the engine vibrations increased dramatically together with the sound of turning screws that seemed to be immediately beneath him; with a slight jolt the small ship moved out to sea.

'We seem to be moving,' said Major Johann Jung. 'I hope that we have a calm crossing.'

'I doubt it, Major,' Captain Conrad Lehman sounded gloomy. 'It's the beginning of January and I don't think this part of the English Channel is particularly famous for mild weather in the middle of winter.'

'I expect you're right; we had better brace ourselves for a rough crossing.' The senior lawyer did not sound enthusiastic. 'I could never understand why the French allowed this piece of water so far south to be called the English Channel by the British.'

'A sign of a degenerate character, Major?'

'Exactly, Captain!' There were guffaws of laughter.

Manfred had to stop himself giving a sigh of despair as he turned over in his bunk to try and get some sleep. He had so frequently taught his boys of the language differences for this stretch of water; the French *La Manche* and the German *Armel Kanal*.

At that moment the ship gave a huge lurch and a massive wave of nausea swept over him. He tried to combat it with some deep breaths and after a few moments the feeling passed. Soon, however, he became aware of a swell that seemed to be taking the ship in an up-and-down movement; this time he vomited onto the cabin floor.

While he was retching with his head held in his hands between his knees the cabin door opened, a head looked in and withdrew, and a few moments later General Meyer entered carrying a bowl with a jug of water and a glass in it. He set it down in front of Manfred. The senior soldier, who was twelve years younger than the schoolteacher, laid a gentle hand on his shoulder.

'I know the feeling, linguist; it affected me in the same way when I first bumped up and down in tanks.'

'Thank you, sir.'

'Don't mention it!' With that he left.

The officers on the upper bunks had remained silent throughout these events. After the door had closed, the Major swung his legs over the side of his bunk. 'Well, Private, you've certainly made an impression there.' He grimaced at his fellow officer. 'We shall have to be careful what we say to each other.'

In between retches Manfred managed to mumble. 'I don't pass on other people's conversations.'

211

The two officers looked down at him with expressions of contempt. 'In the SS we specialize in listening and reporting other people's conversations.' Captain Lehman smiled.

Mercifully Manfred's nausea abated and he was able to keep down the water that the General had kindly brought to him. Eventually he lay down and drifted into a restless sleep.

Although the sea was far from calm, the minesweeper made good progress and slipped into the picturesque harbour of Saint Peter Port at dawn; the vessel was moored with only a few passers-by to witness the party of four men and two women disembark and be driven away in a waiting military vehicle to the Duke of Normandy Hotel.

The early morning of the January 3rd, 1941, was chilly and misty and there was some fine rain in the air; in these conditions it wasn't surprising that the weary party didn't much appreciate the beautiful and varied waterfront buildings of the little capital of Guernsey. When they arrived at the Hotel their leader addressed them.

'Refresh yourselves in your rooms and we'll meet again for breakfast; we've a busy day ahead.'

They all, with the exception of Manfred, gave the Nazi salute, in unison answered 'Yes, sir', and departed; as they were leaving the General put a hand on the interpreter's shoulder and stopped him.

'Private Interpreter, a word in your ear,' Manfred turned and looked the Senior Officer straight in the eyes; 'I had sympathy for you on the ship but don't misinterpret that event.'

'I'm afraid I don't understand what you mean, sir.' Manfred was genuinely puzzled.

'You will see and hear things today that you will neither like nor approve of but Germany is at war and this is an occupied country.' This wasn't the same man who had behaved in such a kindly fashion on the sea crossing.

212

'Yes, sir.' The unwilling soldier turned and walked up the stairs to his first-floor room where he was able to take a very welcome hot shower and shortly afterwards joined the two officer lawyers at one of the breakfast tables. Five minutes later the two SS secretaries joined them. They all helped themselves to delicious bacon and eggs from a hotplate on the sideboard.

'This is a lovely little island,' remarked Lieutenant Millicent Schmitt. 'It was a little bit misty but I could see quite a lot from my bedroom window, although I can't see why the Führer would want to occupy it.'

Major Johann Jung looked up from his plate and laid his knife and fork down. 'I understand that the decision was taken as a precaution against the enemy using it as a base in an attempt to take France back from the Third Reich.'

Millicent smiled. 'I see, Major.'

The party finished their breakfast and no one commented on the fact that the General had not joined them. After a brief visit to their rooms to collect various items, they gathered together at the main entrance and a few minutes later the military transport arrived to take them to the Royal Court House. The small courtroom had dark oak panelling and furnishings, and there was a single court usher in civilian clothes; the two rows of seats at the back of the court for the press and public were empty.

The usher started to speak the curious dialect of French known as Dgèrnésiais, which Manfred quickly penetrated and translated.

'Please be standing for the judge!'

General Kurt Panzer Meyer was in his familiar military uniform, but now wore over the top a bright-red judicial gown with the insignia of the Nazi Party embroidered in gold thread on the right breast.

'Sit down.' The command was businesslike.

'Private Schultz, who is this man?'

'The court usher, sir.'

'Call me Judge!' The face and the voice were stern. 'Ask him why there are fewer people to be seen on the island than German soldiers.'

There was an exchange with the usher. 'He tells me that there are a number of reasons. Many young men with families fled to England before the German occupation: there's also the curfew and fear keeps people in their houses.'

'I see. Bring in the first accused.'

Manfred passed the instruction onto the court official, a door opened at the side of the courtroom and two Wehrmacht Privates escorted a middle-aged woman wearing a navy-blue woollen dress to a chair facing Meyer; she wasn't asked to sit down and her face was noticeably bruised.

Major Johann Jung rose to his feet. 'May it please the court, this woman is Lisette de Lalujé and it was from her house that a prison worker from the defence construction was seen running away.'

The woman was visibly shaking and tears were streaming down both cheeks.

'Does she have anything to say before I pass the mandatory death sentence by firing squad for harbouring an escaped foreign labourer.' The judge's tone of voice was not merciful.

Manfred was horrified by what he heard, 'Lisette, please tell the court what happened at your house before the military arrested you?'

He purposefully didn't mention the threat of the death penalty; he looked into her eyes and saw nothing but goodness.

The Guernsey woman wiped her tears away with the hem of her dress. 'He wasn't even a man; he was a French boy not more than fifteen years of age dressed in old cement bags; he was freezing cold and desperate for some food.' She bit her trembling lower lip. 'I could not send him away!' Manfred emphasized the pitiful aspect of the story while translating to an impatient and unsympathetic court.

'Major, I presume the penalty for this offence has been circulated among the population of Guernsey?' Meyer was conceding a little ground to the interpreter's implied plea for clemency but this wasn't going to be enough to save her life.

'Yes, Judge.'

'Lisette de Lalujé, I find you guilty of aiding the escape of a prison worker; you will be taken outside and shot.' He didn't make eye contact with Manfred, who trembling began to translate the dreadful words; she was led from the room by the two soldiers.

'Bring in the next prisoner.'

An anguished Manfred said to himself, 'I didn't do enough ... not nearly enough.' His thoughts were brought to an abrupt end by a volley of shots from somewhere outside the courthouse.

The following accused was a bent grey-haired man in his sixties. He wore dark-blue woollen trousers, a white shirt and a grey tweed jacket; he stood in front of the judge behind the same chair that had been in front of Lisette a few minutes earlier.

Captain Conrad Lehman addressed the judge. 'The accused is Marcel Mazarin; he is suspected of producing an underground newspaper based on news from the BBC.'

Meyer appeared irritated by the Captain's presentation. 'Is there any evidence, Lehman?'

The lawyer produced a circular Bakelite box about ten centimetres in diameter with an irregular silvery crystal mounted on the top at one side and a whisker-like structure mounted opposite; a pair of wires emerged from the side of the base leading to a pair of earphones. The lawyer flourished the 'crystal set' in the air and there was a note of triumphalism when he said: 'This piece of incriminating evidence was found underneath the bed of the accused.' He turned to the man standing in front of the judge. 'Does this piece of technological equipment belong to you Herr Mazarin?'

Manfred mistranslated his convoluted answer. 'Yes I bought it for my grandson a year ago but we could never get it to work and when he left the island it was stored under my bed.' The accused man ventured a suggestion of a smile at the judge but it faded as soon as he saw the expression on the General's face.

'Captain Lehman, is this the sole evidence against Herr Mazarin?' His complexion darkened. 'Where are the illegal printing presses? Where are the contraband stocks of printing paper?' The judge gave the strong impression that he thought the whole case was a complete waste of time.

'The military are still carrying out house-to-house searches, sir, I mean General...' He visibly shrank into his greatcoat. 'My apologies to the court, Judge.'

'Case dismissed!' Meyer stormed out of the door behind him.

Manfred explained the situation to the usher. Marcel was released from his handcuffs and ushered out of the court. There was no joy or relief on his face, only resignation.

The interpreter addressed the court usher. 'Would you like me to ask the judge when he will be ready to recommence proceedings?'

He received the curious reply, 'Le good idea, isn't it?' but the meaning was clear.

Manfred found General Meyer in a small adjoining room set aside for his use. The only furniture was a small flat-topped desk and two wooden armchairs with red leather upholstery.

General Meyer was sitting behind the desk his chin resting in his left hand. 'What is it, Private?'

'Excuse me for disturbing you, sir, but when will the General be ready to continue?'

'Private Schultz, if the decision were mine to make I would not even be here; I'm a soldier not an avenger for the Third Reich.'

'Yes, sir.' Manfred was at a loss what to say to a man who had, an hour earlier, condemned a woman to be shot for the crime of showing compassion to a fellow human being.

'We never had this conversation, schoolteacher.' There was a note of respect in the voice.

'No sir.'

'I will return to the court in ten minutes.'

'Yes, sir.' Manfred returned to the courtroom and was soon after followed by the General, once again stern and impassive.

There followed a series of what Manfred regarded as trivial cases. One man had driven a van on the left side of the road when Germans had changed the legal side to the Continental right. Other offences that came to court that day included breaking the curfew by five minutes, not changing clocks to Central European Time, and not converting to Reichsmarks in a shop; all the accused had been brought to the attention of the law by anonymous accusers, probably as the result of a long-held grudge. The accused were all found guilty and sentenced to varying periods of hard labour on the construction of the new defences.

However, the final accused to be brought before the court that day was very different indeed. François Zidane was an eighty-two-year-old white-haired retired schoolteacher of history and respected expert on the island's past.

Johann Jung rose to his feet and pointed at the old

historian. 'This person, Judge, was seen painting a Churchillian "V" sign on a poster of the Führer.'

Manfred translated the charge to the elderly but clearly proud former teacher and the accused replied in a firm clear tone: 'The Nazi menace will reap a whirlwind of destruction such has never been seen in the history of this planet.'

'Private Interpreter, I want a word-for-word translation of that statement.'

The judge didn't leave Manfred any room for manoeuvre; he sentenced the accused to life in prison with hard labour.

François Zidane smiled broadly, clasped his chest and fell to the floor clearly very dead.

# 21

## Hitler Youth

One evening late in 1941 the family Zimmermann took shelter in the cellar of their house in the south-eastern suburb of Mahlow, a few kilometres from Berlin's Tempelhof Airport. The bombing raids on the city had not been particularly frequent but that evening the air raid warning sirens had gone off just as the family were about to sit down to dinner.

Kurt was the first one to get his torch and open the newly reinforced door at the top of the cellar steps. Maximillian had had the door covered with a steel plate, sealed around its edges with a rubber rim shortly after Conrad Bauer had made the underground cellar what he called 'bombproof'; he was halfway down the steps when he stopped and turned around. 'Mother, Marlena, Father, hurry the planes will be here soon!' He was nearing his fourteenth birthday and his voice was becoming a little crackly; he was filling out from the slim young boy he used to be.

'We're here, we're here!' Marlena came bounding after him; she too had matured and was now a lovely sixteen-year-old girl. 'Mother and Father are right behind me.'

Kurt could hear his father closing the heavy door which creaked on its hinges; Mitzi's daughter turned her torch back on the upper stairs. 'Can you see your way all right, Mother?'

'Yes thank you, my dear.' Mitzi carried on down into the basement room. 'It's cold and damp down here, Maximillian, can you light the paraffin heater?' Meanwhile she started to unfold some blankets that had been stacked on a shelf.

Marlena, was still wearing her Bund Deutscher Mädel uniform of a black skirt, white winter long-sleeved blouse and a loosely tied black neck tie. 'Can I help you, Mother?'

'Thank you, Marlena... How was the BDM this afternoon?'

'You know how stupid I think it is, Mother; singing all those daft songs; swinging huge hoops around our heads and now it's become frankly embarrassing.' There was an expression of distaste on her face.

At that moment the whole family could hear the drone of aircraft overhead.

'Do you think it's a big raid, Father?' Marlena looked at her father anxiously.

Maximillian listened intently. 'I think there's a lot of planes but they seem to be spread out...'

There was a sound of a far-off explosion, then another and another. 'I think it's a heavy raid but the aircraft are not in close formation and the bombs seem to be widely distributed.'

The family sat close together with blankets over their laps as the noise of the planes gradually faded and the explosions of the bombs gradually came to an end. During this time the yak-yak of the Berlin anti-aircraft guns carried on at a furious pace throughout the attack. When the whole thing seemed to be over Mitzi took hold of Marlena's hand and led her over to the far corner of the room.

'My darling, you were going to say something to me at the beginning of the raid.'

'Well, Mother.' Marlena was blushing profusely, which even showed up in the artificial light of the air raid shelter. 'You remember telling me about nature's clock in ladies?'

'Of course I do, my darling, but that was about a year ago.' Mitzi put an arm around her daughter's shoulders. 'Has this monthly timepiece started to tick?'

'No, Mother, but some of the girls are talking about it.'

'At the League of German Girls!' Mitzi sounded amazed. 'I thought you did exercises in unison and sang patriotic songs, discussing menstruation doesn't seem to fit in with that very well.'

'We had a lecture from Fräulein Jutta Rüdinger today. She is the Reichsreferentin, or leader, of the BDM; there were thousands of girls there today from many of the groups in eastern Berlin and its suburbs.'

'What did she have to say?'

'She spoke into a microphone in a very loud high-pitched voice; she said how proud she was of us girls and that she was sure that we would all make wonderful mothers for the next generation of a pure Aryan race.' Marlena's face betrayed the horror with which she regarded the statement that she was to be used as a bio-political instrument. 'After it was over we broke up into our home groups and that was when some of the other girls started talking about their body clock.'

'I really don't think what is happening to your body is anyone else's business,' Mitzi smiled at her daughter. 'You, my darling daughter, have read more about diabetes than the average doctor and what you've not read Dr Greenbaum told you all those years ago when he first made the diagnosis and saved your life.'

Marlena brightened considerably as she followed the rest of the family back up the stairs when the 'all-clear' sounded after the raid. She had remembered dear old Dr Greenbaum telling her: 'My dear, the diabetes may cause some things to happen a little late.' And now she knew what he had meant.

There were very few further air raids on Berlin that year

but the radio did tell them of intensive bombing of the U-boat ports of Saint-Nazaire and Lorient on the Atlantic coast of Brittany.

'I suppose that was one of the reasons for the invasion of France.' Maximillian observed after listening to the six o'clock news at the beginning of January 1942.

'Why should it make a difference, Father?' Kurt was following events closely and discussed them with his school friends, all of whom were in no doubt that right was on the side of Germany and its Führer.

'It gives them easy access to the Atlantic, whereas previously the U-boats had to leave Germany via Bremerhaven into the North Sea, passing the long way round via Scotland. Still, it's all very sad.'

'What's sad, Father?'

'I have to answer you, my son, in a way that is strictly between ourselves.' Maximillian saw his son listening intently and nodding his agreement. 'You know that I don't share other Germans' enthusiasm for this war and there's something very tragic about U-boats sinking Britain's merchant ships with the loss of their crews.'

Kurt was clearly moved by his father's words. 'Of course you've met a lot of the English when setting up the factory at Slough.' The young man could visualize the seamen thrashing around in the freezing Atlantic and eventually sinking without trace.

'Exactly, my son!' Maximilian searched for the right words. 'Not everything is as black or white as we're told by Dr Goebbels.'

'I understand, Father, but I think things will be more difficult soon.'

'You mean the bombing?'

'No, Father ... I mean for me! It's my fourteenth birthday.'

'I understand you completely, Kurt. You will hear things; be told other so-called truths and in particular be in the company of other fourteen-year-old boys who will be fiercely in favour of the Reich, the Nazi Party and Adolf Hitler.'

'Yes, Father. I will try hard to remain independent, but it will be so hard when everyone and everything around you is saying something different.'

Maximillian was impressed at the maturity of his own son's vision.

Sure enough on the morning of February 9th, 1942, a letter arrived for Kurt in the post instructing him to attend his first Hitler-Jugend, or H-J, meeting that same afternoon; it gave him the address and told him not to be late.

At school that morning he was apprehensive about what was going to happen in the afternoon. After eating the packed lunch of a liver sausage sandwich washed down with a small bottle of fizzy lemonade, he set off for the meeting place in Weisestrasse; there could be no mistaking the venue since there was a large poster on the wooden door depicting a huge portrait of the Führer in the background and a smaller superimposed picture of a blond youth with a cheerful expression and wearing a brown shirt. The poster read: 'Jugend dient dem Führer' – Youth serves the Leader.

Kurt pushed on the door and it opened easily. He went in and was greeted by a rather fat man in a brown shirt, black shorts and a dark blue-and-white scarf held loosely around his neck by a leather ring: 'Kurt Zimmermann, I presume?' The similarly dressed boys behind him sniggered.

'Yes, that is my name, sir.' Kurt was uneasy from the moment he had entered that room. 'I received this letter this morning.' He handed it to the man whom he guessed to be about fifty years of age. As he looked down he saw that he was wearing long black socks and black lace-up shoes. The portly but not unfriendly man took the letter and read it.

'Zimmermann,' he said, looking up, 'welcome to the weekly meeting of the Mahlow cell of the Hitler Youth.'

The surrounding boys all gave the Nazi salute followed by a 'Heil Hitler'.

'My name is Herr Weber and I'm your leader; come with me and we'll soon find you a uniform and then you will feel more comfortable among your colleagues.' He led the way over to a door at the far end of the room. 'Try on a few shirts and shorts; I'm sure you will find something that will fit you.'

Kurt went into the end room and found piles of shirts and shorts. It didn't take him long to find a uniform that fitted him together with some long black socks; he neatly folded his clothes and placed them in his satchel with his school books. He finally placed his satchel with those of other boys near the entrance. This he managed to do swiftly and when he returned to join the other boys, he was greeted by a further round of 'Heil Hitlers'.

Herr Weber produced a blue-and-white square cotton scarf, folded it obliquely, and placed it around Kurt's neck; he slipped the two remaining corners through the leather ring and pulled it loosely upwards.

'Congratulations, Zimmermann, you're now part of our country at war.' The other boys shook hands with the new member of the Hitler Youth; two of them who were much taller than the others and nearing eighteen years of age gripped Kurt's right hand painfully hard. The new member didn't make a sound.

There were about forty boys in the small hall and Kurt knew that there were many other similar meetings taking place in Berlin and throughout Germany involving hundreds of thousands of boys like him and the others in that room.

'Hitler Youth of Mahlow Group Ten!' The group leader was addressing them and before he had finished they started to rapidly assemble into three rows.

'Well done, we'll now recite our motto.'

The boys competed with one another in the energy of

their rendition: 'Live faithfully, fight bravely and die laughing.' This didn't appeal to Kurt at all; still less the constant enthusiastic talk of Aryan superiority and virulent anti-Semitism being enthusiastically expressed. When the meeting finally broke up, one of the older boys came to Kurt and put an arm around his shoulder.

'The motto I prefer is "Blut und Ehre" – Blood and Honour. See you next week, Comrade Zimmermann...' he paused. 'It will be really good; we'll be doing field exercises.'

Kurt was puzzled. 'I don't know what those are.'

'Practising to be soldiers like the Waffen SS.'

'Is that what you want to be?'

The older boy didn't hesitate in his answer. 'Oh yes! I admire them so much – nothing stands in their way.'

Kurt wasn't attracted by such a prospect, but like any boy was curious about soldiering and weaponry. He picked up his satchel with his clothes and school books in it and hurried after his new-found friend.

'What's your name?'

'It's Hermann Jung and I'll be sixteen years old in fourteen weeks, then I can be selected for war duties such as the fire brigade, anti-aircraft defence and recovery work after bombing raids.' There was great enthusiasm in the young man's voice. 'If I do well I hope to join the 12th SS-Panzer-Division Hitlerjugend. Then I will be an elite Nazi soldier in a black uniform with the silver sigrunes on the lapels of my collar.'

'What do those lightning bolts mean?'

'They are the insignia of the Goddess of Victory.' Hermann turned to Kurt. 'I will see you next week, Zimmermann.'

The new but unhappy member of the Hitler Youth hurried off in the opposite direction towards his home and family; he found Mitzi in the sitting room darning a hole in the heel of one of Maximillian's grey woollen socks.

Since yarn was no longer on sale in the shops without using up valuable ration coupons, she had obtained the wool by unravelling one of Kurt's old pullovers, now much too small for him.

'Hello, my love.' Mitzi smiled at her son and took in his Hitler Youth uniform. 'You do look smart!' She was relieved to see that Kurt had chosen a shirt and shorts that were a little bit on the large side and would probably not require her sewing skills for a while.

'Mother, I'm very pleased that these afternoons in uniform are only once each week. I really don't like being in the Hitler Youth.' Kurt had a miserable look on his face.

'You've only been to one meeting.' Mitzi stood up, put down her needlework and kissed her son on his right cheek.

'What is it you found so upsetting?'

'Most of the boys there hate the Jews and can't wait to be soldiers. Liking guns and military exercises and stuff like that is fine as a hobby, but they take it very seriously. They like ... violence. That's what I hate.' Kurt sounded very unhappy.

'You'll get used to it with time, Kurt, and it's just once a week. Try to grit your teeth!'

The fourteen-year-old boy persevered with the weekly meetings but became increasingly despondent.

Then one day Mitzi said to him as he left for school. 'Don't go to the meeting today.'

'Mother, they will come looking for me.'

'I will deal with them.' Mitzi sounded as though she really meant it.

Kurt did exactly as his mother had instructed and that afternoon he was to be found digging furrows in the back garden in readiness for planting potatoes before the winter freeze set in.

While he was doing this useful work there was a furious

knocking at the front door, which even Kurt could hear in the garden. True to her word his mother answered the door to be confronted by two middle-aged men: one portly and wearing an expensive-looking black leather coat; the other slim and bespectacled.

The portly one spoke: 'Kurt wasn't at his Hitler Youth meeting this afternoon.' They didn't introduce themselves nor did they show any courtesy to Frau Zimmerman.

'I'm afraid, gentlemen, Kurt has to work in the garden this week. I'm sure he'll go back soon.'

With that remark she closed the front door.

Kurt now stood behind her.

'I'm afraid, darling, you'll have to go back next week. I don't think I can use that excuse every time and those men looked like they meant business. I'm so sorry.'

The young man had the courage to return to the meeting the following week. At the beginning of 1943 the bombing of Berlin dramatically increased; Kurt was needed by his fellow countrymen and he responded to that need by manning the anti-aircraft guns.

# 22

## *Breslau – November 1943*

During 1943 the aircraft of Germany's enemies became so great in both numbers and quality that massive night-time bombing of Berlin and other major cities now became possible. However, this didn't affect one particular city, Breslau, in the south-east of Germany, close to the Polish border, which was still well beyond the range of the British bombers. Adolf Hitler called it his 'Breslau Fortress'.

It was here that Clotilde's maternal grandparents had their home in an apartment block and where Suzanne had taken her two daughters in 1941 after a telephone conversation with Manfred when she told him of the first air raids on Berlin.

'What do you think I should do, my love?'

'I shall be relieved to know that you and the girls are out of the range of the bombers. It will be one less thing to worry about.'

'All right then, we'll take the train to Breslau tomorrow.'

'It will be a huge load off my mind ... I love you, darling.' The telephone line went dead.

The following day Suzanne, Clotilde, then aged fifteen years, and Margit, aged eighteen, made the train journey from Berlin to Breslau.

'Mother, why are we going to stay with Opa and Oma? I don't want to go! I don't want to see them!' The older daughter was resentful at being suddenly transferred away from her friends and familiar surroundings.

'Margit, that didn't sound very nice.'

'No, Mother, I don't *feel* nice. I'm sorry all the same.'

The two tired unhappy girls with one tired and worried mother eventually arrived in the ancient city of Breslau. None of them were in the mood to appreciate the Lower Silesian town, with its warm climate and famous twin-spired cathedral. The girls were greeted and embraced by their grandma.

'Oma, it's lovely to see you.' Margit did her best to give her grandmother a warm greeting; her grey-haired grandfather remained seated and merely nodded at the presence of his granddaughters.

'Hello, Opa.' Clotilde's cheerful voice would have brought a response from most people but this old man merely grunted; even Suzanne giving her father a hug did nothing to improve matters.

'I've arranged for the Girls' High School to take your daughters, Suzanne; it has a very high reputation with an excellent record for getting students into Breslau University.'

'That is lovely of you, Oma.'

The elderly lady smiled at her daughter and was clearly very happy to have her child and grandchildren so close to her.

However, as it turned out, Clotilde hated her new school. One day in early 1943, she came home with tears rolling down her cheeks. 'Mother, I hate school here; the other girls know so much more than me and I miss my school in Dahlem. Apart from Margit, you're my only friend.'

Suzanne cuddled her younger daughter. 'I'm so sorry, my darling. Oma did her best but there was only a vacancy for you in the older class.' She patted Clotilde's shoulders. 'Of course I realize you were already in a class of girls one year ahead of you but Oma didn't know that in effect it would mean here you would be two years behind your colleagues.'

229

'I'm silly and ungrateful, Mother. I know we're here for our own safety; I will try and make the best of things.' she kissed her mother on her left cheek.

'You won't have to, my love.'

'Why, Mother?'

'I managed to talk to your father yesterday. There has been much less bombing on Berlin; he thinks it would be safe for us to return for the time being.'

Clotilde was thrilled. 'Oh how wonderful! Does Margit know?'

'She's packing her case, we catch the two o'clock train tomorrow afternoon.' Clotilde flung her arms around her mother and ran out of the room; and so mother and daughters returned to their apartment in Dahlem with the two girls rejoining their school friends.

The remainder of that part of the year seemed much happier to Clotilde and Margit, although they were very much aware that their mother desperately missed the presence and support of their father. All three of them were always excited when the telephone rang every few weeks and it was him; whoever picked up the receiver would shout to the others: 'It's Father, it's Father'; each of the girls spoke with him for a few precious moments and then Suzanne took over.

'How are you, my love?' she said as usual on one such occasion.

'I'm all right but I wish that I could come home to you and the girls. The journey back from Guernsey wasn't so rough, no seasickness; Donald left us at Dinard and has returned to military activities in Normandy.'

'Is that good?'

'Unfortunately no, Grumpy has taken over in the Resistance courts and he is a total disaster for everyone.' Grumpy was their codename for the Colonel.

'I hope he can't hear you.'

230

'Oh no he has taken a great liking to French wines, especially champagne. He's indulging himself now and is well gone.' Manfred knew that time was short. 'How are you managing for food and heating, darling?'

'We're fine. Don't worry. We still get coal, though some people are using the furniture of the bombed-out buildings for firewood. It's the food situation that worries me; there's less and less food on the shelves. We've not been able to get fresh butter for the past two months! They tell us it's needed for our brave soldiers in the east.' Suzanne tried hard to laugh it off, but Manfred's anxiety for his family was palpable even from the other end of the telephone. He was silent for a while.

'Can you hear me, my darling? Please don't worry about us!'

'I will do what I can ... I must go now ... I love you all.'

Suzanne spoke into the telephone. 'Go safely, my love!' but there was no longer anyone at the other end of the telephone to hear her.

Suzanne joined Clotilde and Margit in the sitting room. The radio had just been turned on and after a few moments warming up. 'This is the six o'clock news on July 12th, 1943. There was a light air raid over Berlin last night. A few bombs were dropped but our state-of-the-art anti-aircraft guns mounted on the flak towers of the city's defences drove the attackers away and Berlin remains safe.' There was pause in the broadcast. 'A speech to the British Empire follows given by that good friend of the Third Reich and man of vision, Mr William Joyce...'

Once more the family Schultz heard William Joyce's strange Anglo-Irish accent with its nasal twang speak out of the radio. 'This is Jairmany calling. The forces loyal to the Führer Adolf Hitler are in command from the Atlantic coast in the west, to our brave soldiers holding Stalingrad in the east; in due course we will invade England ... Our triumph is inevitable! ... We have developed flying bombs that will soon land on London in their thousands.' His voice rose dramatically. 'I call on the people of the Great British Empire to surrender and join their natural allies the German Empire led by our Führer, Adolf Hitler.'

'I don't believe a word he says!' Suzanne cried. 'And his English is so weird – I can barely understand what he says.'

Clotilde grimaced. 'He sounds as though someone has pushed two carrots up his nose. No wonder he is called Lord Haw-Haw.'

That radio broadcast gave Berliners a false sense of security for on the night of November 23rd a massive raid took place, causing extensive damage in the residential areas west of the centre, including Tiergarten, Charlottenberg, Schönberg and Spandau, which were not so very far from Dahlem. During this heavy raid Suzanne and her daughters sat holding each other and trembling with each explosion. The fifteen-year-old Clotilde had tears running down her face.

'I don't want to die, Mother.'

The following day school was cancelled and the news spread that the raid had caused several firestorms due to dry weather conditions. The Kaiser Wilhelm Memorial Church had been largely destroyed, although its steeple was, amazingly, still standing.

Manfred, who was in Brittany, had heard the news on the radio and was able to telephone his wife after repeated attempts; the conversation was short but they decided on a return to Breslau – the Russian bombers were still far away.

'What did Father have to say?' Margit could not hide her anxiety.

'He thinks we should go back to Breslau for safety.' There was sadness in Suzanne's voice and full of anguish.

'Your father thinks the only thing that will stop the bombing of Berlin will be the approaching Russians.'

Margit had tears pouring down her face. 'Mother, I hate it in Breslau; I hope so very much that we can come back home soon.'

'I promise that we'll come back as soon as your Father tells us it's safe.'

'Thank you, Mother.'

Therefore on November 25th the three Shultzes made the return railway journey to Breslau. On the way out of Berlin they were all horrified to see the vast amount of bomb damage to apartment blocks and public buildings; there was a sea of broken glass in all the open spaces.

From the moment of their arrival they felt hostility from their grandpa and no one called him Opa. He didn't get up from his chair when they arrived but Oma embraced them all and took them into the kitchen.

'Please forgive your father, Suzanne; he is a very proud man. He suffered terribly in the trenches in 1918, then there was no work after the war until Hitler came to power in 1933.'

No one found this easy to accept but Suzanne said, 'It must be very difficult for you, Mother.'

'I manage!' There was hurt in her voice. 'Let's have a cup of coffee and a game of rummy.'

'Oh yes!' Clotilde was really pleased to hear the suggestion. 'Are you going to cheat, Oma?

'Would I do a thing like that?'

Suzanne smiled as she lit the gas for the kettle and reached up for the brown packet with light blue dots on it labelled 'Linde's Kaffee-Ersatz', which was a coffee-like drink that was made from the roasted roots of the chicory plant; at the same time she took down a packet of powdered milk.

They played rummy and as usual they turned a blind eye to Oma bending the rules a little.

'I win!' she cried after a hand was played.

'Well done, Oma!' the children cried and Suzanne poured out the coffee. 'Well, girls, there are a few more days of school before Christmas I'm sure you will both sleep well after ten hands of rummy.'

As the game progressed their eyelids drooped and the two girls didn't take much persuading to go to bed. Children are resilient and the next day they cheerfully set off for school, which had been forewarned by their grandmother.

Margit's school friends greeted her enthusiastically. 'How is beautiful, exciting Berlin?' Ulrike Hofman was a tall handsome young woman of seventeen and the daughter of a German general living on a luxurious estate two kilometres outside Breslau.

'It's had a lot of bombs dropped on it in the last few weeks.' Margit told her what they had seen from the train as she, her sister and mother had left the city.

'I'm not surprised. My father and his colleagues think Germany is going to lose the war and that Adolf Hitler is a madman; some of them feel he should be removed.'

Margit was shocked; she had reluctantly attended the League of German Girls for nearly four years and had not heard anyone express anything like the sentiment she had just heard.

'Gosh!' was all she could manage.

'It's true; ever since the German Sixth Army was destroyed last February and the Russians broke out of Stalingrad, my father and his colleagues have thought the situation was hopeless.' She shrugged her shoulders. 'I'm sure we'll be heading west soon.'

At the end of the schoolday Margit met Clotilde outside the gates and told her what she had heard. 'Don't you think that's amazing?'

Clotilde was thoughtful and looked up at her older sister. 'We have to be careful, Margit; Oma told us both that grandfather is a Nazi, although she is afraid to tell Mother.' They returned to their grandparents' apartment without discussing the matter any further.

They were greeted by Suzanne. 'You look very serious, girls; what has happened?'

Clotilde looked at her mother. 'Is Opa here?'

'Yes, why?'

'Margit wants to tell you what she heard at school, but we know Opa is a Nazi.'

Suzanne was shocked. 'I'm sure you must be mistaken, my darling.'

'No, Mother, it's true. Oma told us but she said she was ashamed to tell you because of Father having to serve in the army even though he is much older than most soldiers.'

There were tears pouring down both of Suzanne's cheeks; the huge strain of looking after her two daughters; worrying herself sick about the welfare of her husband in wartime France, and now learning that her father supported the regime which she abhorred, was just overwhelming. Her two girls put their arms around her.

'I can't believe it.'

'The Military are convinced the war is unwinnable,' Margit said excitedly. 'They say that Hitler directing the German armed forces is an obscene joke.'

The door leading from the sitting room to the dining room suddenly burst open and the imposing figure of Suzanne's father stood there. 'What's all this disturbance about?'

'Father, how could you? How could you when you know what I'm going through. You're ... you're a rotten, vicious, self-centred Nazi!'

The man's face turned puce and the veins stood out in his neck. 'And you and your husband are traitors to the Reich. Get out of my house! Pack your cases and leave.'

'Gladly! You should be ashamed of yourself; come, girls, pack your cases.'

Within five minutes the three ladies of the family Schultz walked out of the front door of the Breslau apartment.

Suzanne knew it was a mistake; her mother had always cautioned her against decisions made in haste; she pulled her coat collar up as the late November wind blew down from the Arctic and set off with a heavy heart towards the town centre where they sought shelter in a coffee house. It was then that reality hit Suzanne as she opened her purse and to her horror found just twenty-five Reichsmarks and forty-three pfennigs; she had left all her cash under her pillow in the bedroom she shared with her mother. Once again uncontrollable tears rolled down her distraught face, she felt as if the whole weight of the world was on her shoulders and she could not support it for much longer.

'We've just about enough for three soups! What do you think, girls?'

All of them dreaded a return to the Breslau apartment. 'Let's have the soup – with full stomachs our brains will work better.' Margit was amazingly cheerful and encouraging. 'Clotilde, you stay with Mother and I'll bring the soup.' Suzanne handed her some money and her daughter disappeared into the crowd.

Mother and daughter snuggled up close together and watched people scurrying about. There was a sense of urgency in the air and occasionally the word 'Russians' could be heard. They were tucking into the steaming hot bowls of delicious soup when a grey-haired elderly lady wearing a maroon felt hat and waving a folded green umbrella came hurrying towards them.

'Mother, it's Oma!' Clotilde waved and shouted. 'Oma, over here.' Suzanne had never been so pleased to see her mother.

Oma was relieved to have found them. 'After I had been

to the United Dairies because I had heard they had some fresh milk I went home and Opa was by himself and would not tell me where you had all gone.'

While Oma regained her breath Suzanne told her the whole sorry story. 'Oh my poor darlings. Give me half an hour alone with him and I promise you he will never be any more trouble.'

They returned to Suzanne's parents' apartment with considerable trepidation but Oma was as good as her word – her Nazi husband didn't trouble them again; he was seen but not heard.

At the beginning of March 1944 Suzanne finally received a telephone call from Manfred, who was now in Normandy. 'I think you can return to Berlin; there has been terrible bomb damage and loss of life but you will be better off there than in Breslau. The Russians are advancing fast and Breslau will fall.'

Oma accompanied the family to the train station. She was in tears.

'I don't know when we shall meet again but you will all be in my thoughts.'

She embraced her daughter and granddaughters and they climbed onto the train that would take them home.

# 23

## *25 Kilos of Butter*

The group of lawyers, secretaries, interpreter and judge prosecutor working on behalf of the German army of occupation in France were now seconded to the Upper Normandy city of Rouen. This fine old city stood on the River Seine as it wound its way from Paris to the port of Le Havre and the English Channel. These small military tribunals were scattered throughout the north-west of the country and were used against the increasing Resistance movement among the French. However, the initial zeal with which the quasi-legal group operated had long since waned. Manfred's deliberate misinterpretations, which had by now kept many French men and women from slavery; imprisonment and death, were allowed to pass without comment. The same didn't apply to other judicial groups which were far more aggressive and ruthless. It continued to be difficult for Manfred to make a telephone call to Berlin, but he was amazed that the engineers had managed to keep these communications open at all.

'Suzanne, is that you?'

'Yes, my darling Manfred; it's so good to hear your voice.'

'How is Berlin?'

'There's bomb damage everywhere. Some buildings are completely destroyed, others partly damaged, but our apartment is relatively good with only a few broken windows.' He could hear her sigh. 'The buildings are not the only problem here in Berlin; there are bodies: dead bodies not yet buried.'

'Have the girls seen them?'

'Yes, they know what they are...' He heard his wife take a deep breath in. 'But your daughters are growing up very fast. There are other things that are worrying everyone in Berlin.'

'What are those?'

'Food and drink! They are becoming scarce...' There was a pause. 'We won't have enough coal or wood to keep us warm for another winter here.' There were other worries too, but she did not mention them. The two 'Rs'– the Russians and rape were the unspoken menace hanging over the populace in what was increasingly a city of women and children. As a mother of two rapidly maturing daughters Suzanne was desperately worried.

'The bottles arrived all right?' Manfred had always sent gifts that he had received from the grateful French, mostly liqueurs, wines and brandies.

'Oh yes, my love, and they are safely stowed away in our apartment.' A note of desperation entered her voice. 'What I'm really worried about is clean water for drinking and washing.'

'I can't do anything about the water until I come home but I can try and help with the food.' For a very brief moment Suzanne's heart missed a beat and she was in much happier days awaiting her husband's return home from school; she came back down to earth with a bump. 'I so want to see you, Manfred.'

'All this nightmare will come to an end and we'll be back together again. Home leave has been refused once more. They say I'm too valuable. I have to go to work now. I love you.'

The telephone line went dead and there was so much more that Suzanne wished to say her husband.

Manfred walked down the rue Jeanne d'Arc from his lodgings towards the Palais de Justice. He could see the damaged Notre Dame Cathedral in the distance beyond the River Seine. His group had taken over one of the courtrooms there but he knew that their hearts were no longer in it; they were preoccupied with the imminent invasion by the massed forces that were now aligned against Germany on the other side of the English Channel.

The translator entered the court and sat down beside Captain Conrad Lehman, one of the two prosecution lawyers; there was no sign of Major Johann Jung, the senior prosecuting officer, but the two tired-looking secretaries, Lieutenants Eloise Weber and Millicent Schmidt, were sitting at a table at right angles to the lawyer's bench. Shortly afterwards the judge, Colonel Engelbert König, entered through a small door behind the high-backed chair on the dais; he had long since discarded the bright-red gown with the gold Nazi symbol; at least two of his colleagues had been assassinated. He simply wore his SS military uniform.

'Bring in the prisoner.' There was no enthusiasm in his tone of voice and above him an electric light hung precariously from a bomb damaged ceiling.

An elderly slim man wearing blue dungarees was brought into the court in handcuffs, escorted by a single German soldier.

'What is your name?' Manfred sensed that the Colonel didn't wish to spend much time here and was thinking of travelling to Paris as soon as possible and from there taking a train to Berlin.

'Claude Girard, Monsieur.' König didn't correct the accused man's form of address.

'Captain Lehman, what are the charges against this man?'

'He is a farmer from the Pavilly region just north of here. Two days ago he was stopped by a patrol while he was driving his donkey and cart; it was carrying twelve

240

aluminium milk churns in two tiers and the soldiers' suspicions were raised by the slow pace of the vehicle, the almost flat tyres and a difference in the noise that the empty churns made.'

Manfred translated for the Frenchman and then told him that the court would hear from one of the members of the patrol. 'He will say that two of the milk churns were welded together and that standing inside was a British pilot who had baled out of his Spitfire fighter that had been shot down two days ago.'

'*Non!*'

'What does he say no to?' The military judge showed signs of irritation; an explosion could be heard outside and nobody seemed to know who or what had caused it. The light above the judge's head flashed off and then back on again.

Manfred spoke to the farmer in French. 'I don't understand your answer.'

'There was no pilot in the milk churns.' This explanation was given to the lawyer and the judge who were both clearly exasperated by the truculent Frenchman.

Captain Lehman beckoned over Lieutenant Eloise. 'I think we should finish this by calling the witness who was a member of the patrol; will you fetch him, please?'

'Yes, sir.' She left the room and returned a few moments later with a distraught look on her face.

'He has gone, sir.'

König rasped, 'Who has gone?'

'The witness from the patrol, sir.'

'Where is he?'

'He said he had to go and search for the escaped pilot.'

'Captain Lehman, will you please make some enquiries as to what exactly has happened to this enemy fighter pilot and his guards; we'll reconvene in fifteen minutes.' Colonel König left the dilapidated courtroom.

241

'Yes, sir.' The Captain Lawyer picked up the telephone and wished that he was in another place.

Precisely a quarter of an hour later Judge Colonel Engelbert König returned to the court. 'Just what has been going on, Lehman?'

'We've a great shortage of military personnel here in Rouen. There's concern about an invasion from across the English Channel and there are extensive troop movements up towards the Pas-de-Calais; our manpower was halved last night and the pilot escaped in the confusion.'

'Things are starting to go very badly for us, Captain. We'll have to release Claude Girard; we don't want to make ourselves even more hated than we are already.'

'Yes, sir.' The lawyer turned to Manfred. 'Tell him, Private.'

Manfred explained the situation to the incredulous Claude who, up until that moment; didn't think he would see another sunrise and a broad grin spread across his face. 'You're free to leave, Monsieur.'

The man in blue dungarees walked out of the court a free man. There was no relative there to greet him; no one in his family had been informed of his indictment.

'Oh by the way, Private, Major Johann Jung is returning to Paris and then on to Berlin tomorrow; the Colonel is closing down our operation and he would like you to accompany Major Jung to Paris and then rejoin your unit.'

Manfred walked back to his lodgings with Suzanne, Margit and Clotilde very much on his mind; he packed his few possessions and crossed the street to the café for a sandwich and coffee. He sat at a small round marble-topped table and asked the waiter for half a baguette, butter and a cup of coffee with milk; he was well known here and appreciated for his knowledge of the French language and culture. He was also grateful that here he was able to drink real coffee and he imagined the difficulties his family was having getting food and drink in the increasingly besieged Berlin. He felt guilty.

As his thoughts swirled around in his mind he felt a light tapping on his left shoulder; he looked up and saw Claude Girard smiling down at him.

'Bonsoir, Monsieur.'

'Bonsoir, Monsieur Girard.'

'I think you're going to Paris tomorrow, Monsieur.'

The coffee and baguette arrived. 'Please sit down, Monsieur Girard.'

'Thank you, Monsieur.'

'How did you know I was going to Paris tomorrow morning?'

'These things get around, Monsieur.' Claude was still in the same blue dungarees and the black stubble on his chin was more dense than earlier in the day. 'I thought that I was going to be put in front of a firing squad today, Monsieur.' The Frenchman gently took hold of Manfred's right hand with his own, 'I can't fully repay you for telling me I was free to leave when I thought I was going to die, but I will bring a wooden box to the station and perhaps you can send it to Berlin to help your family.'

'That's very kind of you, Claude.'

At nine o'clock the following morning Manfred arrived at the main railway station of Rouen. Claude was standing beside a substantial wooden box with rope handles at the barrier of platform nine.

'Take one end, Monsieur, and we'll put it in the luggage van.' It was labelled 'Manfred Schultz'.

Manfred did as he was asked. 'It's heavy; what's in it?'

'Twenty-five kilograms of butter and...' At that moment Major Johann Jung could be seen striding towards the platform. '...Half a pig!' whispered Claude giving Manfred a theatrical wink and walking away with a spring in his step.

The Major handed Manfred his ticket. 'Nothing changes,' Manfred murmured; he was going to travel third class on a wooden bench in a carriage right next to the goods van while the Major hurried off to the first-class carriage at the front of the train next to the locomotive. How things had changed since the General had departed. He climbed into the sparsely furnished carriage and found a compartment occupied by four or five glum-faced Privates, all sitting more or less motionless, with tired eyes staring straight in front of them. One of them had a face that seemed familiar but he could not be certain.

His dilemma was solved by the fair-haired man sitting opposite him.

'You're Herr Schultz, I believe?'

Manfred was pleasantly surprised to be addressed as 'Herr'. 'You're quite correct, young man but I have to apologize for not remembering *your* name.' He stood up to shake his former pupil's right hand and was horrified to see an empty sleeve and gratefully took the proffered left hand.

'I didn't distinguish myself at school, sir. My name is Heinrich Schäfer.' The young man smiled. 'I remember you very well as a greatly respected teacher, Herr Schultz.'

'I do remember you, Heinrich; you were always quoting Goethe to me.'

' "A noble person attracts noble people and knows how to hold onto them." ' He paused a moment, '... Sir.' For the first time in ages Manfred shared in spontaneous laughter.

Heinrich then answered the unasked question. 'I lost my arm five weeks ago while disarming a landmine placed under a railway line by the Resistance; I'm on my way back to Berlin.'

Once more Manfred was witnessing the senseless violence inflicted by war. 'I'm so sorry, Heinrich; with your physical loss it must seem insensitive of me if I ask you a favour?'

'No, sir, ask away.'

He told him about the wooden box, its contents and his family in Berlin. 'I will telephone when you've left Paris and my two daughters, Clotilde and Margit, will meet you at the Anhalter Bahnhof.'

'Sir, it will be my privilege to help. You can trust me to take care of things; I will see that it gets to its destination safely.' Heinrich Schäfer's voice had changed; it was full of a sense of purpose and he was smiling broadly at Manfred.

With the willing and energetic support of Heinrich the large wooden crate was transferred from the Rouen goods carriage to the D- or through train to Berlin. Manfred thanked him and then used a public telephone to speak to Suzanne in Berlin; he was amazed that he was able to get through quickly.

'Hello, my love; a troop steam train has just left Paris with a large wooden box in the goods van for you; it's being looked after by one of the boys that I used to teach.'

'How exciting! When will it arrive?'

'It will take eighteen hours to reach Anhalter Bahnhof. There are two scheduled stops but I think they will be short in case they are spotted by dive bombers. Can Margit and Clotilde be there to collect it?'

'Oh yes, what is the name of your former pupil?' Suzanne was trying to gain as much information as time allowed on the call from her dear husband; she loved the sound of his voice.

'Heinrich Schäfer...' the ex-schoolteacher hesitated for a moment. 'I will tell you something about him and leave it to you to decide if you pass it on to the girls.'

'What is it?' Suzanne was alarmed.

'Heinrich lost an arm in a mine explosion five weeks ago.'

'Oh how sad! I will tell them; they have grown up very

quickly in this war...' It was now her turn to hesitate. 'Both emotionally and physically.'

'I'm pleased about that.' He glanced at his watch. 'I have to rejoin my regiment. Love you all.'

'Manfred, Manfred!' Suzanne wanted to know more; it sounded as though his interpretation work had come to an end and that would mean back to military service and danger, but the phone was dead. She looked at her watch and went to find her daughters.

At six o'clock on the evening of March 28th, 1944 the D-train from Paris drew to a halt at the Anhalter Bahnhof in Berlin. What once had been the most elegant railway station in Europe was now a shadow of its former self. Much of the glass in the roof was broken, and the great steel girders of the main arch looked like a battered skeleton resting on shrapnel and bullet pock marked walls; it was amazing that it still functioned at all.

In this intimidating wreckage Clotilde and Margit walked confidently along the platform beside the newly arrived train until they reached the luggage van at the rear. Its sliding door was open and a private soldier stood beside a wooden crate approximately one metre in length with water dripping through the lower horizontal slats; the right sleeve of the soldier's jacket contained no arm.

Clotilde pointed to him. 'Look, Margit, I think that must be Heinrich!' They both hurried over to him while soldiers started to pour out of the carriages behind them; many were wounded.

'Hello!' The young one-armed soldier jumped down on to the platform and dragged the box by one of its rope handles to the edge of the goods van. 'You two lovely ladies must be Margit and Clotilde.' He pulled the crate so that part of it was over the edge. 'Can you hold this handle?'

The sisters took hold of it and Heinrich reached in to take the other rope handle.

Together the three of them carried the load towards the station entrance. 'How did you feel about my father teaching you at school, Heinrich?'

'He always tried to believe in me, even if I disappointed him over and over. He did succeed in giving me my love of Goethe.'

He led the way to the still-functioning 'Stadt-Bahn', or town train. 'You will find it easier to take it in turns to hold the other rope handle.'

'But you've only got one...' Margit stopped herself just in time from drawing attention to Heinrich's missing limb.

'Don't be embarrassed! There are millions much worse off than me lying in Russia, France and the bottom of the Atlantic.' They entered the town train station.

'Here we are; I can travel free because of my arm.' A train arrived after a short wait of about twenty minutes. Heinrich felt he was useful again; 'I will help you all the way home.'

'That is very kind of you, Herr Schäfer.' Clotilde was genuinely grateful since she was beginning to worry about the walk home from the station.

Heinrich was delighted to be given back his civilian title.

'What will you do afterwards?' Margit asked.

'I've been promised training as a searchlight operator, I report to my new unit tomorrow; I'm really pleased to be back here defending Berlin.'

Clotilde, now nearly sixteen years old. thought this was a really significant statement.

'Do you think we're losing the war, Heinrich?'

'I can't say exactly, Clotilde, but things are not going well for Germany.'

The remainder of the journey was made in silence apart from the occasional 'Oh my God' from one or other of the party as they passed badly bomb-damaged buildings. Eventually the train stopped at Dahlem station in south-west Berlin. The three young people carried the box to the Schultz apartment and Suzanne opened the front door to greet them. The box was awkward to handle. It was dripping water and there were salt-like stains on the lower planks.

'You must be, Heinrich. Please come in. Perhaps you can remove the wooden top for us?' She suddenly remembered the amputated arm. 'Oh I'm so sorry; we'll all help.'

After a few minutes with a screwdriver the top of the crate was removed revealing a vertical division into two compartments: one containing butter surrounded by ice and the other containing half a pig packed in salt.

# 24

## *Kurt's Air Defences*

Since January 1943 Kurt's Hitler Youth activities were changed and at the age of fifteen years he became part of the Luftwaffe as an anti-aircraft helper. After the devastating bombing of London, Coventry and other cities in England and with the failure of a follow-up invasion; it was clear to the German High Command that cities in Germany would be similarly attacked and in order to defend Berlin three massive *Flaktürmer*, flak towers, were constructed in the centre of the city.

These Flak towers were massive reinforced concrete structures, over forty metres high; taking only six months to build and serving many purposes; there were anti-aircraft guns mounted on platforms at each corner, a radar tower which gave a five to ten-minute warning of an air raid, an observation post, a hospital, an air raid shelter, a communications centre and a storage area for all the great works of art and valuables from Berlin's museums. Once completed, they were staffed by one hundred members of the Hitler Youth commanded by Luftwaffe officers in addition to the military staff who manned the radar and the medical staff in the hospital.

Kurt was allocated to Flakturm Number Two in the Friedrichshain Park. Throughout 1943 there were increasing air attacks on Berlin made worse by the United States of America bringing their massive bombers into the war. On the night of November 22nd, Kurt and his school friend, Fritz Keller, also aged fifteen, were passing shells to the gunner of a ground mounted anti-aircraft gun. School had been cancelled that afternoon, and the two boys had reached their assigned gun just after dusk; they were both wearing heavy blue woollen jumpers and scarves and long black trousers.

Kurt shivered in the cold. 'Here, Fritz, have some of this.' Kurt produced a Thermos flask with some hot pea soup in it.

'Thanks, Kurt; your mother is an absolute star.' He poured himself a cupful of the steaming liquid. 'I think these raids will get less after Christmas.'

'What makes you think that, Fritz?'

'Peenemünde.'

'Do you mean on Usedom Island?'

'Yes, Germany is building a fantastic rocket there which will stop England and America attacking us while we send the Russians back where they came from.' Fritz sounded pleased with the information he was able to give his friend.

'I used to go for my summer holidays on Usedom Island; it was lovely.' For a moment he was back there and thought he could hear the sand singing. The sound of the air raid warning siren brought him swiftly back to the present.

'Here take this.' Fritz handed an artillery shell to Kurt. 'My brother told me about the rockets.' He turned and walked the twenty metres to collect the next one for his friend to hand on to the gunner...'

Suddenly Kurt could no longer hear what his friend was saying.

'It's that singing sand again!' Kurt could not believe his ears. 'Fri...'

But there was nothing, no pain, no sound, no light. He coughed; earth and a few blades of grass came out of his mouth. Slowly the pain made itself more and more insistent in his right ear; nature forced him to take a deep breath and he became aware of movement in the distance as he rolled over onto his hands and knees.

Gradually he heard people's voices but they were far away.

Unsteadily and unaided he stood up and looked around him. The anti-aircraft gun to his right was lying on its side; the gunner lay crushed underneath it with his legs protruding at a weird angle. Kurt recoiled from the gruesome sight; instinct drew him towards his school friend.

'Fritz ... Fritz Schäfer, where are you? Can you hear me?' There was no reply and then Kurt stumbled over something soft just as a shell exploded high above him. He looked down at an arm, just an arm; bloody but unmistakable in its navy-blue woollen sleeve. 'Oh...' He vomited the pea soup and staggered towards the unlit road to Mahlow.

Without any idea how, he found his way home and slumped against the front door. Mitzi was just emerging from the cellar after hearing the siren sound the 'all clear'. She heard the thump that her son's body had made; she walked briskly to the front door. On opening it the unconscious Kurt fell onto her feet.

'Maximillian! Marlena, Mother! Come here quickly.'

Together they carried him into the sitting room; Romhilde was the first to speak.

'Fetch some strong scissors, Marlena, and then a warm blanket from the cupboard; Mitzi, be a darling and boil some water.'

While his grandmother was cutting off his shirt and jumper Kurt regained consciousness. 'Grandmamma, what has happened? How did I get home?'

'I don't know, Kurt, but you were clearly wounded during the air raid.'

Marlena came and wrapped the blanket around her

brother's shoulders; the front door could be heard being closed.

'Maximillian has gone to see what happened at your gun emplacement, Kurt.'

'I can't remember anything about it...'

Romhilde was gently cleaning the outside of his bleeding right ear. 'Ouch! It hurts, Grandmamma, especially if you move my ear.'

Romhilde stood behind the wounded young man and gently placed two fingers of her left hand over her grandson's left ear. 'Does it hurt on this side?' There was no reply, she took her hand away. 'Kurt, I think there may be an internal injury to your right ear.'

'If that is the only damage, it's truly amazing.'

Maximillian had quietly entered the room. 'Everyone at the flak tower thought that Kurt had been blown to pieces by the bomb; his friend and the anti-aircraft gunner are both dead.'

Mitzi put her arms around her son, as Marlena placed a tray of warm borscht in front of him and he gratefully started to eat.

Romhilde put a hand on Mitzi's left forearm. 'I will take Kurt to a doctor tomorrow; I think he will need an aspirin to help get him off to sleep for the rest of the night. Maximillian, do you think that the raid is over for tonight?

'Yes I do. The most amazing thing is that I think Kurt made his way home during some of the heaviest bombing we've had so far.' He paused a little then grimaced. 'There are still those posters on walls in the streets with a picture of Adolf inscribed "For all this we thank the Führer". I think it's taking on a new meaning.'

Marlena and Mitzi helped the exhausted and still confused young man up to his bedroom.

'I really can't remember what happened this evening.'

Kurt looked up at his mother and she was ready with the reassurance that he so urgently required.

'Kurt, my darling.' She leaned down and kissed him on the forehead. 'Bit by bit you will remember what has happened; we're so very grateful that you've survived this terrible night.'

The following morning, refreshed by a warm bath and clean winter clothes, he came down to the dining room. 'You look so much better today. Here are two boiled eggs with toast and honey.'

Marlena placed more than his ration in front of Kurt.

Romhilde appeared resplendent in her thick black wool winter coat with a brown fur collar together with her olive-green felt hat.

'Right, young man, when you've finished your breakfast please put on your coat and we'll go and see the doctor about that ear. Has there been any more bleeding during what remained of the night?'

'There was a little blood on my pillow.'

'I'm sure we're right to visit the doctor even though the medical services are tremendously busy with all the other casualties due to the bombing. We're going to see my old doctor, Jürgen Schmidt.'

Romhilde led the way through the front door into the street where women young and old, together with old men, were clearing up the scattered broken glass, masonry and shrapnel from exploded bombs and anti-aircraft shells. As they walked along the road they saw that a few of the buildings had taken direct hits and were largely destroyed but most of the damage was due to the bomb blasts causing broken windows, tiles lifted off the roofs and a few shattered doors.

'How old is Dr Schmidt, Grandmamma?' Kurt was curious.

'I think he must be seventy-four; he always had a very good reputation and I liked him because he was always kind and polite.' Romhilde felt that she had reassured her grandson but she did wonder how all these elderly people were managing as doctors, builders, plumbers and electricians again when they should have been in peaceful retirement.

Grandmother and grandson arrived at the consulting room door; it was open and they walked in to find some women, children and one elderly man who was coughing into a blood-stained handkerchief; they sat down to wait.

'Good morning, everybody.' Dr Jürgen Schmidt walked over to the man. 'I will see these good people, Herr Braun, and then I will take you to the hospital in my car.'

'Thank you, Doctor; you're very kind.' Wolfgang Braun again had need of his handkerchief.

The doctor worked quickly and efficiently, despite the fact that Kurt heard him tell one lady that his receptionist had been injured in the raid.

Kurt and Romhilde went into Dr Jürgen's consulting room, sat down and Kurt told his story, which was necessarily short because of his partial memory loss, but he did complain of continued right ear pain and bleeding.

'Kurt, young man.' The voice was gentle and kindly. 'Am I correct in thinking you can hear normally on the left side? ... Good, I'm not going to do anything at all on that side.' He turned Kurt around on a swivel stool and looked at the right side, noting the congealed blood on the outside of his ear. 'I am not going to hurt you.' He gently lifted the dried blood off the skin of his outer ear with fine stainless-steel forceps; it was clear from Kurt's face that this didn't cause any pain.

Dr Jürgen leaned back in his chair and Romhilde was pleased to see the relieved expression on her grandson's face.

'I'm not going to do anything more, Kurt; neither should anyone else; no cotton wool buds and no internal examination with an auroscope.'

'Will it recover on its own, Doctor Schmidt?' Romhilde asked.

'Yes, my dear, we're seeing many of these perforated eardrums at present which are blast injuries from the exploding bombs, you've already given your grandson the appropriate treatment with a mild painkiller.'

'Oh, that is very good news, Doctor.'

'Kurt, this is definitely a time when nature does know best and she should be allowed to heal you, which she will do given time.' Dr Jürgen smiled and patted Kurt's knee.

The consultation was over; the patient and his grand-mother stood up. 'Thank you very much,' they said in unison and smiled at each other before leaving with a spring in their steps.

When they arrived home, Maximillian opened the door for them. 'Father, didn't you go to the factory today?' Kurt was surprised to see his father, whom he always admired for keeping to his work schedule whatever the circumstances.

'I've been to see the Flakturm Two Commander and he was very relieved to hear that you arrived home safely,' He followed Kurt into the sitting room and found the rest of the family and Romhilde told them the good news about Kurt.

Kurt's memory for that terrible night gradually returned, although he never recalled the bomb actually exploding. 'But,' as he explained to Marlena a week later, 'I can remember thinking I was on holiday on Usedom Island and I could hear that singing sand that Grandmamma was so fond of recalling.'

'What can you remember after that? I saw the damaged anti-aircraft guns when I went to collect my insulin from the hospital in Flakturm Two this morning.'

'I remember bits of my walking home and then seeing you all.'

'I think nature is protecting you from remembering

terrible sights; the officer commanding the gun emplacements told me how your friend had been found.'

On the morning of February 1st, Maximillian came home from the factory early.

'Ah, Kurt, I hoped that I might find you here. Come into my study.'

The young man followed his father into the room that usually no one else entered: the roll-top desk was open and on display was a mahogany box approximately twenty centimetres in length and half as much in depth and width.

'Have a look in there, young man.' Maximillian lifted the lid and his son peered inside.

'Wow, wowee, that is amazing! I can't believe my eyes,' Inside the box he saw numerous gold coins of varying sizes. 'These are fantastic, Father, here is a German Wilhelm the First 1872 twenty-marks coin and one of Wilhelm the Second dated 1913.'

Maximillian found Kurt's enthusiasm infectious. 'Here look at this: a Belgium Leopold the Second 1877 twenty-franc piece; a British sovereign of 1890 and a French rooster twenty-franc dated 1874.'

'They must be worth a lot of money, Father.'

'They certainly are! We must put these coins somewhere the Russians won't find them.'

'Do you think the Russians will reach Berlin, Father?'

'I'm sure of it! From what I here on the radio, especially the BBC, we're losing this wretched war, Kurt.' He closed the lid. 'It's better we do this before your mother and Marlena return from their shopping.' He picked up the box, led the way into the garden and headed towards a small rhododendron bush, with a spade and a garden fork already lying beside it.

It didn't take long for the father and his son to dig a substantial hole in the garden and then bury the box containing the valuable items.

'I think we must both bear in mind exactly where we've buried the gold.' Maximillian sighed. 'We don't know what this garden will look like after the coming year has passed.'

'I will do my best to remember, Father...' He paused for a moment. 'When do you think I should return to Flakturm Two?'

'What did Dr Jürgen say about that?'

'He said that my perforated ear drum would heal and that I should just let nature take its course, but he didn't say how long nature would take.' There was a broad grin on the young man's face.

'Well, Kurt, I think you should wait until next week. It was a big explosion.' Maximillian led the way back into the house where they found Mitzi and Marlena had just arrived home.

One week later Kurt returned to Flak Tower Two and went to see the commander of his unit, Oberleutnant Wolfgang Wagner.

'Hello, Kurt, I was very relieved to hear that you had survived that terrible air raid.' He looked up at the sky. 'We thought we had lost you.'

'I was very sad about Fritz and the anti-aircraft gunner.' They had stopped beside a new gun that had already replaced the one destroyed on the night of their particular disaster and Kurt noticed red staining of the ground close by.

'It was all very distressing...' The lieutenant stopped in mid-sentence. 'We've had another piece of good news as well as your survival.' He smiled reassuringly.

'Does it concern anyone that I know?' Kurt's spirits rose.

'I don't think so ... Ah here he comes.' A young man in his early twenties was approaching in a dusty blue uniform. He was moving slowly and only helped by a similarly dressed colleague lightly holding his left upper arm. 'Let me introduce our walking miracle, Hans Weiss.'

The young man with the unsteady gait shook hands with Kurt.

'Nice to meet you. I was told that you were lost and now you're found.' he joined in Kurt's laughter and there was a clear bond between the two young men. 'A bomb blast threw me up in the air and I landed with my left thigh across a metal fence surrounding a pile of shells and I can still remember hearing my thighbone breaking with a loud crack; it wasn't until I tried to move it that I felt any pain.' He smiled. 'I will be back on duty tonight.'

'He was taken to the Flak Tower's own hospital and seen by our orthopaedic surgeon on duty who had recently been trained by Dr Gerhard Kuntschner. I think you should tell Kurt what happened next. Hans.'

'I was taken on a stretcher to the casualty centre in the hospital which was very busy with many other injuries from that heavy air raid but I didn't have to wait long after I had been given a painkiller and my left thigh was put in splints. An X-ray was taken, a Dr Neumann came to speak to me and said that either I could have my leg immobilized in traction, which would mean being in bed for three months, or I could have a new operation that had only recently been invented and I would be walking in two days; I was told there were risks as it was such a new procedure but here I'm up and walking.'

'That's amazing!' Kurt could not believe that Hans was walking on a broken leg. 'It's magic.'

'No, it's not; it's a long stainless-steel nail passing right down the middle of my left thighbone.'

'Congratulations, Hans, I think you're fantastic.'

'With a fantastic Kuntschner nail.' The two young men embraced each other.

There were continued heavy bombing raids for the remainder of the year and during that time Kurt returned to his duties at Flak Tower Two. Then, soon after his sixteenth birthday, Kurt received his orders to report for army training.

'Where do you have to go?' Marlena asked the question on behalf of the whole family.

'Schleswig-Holstein. There's a railway pass here with the papers.' The sixteen-year-old young man sounded apprehensive. 'It's dated for tomorrow.'

Mitzi put an arm around her son's shoulder and hugged him firmly but Maximillian had words of encouragement. 'You will only be about two hundred and fifty kilometres away.'

That evening Kurt's mother cooked a wonderful-smelling bratwurst from a small piece of pork she had obtained using the rest of the month's ration allocated to the family.

The following day Kurt set off from Mahlow grateful for his jumper that Marlena had given him for his birthday and boarded the train for Schleswig; he had preferred to say his goodbyes in the privacy of his own home where a few tears had been shed; when he arrived at the assembly point he was amazed to see so many old men and other boys who had been conscripted to take part in Hitler's final throw of the dice: 'There must be thousands,' he whispered to himself. Two men climbed up onto a platform, one dressed in a raincoat, the second one was in an officer's uniform. As the officer held up his hand silence descended on the obedient throng.

'I'm Lieutenant Schwarz one of your group leaders and this is Gauleiter Krause who is the political leader of the Volkssturm of which each of you are a Volkssturmmann.'

'You're all here for the training of your minds and bodies; your generation will save Germany!' Krause didn't seem to appreciate that he was addressing two widely separated generations. 'You will think like the English Admiral Nelson at Trafalgar when he told his men "England expects that every man will do his duty." ' He was appealing to fanaticism.

'My fellow officers and I will instruct you in the use of the Karabiner ninety-eight K rifle and the Panzerfaust anti-tank weapon.' Lieutenant Schwarz tried to sound enthusiastic and Kurt wondered where all this would lead.

But the young man's thoughts were far away from anti-tank weapons and wondering what had become of his beloved Grandmamma, Romhilde, who had mysteriously disappeared two days previously.

# 25

## *Northern France – August 1944*

Manfred saw his box start its journey to Berlin and having telephoned Suzanne he slowly made his way to the address he had been given to rejoin the military. He found the building behind the Gare St-Lazare but apart from two sentries either side of the entrance it looked and sounded empty; he presented his papers to the more friendly-looking of the pair. 'I'm reporting back to my unit after a period of secondment.'

'They have all left for the day.'

'May I ask where they have gone?'

The sentry wasn't accustomed to such politeness. 'Are you trying to be funny, matey?'

'No, I'm just trying to rejoin my unit. I've just returned from my attachment to General Kurt Meyer as his chief tribunal interpreter.' The sentry saw a man who looked and sounded as though he was who he said he was and his attitude changed immediately.

'Your colleagues are on manoeuvres in or around the Pas-de-Calais region. They go for two or three days, come back, and after a day off they go again to somewhere different but in the same region: it seems our masters know that there's going to be an invasion from across the English Channel but they don't know where.'

'When do you expect them to return?'

'We expect them back tomorrow afternoon. Meanwhile

you can go and find a bed and a locker; we're short of men due to air raid injuries and so you will easily find a vacant place. There's no food served while the unit's away; we go to the small café fifty metres down that road. The food is cheap and they do a good omelette; eggs are difficult to get in Germany these days.' The sentry gave a hesitant smile.

'Thank you very much.' Manfred made a mental note as he entered the building to find a different café whatever the distance; he didn't have any difficulty in finding his accommodation and deposited his few belongings and left the building.

'We go off duty at six o'clock and are not relieved for the night but you can get through this door which is not locked.' The sentry clearly thought an explanation was in order. 'We've lost so many men recently that it's even affecting sentry duty.'

'Thank you.' Manfred pulled up his coat collar and went on his way in the opposite direction from the café frequented by the sentries. 'Ah this will do nicely,' he said to no one in particular when he saw a café with pavement chairs and tables halfway along the rue de Lisbonne. He enjoyed both his freedom from the soul-destroying work of the mobile tribunal and the fresh bread, cheese and steaming-hot coffee. He slept well that night knowing he had done his best for Suzanne and the girls but when he woke up the next day he had an overwhelming wish to see his family. On going outside he was told by one of the sentries back on duty that his unit would return at midday.

The returning men were not the proud Wehrmacht that had marched down the Champs-Elysée nearly four years before; these men were tired, thin and dispirited; few remembered Manfred since he had been recruited as interpreter to the courts a few days after the German victory parade. They told him to eat well and get a good night's rest because he would join them the next day on exercises to the north-west of Paris.

These excursions continued two or three times a week with monotonous regularity until June 6th, 1944, when one of Manfred's colleagues back at the barracks hurried up to him and said, 'It's happened.'

A puzzled Manfred enquired. 'What has happened?'

'The British and Americans have landed on the Normandy coast; it's not the Pas-de-Calais region at all.' He shrugged his shoulders. 'The top brass got it wrong ... of course.'

'What does that mean for us?' Manfred was very conscious of his lack of combat experience and his own opinion was that he wasn't trained properly to defend the northern coast of Normandy.

'Three-quarters of our unit will set off in large transport vehicles tonight; all personnel who are going have already been informed. I presume that doesn't include you?' The fellow soldier smiled. 'It's going to be good to have some action after all this going backwards and forwards.'

Manfred was relieved not to be going to the Normandy coast. 'This will leave us very thin on the ground in the north Paris region.'

Manfred felt that was far less risky than the confrontation that the greater part of his unit were heading for to take on the British and Americans in western France but said nothing.

'Good luck, my friend. I have to be on my way.'

They shook hands and the older man watched the young soldier set off to prepare for his departure. Shortly afterwards the large contingent from Manfred's unit swept out of the barracks heading west. The commandeered building not only seemed quiet to the schoolteacher and his few remaining Wehrmacht colleagues but it also appeared that way to a Frenchman apparently mending a puncture in his front bicycle tyre fifty metres away from the single sentry at the entrance of the barracks.

The following few weeks were quiet for the skeleton garrison in the north of Paris but short small daily patrols did take place in the suburbs surrounding Manfred's unit's barracks. He was taking part in one such exercise on August 20th when he with his seven colleagues were fired on from windows in a building on the opposite side of the road along which they were moving; no one was injured during the initial burst of firing but it was clear to those taking cover that they were heavily outnumbered by French Partisans.

'Come out with your hands above your heads!'

Manfred understood the command in French immediately and, with a nod from one of his comrades, he slowly emerged from where he had concealed himself. Immediately he started to appear around the corner of the building that had been hiding him there was another burst of gunfire.

An agonized scream came from the schoolteacher as he fell to the ground clutching his left hip.

There was a furious shouting by different voices in French from the other side of the road. 'You idiot, he was surrendering!' Another speaker: 'You wait until Claude hears about this.'

Meanwhile the remainder of Manfred's party had showed themselves and no further shots had been fired. Men crowded around Manfred with the French showing more concern about him than his German comrades. 'Stretcher coming' was heard from down the road; one man produced an enormous handkerchief and rolled it into a ball which he then pressed into a very blood-stained area at the top the injured man's left thigh. 'He's bleeding a lot; we must get him to the Hôtel-Dieu Hospital.'

The French Partisans tenderly lifted the injured man onto a crude stretcher and transferred him onto the back of a battered farm lorry. Two of the Partisans accompanied Manfred towards the famous and historic emergency Hospital on the Île-de-la-Cité.

'Quick, driver!' shouted the second man from his place beside the injured man. 'He really is losing a huge amount of blood.' The man who had been Manfred's sworn enemy only a few minutes earlier was now his devoted carer.

At the hospital they were received by French staff and Manfred, who was in great pain, realized that he was a prisoner of war; a nurse in a pale-blue uniform with a starched white apron and cap said, 'I'm going to give you an injection of morphine to ease the pain before you have an X-ray.' He was transferred to a trolley and noticed less pain but felt a little sleepy. A young doctor in a white coat put a needle in his arm and attached it to a red rubber tube which went up to a bottle containing clear fluid.

'We'll change that to blood as soon as we know your blood group, Monsieur.'

Manfred was aware, and amazed, that the French were treating him with great kindness and respect. A little while later he was in a bed receiving a blood transfusion and a white-haired doctor was speaking to him in German.

'I'm Doctor Maurice, your surgeon. You've a bullet in your left hip; it's damaged the neck of your left thigh bone; you're losing blood and need an urgent operation.'

Manfred felt in no position to argue and nodded his agreement.

The next thing that he knew was waking in a semi-darkened room and when he stirred he found that he was immobilized in some way. In response to his struggles a nurse came to his bedside.

'Be calm, Monsieur Schultz; your operation is over and all went well. Are you in pain?' She gently laid her hand on his forehead and he immediately felt relieved.

'Not nearly as much as before the operation,' he smiled back up at her. 'I feel much better now.' His eyes closed and he drifted into dreamless sleep.

The next morning his dressings were changed. He was

made comfortable in his bed and was given a light breakfast of bread, butter, jam and coffee following which Dr Maurice appeared at Manfred's bedside. 'I understand from the nurses that you speak perfect French, Monsieur. I'm sure you will make a good recovery but it will take a long time. The bullet had partly shattered the neck of your femur and new bone is going to grow in place of the shattered pieces that had to be removed with the missile; in order that this can take place your hip has been immobilized in what is called a "hip spica"; it's a plaster cast and I'm afraid makes normal bodily function very awkward, requiring great patience on your part.'

'How long will I have to be in this cast, Doctor?'

'At present it's very difficult to predict and where you're treated depends on the progress of the war. Your colleagues were taken prisoner by the French Partisans and I expect they will be handed over to the advancing Allies.' Another man came and stood beside the surgeon and Manfred was amazed to see Claude Girard.

'I have to apologize, Herr Court Interpreter; you were the very last person that we wished to harm. Your help to our people is now legendary throughout Occupied France.' He shook Manfred's hand. 'Please forgive us.'

The schoolteacher smiled. 'Of course.'

He watched the two men as they left the ward; he was treated with great kindness and what he felt was excellent medical and nursing therapy but he did find being more or less confined to bed humiliating; he was entirely dependent on the nurses for managing his bowel and bladder function. These 'angels of mercy' dismissed his embarrassment with such comments as 'It's the least we can do for you' or 'It's our duty', but these kind words didn't completely allay his feelings.

After six weeks he was informed that he was an American 'prisoner of war' and was going to be transferred to a suitable facility in Bavaria, which gave Manfred an indication as to the progress of the war.

Two days later a nurse bustling with efficiency came to Manfred's bedside. 'Monsieur Schultz, we've to get you ready for your transfer to Bavaria; I expect that you will be much happier in your own country.'

'Even there I shall still be a prisoner of war.' Manfred was under no illusions about his situation. 'I'm seriously wounded, I'm totally dependent on others for all my needs and I'm on the wrong side of a lost war.'

The nurse was understanding and realized that Manfred's morale needed boosting. 'I think you are quite correct to be realistic about things but with patience, endurance and perseverance I'm sure all will come good for you...' She took his right hand in both of hers. 'Believe me.'

'Thank you very much.' He looked deeply into her eyes.

'You don't have to thank me! I've heard great things about what you've done.' At that moment a colleague brought a trolley to the side of the bed and the nurse started to arrange some extra pillows to support the patient and his massive plaster cast.

'We need to have you quite secure with no chance of an accident during your journey.' More helpers appeared and Manfred thought there were six who eventually lifted him from his bed.

He was wheeled, together with his few possessions, out of the hospital that had been so good to him to a waiting ambulance. As he passed out of the building he said to the accompanying nurse, 'Will my family in Berlin be told about my transfer?'

'I'm sure they will but these are difficult times and it may be some time before the news gets through.' The young Frenchwoman tried to reassure him but there was a note of doubt in her voice. 'Try not to worry about that at the moment.'

'You're very kind, my dear.' He was still thinking about Suzanne and his daughters as he was lifted into the ambulance and in a short while he was being driven towards the railway station on the first stage of his journey to Bavaria. It was only when he heard and saw all the Americans attending and checking all those around him at the Gare du Nord that he asked someone lying on a stretcher next to him: 'When was Paris liberated?'

'On August 19th, my friend.'

It was then that the irony of his injury struck him. 'I was shot the day *after* the Liberation had taken place but of course I'm a German and was in a German uniform!' Manfred said to no one in particular.

There was seemingly endless checking, rechecking and assigning of positions on the train and the language teacher was quite exhausted simply by lying and waiting; eventually it was his turn and no one was prepared for the massive cast.

A large American serviceman looked confident. 'We'll place him sideways on a bench seat.'

But it wasn't to be; the cast hung perilously over the side of the third-class accommodation.

'It's not going to work,' admitted the soldier from the new army of occupation. 'It will have to be the whole trolley and the patient in the guard's van.'

In due course Manfred was apparently secure in the goods carriage with an attendant American male military nurse and there was some mutual hostility between the two as the repatriation train drew out of the Gare du Nord.

Manfred looked around his new prison; his trolley had been wedged into the rear nearside corner of the carriage with cases piled on one another. 'They need not have bothered; I'm not going anywhere,' he said in English.

'If you're referring to the suitcases and boxes that surround you, they are put there to stop your trolley from moving around, banging against other items and probably causing you pain!' The military attendant glowered at his charge; there was no sympathy in his tone of voice.

The locomotive gathered speed and the schoolteacher in the cast felt every swaying movement of the goods van, finally making him aware of his full bladder. He was reluctant to ask the American for assistance, although he knew he would have to ask for his help soon.

'I need to empty my bladder, Corporal.'

'You need to what?' The attendant was used to much more colourful language from injured soldiers. 'You mean you want a piss?'

'Yes!' was Manfred's brief response to this crude language.

The military medical attendant roughly pushed some of the luggage to one side in order to gain access to his patient and attend to his need. 'Here you are.' He glared at his charge. 'Though it's more than you deserve, you rotten Nazi.'

Manfred relieved himself but was astonished at the way he had just been addressed; he had never been spoken to in that way throughout his four years in France. 'I wonder what is behind that,' he thought to himself. He was physically comfortable again but felt very tired and started to doze off; as he did so he was aware that the train was picking up speed.

He never knew how long he had been asleep but suddenly became aware of his trolley jerking around and causing pain in his left hip.

'This can't be right! Please secure my trolley and plaster cast,' he shouted.

Cases and parcels started to slide across the floor and the train suddenly came to a halt with a screech of brakes. Manfred's personal transport hurtled down to the front end of the van where it struck the wall of the luggage container with a sickening crunch.

Manfred screamed in agony; the side door of the van slid open and a massive American army sergeant peered inside.

'Is everything all right in here?'

'No it's not!' The answer was aggressive and quite out of character. 'This attendant is totally neglecting his duty of care and as a result I'm in great pain and I think my plaster cast has been broken.' Manfred looked to this man to put things right but was amazed at the response.

'You listen to me: as far as the United States military is concerned you're just another member of the Nazi Party; if you've to go through a bit of discomfort while we're transporting you from Paris it's nothing compared to what you evil bloody Nazis have done to millions of people.'

The stunned schoolteacher was truly lost for words and he stayed silent for a few moments; anything he could possibly say would only make things worse but one thing he was sure about was that he somehow had to speak to Suzanne on the telephone as soon as possible. The amazingly large sergeant was speaking again.

'For your information the Allied advance into Germany has been stalled by heavy fighting near the Belgian border at the city of Aachen; we've made good progress travelling south-east but we will have to make a temporary camp here forty kilometres from Dijon...' He spread his hands. 'We could be here for the winter.'

As Manfred listened to this his heart sank deeper and deeper; he became more aware of the pain in his hip with the broken plaster spica; in the half-light of dusk coming in through the open door of the goods van tears could be seen trickling down his cheeks.

# 26

## *Soldier-Philosopher at Sixteen*

Kurt didn't enjoy his military training at Schleswig-Holstein. He found the drilling and instruction in basic military strategy pointless at this stage of what was clearly a lost war and never really engaged with it all, in spite of the intimidating rantings of the Gauleiter.

Major Krause had been with Kurt's unit since his recruitment and over that period of time his fanaticism had steadily increased. 'Germany is going on to victory and I've received orders that all traitors will be summarily hanged for all offences against the Third Reich including abandoning your weapons, showing a white flag or doing anything that doesn't fit in with fighting unto death.'

Most of the young men listening to the man in the black uniform with the four square silver studs on his collar and woven silver insignia on his shoulder tabs realized that they were listening to a dangerous man who was to be avoided where ever possible. Kurt, like his colleagues, was relieved when their army training came to an end and they were assigned their various postings.

Kurt received his instructions in a poor-quality brown envelope and when he opened it he read that he was to report to an anti-aircraft battery at Stettin near Usedom Island in north-east Germany; this inevitably brought back memories of holidays with his family in 1935. As he looked at the piece of paper he whispered to himself: 'So much change in so short a time.' He took the train to his new post and the nearly 400-kilometre journey via Lübeck was uneventful and he found himself assigned to an 88mm anti-aircraft gun similar to the one with which he had become familiar in Berlin.

'Hello, my name is Werner Hofman.' A young soldier of the same age and with a Berlin accent gave Kurt a cheery welcome. 'Let me show you to your quarters.'

'That's very kind of you.' Kurt was grateful for the offer but was wary of getting too close to a colleague after the terrible death of his good friend Fritz Schäfer beside Flak Tower Two. 'I'm a little tired after the journey: do I have to be available tonight?'

'No, that's all right; I will cover for you.' Werner said with a smile. 'I will also show you to the canteen, although it's always the same menu of potatoes and bratwurst.'

This new friend gave the impression he really wanted to be a help and Kurt felt that he could not be rude to him. The dark-haired young man wore the same outfit as the recent arrival, which consisted of their everyday clothes with a black armband on which was inscribed in silver words 'Deutsche Volkssturm Wehrmacht'

'Rumour has it that we'll have woollen uniforms in field grey for the winter,' Werner cheerfully told his new friend; belatedly he remembered to ask, 'What is your name?'

'I'm Kurt Schultz.' He thought his new acquaintance was very nice but there was something about him that was disturbing. 'Are you OK, my friend?'

'Not really,' was the unsurprising reply.

'What has happened to you?'

'Here is the canteen...' Werner seemed reluctant to answer his new comrade's enquiry. 'I don't want to talk about it.'

They helped themselves to mashed potatoes and pork bratwurst. Werner led them over to a rough wood table where the two of them sat down and began to eat in silence.

Suddenly he said: 'My mother, father and two sisters were all killed on the night of the November 22nd last year. Our house was near the Charlottenberg Palace; I was on anti-aircraft duty that night and when I arrived back in the morning: there was no home, no family; their bodies were lying under blankets beside the ruins.'

'I'm so sorry, Werner.' The two boys ate in silence.

'I mean it!' Kurt said.

After the pair had finished eating Werner showed him where his sleeping quarters were and left his weary colleague to have a well-earned night's sleep.

The two young men met at breakfast the next morning. 'Hello, my new-found friend.' Kurt greeted him with a smile. 'Was there much activity last night?'

'No, it was quiet; the RAF bombers don't come every night.' Werner had worked up an appetite and was tucking into his breakfast.

'Why is it so important to defend this remote area of Germany?'

'Because of Peenemünde – that western end of Usedom Island is where the V2 rockets are being manufactured and tested.'

'Aha, the not-so-secret secret weapon!' Kurt remembered his friend Fritz telling him it would bring about less bombing on Berlin. 'And so that's why we're here?'

'Exactly, my friend and we do the job with those massive 88mm anti-aircraft guns.' Werner seemed to be lost in thought for a moment. 'I've something to show you after breakfast.' He seemed very excited but didn't say anything further.

When they had finished eating the still-grieving young man led the way to his bedside locker. He opened the little wooden drawer, took it out completely and emptied the contents onto his bed. Then he turned the drawer over revealing a brown envelope stuck to the lower surface using an Elastoplast dressing; as he removed it and took a white sheet of paper out he said quietly to Kurt, 'I've not shown it to anyone since I saw it floating down from the sky lit up by the searchlights during an air raid in Berlin. Please read it.'

Kurt took the piece of paper and read out loud: 'Manifesto of the Students of the University of Munich.' He looked down the white sheet and read on: 'Fellow students, the day of reckoning has come for the most contemptible tyrant our people has ever endured.' It then listed a whole raft of atrocities and finished up with: 'We will not be silent.'

Kurt handed the highly dangerous piece of paper back to Werner. 'I've never seen anything like it.'

The slightly older young man put it back in its hiding place, shut the drawer and turned back to Kurt. 'I apologize for putting you in danger by showing you this piece of paper but after the deaths of my family it fits into my feelings about how our country is treating us and others.'

'How do you think it came to be written and amazingly to be floating down out of the night sky of Berlin?' The newly arrived soldier was astonished by what he had just read.

'I've not told anyone else about this but some boys from Munich manning the gun emplacements here told me about an anti-Hitler organization called the White Rose; they say that the students involved were killed in a horrible way.' He placed a hand on Kurt's left shoulder. 'Thank you for listening; we'll never speak of this matter again. I just had to get it off my chest...'

And that was how it remained.

That winter Kurt did his part in trying to protect the Peenemünde V2 Rocket site but his heart wasn't in it and his thoughts started to turn to his own situation; he had already noticed that others were making preparations to take care of themselves and he knew that he too had to take control of his own life. As time passed rapidly into 1945, the Russians were reported to be advancing via Poland from the East and the Allies in the form of the British were approaching from the West.

Kurt finally made up his mind. In late April, taking advantage of the gathering chaos he made his way back to Schleswig-Holstein, occasionally gaining a lift on a horse-drawn wagon but mostly going on foot. He reached Flensburg on the Danish border on May 8th; on the outskirts of the city he saw some British soldiers running after a dishevelled slightly built man.

'Halt or we fire!' they shouted in English.

The man continued running and four shots rang out, the man fell to the ground and two soldiers pulled him to his feet; he was then half walked and half dragged towards what Kurt thought was a military camp. Kurt followed at a distance; his father's association with Slough led him to trust the British.

The small noisy party entered the wood and barbed-wire gate. Kurt, who was now a strong well-built young man of seventeen years of age – his birthday in February had passed almost unnoticed – had no difficulty in scrambling up a grass bank near the entrance where he had a good view of the tented encampment. He could hear the little man protesting.

'I was only reaching for my passport to show you gentleman.'

The party had disappeared into a large khaki canvas tent and shortly afterwards he heard a loudspeaker announcement: 'Calling Captain Glanvill; you're urgently needed to give an anaesthetic...' then the announcer added, 'for Lord Haw Haw.' Kurt remembered hearing him on his father's radio, with his odd nasal 'Jairmany calling'.

While he was thinking out his next move he heard the 'click' of a rifle being cocked behind him.

'Don't move or I will fire!'

The young man realized that he was being taken prisoner. 'Turn around and face me!'

The voice spoke in English, which was no problem to the soldier not in uniform, and he did as he was asked.

'Now come down from that little hill, then stand with your arms in the air!'

Kurt was finally on the ground with his arms above his head and could see that his captor holding a rifle pointed at him was probably only a few years older than himself.

'Now march towards the camp gates.'

The seventeen-year-old prisoner was guided to a smaller tent beside the one from which Lord Haw Haw could still be heard protesting. He went inside, sat on a wooden chair by a table and waited; after a few minutes a different young British soldier came in with a steaming cup of liquid.

'Nice cup of tea, mate?'

Kurt was well aware of the legendary 'English cup of tea' and replied 'Thank you very much!' He took a sip of it and found that a lot of sugar had been put in but it tasted good and warmed him up on the cold May morning in northernmost Germany.

'What is going on in the next tent?' he asked.

'You speak bloody good English ... That's Lord Haw Haw having a bullet removed from his arse; our very own Captain Glanvill is giving the anaesthetic and a surgeon officer has been sent down from headquarters.' The soldier took the now empty cup. 'There's no point in trying to run away; the war is over.' He turned and left.

Half an hour later a British officer entered the tent.

'Hello, young man, I'm Captain Glanvill and I've been asked to take a look at you; have you any injuries that have happened to you on the way here?' The soldier asking

276

the question had a soft gentle voice. 'Any wounds or illnesses?'

'No. Thank you, but I'm very hungry.'

'If you've nothing to show me or tell me about I will arrange for you to be fed.' Captain Reginald Glanvill of the Royal Army Medical Corps was a sympathetic doctor and seemed to Kurt to be a very fine human being. 'Is there anything else that I can help you with?'

'I'm just curious really but that man you've just anaesthetized, I think I heard his voice on my father's radio; who is he?'

'His real name is William Joyce but in England he was called Lord Haw Haw. He was given that name because he broadcast from Germany trying to influence the British to abandon Churchill and join Hitler; although we've just treated his wound he will probably be executed as a traitor.' The doctor shook Kurt's hand. 'We may be on different sides but I hope that everything goes well for you so that when you eventually get back to your family you'll be able to finish school and then go on to university. You seem a smart lad, just like my son at home. Goodbye.'

Kurt was sad to see the kindly British doctor leave; he detected sadness in his eyes and felt sure that he desperately missed his wife and children; he didn't see him again.

Nothing much happened for the rest of that day. He was given English corned beef, potatoes and cabbage and then spent a restless night on a camp bed that had been brought into the tent. He was tormented by the fact that he was now a prisoner and his destiny was no longer in his own hands.

The following day he sat in weak sunshine outside the tent flap watching the comings and goings in the camp. In the middle of the morning a young man was marched through the camp entrance; as he drew closer, Kurt, to his amazement, recognized his friend from Stettin.

'Werner! Werner Hofman, over here, over here...' He was overjoyed to see his friend and they embraced.

'Kurt it's really good to see you.'

The British soldier who had escorted the prisoner into the central compound lifted up his gun a little in a slightly threatening way.

'There will be plenty of time for that sort of thing later ... Inside please!' He indicated the interior of the tent. 'In there and sit down.'

At that moment an officious-looking soldier, who, Kurt thought, was a low rank but felt important, followed them into the tent carrying a board with some paper clipped to it.

The two prisoners, who must have looked very young to their captors, were reunited for more corned beef for lunch. 'I could not stay after you had left, Kurt, and so I followed two days later and picked up news of you as I passed along and guessed that you were heading north.'

'I'm so very pleased that you did.' Kurt smiled at his friend. 'There were times when I felt uncertain and lonely.'

'I think the two of us will get on better together, my friend.'

'I agree! In these uncertain times we need each other.' There was a new maturity in his voice.

The following day the two prisoners were taken to a nearby small town where they were able to take a shower and were given some well-used but clean clothes.

'Anyone speak English?' a soldier, whom Kurt now knew to be a sergeant, asked in a loud voice.

The two young friends responded quickly. 'We do.'

'Good lads. Stay close to me.'

And this the two young men did over the next few days during which they helped with translating the words of the numerous refugees fleeing west, of German soldiers surrendering and of the numerous people who could not, at first glance, be identified; all intermingling in the newly occupied territory.

The two young men were well treated over the succeeding days but the time came when all the prisoners who had been assembled in the region were to be transported south to a larger POW camp. As they were watching the people in front of them climbing onto the transports Kurt turned to Werner.

'My friend, I'm not going to arrive at that camp where we're supposed to be going!' He pointed to the first and then the last vehicles. 'It's only those two lorries that have British drivers; all the ones in between are German.'

'What are you thinking of doing, Kurt?'

'I'm going to leave the transport just before the Kiel Canal; I'm just going to have a word with our driver.'

The two young men climbed onto the battle-scarred vehicle and positioned themselves just behind the driver's cab. A few minutes later the convoy was on its way and as their vehicle neared the crossing of the Kiel Canal, Kurt rapped on the roof of the driver's cab; it slowed almost to a halt and the two prisoners jumped to freedom without giving thought to the danger.

They hid behind a hedge for an hour before daring to move. When they eventually emerged Kurt carefully checked in all directions.

'All clear, Werner; no one in sight!' Indeed, they seemed to be in a desolate part of the country with the Kiel Canal disappearing away from them towards the south-west.

Werner joined his friend and looked around. 'Which way do you think?'

'West is best! We show our backs to the Russians.'

They set off leaving the canal and heading into deserted agricultural land. After a few hours with daylight fading they came upon a farmhouse in a poor state of repair but apparently not affected by war damage. Kurt looked at his friend.

'This is as good a place as any; shall we give it a try?'

'We might as well.' Werner opened the creaking five-bar gate; they walked along broken paving stones with uncut grass partly concealing them and could hear the sounds of cows and sheep.

Kurt knocked on the front door and waited. The door opened by a thickset man with his right arm missing; the stump was concealed by his folded-up light-blue shirtsleeve fixed with a safety-pin; his hair was greying but his face was friendly.

'Yes?' The tone was kind and a smile hovered around his thin lips.

'We're looking for work.' Both young men spoke at once.

'Come in, come in, lads! I could do with some help.' He opened the door a little wider.

# 27

## *Clotilde amid Devastation*

The twenty-five kilograms of butter and half of a pig were greatly welcomed in the Schultz family home.

'I think we should divide up the butter into small portions and try to preserve them by adding more salt and wrapping them in silver foil.' Suzanne was really excited about the arrival of the box from Manfred; it was as though he had sent her part of himself. 'Heinrich, I will make you a parcel with butter and pork in it.'

The young disabled soldier was clearly moved by being in the Schultz household. 'That is very kind of you Frau Schultz; you know that I was a pupil of your husband?'

'I didn't know. How wonderful! Did you hear that, girls?'

'What is wonderful, Mother?' Margit had found the silver foil that she knew that her mother had collected since before the war from chocolate bars.

'Heinrich Schäfer was one of your father's protégés and they met in France.'

'I didn't think he would know me but he did because of my once quoting Goethe to him. I was amazed at his memory; we admired and liked him very much at school.'

'It's good to hear that coming from one of his pupils...' Suzanne paused for a moment; 'Perhaps it sounds strange but I feel closer to Manfred by hearing and seeing you, Heinrich.'

She was interrupted by Clotilde running onto the balcony

chasing Fräulein Müller. 'We would love to hear him on the telephone now.' The discerning pussycat stopped in mid-leap as she headed towards the delicious aroma from the pickled pig. She turned and approached the one-armed soldier and rubbed her body backwards and forwards on his trouser legs.

'Please meet Fräulein Müller! You must be a wonderful person because she doesn't do that to people she takes a dislike to.'

'I feel very honoured.' Heinrich smiled broadly at Clotilde. 'In fact, it's been lovely meeting you all. I will take my packages of butter and pork and be getting on my way to register for my searchlight training.'

He took his parcels and everyone thanked him for his great help. The Schultz family watched him leave from their front door with sadness in their eyes; defending Berlin was becoming in an increasingly dangerous occupation.

Clotilde and Margit continued to go to school but the air raids had now become so frequent that ordinary life was well-nigh impossible. Suzanne was busy when the girls were at school, although she was increasingly anxious at the lack of contact from her husband, who had phoned her at the beginning of August 1944 with the news of the box being put on the train to Paris. She had no idea of his injury a few days later, and subsequent misery.

From early 1944, at the beginning of each month Suzanne always placed her and her daughters' ration books on the dining room table and worked out exactly how to use the coupons to maximum effect for food, which included bread, potatoes, butter and meat, together with their clothes. The following day she summoned the girls to the kitchen.

'I'm going on my monthly trip to the farmer's.'

'Have a safe journey, Mother!' Clotilde always worried that something awful might befall her darling mother on one of these trips, especially as she always travelled on open goods wagons on the railways. Not only did she run the risk of air-raids but also a confrontation with other civilians, desperate for food. Moreover, if she were caught by the authorities she would probably have to pay a significant fine or worse for travelling illegally.

This dangerous way of life continued. Clotilde's sixteenth birthday came and went on May 28th. Every day the Schultz family saw another bit of the city destroyed by the bombing and more lives lost. The spirit of Berlin's people wasn't crushed, however – symbolized by the clock tower and spire of the Kaiser Wilhelm Church standing above the ruins.

The intermittent heavy bombing continued through 1944 and there was speculation in the shelters and queues for food that part of the Allied effort was being diverted to support the invasion of France – these gathering points were the most reliable places for information. In July there were rumours that there had been an attempt on Hitler's life. A bomb had failed to kill him at his headquarters in the 'Wolf's Lair' at Rustenburg in western Poland: the conspirators had been apprehended; tortured and executed.

The German counter-attack in the Ardennes Forest also known as the 'Battle of the Bulge' was finally overcome on the January 25th, 1945; it was Germany's final offensive of the war in Europe and this allowed the Allies to proceed towards the German border, which was supported by a massive air raid on Berlin that destroyed the Reich Chancellery, extensively damaged Unter den Linden, Berlin's loveliest avenue, and the People's Court.

By the middle of March 1945, the invading Allies had crossed the River Rhine and fanned out to engulf Germany from the west; the Soviets reached the River Oder in the East. In the Berlin suburb of Dahlem the telephone rang in the entrance hall of the Schultz apartment. Suzanne had just returned from the increasingly difficult task of finding food in the shops, often bartering with the brandies and liqueurs sent to her by Manfred to obtain her rations.

'Hello, Suzanne my daring.'

'Manfred, oh Manfred! How wonderful! We've waited so long for news of you; where are you and how are you?'

'I'm in Germany, in Pfaffenhofen forty-five kilometres north of Munich; I have a hip injury and am a prisoner of the Americans who think that I'm a member of the Nazi Party.'

'That's ridiculous! Nothing could be further from the truth.' Suzanne thought that her husband's voice sounded strained. 'What can I do to help?'

'There has been a legal process opened against me. The only way I can see to get me out of this predicament is to find a school colleague who will make a statement on my behalf.'

'I will get on it first thing tomorrow but please tell me more about your injury?' Suzanne had so many questions she wanted to ask but realized that her husband was exhausted.

'I was captured by the French and while I was being taken prisoner I was shot in the left hip and some of the bone was shattered. I've had an operation to remove the bullet and broken pieces of bone but I've had the joint immobilized in a great plaster cast. I'm going out of my mind with boredom, darling! But, more importantly, how are you? ... How are...?'

There was a pause and Suzanne could hear angry shouting in the background and then Manfred was back on the telephone. 'I have to go now.'

'We'll speak again and I will ensure the girls are here. I love you so very much, my darling Manfred.' The line went dead but she continued to grip the instrument as though it was his hand.

She was still sitting beside the telephone when her sixteen-

and nineteen-year-old daughters came home from their remnants of a school which was now little more than a ruin; they spent most of the time there in the basement shelter.

'Mother, there are planes flying over Berlin and we keep on hearing explosions.' Clotilde could barely get the news out quickly enough and Margit nodded in agreement.

'Oh darlings! I've such news. Your father telephoned two hours ago. He is wounded and a prisoner of the Americans but he *is* in Germany!' She didn't know whether to laugh or cry. He was safe … for the moment.

'Where is he, Mother?' Clotilde's excitement didn't immediately take in the fact that there could also be bad news.

'He is in Pfaffenhofen, near Munich … He has an injured hip joint, but on top of all that a process has been taken out against him for being a member of the Nazi Party.' Suzanne spread out her hands in a gesture of helplessness.

'That's outrageous.' Margit was incandescent with rage. 'He was firmly opposed to the Nazis; that's why he was victimized and conscripted into the military before men much younger than him.'

'I know you're quite right to be angry, Margit, but we are where we are and we have to make some decisions.'

It seemed to Clotilde that the strength that her mother had shown throughout the war was going to continue to be tested over the next few months.

Suzanne decided to take the initiative. 'I think it's too dangerous for you to go to school any more, darlings. Berlin is now the objective for both the Allies and the Russians to seize and occupy. From now on, we'll stay here and only go out for short distances for food and fuel.'

'Is it really that serious, Mother?' Clotilde was shaken.

'We can see it all around us, my darlings, There's hardly any buildings untouched by bombing; the city's defences are manned by young boys and old men and even some girls. Dr Goebbels' rantings about no surrender and fighting until death don't fit in with what's clear to all of us.'

The three women clung to each other in an embrace of strength, purpose and love.

The following day Suzanne set off alone to make her way to the Fichte Gymnasium in the neighbouring suburb of Wilmersdorf, the school where her husband Manfred had taught languages for most of his career. The building was nothing but a skeleton and a heap of rubble spilling out onto the street; she was deeply shocked to see the state of her husband's beloved school. On the opposite side of the street a grey-haired man wearing a black coat and matching homburg stood shaking his head sadly. Suzanne crossed the debris-strewn road to speak to him.

'It only happened in the raid last night; it was a good thing that we closed the school six weeks ago. It will open again eventually.'

'Did you know the school, sir?'

'I certainly did. My name is Herr Wilhelm Weiss; I used to teach history in the Fichte Gymnasium.' He looked across the road. 'So many young men educated with dedication; so many of the same young men slaughtered in the east and in Western Europe.'

'But why are you here today, Herr Weiss?'

'While I was in the queue for the baker I was told about the school being bombed last night; I get most of my reliable news in the queues these days. But how can I help you, my dear?'

Suzanne was surprised and relieved to have found this schoolteacher. 'I wonder whether you knew my husband, Manfred Schultz? He was a teacher here too.'

'I most certainly did!' He smiled and shook hands enthusiastically with his new acquaintance. 'He was much admired by all of his colleagues except for an obnoxious few...' He looked up and down the street and showed his nervousness by hesitating before speaking again. 'On my way here I saw two people with Volkssturm armbands who had been hung from lampposts by the SS; there were notices pinned to their coats saying "coward" – one was a boy barely sixteen and the other a very old man.'

'We live in terrible times!' Suzanne didn't wish to press her new-found friend for fear of losing his cooperation. 'Were you one of those who admired my husband?'

'Most definitely, but I don't think that we should continue our conversation here in the open.'

He offered his arm to her and they walked arm in arm to a small café with steamed-up windows serving ersatz coffee. It was almost empty.

'We can talk safely here. ... Frau Schultz, why are you asking me these questions?' The history teacher glanced gloomily at the café proprietor. 'Please don't misunderstand me; I want to help but trust is a scarce commodity.'

Suzanne told him Manfred's story and that he needed a colleague to sign an affidavit that he had never been a member of the Nazi Party. A flicker of a smile hovered on her lips. 'Is there anything you can do? It would mean so much to us.'

The history teacher smiled back at her. 'Of course I will do it!' He thought for a moment. 'I couldn't live with myself if I refused.'

Suzanne squeezed his arm across the table. 'I'm so very grateful.'

'I've headed school writing paper and an official seal of the district of Wilmersdorf.'

'How very impressive.'

'There are compensations for being a history teacher. I had access to the archives in the Town Hall and rescued one or two items, so to speak.'

'How wonderful to have found you! I'm a lucky woman.'

There was jubilation in her voice. 'How can I help and when will it be ready?'

'There's something you can do to streamline matters; we'll need the signatures of two witnesses. Do you know of such persons?'

'Yes I do, although one of my daughters may not be pleased – the lady concerned used to be her primary schoolteacher – and perhaps a colleague of hers.'

There was a spring in Suzanne's step as she left to do her part to certify that her husband wasn't, nor had ever been, a member of the Nazi Party.

Once she was back in the family apartment she found Clotilde putting out Fräulein Müller's lunch. 'That cat gets fed better than anyone else in Berlin, young lady.' It may have been a mild complaint but there was laughter in the voice. 'I've a little job for you, my darling daughter.'

'Mother, I think you must have had a good morning.' She stood up and gave Suzanne a big hug.

'I did indeed! I want you to go and see the other Fräulein Müller.'

'Did I hear what I thought I heard?'

'You did indeed. I want you to ask her if she and a colleague would be kind enough to come to our apartment tomorrow and sign a document to help your father.' Suzanne smiled sweetly at her daughter and there was no protest.

'I will go to her apartment. Mother; it's not far away from my old school.'

She set off on her errand. As she left, Suzanne suddenly saw her daughter in a new light – as an almost fully grown woman, lithe and attractive. This worried Suzanne with Berlin nearly under siege.

'Margit my love, please go with Clotilde.'

All went well. Herr Weiss brought a beautifully prepared affidavit to the Schultz apartment the following day and it was witnessed by Fräulein Müller and a colleague an hour later. After a further twenty-four hours – it was April 1st, 1945 – the telephone rang in the entrance hall of the Dahlem apartment.

Suzanne picked it up and Manfred's voice was at the other end of the line, louder and clearer.

'Hello, my love, how have you been getting on?'

'My darling, it's so good to hear your voice again. I've got the document that you need, I'm going to get it to you with the help of a train driver who has a special pass that he says will enable him to find you, with the German genius for organization in chaos.' There was a note of cheerfulness, almost of levity, in her voice.

'Who signed it?' Manfred was very curious.

'You know him.' She told him about meeting Wilhelm Weiss, his former colleague. 'The train driver is Weiss's son, Hermann.'

'I remember Wilhelm well. He was a first-class history teacher and a very nice person; I'm afraid I don't recall his son.'

'Wilhelm thought you might have difficulty in remembering Hermann academically but he thought you might recollect the incident of the headmaster's motorcar being driven away from the school and returned three days later in perfect polished pristine condition, with a full tank of petrol and neatly parked outside the school with no sign of the driver.'

Manfred laughed. '*That* I do remember and it gives me confidence in my train driver.'

'It's lovely hearing you laugh, my darling! Please telephone me when the affidavit arrives; I think of you so much and long to see you!' The telephone went dead.

Clotilde was awoken on April 16th by a deep rumble apparently coming from the east. She got up out of bed and knocked on her mother's bedroom door.

'Come in!' Suzanne was half asleep.

'That sounds like thunder, Mother, but there isn't any rain.'

'It's guns, my darling.' She looked up at her ceiling as the light with its glass shade shook. 'Russian heavy guns that they have brought across the River Oder to its west bank.'

A picture of Suzanne's favourite view of the Grand Canal in Venice on the bedroom wall shook, falling to the floor. The glass shattered ominously.

'Perhaps Berlin is about to be demolished like that picture!' Clotilde climbed into her mother's bed and snuggled up to her. 'I'm afraid. Mother!' Suzanne heard fear in her daughter's voice.

'I'm sure that is not going to happen, my darling daughter.' She so very much hoped that she was correct but at the moment her anxiety about the future for her family could not be greater. 'Try to get some sleep, my love.'

The rumble of heavy gunfire continued through the night and at dawn Suzanne ventured out onto the street, where other women were now gathering.

'Those are heavy artillery,' she observed to the gathering in general.

Another woman spoke up. 'The bombardment has started; the occupation will follow.'

'Who will get here first – the Russians or the Americans?' another voice said.

'It seems as though it's going to be the Russians; it's their guns we can hear,' Suzanne joined in; she pointed to some graffiti on a wall opposite: 'Protect our women and children from the red beasts.'

'How far away are those guns?'

'About eighty kilometres. Goebbels said so on the radio last night,' said yet another female voice.

'What did he say?' Frau Schultz pushed her way to the front of the noticeably growing group. 'I don't believe a word he says.'

'Why do you want to know what he said then?' came an unsympathetic comment.

' "For those who wish to know," he said, "the Asiatic hoards will smash themselves on the line of the Oder"...'

'Oh great! I presume that is what we can hear them doing now!' Suzanne chipped in, She now felt no hesitation about showing her mistrust of the regime.

'He also said, *if* you will allow me to continue'– the sarcasm was unmistakable – 'that any male in a house flying a white flag will be shot.'

'Fantastic, so the way we're going to win this war is by shooting Germans!' There were murmurs of agreement as the women of Berlin drifted back into their apartments.

Suzanne returned to her home, angry with herself for showing her feelings. Clotilde and Margit were waiting for her fully dressed.

'What has happened, Mother?' The two sisters spoke in unison, which was a measure of their anxiety.

'Our city will be occupied, my darlings. It's inevitable. Berlin will be soon swarming with Russian soldiers; we must make some preparations.'

During the following two days the capable and ingenious family Schultz strengthened the front door with two massive beams of wood that could be slotted into steel brackets; they themselves were amazed at their abilities with Manfred's tools. Following this they started to store essential foods in the attic which had not been used by the family for years.'

'This place needs a good clean and I think we'll have to install three camp beds. We'll each bring up our own.' The loft had an opening with an adjacent folding ladder that could be pulled down with a strong string. 'I think they will come through here quite easily but the hinges need some oil and we'll have to use some heavy wooden beams like we did at the front door.'

'Don't you think we're overdoing the barricades, Mother?' Margit had an uncertain look on her delicate features.

Suzanne had not fully discussed with her daughters her fears about the coming Russian occupation, that women would now bear the brunt of the victors' revenge.

'It's a precaution, my darling.' Nothing further was said about the matter at that time. 'I think we should remember to bring up some bottles of water, and a supply of candles and matches.'

The following morning, Clotilde was helping Margit to practise her spoken English – she felt sure this would help her find work when the Americans and British needed translators – when, at approximately eleven thirty in the morning, the telephone rang. Calls were rare and Clotilde won the race to the receiver.

'Hello, is that you, Father?' There was a short pause. 'It's me, Clotilde; it's fantastic to hear your voice. You sound really cheerful ... Mother's here.'

Suzanne took the receiver, while her daughters stood by, desperate to catch her every word.

'Oh how wonderful! That's such good news, darling. The affidavit arrived safely yesterday and had an immediate effect and you are now at Wöllershof for rehabilitation.' the mother and wife was overjoyed by the news ... We'll be able to visit you when the war is over. People say it will only be a few days ... Oh I know, darling ... We all love you, too. you. Au revoir.'

Suzanne had more or less repeated every word her husband said partly to let her daughters know the news about their father and to ensure that she herself had understood every word.

'Oh Mother, everything's going to be OK, isn't it? Father will come home?' Clotilde was almost crying with relief.

'Yes, darling, but Father will still need our help when he eventually comes home.'

'When do you think that will be, Mother? ... I really can't wait to see him after such a long time.'

'We'll have to be patient. He still has a serious hip injury and is still a prisoner of war of the Americans.' Suzanne feared it was going to be a long wait. 'Meanwhile we have to prepare for what's going to happen here. Father is safe and now we must make sure we are safe too! I have a little chore for you both: will you both go out to that little electrical shop on the corner? It's still in business. I want you to buy a small electrical heater that we can install in the attic for cooking when things get dangerous and too risky to come down.'

Susanne watched her two lovely daughters leave the apartment and she thought it would be the last time that they would go out alone for some time. They soon returned with the heater.

'Mother, Mother!' Clotilde was shouting with excitement. 'We've just seen two Ilyushin airplanes fly over Dahlem towards the Tiergarten; they had huge great red stars on each side. Then we heard two massive explosions and saw plumes of smoke coming from central Berlin.'

'It means the Russians are now confident enough to bomb us in daylight! Their guns are getting louder and we'll soon have their shells landing here!' Suzanne's anxiety was clear.

Margit had a mischievous grin on her face. 'It's "that man's" birthday today – April 20th. Perhaps they were sending him a birthday present.'

Suzanne laughed heartily. 'Well done, Margit; it's good that our worsening situation hasn't dampened our sense of humour.' She smiled at both her daughters. 'I don't think it will be an excuse for massive military parades as in previous years.'

In fact, the Führer was outside his bunker pinning medals on the malnourished old men and young boys of the

Volkssturm; it was the last time that he was seen in public. Shells from the ever closer Russian heavy guns were landing around the pathetic little ceremony.

# 28

## *Mahlow, East Berlin – April 27th, 1945*

In Mahlow the Zimmermann family were sitting in their comfortable living room. The guns were now silent and there were no planes flying in the skies above Berlin; the quiet, however, was menacing.

'I do so miss Kurt. I dread to think what may have become of him,' his mother lamented.

'He is very resourceful,' his proud father responded. 'We'll see him again.' Maximillian took a deep breath. 'This is such a beautiful house; we've been here throughout the war and the house has sustained only minor damage and broken glass which we were easily able to repair.' His brow puckered. 'I've no doubt that the senior military personnel of the Russian army will have already earmarked it for themselves.'

'You mean they already know about our home?' Mitzi was appalled.

'I certainly do. The Russians have had excellent aerial surveillance and intelligence; that is one of the reasons that they are knocking on the gates of Berlin now.' Maximillian's face was grim. Suddenly he leaped to his feet.

'We can't just sit here waiting for them! Beautiful as our house is, what matters is us! It will have to fend for itself.' His voice was filled with determination; he had long since guessed what was coming. 'Marlena, go and pack your case especially with your diabetic requirements; remember food is going to be one of our greatest priorities.' He got up and went over to his wife. 'Mitzi, my love go upstairs and pack your suitcase but don't leave it in a conspicuous place; we don't want the Russians to think we're one step ahead of them.'

'Very well, my love.' Mitzi trusted her husband; she knew he would always know the best thing to do. But oh, her lovely house ... Would she ever be able to return?

'While you two ladies are attending to your packing I've got a little job to do in the garden.' He headed towards the garden door.

Mitzi and Marlena exchanged curious glances as together they climbed the stairs for the last time. Mitzi sighed deeply.

Maximillian went into the little tool shed just outside, put on his galoshes, took a garden spade and strode over to the rhododendron bush. Twenty minutes later he returned to the house with a stout canvas bag and took it upstairs to pack in his suitcase with a few clothes and toiletries.

An hour later they were gathered together again in the sitting room when they heard a sudden clattering noise outside.

'Here they come now!' Mitzi peeped around the edge of the curtain. 'It's not a very impressive start. I think their first priority was to break into a liquor store.'

Maximillian and Marlena joined her and their first sight of Stalin's massive Red Army was of two very drunk khaki-clad individuals, with large flat-brimmed hats awry, weaving their way down the street on a single stolen bicycle. This weird sight was followed shortly afterwards by a mobile anti-aircraft battery with their great barrels pointing up towards the sky; then the men in no particular formation, broad backs in leather jackets and high boots; and after this jeeps, howitzers, the stench of petrol and noise noise noise. The rear of this unit was taken up by horses, cows and foals, all of which were dropping faeces to varying degrees, and finally a more luxurious jeep in which were sitting four officers with red shoulder flashes and red hats with massive brims.

'It will be those last four whom we'll be dealing with.'

It was no great surprise, then, when the officers' vehicle drew up in front of the sturdily built house of the family Zimmermann – it was, after all, the only house in the street that had not been flattened or severely damaged by the devastating bombing of Berlin. The four officers climbed out of the jeep leaving the driver at the wheel, crossed the shell-pocked front garden and knocked forcefully on the front door.

Inside, the three occupants sat up sharply in response to the apparent attempt to shatter the wood.

'I will go.' Maximillian stood up and marched towards the sound of the banging. He returned followed by four very big uniformed men.

'My name is Colonel Vladimir Orlov,' announced one of them in a heavily accented German that was barely comprehensible. 'We will take this house for our headquarters; my colleagues will carry out a quick survey.'

Mitzi stood up. 'May I conduct them around the house?'

'That will not be necessary.' The leader nodded to his fellow officers; they scuttled off in different directions and returned five minutes later and this was followed a brief conference in Russian.

'We like the house. You have one hour to pack a single suitcase each and leave the premises; you will then be transported to your new accommodation.'

Mitzi and Marlena had carefully rehearsed for this moment and now swung into action, 'One hour!' Frau Zimmermann leapt to her feet and tears started to cascade down both cheeks. 'It's impossible.'

Marlena produced a similar diva performance. 'You can't

evict us from this house where we've lived all our lives.' Huge tears appeared in her eyes and welled over to drop ostentatiously onto the floor. 'What will become of us?'

'Get upstairs and pack!' The Colonel's tone was menacing. 'You now have only fifty minutes.'

The two ladies rapidly climbed up the stairs, and Maximillian followed behind more slowly. Exactly fifty minutes later three pairs of legs and three suitcases could be seen descending the fine oak staircase of the last house standing in Mahlow. Colonel Orlov opened the front door; the mother, father and daughter walked out of their house for ever and clambered on to the back of an open topped lorry.

They were taken to a three-storey house in a poor part of the suburb that had miraculously survived the bombs and shells; they climbed out of the back of the vehicle and walked towards the dark-green shrapnel-pocked front door. Maximillian pushed against it; it was unlocked and opened easily. Just as the three of them were about step inside a female voice behind them stopped them in their tracks.

'What do you want?' They turned around as one and saw a painfully thin middle-aged woman with greying unkempt hair in a threadbare Prussian blue overall.

Maximillian answered in a gentle voice, 'We've been brought here by the Russian military who have compelled us to leave our house; they said there would be rooms for us here.' He then took a step towards her holding out his right hand. 'My name is Maximilian Zimmermann. This is my wife Mitzi and my daughter Marlena; may I ask who you are?'

'I'm Bertina Schwarz. I've heard that you run the battery factory, don't you?'

'That's correct. Do you have anything to do with this house?'

'Yes, Herr Zimmermann, I'm the caretaker and I've kept

some rooms available for you and your family; it's not much but I promised the councillor I would do my best for you.' She smiled revealing one central incisor tooth missing and the remainder in a poor state of repair, but she had a friendly face. She gently pushed past the three of them. 'This way please; I apologize for the poor state of repair and the smell of the drains but together with the other residents we'll start to clean the place up tomorrow.'

'We'll help!' Mitzi realized that rolling up her sleeves and getting her hands dirty was the only way forward. 'What was that you said about a councillor?'

'She's the lady who has been put in charge of rehousing; her name is Helga Schmidt; she says that your husband treated her very kindly when she worked in his battery factory.'

Mitzi turned to her husband, who had just finished carrying the family's suitcases up to their three rooms.

'Do you remember Helga Schmidt?'

'I most certainly do! She was a most wonderful person to have among the workers of the Berlin factory; when she was there we never had any problems if she was around but whenever she was away there were frequent squabbles among the women.'

'She is here organizing the accommodation and after that she is taking on the job of supervising the *Trümmerfraue*, rubble women, who are clearing the bomb damage by hand. In fact, I'm going to join them.'

'And so will I!' Marlena bounced down the stairs from the new rooms. She gave her father a hug and kissed him on the cheek. 'But before that I must get more supplies from the pharmacy.'

'I hope you will take care of your hands, my love. Remember what Dr Greenbaum told you about the risk of infected wounds in diabetic patients when he first made your diagnosis.'

299

'I certainly have not forgotten anything which that lovely man said, I'll get hold of some strong canvas gloves to protect my hands. Poor Dr Greenbaum! Father, is what they're saying really true ... about the camps for the Jews out east?'

There was a deathly silence for a moment.

'I'm afraid it is. We should have guessed...' Maximillian said.

'How could we have known?' protested Mitzi.

'We should have made it our business to know where our neighbours disappeared to!' He looked around at the assembled people. 'There will be no words to describe the horror that is going to unfold and we will be reminded of it forever.'

Maximillian felt angry and powerless.

'What are you going to do while we're working with the rubble?' Mitzi said, trying to change the subject.

'The branch factory in Thüringen is a little bit damaged but it's still functional. When I've made the three rooms upstairs habitable I'm going to start producing batteries again. What else?'

Half an hour later Marlena came rushing back in, leaving the door open. 'Mother, Father, it's Kurt! I know where he is.'

Both Mitzi and Maximillian ran to their daughter. 'How is he? Is he coming home?'

Marlena had just returned from the Mahlow pharmacy. While she had been waiting for her insulin supplies a young woman she knew had come into the bomb-damaged building and told her about some temporary work she had been doing for two months on a farm in Schleswig-Holstein, thirty kilometres north-west of the Kiel Canal.

'Is that where she met Kurt?' Mitzi could not hide her impatience.

'That's right,' she said. 'Kurt and a friend of his had

escaped as prisoners of war of the British and had walked until they found this farmer who didn't mind where they had come from provided they could do the work.'

'There was no possible mistake?' Maximillian wanted to be absolutely certain.

'Oh no she described him perfectly and in any case he mentioned us by name.'

'Well, that is wonderful news!' The three of them embraced.

Late one evening a few days later there were excited shouts, fists punching the air and cheers among the Russian guards who supervised the brick cleaners who gathered in the shattered central square of Mahlow. Many of the occupants of the shell and bomb-damaged apartments came out onto the streets to find out what was the cause of all the noise. One of the few Russian-speaking residents walked over to the celebrating group and returned with some humiliating information.

He stood on a pile of bricks. 'A young Russian soldier named Mikhail Petrovich Minin has just climbed up on to the Victory statue on the Brandenburg Gate and planted a Hammer and Sickle flag into the crown on the head of the eagle.'

Although this act was an ignominious insult to Germany it coincided with a wonderful event for the Zimmermann family, for as the news of the flag raising sank into the minds of the Germans, Mitzi, Marlena and Maximillian saw a lone figure striding purposefully along the debris-strewn pavement.

'It's Grandmamma, it's Grandmamma!' shouted Marlena as she ran towards her grandmother. She ran up to her and flung her arms around the elderly lady with tears streaming down her cheeks.

'My darlings, how lovely to see you all again!' She embraced each member of her family in turn.

301

'I owe you all an apology because I slipped off to see my sister Brunhilde in Potsdam; she broke her ankle going down the air raid shelter steps and I had to stay to look after her. Well, you know how chaotic it's been since then! And I've only just managed to get back again.'

'We were so worried,' Mitzi smiled; 'but I know that when your mind is made up it's set in stone.' Romhilde's daughter put her arm around her mother' shoulders.

'Anyway you're safely back with us now!' Marlena gave her Grandmamma another hug; no one ever discovered how this remarkable lady found her way back from Potsdam.

# 29

## *The Bear at the Door*

The Russian troops entered the eastern suburbs of Berlin on Friday, April 27th, 1945. Their first priority proved to be the liquor stores, followed by looting more or less anything on which they could lay their hands; and then they turned to rape. The perpetrators broke into houses and apartments everywhere and sexually assaulted women of all ages. Looking for prey, they rampaged through the upper parts of the bomb-damaged buildings, and penetrated into the cellars where mothers and daughters cowered in fear.

News of this outrage rapidly spread across Berlin by word of mouth, principally from woman to woman carrying pails in the queues for the standpipes at street corners. On April 29th Suzanne's water reserves had already nearly run out. She joined the queue carrying two empty buckets. The woman in front of her who was in her mid-forties, shabbily dressed in a floral overall and had prematurely greying hair turned around to greet her.

'Morning love, it's a long wait.'

Suzanne's new acquaintance then proceeded to tell her the news about the rapes in the east of the city. 'I reckon they will be here in Dahlem tomorrow or the next day; we'll have to barricade our doors.'

Suzanne was unwise enough to make one final defence of her country. 'Goebbels said on the radio this morning

303

that the Volkssturm was already repelling the invaders and would retake Berlin in less than one week.'

The woman spat into the street. 'And that same lying bastard said in September 1941 that the one-thousand-year Reich would take Leningrad in a few days with minimal casualties; nearly 900 days later the glorious Third Reich had to retreat over the corpses of thousands of dead German husbands including mine.'

The sarcasm wasn't lost on Suzanne. 'I'm so sorry, Frau...'

'Schmidt ... Heidi Schmidt.'

'Frau Schmidt, I didn't wish to raise painful memories; please forgive me.'

'Of course, there's no reason why you should know; no one will ever know about the thousands of German husbands, sons and fathers who froze or were blown up or starved or shot in the east.'

'No one yet knows what those loved ones were doing there apart from being soldiers in those vast little observed lands.' Suzanne had at last put into words thoughts that had been gnawing at her ever since the blitzkrieg in Poland.

'We German women are going to pay for that for weeks, months ... years!' By now the two women were near the head of the queue. 'I don't know what will be in the Russians' minds – hatred or revenge or a mixture of the two – but we'll suffer.'

Suzanne felt shivers go through her spine. 'I hope not,' she said, shuffling forward. 'It's your turn next.'

Heidi Schmidt filled her two buckets and wearily made her way back to her apartment.

'See you, love,' she hurled over her shoulder as she disappeared around a street corner.

Having filled her own two pails of water Suzanne wanted to hurry home to her daughters but halfway there she had to stop and put the water down on the rubble-strewn pavement. 'Next time, I will have to bring one of the girls,' she said to no one in particular. She plodded on and with each step her load seemed heavier and when she reached the front door it seemed as though she was carrying lead, not water.

Clotilde let her mother in. 'Oh my poor darling. I'm so sorry that one of us didn't come with you.'

'Next time I will have to take one of you with me.' She sat down in the hallway while Clotilde carried the buckets, one after the other, up the stairs and hauled them up to Margit in the attic.

During the night of April 28th the Russian forces overcame the light resistance of the Volkssturm and entered the suburb of Dahlem. Although Suzanne and her daughters Clotilde and Margit had planned their going into hiding in the attic in detail, with an electric water heater, food, blankets, clothes and cutlery, in reality they had very little to eat apart from potatoes. The three of them formed a chain to pass all the items up the stepladder into their refuge.

'Margit, while you start to organize things up there your sister and I will go down to see to the front door.' The older daughter could hear their footsteps fade as they descended the two flights of stairs.

'Very well, Mother,' she replied, her flat tone betraying her anxiety about the imminent occupation of Berlin by Russian troops.

Meanwhile Suzanne and Clotilde had reached the door.

'I will do the locks while you fetch one of the cross bars, my dear.' Her younger daughter did as she was asked and helped her mother place the first of three strong wooden beams in two steel brackets on the doorframe.

Together they placed the other two beams across the front door of the Schultz apartment.

'Mother, I can't see that door being broken down without some sort of mechanical aid!' Clotilde smiled up at Suzanne. 'I'm sure we'll be safe.'

'I hope you're correct, my darling daughter.' Together they climbed back up to rejoin Margit in the attic. They sat down and waited.

All day long screams reached the ears of the terrified three and from time to time they could hear drunken shouting and a thunderous hammering on their front door.

'Mother, I'm so frightened that these Russians will break down the door and come up here.' Clotilde was trembling.

Suzanne extended a hand to each of her daughters. 'Do I need to tell either of you what these men may do to us? I don't want to frighten you, but...' Suzanne then described in plain and simple terms what had been happening elsewhere in Berlin. 'Whatever happens we must remain calm. Chances are they won't find us.'

Clotilde hugged her mother even more closely and the three women remained entwined the whole night long, waiting in the darkness. There were intermittent attempts to batter down the front door and from time to time shrieks and wails from adjacent apartments punctuated the night. By the morning of April 29th the three of them were exhausted by lack of sleep and anxiety. Margit was the first to say what they all felt but dared not come out with it.

'Mother, I'm so hungry.'

'My love, there's one thing we have in abundance and that is potatoes.'

'We've nothing to cook them in, Mother.' Margit was desolate.

'It's raw potatoes then...' Clotilde grimaced. 'At least it will fill our stomachs.'

'Let's make a start then, girls,' Suzanne walked over to a large sack in the corner of the attic, removed three medium-sized potatoes and began washing, peeling and slicing them. 'Mmmm, smells good!' Suzanne smiled at her daughters and the tension was broken as each one took

bites of the strange fruit of the earth and started chewing.
Little by little their hunger abated.

'I will have to fetch some more water today; I was going
to take one of you, but I think that it would be better if
I just took one bucket.'

'Are you sure that will be all right, Mother?'

'Yes, darling, but please don't come out.'

'You're very brave, Mother.' Clotilde was quite emotional.
'We love you.'

Suzanne got to her feet and picked up the empty pail.
'Who is coming with me to deal with the barricades?' She
turned to her younger daughter. 'I think Clotilde is more
used to it.'

Very gently Suzanne was taking command. Margit opened
the trapdoor to the attic and let down the ladder. Mother
and daughter went down to the front door together and
Clotilde let her mother out into the street.

There were very few people about; there were a few
drunken Russians who had passed out on rubble-strewn
grass banks; she walked at an unhurried pace along a
different route from her first visit to the standpipe. She
was horrified to see a man hanging from a lamppost just
like Manfred's old colleague had described. She eventually
reached the queue for the standpipe and noticed there
were far more people waiting for water than two days
earlier. She could not help but notice that the woman
standing in front of her was dishevelled and weeping
continuously.

She gently tapped the woman on the left shoulder, who
turned nervously to look at her directly. The whites of
both eyes were red; there were scratches and multiple
bruises on both of her cheeks, and her navy-blue dress
with white flowers on it had one sleeve torn off revealing
the dark purple of the flesh beneath.

The woman almost fell into her arms, sobbing.

'There were three of them ... They caught me in the stairwell of my apartment at about ten o'clock last night ... They were all drunk and stunk of booze and sweat. One of them asked me in German, "Husband"? I didn't say anything but two of them held me by each arm and forced me back onto the lowest stair ... I screamed but they punched me twice in the face. One of them took me, then the others ... It happened in about twenty minutes but it seemed an eternity...'

Suzanne held her tightly; there was nothing to say, no words that could comfort her.

'What is your name, love? Mine is Suzanne.'

'Eloise, my husband is in the East; I haven't heard from him for two years,' she buried her head in Suzanne's bosom.

Her comforter felt almost certain that this poor lady's husband was dead. 'We're nearly at the head of the queue. Let me fill your bucket?' It was a small gesture, but what else could she do?

Suzanne watched her neighbour walk away, the picture of desolation.

A week or so later, as the occupation settled in, the women of Dahlem, some dressed in rags, were sent to clear the rubble from the streets and cleaning any reusable bricks. As the three Schultz women worked together Margit commented, 'It's as if the world has stopped, Mother.'

'What do you mean, my dear?'

'No radio, no newspapers, and so we know nothing.'

The slow process of cleaning up Berlin was made particularly unpleasant for these valiant women by the piles of faeces, both human and animal, covered in swarms of flies in the bombed-out buildings.

'The smell is terrible, Mother, can we leave this building?' begged Clotilde.

'We must do our best. Tear a strip off your skirt and tie it around your mouths and noses.'

308

The girls followed their mother's example and toiled on.

Sunday, May 13th brought peels of bells all over the city and there were rumours of a victory parade taking place somewhere. The following day the Russians returned but this time it was with lorry-loads of flour and as a result queues started to form for bread. Bulletins were posted on buildings, trees and lampposts declaring the unconditional surrender of Germany to the Allies signed by Keitl, Stumpff and Friedberg. The other two items of news were that Goering had been captured following which he had burst into tears and that new, more generous ration books were being prepared.

There was a slow return to a sort of normality, but at the beginning of July Suzanne began to have sharp abdominal pains and this became associated with vomiting. Clotilde took charge. 'Mother, this can't go on; I'm taking you, and a bottle of father's Benedictine from Paris as payment, to the Gertrauden Krankenhaus ... immediately.'

Margit stayed at home to look after the apartment while her sister accompanied their mother on the slow walk to Dahlem railway station.

'It's wonderful that the railways are working again, Mother.'

They walked arm in arm onto the platform of the partially repaired station and didn't have long to wait before a locomotive puffing blue–black smoke pulled to a halt. They climbed aboard one of the two carriages and both of them were relieved to sit down.

'Ah, that's better!' Suzanne was clearly in some pain and a little short of breath.

The journey north-east to Wilmersdorf was slow but quite short, and they soon were making their way towards the Gertrauden Krankenhaus which was their local general hospital.

'You're quite correct, Clotilde, I couldn't have gone on

much longer!' She squeezed her daughter's hand with her own.

The hospital building was badly damaged but there were a number of new prefabricated single-storey annexes in the surrounding gardens. Clotilde made a few enquiries which led her to a white-haired German surgeon; she gave him the bottle of Benedictine liqueur and he wrote something down on a small piece of paper.

'I've matters in hand, Mother.' Clotilde consulted her piece of paper. 'This way.'

Twenty minutes later Suzanne was climbing into bed in a small women's ward in which there were four other beds all occupied. The nurse who had escorted mother and daughter into the room left and returned a few moments later accompanied by the same white-haired doctor to whom Clotilde had spoken earlier.

'My name is Doctor Engelbert Richter and this is nurse Hannah Peters.' He turned to Clotilde. 'Would you kindly wait outside while I examine your mother and then I will speak with both of you together.' The patient's daughter left the room. 'Nurse Peters, the screens please.'

When the medical activity was finished Nurse Peters brought Clotilde back into the room and cleared away the screens and removed other items on a trolley.

'Well now, Fräulein Schultz, you were quite right to bring your mother here today.'

'What do you think the diagnosis is, Doctor Richter?' Suzanne was typically direct.

'I think you have an ovarian tumour that is undergoing recurrent torsion.' He smiled at her. ' Shall I explain further, Frau Schultz?'

'I understand most of what you've said but I have two questions.'

'Go ahead, my dear.'

'This tumour ... is it cancer?'

'Probably not.' The elderly doctor's smile was reassuring. 'During the war we've learned to rely on a clinical diagnosis based on taking a history and examining the patient without sophisticated tests; we usually get it right.'

'Thank you. And what will happen if I don't have an operation?'

'It will eventually twist so much that the arterial blood supply will be cut off. It becomes gangrenous and ruptures, causing fatal peritonitis.'

Suzanne managed a smile. 'I'm in your hands, Doctor Richter.'

Three hours later her operation was performed and the diagnosis was correct. Two days afterwards the grateful patient was sitting out of bed in an old armchair, drinking some delicious clear chicken soup and watching Clotilde leave. Her daughter had told her that she had had a telephone call from Manfred and that she, Clotilde, was going to visit him.

After her daughter had left, the customary silence descended on the room.

'Now you listen to me, ladies,' Suzanne said, finally unable to take it any more. She looked around the room and saw two trembling girls aged twelve or thirteen years together with two much older women in their late sixties or even early seventies. 'There's nothing, absolutely nothing, that is not made better by talking about it.'

There was no response.

'I'm going to ring this bell then I will ask Nurse Peters to put the screens around the bed of the first of you four who is prepared to let me come and sit on the edge and have a private little chat.' She reached for the bell and slowly one of the girls raised her arm. The bell rang, Nurse Peters bustled in and Suzanne whispered in her right ear. The nurse nodded and pulled the screens around the bed of the young girl with her arm still raised; there was a flicker of a smile on her face which was framed by long fair hair. Suzanne heaved herself out of the chair, which still caused her a fair amount of pain, slipped on her shoes, put a blanket from her bed around her shoulders, crossed to the screened-off area and went inside.

'Hello.' The pale freckled face said the first word that Suzanne had heard from her.

'Hello, my name's Suzanne; I live in Dahlem and have been there for a long time.' She took one of the girl's hands in both of hers. 'My husband is a teacher in a boy's school but was conscripted into the military four years ago and I've two grown-up daughters.'

'Are they all right?'

'We hid in the attic and they never found us.' She squeezed the girl's hand.

'My name is Gisela, I wasn't so lucky. When the Russians came I was staying in my grandmother's apartment...' She nodded in the direction of one of the elderly women. 'That's her over there; they damaged her too.' Now she had started she kept going. 'There were eight of them who broke into our small home; all Russian with close-cropped hair: three of them boys not much older than me and too drunk to do anything.' Tears rolled down her cheeks. 'Two big men took Grandmamma into her bedroom and she started screaming; my grandfather, you know, died thirty years ago...'

She continued with her account; it was so terrible, hellish, but Suzanne remained calm, listening carefully and patiently. At last the girl finished. '...I opened the window and remember shouting for help.' Suzanne put an arm around the girl's shoulders. 'We've already had surgery but we've been told that there's more to come.'

Suzanne kissed Gisela on both cheeks, returned to her bed and rang her little bell. Nurse Peters came and removed the screens and walked over to Suzanne. 'Thank you, Frau Schultz that poor girl has not spoken until today.'

The following day Dr Richter came into the small hospital ward.

'Good morning, Frau Schultz, how are you feeling today?' His smile was a reassuring oasis in the desert of tragedy and destruction that was Berlin in July 1945.

'Good morning, Dr Richter. I'm feeling much better today; I had a good night's sleep and hardly feel any pain at all but I do find that walking is still a little painful.'

'That will be the surgical wound; it will feel much better when the stitches have been removed.' He felt her pulse while the ever attentive nurse pulled the screens around the patient, drew back the bedclothes, and gently removed the dressing, exposing a healthy-looking abdominal wound extending downwards from her belly button with white thread stitches neatly holding it together. She then took some forceps from her trolley and used them to dip a cotton-wool ball in some ether she had poured from a brown-glass bottle into a little galley pot beforehand and gently cleaned the skin around the wound.

Dr Richter gently palpated Suzanne's abdomen.

'Nice and soft,' he murmured.

He then took his stethoscope and listened to her abdomen for a full two minutes: 'Normal bowel sounds, I expect you've been to the toilet?'

'Yes, Doctor!' She looked up at him hopefully. 'I think you can go home tomorrow and come back in ten days to have your stitches removed. I am sorry that you're not going to stay in hospital for the full two weeks but we've a large number of patients waiting for surgical treatment.'

'I quite understand.' Suzanne was really very pleased. 'May I ask you a question, Doctor?'

'Of course.'

'How old are you?' She smiled sweetly at him.

'I'm seventy-four and apart from my creaking knees I feel like thirty-four.' He thought for a moment. 'Coming

313

out of retirement to work in the war has been good for me.'

'It's certainly saved my life, Doctor.' She looked towards the door. 'Hello, dear!'

The doctor turned to leave. 'Your mother will be fine; good afternoon to you both.'

'Good afternoon and thank you,' mother and daughter said in unison.

'What news do you have, love?'

'I'm catching the eight o'clock train to Munich tonight, Mother. I will then get a local train to the rehabilitation centre at Wöllershof where father is now being treated.' She smiled at her mother. 'Things are going better at last.'

'I think you're right, my darling daughter. Oh, let me introduce you to a new friend.' She waved across the hospital ward. 'Gisela my dear, come over here.'

The twelve-year-old girl responded immediately to the softly spoken request; in spite of her wounds her face lit up and she bounded out of bed and came over to Suzanne's bed.

'Hello, Clotilde!' she giggled. 'I've been eavesdropping.'

'It's lovely to meet you, Gisela.' She kissed her on the cheek. 'I have to go now; my mother will explain why this is such a short visit.' She kissed Suzanne goodbye and left the little hospital ward.

That evening Clotilde caught the eight o'clock train at the Anhalter Bahnhof. The locomotive drew hesitantly out of the heavily bomb-damaged railway station on the late-July evening. It was still daylight and the seventeen-year-old girl was horrified to see block after block of apartment buildings flattened to the ground, lamp posts at impossible angles; burnt-out cars and military vehicles. Eventually the railway train left the devastated city and passed into the countryside shrouded in dusk and the weary young woman dozed off to sleep. She awoke when the locomotive pulled into Leipzig and came to a halt with a muffled announcement over the loudspeaker system: there would be a twenty-minute delay before the train moved on south; Clotilde stood up and looked out of the window and saw a large urn with steam pouring out of the top and an old woman with a bright-green headscarf tied under her chin ladling soup into paper cups for a queue of passengers. The smell reached the girl's window – it was a delicious aroma; she stepped down onto the platform and joined her fellow passengers.

Once back on her seat she held the cup in both hands enjoying the warmth before she took a sip; it was a thick meat and potato mixture that immediately warmed her throughout her body; when she had emptied her cup she felt revitalized and strong. Finally a peaceful dreamless sleep engulfed her exhausted body. She slept through the brief halt in the early-morning hours at Nuremberg and awoke as the amazing journey through war-ravaged Germany came to an end in Munich railway station. She had little difficulty in finding the local branch line to Wöllershof; she waited three hours for her connection but finally arrived at the rehabilitation centre and was conducted by a smart white-uniformed nurse to a room full of men. They were either lying on beds or sitting in armchairs supported by pillows, which is how she found the grey-haired man, with crutches leaning against his left shoulder, when she came to a stop behind the nurse; he was staring into space and there was no hint of recognition after five years of family separation.

Clotilde looked at the nurse who nodded. 'Father, it's me, your daughter Clotilde.' She bent forward and kissed him on his right cheek. Slowly, very slowly, recognition dawned on the broken man's face; tears rolled down both cheeks.

'Clotilde, is it you … is it really you?' The eyes of the

formerly brown-haired schoolteacher were pleading with the young woman who stood before him.

'Yes, Father, it really is me!' The two weeping souls embraced.

# 30

## *Hunger*

Marlena, Maximillian and Romhilde sat at the improvised dining table in their squalid accommodation; in reality the 'table' consisted of two planks of wood supported by two old trestles; it was very awkward to sit at but was made presentable by Mitzi's tablecloths. She had embroidered seven pieces of white silk cut from a parachute that had floated down with a dead British bomber pilot attached during one of the heavy bombing raids on Berlin. Maximillian's wife and Marlena's mother was attending to a steaming saucepan on a paraffin heater perched precariously on an upturned wooden packing case.

'The delicious aroma coming from this pot is potato soup!' She smiled at her family but it was a thin humourless countenance.

'Please, Mother, don't say "to be followed by boiled potatoes"; I can't stand it any more; it no longer takes away the hunger and my diabetes is becoming incredibly difficult to control.'

Mitzi put both her hands on Marlena's shoulders. 'I apologize, my love. I'm sick of potatoes too; but what can I do!' She was nearing the end of her tether.

Maximillian looked at each woman in turn. 'I've been thinking what the best thing to do is and it's time we went to find Kurt.' All the ladies perked up immediately. 'He is probably eating very well on the Bruhns farm.' Marlena

317

was brightening up by the minute. 'We're just getting more and more miserable here in Berlin.'

'What will you do about managing the branch in Thüringen, my dear?' Before her husband could answer there was a furious knocking on the fragile front door.

'I'll go before that poor door falls into the apartment.' Maximillian stood up and left the room.

Romhilde had remained silent up until this moment. 'I think we're in for a very pleasant surprise.' She smiled at her daughter and granddaughter.

Maximillian returned. 'You will all be amazed when you see our visitors!' He stood to one side and there behind him stood a very dishevelled but large-as-life Lothar with an arm around the shoulders of Lorelei.

'Hello, my dears.' Romhilde went and shook hands with both of them and each kissed her on the cheek. 'You found your way here without any difficulty?'

'Oh yes thank you, Romhilde.' Lorelei was dressed in a partly torn navy-blue tunic, light-blue shirt and khaki trousers. 'That was such a fantastic idea of yours all those years ago to have a box number in the post office at Seebad Ahlbeck on Usedom Island.'

'Lorelei is quite right; the money and information that you sent us was a godsend; the Nazis never spotted it and you saved our lives when you told us to get out of our house.' Lothar put his other arm around Romhilde's shoulders and she wasn't bothered by his mud-stained dungarees. The other three people in the room looked at this trio open-mouthed, Mitzi broke the stunned silence.

'Am I to understand that my own mother has been a secret agent involved in some grand espionage under our very noses.'

'Absolutely correct, Frau Zimmermann ... a very successful one as well.' Lothar was clearly relieved to be in the presence of this family. 'Both of us now feel safe after months of signalling to the RAF the location of the Peenemünde V2 rocket factory and launchpad.'

'Things are so confused at present that I've advised them to lie low for a few months.' The older woman spread her hands. 'The problem is that I don't know what to suggest they do now.'

A broad grin spread across Maximillian's face. He briefly explained that at present there was no one in charge of the Thüringen factory. 'It's the last of the three factories but it's really working very well. It just needs supervision: would you two take it over while the rest of the family sets out to find Kurt?' He looked expectantly at Lothar and Lorelei. 'Before you ask there's food down there; the staff have found wild boar in the forest and one or two have already been caught and slaughtered for their meat.'

'That is very nice for us but couldn't you've brought some to Berlin?'

'The authorities have put a veto on any such movement of food for fear of a riot,' He looked at Mitzi. 'Can we have them here tonight and I will take them down on the train tomorrow?'

'Of course we'll manage for these two lovely people; it's so wonderful to see them again!' She grimaced. 'I apologize for the terrible apartment.'

The following morning Maximillian accompanied Lothar and Lorelei to the factory, got them settled in and was able to return to Mahlow on the same day. He found Mitzi, Marlena and Romhilde already prepared to set off to find Kurt the next day; they had also had a successful shopping expedition which enabled Mitzi to cook a delicious-smelling pork bratwurst.

'I used that one-half of a gold sovereign that you gave me; it opened cupboards, drawers and back rooms that I never thought existed and we were treated like royalty; I will also have enough food left over for our trip.'

Maximillian embraced his wife. 'I think you've all done brilliantly; I almost feel like staying on in this luxurious apartment.'

Marlena glowered at her father. 'It may be a joke, Father, but my sense of humour is run dry.' Her face reflected what she was saying. 'I can't wait for us to be on our way to Schleswig-Holstein tomorrow.'

That night they all slept well with full stomachs. Maximillian reflected to himself that 'Starvation is worse than rape', then he thought further and murmured: 'Only a woman can make that judgement.' Mitzi was fast asleep and his tired body and exhausted mind joined her.

At nine o'clock the following morning the family Zimmermann set off from their squalid accommodation and walked to Mahlow railway station, from there they took the city train to Lehrter Bahnhof. The old mainline station had been heavily bombed but an amazing partial clearance by the women of Berlin had opened a railway line to Hamburg. The locomotive plus two carriages was waiting, idly puffing light-grey smoke from its stack; the Zimmermanns and Romhilde boarded and took their seats. Twenty minutes later they began their journey north-west to the province of Schleswig-Holstein.

'We're on our way at last.' Maximillian was in a relaxed mood as they wound their way out of the devastated city. The railway train took them into the more or less flat north German countryside. Roads were visible crossing the mainly agricultural land and Marlena could see people with luggage on their heads or handcarts or horse-drawn vehicles of various descriptions mostly moving in the same direction as them.

'There are a lot of people on the move, Father; I wonder where they are going?'

'They're refugees, Marlena; they are fleeing from the Russians.'

'I don't blame them after our experience though it could have been so very much worse. But how do we know that they will come this far west?' She looked enquiringly at her father.

He shrugged his shoulders. 'I don't think the Russians will come to this part of our country but we're now in the hands of foreigners and from all points of view I think we're quite right to find Kurt and Farmer Bruhns.'

'I agree completely.' Romhilde didn't speak very often but Maximillian was always reassured by what she had to say. 'Do you know how to find him?'

'A very good question!' Mitzi took after her mother and was a woman of few words but she made them count. 'If I know my son he is already the master of his destiny and will have established a very good situation.'

'I'm very pleased to hear it. That young man will go far in my opinion: of course he will have to find the right wife to be *totally* successful.'

The journey was delayed from time to time where the locomotive slowed to pass over damaged lines, but their trip was helped along by a cold snack handed out by Mitzi and they eventually drew into the railway station in Hamburg in the early afternoon. The scene that greeted them was familiar to the travellers – bomb damage devastation.

'It's worse than Berlin. I think we should move on as soon as we can, Father.'

There were general noises of agreement. Maximillian had done some research and had discovered the little town of Rendsburg on the south side of the Kiel Canal and that a once-a-day train service from Hamburg had been restored. He found a booking office in the ruined station.

'It leaves at four o'clock, sir.' There was an old-fashioned politeness from the clerk that seemed to Maximillian to be an echo from an era before the war.

The timing was good. During the short trip Maximilian

told them what to expect. 'Rendsburg is on the south side of the Kiel Canal and the bridge that this train crossed in former times is badly damaged but there's a pedestrian tunnel that is the longest in the world and is usable.' Sure enough, they found the tunnel quite easily shortly after leaving the train and Maximillian led the three women down the steps into the dark and dank passageway. There was a click and some light appeared in the gloom.

'You don't manufacture batteries without having some benefits, my love!'

Mitzi's comment was greeted with a mixture of giggles and relief as they followed the illumination from the torch. Eventually the little group of people emerged on the north side of the canal and, to their surprise, found themselves on a road crowded with refugees. For a moment they did not know what to do.

'We can't stand here all day, Father.' Marlena was visibly tiring.

Maximillian waved at the driver of a donkey and cart with a load of two mattresses; he pulled over to the side of the road and came to a halt.

'How can I help you?'

'Do you know a Farmer Bruhns?'

'I most certainly do, sir; I'm on my way there now – we expect to arrive at the farm within two hours, if this modern piece of equipment here lasts the course.'

'I would be most grateful if you and your fine piece of modern engineering would take these lovely ladies and myself to the good farmer.'

Fortunately this good-natured banter was well appreciated by the driver. 'With pleasure, sir; it's Wolfgang at your service.'

The three women climbed up onto the mattresses, followed by Maximillian, and the donkey and cart, together with its passengers on their improvised upholstery, set off at a steady but quite slow pace along the road in a westerly direction; leaving the Kiel Canal curving towards the south-west.

'This is really very comfortable; I'm beginning to become rather fond of Farmer Bruhns!' Romhilde had never said anything like this before. 'Mother, you're showing me a side of you I've never seen before. I can see Farmer Bruhns' wife will have some competition.' Mitzi had a broad grin on her face as she looked admiringly at her mother.

'There's still life in me, my dear.'

'Hidden depths as well,' Marlena chortled.

'There certainly are, my dear. In 1925 I danced all night in the ballroom of the Hotel Adlon and none of the young men could match my "Lindy Hop"; one by one they collapsed into chairs exhausted.'

'It must have been a great sight, Grandmamma.' Marlena's voice held genuine admiration.

'I wonder if we'll ever see those days again?'

'Oh yes, Germany will recover and happy times will eventually return.' Romhilde had certainty in her voice. 'It may take years and will not be the same, but it *will* happen.'

'We're making good progress,' said Wolfgang, pointing to a thin wisp of smoke rising from the horizon. 'That's Farmer Bruhn's house.' The driver gave his donkey a gentle prod of encouragement. 'His wife still likes to have a warm fire in the evenings and he finds lighting it a little difficult.'

The donkey seemed to instinctively know it was near home as he picked up speed, and slowly the wisp in the distance grew closer; the cart came to a halt at a wide five-bar wooden gate. Wolfgang climbed down from the cart and opened the creaking structure and as he did so a fair-haired young man in a red-and-white check shirt with rolled-up sleeves and light-blue canvas trousers came striding along the path to offer assistance. He had an air of strength together with self-assuredness.

Slowly light dawned on Marlena. 'Mother, it's Kurt!'

Everyone sat up and screwed up their eyes against the setting sun. 'It is! It's him! We've found Kurt!' The passengers on the mattresses slithered off the back of the cart, their excitement sweeping away any thoughts of dignity.

'Marlena is right; it's our son Kurt.' Maximillian ran forward followed by the three women.

As they approached, Kurt recognized them and also ran forward with his arms spread wide; they met and hugged as a group with Romhilde gallantly joining them a little later and a little short of breath. The astonished young man kissed his mother, grandmother and sister.

Maximillian embraced his son, 'It's wonderful to see you ... You've grown up very quickly.'

'Thank you, Father. I'm still amazed and thrilled that you've found me.' He put his arms around his mother and grandmother. 'Come into the farmhouse and meet Farmer Bruhns.'

They walked along the stone path followed by Kurt's father and sister with Wolfgang bringing up the rear with his donkey whom he was promising an excellent dinner as reward for his day's work. As they approached the front door it was flung open and a well-built man in navy-blue dungarees, Wellington boots and his red shirt had the right arm folded up over his missing upper limb.

'This is my boss. Please meet my very hungry family, Herr Bruhns.'

'Delighted to meet you!' There was a lot of left hand shaking. 'Kurt has become my right arm!' Farmer Bruhns convulsed himself with great guffaws of laughter as he ushered his guests into the warm farmhouse. Standing beside the log fire was a tall young man smiling at the joyous reunion; he stooped to draw up chairs for the three ladies.

Romhilde was characteristically direct. 'And who are you, handsome young man?'

'I'm Werner Hofman and I accompanied your grandson when we decided to leave the protective custody of the British and pursue agricultural careers with Farmer Bruhns. We've been well trained in milking, looking after the herd and, what's more, we've been well fed.'

'I can see that!' Romhilde looked over at her seventeen-year-old grandson and saw a sturdy well-nourished young man. 'Have you been the only workers passing through here?'

'Oh no but we've stayed longer than any others.' Werner pulled up a chair and sat down. 'There were two men working here already.' He looked up at Farmer Bruhns who was in animated conversation with Maximillian. 'Their names were Peter and Max who had the same birthday as Kurt.' He smiled and seemed to be enjoying telling the story to Romhilde.

'Where are they now?'

'They left a few days after we arrived; they said they were going to South America!' Werner lowered his voice. 'We think they may have been Nazis.' He continued in lower tones. 'Kurt and I came to the conclusion that the boss knew they were leaving and was pleased to see the back of them; our arrival was very convenient.'

Their tête-à-tête was interrupted by the door at the far end of the room being flung open and a tall handsome woman in her mid-thirties stood with her hands on her hips, her ample bosom and posterior encased in a brilliant white apron. The aroma that emerged from around her was a mouth-watering one of boiled meat, vegetables and potatoes; her deep booming voiced announced 'Supper's ready!'

The men hurriedly arranged the chairs around the table. The lady of the house brought in a huge steaming earthenware tureen and set it on a thick matching brown plate.

'Gentlemen, serve the ladies and then yourselves! Bruhns will lay out the dishes and spoons.'

The farmer meekly but skilfully carried the plates in the crook of his left arm, tilting the pile at each place setting, allowing the top one to slide off accurately so that it landed exactly where it was directed.

'Come and be seated, ladies.' The powerful lady returned from the kitchen with a handful of spoons.

'Here you are, Helmut; hand those around then come and sit by me.'

Kurt's family looked on in astonishment as he responded to the unfamiliar name with a wink at his mother.

'Have plenty to eat, Mitzi; you look as though need it.'

There were a few moments of silence except for the sound of spoons on plates. Marlena was the first to break the spell after swallowing a spoonful of meat and cabbage.

'Frau Bruhns, this is a feast and it's absolutely delicious.'

The farmer's wife basked in the murmurs of agreement that echoed Kurt's sister's heartfelt praise. Her husband's left hand gave her a robust congratulatory slap on the back; his wife's facial expression didn't register pleasure.

'Frau Bruhns is a great cook,' Kurt joined in. 'She manages to produce mouth-watering food in the most difficult times.' He smiled at the gathering around the table. 'When I go out to work in the mornings I have delicious sausages in my lunch box.'

The lady who was the subject of the compliment showed a light blush in her cheeks.

'Quite right too.' Farmer Bruhns wasn't offended by his wife's treatment of Kurt whom she called Helmut; 'Good workers need properly feeding.'

Frau Bruhns had plenty to say. 'We've had many refugees passing through this farm wanting work; my husband has been very good to them but some wanted money or food for no work.' She looked around at her audience. 'A short while ago two older women came here to the farm; they were in their forties and dressed in warm clothes including leather coats together with fur-lined hats. They were definitely weird and we saw them looking furtively at Helmut, whispering and plotting.'

Farmer Bruhns took up the story. 'We thought they were planning to seduce Helmut ... Kurt ... kidnap him and take him away to be their toyboy.'

Frau Bruhns stood up. 'I would never have let that happen; those women would have destroyed this wonderful young man.' Again she looked around her. 'I want you the lovely family of Helmut to know that you can stay here for as long as you wish, and certainly until you all have gained some weight and no longer look as though you're starving.'

'That is very generous of you, Frau Bruhns.' Mitzi sounded both grateful and relieved. 'We'll all work to help you and your husband while we're here of course.'

'Tell them what they may have to do, Kurt.' The farmer was smiling. 'Not only milking the cows but also the maternity work.'

Marlena looked puzzled and Kurt explained.

'A week ago we had a calf that became stuck while it was being born. I saw the mouth with a swollen tongue protruding from it but beside the head were hooves.' Kurt increased the drama by pointing exaggeratedly to his own face and feet. 'When I saw the situation I ran in to tell the boss and he went to fetch our neighbour Herr Fredericks.'

'He is a very helpful man and he has two arms.' Farmer Bruhns laughed uproariously at his joke. 'He also knows a lot about cows!'

'He came over on his horse very quickly, had one look at the poor calf, took off his coat and grasped the hooves and pulled.' Kurt put his hands together and imitated pulling really hard but there was no movement.

327

'What happened then?' Marlena was fascinated.

'He told me to put my arms around his waist and when he gave the word we pulled together. First the hind legs came out, then he was able to pull out the front legs and finally the head...' Kurt finished the story with a flourish of his right hand. '*Voilà!*'

The family Zimmermann stayed with Farmer Bruhns and his wife who mysteriously referred to Kurt as Helmut for two weeks. They were now in a much improved nutritional state for their journey back to Berlin.

'Please return here as soon as you wish.' Farmer Bruhns had established a very nice relationship with Maximillian and put great value on his business acumen.

'It will be difficult to keep us away from your wife's delicious cooking!' Mitzi had a smile on her face and a spring in her step as she set off with her mother, Marlena and Maximillian back to Berlin.

Farmer Bruhns had arranged transport for the start of the return journey and the whole trip was much easier and much less uncertain than when they had set out to find Kurt. Berlin was still seriously damaged but there had been further clearance carried out by the city's women. Maximillian managed to find some improved accommodation; he made a trip to Thüringen and returned pleased with the way Lothar and Lorelei were handling things.

In July American soldiers entered the city but Maximillian was disappointed that the suburb of Mahlow remained under Russian occupation. The year drew to a close and still the occupants of the eastern suburbs struggled with shortages of food and fuel.

Some things did gradually improve, for the telephone exchange was up and running again. And thus it was at the end of January 1946 the telephone rang in the Zimmermann apartment.

'Hello, is that you, Kurt?' Mitzi's face lit up.

'It is indeed, Mother. Farmer Bruhns feels that you all need a week's holiday and after that I will probably return to Berlin with you.'

'How wonderful, my darling, I can't wait to tell the family. I know they will all want to come to see you as soon as possible.' She waved at Romhilde and Marlena with a huge smile. 'I'm sure that we'll be able to make the trip the day after tomorrow.'

The Zimmermann family spent a very happy and nourishing first week of February 1946 in Schleswig-Holstein, and following this they returned to Mahlow and reality, but this time Kurt was back home with his family.

# 31

## *Carer and Student*

Clotilde found an unoccupied chair and drew it alongside her father's armchair.

'How long can I stay with my father, Nurse?'

The starched white uniformed nurse spoke English with an accent that the young woman from Berlin assumed to be American. 'Normally we allow one hour visiting because rehabilitation is necessarily a time-consuming process, but your father needs cheering up, so I think we can bend the rules in this instance.' She leaned forward and stroked Manfred's cheek. 'I'm sure you would like your daughter to stay a little longer than the usual one hour?'

A flicker of a smile played across his pale lips. 'Yes.'

'I've lots to tell you, Father.' Clotilde turned back to the nurse. 'Is there somewhere I can stay tonight and then I will be able to come back in to see my father before I catch the train for Berlin tomorrow evening?'

'It's most unusual but I will see what I can arrange,' she smiled. 'My name is Nurse June Cash ... I can see that your visit will greatly help your father.' She turned to leave. 'Would you like a cup of coffee, I mean *real* coffee?'

'That is very kind, yes please.' Clotilde liked Nurse Cash and felt that it was in the sick man's interest that she had a positive relationship with the woman who had just left the room. She turned back to her father. 'I've brought letters from Margit and Mother who is still in hospital after

330

an operation for an ovarian cyst but she is making a good recovery; we paid for the hospital and the doctor with a bottle of the Benedictine liqueur that you sent us! It was truly a lifesaver.' She handed the letters to Manfred. 'Their eyes really lit up when they saw that black bell-shaped bottle with the red seal.' She grinned at her father. 'But you know Mother; she is doing the doctor's work for them now.'

Manfred gave her a weak smile back. She opened the drawer in the small table beside his chair; it was empty except for a toothbrush and a tube of toothpaste. 'Do you have a comb, Father?'

'I don't think so.'

'Well, never mind then.' Clotilde reached inside her shoulder bag and produced her own comb. 'Your hair was a deep brown when you were conscripted into the military!' She combed his hair forward and then created a neat straight parting in the thin grey strands. 'That looks much better, Father.' She looked at the bulky dressing on his left hip pushing his pyjama jacket upwards. 'Does that hurt?'

'When I try to walk, it does.'

The young woman far from home in a strange rehabilitation centre run by American occupiers realized that she was on the wrong route to raise her father's spirit.

'Father, do you remember Fräulein Müller, my lovely lovely pussycat?'

'I do indeed!' His face lit up immediately. 'How is she?'

'She is very well. Mother thinks it's because she is the best-fed lady in Berlin.'

Manfred produced a much improved smile. 'I'm sure she is.'

'Do you remember how we found her, Father?' Clotilde had sparked some interest at last.

'If I remember correctly she found us and jumped into

331

Margit's saddlebag when we were out on our bicycles on Rügen Island.'

'You're absolutely right, Father, and she sent you this kiss.' She wrapped her arms around Manfred's shoulders and gave him a prolonged and affectionate kiss on his left cheek.

After Clotilde had stood up her father laughed for the first time since she had arrived. 'I don't think I will ever wash that part of my face again; it's the most valuable kiss I've ever received.'

Clotilde thought she detected a glimmer of a mischievous grin; she was a much happier daughter when a loud rustling heralded the starched white uniform of Nurse June Cash marching briskly towards them.

'I can see you've had a wonderful effect on our patient. I could hear you talking from outside the open window on my way back from finding you a bed for the night in the staff quarters.' She spoke encouragingly. 'Fräulein Müller must be a very special person to have brought out laughter in your father for the first time since he arrived here.'

'Oh she certainly is a very special lady and is so very much looking forward to his coming home; do you have any idea when that will happen?'

'Wish your father a good night's sleep and I will show you to your room and give you a medical report while we're walking together.'

Nurse June Cash seemed to be a very senior person in the unit; once or twice Clotilde thought she had seen soldiers and other nurses alike saluting her.

'Yes, Captain!' The seventeen-year-old had a twinkle in her deep-blue eyes; she turned back to her father. 'We're a family again! I hope you sleep well tonight and I will come back and see you in the morning.' She took his right hand in both of hers, lifted it up and pressed it to her cheek. 'Goodnight, Father.'

She was hugely gratified when he said: 'Goodnight, young lady, and Fräulein Müller.'

She walked side by side with June out into the warm early-August evening air.

'I'm sure you've noticed, Clotilde, that your father has been injured both psychologically and physically. The doctor who is in charge of him thinks that he has been under enormous stress throughout the war; this was made much worse by being accused of being a Nazi.'

'Oh yes, he was conscripted at a much older age as a punishment by his colleagues for being *against* the Nazis and in France was a court translator working in such a way that he saved many of the French Resistance people by mistranslating the evidence.'

'I expect he was under more or less constant stress of being found out by the Gestapo. Was he able to say anything about this in his telephone calls to you?' Nurse June was very interested.

'Absolutely nothing! The irony was he was shot accidentally by the French Resistance, then accused of being a Nazi by the Americans and I think no one cared for him properly after he left Paris.' Clotilde's voice was sombre but not accusatory.

'I regret to say that I think you're quite right. I'm sure there were times when your father felt very low and that would have been made much worse by all the poison from his infected wound passing into his bloodstream affecting his brain.' The nurse stopped walking and turned to her patient's daughter. 'I can only apologize to you ... We've reached your accommodation.'

They shook hands.

'Thank you, Nurse June; you've been very kind. What time may I visit my father tomorrow?'

'I think it will be fine after his dressing has been changed and he has been helped out of bed into his armchair,

333

which will be about eleven o'clock in the morning.' She handed Clotilde a ticket. 'This will enable you to have some breakfast in the staff canteen.'

'Thank you and good night, Nurse June.'

Clotilde went into the single-storey building the nurse had indicated to her and was met by an elderly slim little lady in a light-blue overall.

'Come in, love, your bed is this way; would you like a hot drink of milk before you go to sleep?'

'Oh yes please, Fräulein...'

'Frau Greta Schneider; my husband was a sergeant-major and never returned from Stalingrad.'

'I'm so sorry, Frau Schneider.'

'It doesn't matter. He knew what he was doing; he had been in the Nazi Party since 1938: after that he rapidly rose in the ranks.'

She showed Clotilde to a little room with a newly-made bed. 'You get into that and I will bring the hot milk with a big spoonful of sugar.'

Ten minutes later the milk had been drunk, a very tired young head lay on the clean white pillow and deep refreshing sleep overtook Clotilde.

The following day the seventeen-year-old woman from Berlin awoke on a bright summer's morning. She washed and dressed and a delicious smell of toast and sausages wafted under her nose; it lead her to a small kitchen.

'My word, you look a new woman, my dear.' Frau Schneider was standing in front of a small gas cooker with a sizzling frying pan perched on top with what Clotilde could only describe as a pre-war aroma coming from it.

'I had a wonderful night's sleep!'

A plate was put in front of Manfred's hungry daughter. 'I have to go to the staff canteen and give them my ticket for breakfast there.' She handed the pink slip of paper to Frau Schneider who took it and put it in her pocket. 'You slept right through breakfast which finished at half past nine. I looked in on you twice; you were so very peaceful that I felt it would be a shame to disturb you: so I've done a special extra breakfast.'

The smile was beaming lovely warmth towards Clotilde. 'There's plenty of time to get that inside you before visiting time.'

By eleven o'clock she was walking towards her father's armchair and was thrilled by his cheery smile and enthusiastic wave.

'You look so much better today, Father.' She sat beside him and held his hand. 'My dressing was changed earlier today and the nurses were very pleased because they were able to remove some dead bone with a piece of my trousers attached to it.' He squeezed his daughter's hand. 'I feel better already.'

'Wasn't it painful while they were poking inside your open wound?' Clotilde was horrified. 'Amazingly I didn't feel any pain at all.' He looked at his crutches. 'My next step is learning to walk again!'

'Your next step, Father? Then you've already made it!'

'Thank you, my darling daughter. You've made such a difference.' A sad expression crossed his face. 'I expect you will have to return to Berlin soon.'

'I've made an appointment with Nurse Cash who is going to give me a written report to take back with me.' She lowered her voice. 'She seems to know more about your recovery than any doctor.'

Manfred became more cheerful: 'There's a cloud lifting; I'm remembering more and more about my Clotilde, Margit and Suzanne.'

'Father, we're going to be back together again one day, but next month is September and it's time for me to get back into school to prepare for university.'

'You're quite right. I was so proud of you when my

Clotilde did so well at school to be advanced a year.' He patted the back of her hand.

'You remember that, Father! How wonderful – what a change since yesterday.' She stood up. 'I am going for my appointment with super-efficient Nurse June Cash.'

The increasingly confident young woman walked happily out into the midday August warmth. She easily found the nursing office and knocked on the door.

'Come in, young lady.' Nurse June was sitting behind a small desk with an open file in front of her. 'This is a full medical report on your father compiled by the US Army Medical Service which includes an opinion on both physical and psychological injuries.' She tapped the file in front of her. 'Eventually these papers will travel with your father when he leaves this centre.'

'Thank you.'

'My dear there's still a long journey before we reach that happy point.' She opened the folder, took out an X-ray picture and held it up to the light coming through a large window behind her. 'This is your father's left hip joint.' Nurse June's finger pointed out the shattered bone. 'That missing part of the bone will be filled in by nature and then strengthened by calcium being deposited from the bloodstream.'

'How long will this take?'

'Providing all the dead bone and clothing has come out it will be six months before we can get him onto crutches. During that time he will have physiotherapy to build up the surrounding muscles; continued dressings until the wound has healed and he has no pain or fever.'

'That is a very long time.'

'It is but during that time he will also be helped to recover psychologically.'

'Do you mean a psychiatrist?'

'Yes.'

'I don't think he would like that; he is a very independent-minded person.' Clotilde grimaced.

'It won't be forced on him but will be offered as support.' The nurse produced her most disarming smile. 'I certainly know he will benefit in every way by family visits.'

Clotilde smiled back. 'Thank you very much, Nurse Cash; I feel he is in very good hands.'

She stood up, accepted the firm handshake from the American and went back to spend a little more time with her father before making her way to the railway station for her return journey to Berlin. When the moment came there were tears but now it was Manfred who was comforting his daughter from his armchair.

'I will return, Father.'

'I know that, my darling daughter; I wish you the safest possible trip home and will be thinking of you in your studies; give my love to Margit and your mother.'

Clotilde squeezed his hand, kissed his cheek. '*Aufwiedersehen, Vater.*' She wiped her eyes and set off to catch the train home.

The first telephone call from Manfred came in mid-November. Suzanne, now fully recovered, picked up the instrument.

'Manfred is that you, my darling? Is it really you?'

'It is.' The voice was stronger than Suzanne had expected. 'I'm so happy to hear your voice and so very much has happened since we last spoke together.'

'I know, my darling; I've been so worried about you!' She paused and sat on a chair by the telephone. 'You know that I've had an operation?'

'I do, Clotilde told me about it; I hope you're making a good recovery.'

'I am but things are so difficult here in Berlin. There are food shortages; fuel for heating is a problem and we have to help in cleaning up the city.'

'I understand!' Manfred felt for his family. 'I think it's much the same in Munich but conditions are better here in the rehabilitation centre. I'm getting stronger although I've not attempted to walk yet.'

'I think you're in the best place. I must tell you Manfred that I'm proud of my fellow women here in Berlin. They have started to clear the ruined city brick by brick with damaged but determined hands, they disregard broken fingernails, grazed knuckles and calloused palms; these heroines of the ruins handle broken pipes, fallen beams, electric cables and lumps of concrete.'

'You're quite right to be proud of them; they are the beginning of a new age.'

'We plan to come and see you in January when I think things will be easier and I will feel stronger for the journey.'

'That will be good; I'm looking forward to the visit already.'

'I almost forgot. Clotilde had a telephone call asking for your postal address; he will call again.'

'I'm quite happy for you to tell anyone where I am. Goodbye, my love.'

'Take care, good bye, Manfred.'

# 32

## *University Entrance*

The Zimmermann family's return to the eastern suburb of Mahlow was something of an anti-climax. The new apartment that Maximillian had found was in a sturdily built block with four bedrooms that had withstood the bombing which had flattened all the surrounding buildings. On opening the front door they were struck by the extreme cold, although it was the middle of March 1946; midwinter seemed to have lingered in the unheated rooms.

Kurt shivered and kept his coat on. 'It's really freezing in here; have you any coal sacks, Father?'

'I had to have some made at the factory in Thüringen and I brought two of them home with me; you will find them behind that awful old stove.'

Kurt retrieved them. 'Can you start a little fire with wood while I fetch some coal?'

'We'll do our best.' Marlena gazed at her brother. 'Do be careful!'

The young man slipped out of the substantial front door into the night. Everybody's attention turned away from the exit towards the ancient heating appliance; no one noticed the second opening and quiet closing of the same door.

'Will he be all right, Maximillian?' Mitzi asked.

'He has had a lot of experience of survival in his young life; I was amazed how much he has matured.'

The young man meanwhile went to the side of a locomotive

in the railway siding. The boiler had a small amount coal in it on a slow burn, producing a thin wisp of steam out of the funnel. The tender coupled behind, however, was piled high with coal. Kurt silently climbed up on to the top, filled his two sacks with coal and slipped quietly down onto the track. 'Halt!' Kurt didn't understand the language but he was in no doubt about the meaning especially when a torch shone on his face. After his eyes recovered from the sudden bright light he saw the rifle pointing at his head; he put down the two sacks and started to raise his hands.

Suddenly there was another figure. 'Do you like vodka, comrade?' the soft female voice speaking Russian took Kurt by surprise. It was Romhilde! She continued unabashed. 'Have a little swig from this bottle and then you can carry one of these sacks to the gates of the Mahlow railway siding.'

'Yes, madam!' The Russian soldier picked up one of the sacks full of coal.

'This will be your reward!' She pulled a bottle of schnapps out of her other pocket.

Grandmother and grandson were well clear of the railway siding with two canvas sacks bulging with coal before anything was said. 'You were simply amazing, Grandmamma; I never heard you come up behind the Russian guard.'

'If I hadn't followed you here I think that you would be on the next train to Siberia.' She let Kurt take both the sacks, which his farm-strengthened arms easily managed. 'I think we'll keep quiet about our little encounter otherwise the whole family will always be worrying when either of us goes out.'

That was how the matter was left.

Kurt was anxious to get back into education and at the time of his conscription to the Volkssturm he had managed to get well ahead in his studies at his school; as 1946 proceeded he looked forward to the school reopening and met some of his former colleagues and teachers in the streets. In their discussions they reported to one another changes that they could see for themselves in East Berlin: the Russian military were less conspicuous and emerging in its place was a communist civilian and police authority which was German.

Meanwhile Maximillian was combining his work in the branch factory in Thüringen with improving his new home. He had no influence in this part of Berlin; in fact his entrepreneurial spirit was looked on with suspicion by the authorities. That first post-war year was a struggle for the whole of Europe with widespread shortages, devastated cities, and food and fuel rationing; a huge shadow of political uncertainty loomed over the continent from the east.

However, Kurt returned to school early in the following year and his performance received both encouragement and praise. In early June 1947 an official from the local communist council, Herr Fritz Fuchs, marched into the headmaster's office without previously knocking. 'I wish to make a speech to the class in this school that is preparing pupils for admission to the University of Berlin.' There were no courtesies such as 'good afternoon' or 'I'm your local council official'. The class into which Kurt had settled so well was duly assembled in the temporary school hall that had been hastily built during the preceding year using prefabricated materials. Herr Fritz Fuchs was introduced to the boys and the headmaster, Herr Walter Weber, sat down, crossed his legs and looked apprehensively at the visitor.

'Comrades, I'm here to tell you about the new world order and how it applies to you.' The young men looked from one to another with puzzled expressions on their faces. 'After centuries of toil for little or no reward the workers in the factories and farm labourers will finally be properly recognized.' He was a middle-aged fat man with greying hair combed straight back, wearing a grey woollen suit and a loosely knotted dull-red tie on a light-blue shirt. His last statement did nothing to change the look of bewilderment on the boys' faces.

'You disappoint me, boys. I had expected the whole class to rise to its feet cheering and throwing your books into the air and embracing everyone in sight.'

'Books are the art of literature and the foundation of education. No one but absolutely no one should throw books in the air!' The remark was greeted with silence by the mature pupils but if anyone had looked closely they would have seen a glimmer of a smile on Herr Weber's lips

'Who said that?' The words were delivered in almost a high-pitched scream. Kurt stood up.

'I did, Herr Fuchs.'

'Who are you to raise a voice against the state?'

'Kurt Zimmermann, Herr Fuchs.'

'Are you any relation to the Zimmermann battery factory?'

'I'm not related to the building but my father did found the company that built the factory that has manufactured dry batteries since 1919 and provided gainful employment for more than one hundred and fifty people. My father has always cared for the welfare of his staff and my family is very proud of him.'

'That is just the sort of bourgeois nonsense that I'm here to ensure doesn't find its way into the University of Berlin.' He glowered at Kurt. 'I shall personally make certain that you're excluded from even setting foot on the pavement outside the walls of the new university.'

Headmaster Weber stood up from his chair. 'Herr Fuchs, I must protest; Kurt Zimmermann is one of our most outstanding students and I'm absolutely certain that he will gain university entrance.'

'Sit down, Comrade Weber; there's nothing safe about your job either.' Fuchs sneered at the sensitive headmaster. 'I shall be making a report about you as well.' The humiliation of Walter Weber in front of his pupils and the labelling of at least one of the boys as bourgeois seemed a very good day's work to Fritz Fuchs.

The officious fat man turned his back on the headmaster and sauntered past the assembled boys. He came to a halt in front of Kurt; there was recognition in the young man's eyes. It took him back through the years to the railway train journey with Marlena and Romhilde to Usedom Island in 1935. Kurt said one word, 'Brownshirt!', and fat Fritz Fuchs scurried out of the assembly hall.

Unfortunately a directive was issued, later that year, to the University of Berlin academic authorities insisting that they admit only the children of farmers and industrial workers but not the children of capitalists. Accompanying the directive was a list of the wicked business owners who oppressed the workers; it was detailed and lengthy and included Maximillian Zimmermann. Kurt was barred from University!

He nonetheless continued his studies at school and took a philosophical view of the affair. 'Well, Mother I am where I am – a lot can happen in Berlin in a year.'

'You sound just like your father.' Mitzi admired her son's resilience in the face of adversity. 'I have absolute faith that you will be in university education next year wherever that may be.'

Kurt, reassured by his mother, continued his studies but also took a keen interest in events occurring around him. As 1948 dawned he saw Berlin as an island in Soviet-occupied East Germany with its American, British and French sectors in addition to the Russian sector. He observed that the three western sectors were supplied with provisions brought in by road and rail from West Germany. He also noted that in this period of shortages and rationing the inflated Reichsmark was becoming corrupted in a black market which seemed to be being made worse by what were called 'price controls'.

At last Maximillian arranged for the family to move into an apartment that he had bought from one of his ex-employees. A good sale arrangement had been agreed and the Zimmermann family moved in at the end of January. One day, soon after they had settled in, his father came home from work with a broad smile on his face. 'I've good news for you. I met our old friend Jack Thornberry today – you remember, the attaché at the American Embassy – and I told him about our university difficulties.'

'I don't suppose that he can help.'

'No not *him* but the United States together with their British and French allies.'

Kurt's eyes lit up. 'Tell me more, Father.'

'Well, Jack is now first secretary at the reopened American Embassy and he told me there were horror stories coming out of the Humboldt University in the Soviet Sector involving students and scholars being persecuted; in some cases it had ended in murder.'

'In a university?' Kurt was astonished. 'That's outrageous.'

'The Allies are particularly concerned that the new Germany should not be born out of violence and that academic excellence should not have political interference; they are therefore supporting the establishment of a "Freie Universität Berlin" which is free of political interference; the campus is already being built in the south-western suburb of Dahlem. He suggests that you apply for the semester beginning in October.'

Kurt did indeed successfully apply for a place to read law at the exciting new university but clouds were gathering on the horizon.

# 33

## *Manfred Comes Home*

The letter had two rectangular postage stamps affixed to it: one ultramarine and marked twopence halfpenny and the other a threepenny one in violet and depicting peace and reconstruction alongside a portrait of King George the Sixth; they had been franked by a circular date stamp of Nottingham for June 11th, 1946. Handwritten on the top left of the envelope was 'First Day of Issue' and it was addressed to: 'Herr Manfred Schultz, Formerly Languages Teacher, Fichte Gymnasium, Berlin.' This part of the address was neatly underlined and there followed: 'Now thought to be at the Wöllershof Rehabilitation Centre, Near Munich, Germany'; there were additional circular date stamps on the reverse of the envelope indicating that the letter had been through post offices in Berlin and Munich.

At the familiar rustle of Nurse Helen Hofmann's starched white uniform, Manfred glanced up from his newspaper and saw that she was waving a letter in the air with her left hand.

'This letter has travelled a long way to find you, Herr Schultz.'

Manfred took the brown envelope from her. It was the first letter he had received from outside the country since before the war; he took out the thin pale-blue writing paper and saw the handwritten address at the top: 'Nottingham University, England'. His heart skipped a beat:

345

Dear Herr Schultz,

You may not remember me after such a long time but I was the pupil you used to call Günther S. to distinguish me from Günthers P., T. and W.; in 1936 you advised me and the rest of my Jewish family to leave Germany. We took your advice and came to England. Life was difficult but the excellent English you had taught me made things much easier; I passed an entrance exam in English and enjoyed my school and eventually won a scholarship to come to university here in Nottingham.

We initially settled in among the Jewish community in the East End of London. My father joined the fire brigade as a volunteer at night and set up a tailoring business during the day; my mother became a member of the Women's Voluntary Service providing hot soup and blankets to people bombed out of their houses. We survived with lots of hard work and community spirit. It was of course difficult to accept the bombs being dropped on us were from German crews in the airplanes.

Since April last year I've been trying to find out where you are and what has happened to you; and how you and your family are; I owe you a massive debt of gratitude that I can't possibly repay for saving my life and that of my family.

Yours most sincerely,

Günther Schmidt

By the time Manfred had finished reading the letter tears were streaming down both cheeks. He reread the moving words, laid the letter on the table beside him and quietly said to himself, 'Then my living has not been in vain.' He felt an urgent need to telephone Suzanne. He had worked so hard to walk with crutches since his wound had been

346

pronounced healed in April and the letter raised his spirits to such an extent that his progress to the telephone was completely painless.

'Suzanne, I'm nearly ready to come home.'

'I'm so very pleased, my darling. Clotilde and I are coming down to see you next week. We'll be able to check on your progress; you sound so very much better.'

'I'm looking forward to seeing you. I've been in this place for over a year now and am getting to know every knot in the floorboards; will Margit come with you?'

'She is our main breadwinner at the moment, doing translation work for the Americans; she is worried about losing her job if she stays away for even a day.'

'I quite understand but please come as soon as you can.'

'We will, my darling, Goodbye.'

'Goodbye, I hope to see you soon.'

Two weeks later Suzanne and Clotilde arrived at the rehabilitation centre. They were greeted by the ever-present Nurse Captain June Cash, who took them to a wonderfully improved Manfred. His wife was shocked by his grey hair and loss of weight; there was a tearful embrace and Suzanne was the first to speak.

'You look so much better than I had imagined after Clotilde's report on her visit last year.'

'You really have greatly improved, Father.' She kissed him on both cheeks. 'I'm sure that your walking will progress by leaps and bounds now that your wound has healed.' She had some doubts after seeing him struggle to his feet to embrace her mother.

He had now collapsed back into his armchair. 'Leaps and bounds I think I can manage but I plan to give the next Olympic Games a miss. I seem to get a twinge of pain up here from time to time...' He pointed to the region well above his hip joint in the region of his left kidney. 'I expect it will go away as my hip joint heals; they have put me on a four-hourly temperature chart just to be certain.'

'I'm sure you're correct, Father; Nurse June Cash is going to give us an update on your progress.' She perched herself on the arm of his chair and put a reassuring arm around his shoulders. 'Next year I take my high school examinations and I hope that will ensure my entrance to university.'

Suzanne felt she had to intervene. 'We're hearing disturbing reports about the Humboldt Berlin University in the Soviet sector of the city.' She lowered her voice. 'I'm not altogether happy that the university specializing in the education of the children of farmers and industrial workers is taking academic achievement properly into consideration.'

'I'm sure all will be well when I get there, Mother.'

Manfred was puzzled. 'I've never known German higher education to be subject to political considerations; I'm sure it will all turn out for the best.' He clearly wanted to change to another subject. 'I must show you my letter from Günther S.'

'Oh yes please!' Suzanne knew instinctively that it was important to keep his spirits raised. 'I have been looking forward to seeing that letter for a long time.'

He handed her the letter which by now was in a very delicate state having been reread by him so very many times and refolded along the original creases. She studied the interesting postage stamps which were quite different from the former Nazi stamps which had either depicted military might or the Führer. The light-blue paper was carefully unfolded and Suzanne read the letter in absolute silence; she turned it over to read the other side and her shoulders shook as she silently sobbed and tears of pride cascaded down her cheeks.

'My darling, I'm so very proud of you.' She leaned over and embraced Manfred where he sat; at the same time she handed the flimsy piece of paper to Clotilde who started to read as well as feeling deeply for her mother and father.

'I share Mother's pride in what you did for that young man and his family; it was a very brave of you to speak up; perhaps it was that which drew the Gestapo's attention to you and which eventually led to your early conscription.'

Manfred was still in his wife's arms. 'I've thought about the sequence of events so many times now but I don't think we'll ever know what really happened.'

A young orderly in military uniform approached the group. 'Frau Schultz, Captain June Cash wondered if you could come and talk to her; she thought it would be appropriate if your daughter stayed with your husband since she has already had his injuries and X-rays explained to her.'

'Of course!' Suzanne followed her escort out of the room and shortly found herself sitting in a small office on the opposite side of a desk looking at the Chief Nurse of the Wöllershof Rehabilitation Centre; there was a brief smile from Captain Cash and then her face assumed a more serious expression.

'I expect your lovely daughter Clotilde has told you of the serious injury that your husband suffered when he was shot in the left hip. It's been a long process and I'm afraid there's still a long way to go.'

'How long will this take?'

'It could take another year.'

'Another year! It will seem like a lifetime to him, Captain.' Suzanne was horrified. 'He just won't survive that long, I mean psychologically. He's ... he's a different man from the one who went off to war.'

'It will be a bitter blow and we have to soften it, First of all, I understand that you live in an apartment with no elevator, so we have to get him fit enough to tackle climbing the stairs...'

349

For a few minutes they discussed the practicalities that would best aid Manfred's recovery. When they returned to the ward, Manfred was in animated conversation with Clotilde and looked very happy. Gradually, they brought the subject around to getting Manfred fit enough to climb the stairs to the apartment. Manfred took the disappointment very well – at least now he had a finite objective. Suzanne and Clotilde could not stop a tearful departure.

In June 1947 Clotilde telephoned her father with the news that she had passed her high school examinations and had won a place in the new Freie Universität being built in Dahlem. She had been accepted to study English and French philology, just as Manfred had done before her at Breslau University. Her father gave her equally good news: he was coming home.

# 34

## *The German Economic Miracle –*
## *The* Wirtschaftswunder

Ludwig Erhard, the Economics Minister of the American-occupied province of Bavaria, made a much publicized broadcast on June 18th, 1947. Kurt and Maximillian sat in their new living room with their heads close to the radio; Marlena and Mitzi were listening at a rather greater distance.

'People of Germany, the rebuilding of our country has almost come to a halt and I am therefore taking measures to stimulate our recovery and growth. I am bringing in the following measures with immediate effect. Firstly I am withdrawing all the inflation-corrupted Reichsmarks and they will be replaced by a small number of Deutschmarks; in the first instance forty will be issued to each person...'

'What does that mean, Father?' Kurt was following what was said but wasn't sure of the implications.

'It means that the money supply is being cut by 90 percent.'

'Father, people are already short of food and money; won't it make things worse?' Marlena's anxiety was apparent. 'Everyone will suffer.'

'I think we should hear him out.' Maximillian felt sure there was more to come.

'... All price controls are of this moment revoked,' the calm measured tones continued. 'Personal tax will be

351

reduced from 85 percent to 18 percent.' The listeners all smiled – this everybody understood. 'Rationing will be discontinued and honest governance will be restored.'

Maximillian frowned. 'I believe this is good economics for the zones in the West but the Russians won't like it and we may be in difficulty here in Berlin.'

By Monday the streets of Western-occupied Germany sprang to life as the shelves in the shops filled with produce; the spirit of the country seemed to have changed overnight. The Soviet response, however, was swift and much more severe than Maximillian had predicted. The Ostmark was announced as the currency for the Russian-controlled East Germany together with East Berlin. In addition Russian guards stopped all rail and road transport to the American, British and French sectors of Berlin and on June 25th all water, electricity and food supplies were cut off from the three allied sectors of the city. Constant radio and loudspeaker propaganda bombarded the ears of the people of East Berlin.

The Western Allies responded with the famous 'Berlin Airlift' in which the RAF and USAF brought in to Tempelhof Airport the essential supplies for their respective sectors of the city, transporting thirteen thousand tons daily. By May 1949 the humiliated Soviets lifted the blockade, having failed to take control of Berlin, but brought down the 'Iron Curtain' – the political and economic barrier – that extended from Stettin on the Baltic to Trieste on the Adriatic in the south. The new West Germany prospered; stagnation reigned in the new East Germany.

It was against this background that Kurt started the third semester at the Faculty of Law at the new Freie Universität in Dahlem in October 1948.

In the same semester but in another faculty of the university, Clotilde Schultz took her place in the Department of English and French Philology. Her heart was full of joy as she joined the other students in the registration queue and without realizing it she began humming Johann Strauss's 'Radetzky March'

The young woman in front of her turned around and smiled. 'You seem very happy today.'

'I am indeed. I've been so very much looking forward to this day; I think that this university course will be great.'

She smiled back at her new acquaintance. 'My name is Clotilde Schultz. My father studied the same subjects at Breslau University before becoming a teacher at a boys' school here in Berlin. I'm particularly happy because fourteen months ago we brought him home after he was seriously injured in France but he is much better now.'

'That *is* good! I'm very pleased.' The friendly girl in a navy-blue flannel skirt with a light–blue cardigan looked more closely at her new friend; 'I know you from primary school, don't I?'

Recognition dawned on Clotilde. 'You're Lilli Hahn! Fräulein Müller was always scolding you for being naughty.'

'Right first time.' The two young women who had shared a primary schoolteacher embraced. 'I presume we're going to be university colleagues as well.'

'That is truly wonderful!' Clotilde was excited. 'Do you know what happened to my friend Eloise Hoffmann?'

'I'm afraid I heard she and all her family were killed in the November 1943 bombings here in Berlin.' Lilli saw Clotilde's horrified expression. 'You didn't know?'

'No we were sent off to Breslau to stay with my grandparents at that time.'

'I'm so very sorry ... There were so many killed by the bombs from the air raids, and after that came the shelling from the Russian guns...'

'Please stop, Lilli; I can't bear it!'

'You're quite right, Clotilde; we must now think of the future. That's why we're here.'

353

'I think we're nearly at the front of the queue. Oh I know this is the course for me!'

Clotilde plunged headlong into the works of Shakespeare and Dickens, Rousseau and Molière, feeling fulfilled by the new world opening up to her at university.

Elsewhere in the institution, the Faculty of Law had a less well-settled student, Kurt didn't find the lectures, course books, discussions with his fellow students and the lack of precise measurement in legal matters to his liking; it was only natural for him to speak to his father.

'I understand your reservations about studying law. As you know I'm not the sort of person who makes instant decisions without having a backup plan based on experience and research.'

Maximillian sat down in an armchair, crossed his legs and indicated with his right hand for Kurt to sit opposite him in the sitting room.

'My only experience of the law is the first semester at university.' Kurt was despondent.

'I think that is a very good start; you will gain more by completing the first year and during that time you can research what different course you think would better suit your temperament and interest.'

Kurt's father spoke with the authority of a businessman who had adapted to circumstances without compromising his principles, a luxury indeed in the chaos that had enveloped Europe for most of his working life.

'It's the research that bothers me, Father. I find it difficult enough to keep up with law lecture notes, let alone opening up another set of studies.' Despondence was creeping back into his tone. '... And I can't see that I will have the time.'

Maximillian laughed. 'I'm not suggesting that you work twice as hard as your fellow students; that would leave no time to breathe let alone enjoy university life.' Kurt's father uncrossed and then recrossed his legs. 'I would have loved to be in your position; you've the remainder of the academic year to talk to your fellow students in the cafés and bars of the campus – that's where you do your research.'

'Father, I had never looked at things from that point of view and I'm grateful for you giving me a different perspective. Thank you!' He shook his father's hand.

Maximillian drew in a deep breath. 'There's one more thing I would like to say to you. Berlin is still a dangerous place to be and I feel you will have a much more secure future at the New Free University in Dahlem in the American Sector of the city, especially as you were refused a place at Humboldt Universitat.'

At the end of the academic year in June 1949 Kurt applied to the university authorities to change his studies from Law to Economics at the Freie Universität of Berlin.

# 35

## *Tristan and Isolde*

Clotilde, meanwhile, continued to thrive in the English and French Philology Department and loved every aspect of her University course. As the year 1950 began she saw a notice placed on the main campus noticeboard giving details of a skiing trip that was being arranged for March 4th – the twenty people who signed their names were to meet under this board no later than six o'clock on the evening of March 3rd to finalize arrangements. Shortly after she had signed her name and written down the details she set off home.

A little after, Kurt arrived and signed up his name followed by that of Marlena. The feline Fräulein Müller was in her basket in the corner of Clotilde's bedroom underneath the window. Through her half-closed eyes her attention was drawn to a piece of yellowish paper protruding from between the two layers of the well-worn cushion in her basket; the curious cat dragged out the trophy and set off at the pace of the elderly lady which she had now become to find Suzanne and Manfred.

'Hello, Fräulein Müller. What do you have there?'

Suzanne bent down to stroke her. The much-loved cat dropped what was, in fact, vellum parchment at Frau Schultz's feet; she picked it up and glanced at the beautiful embossed gold. Her other hand flew to her mouth.

'Oh my God, the Nobel Peace Prize from Rügen Island.'

She took the impressive document to the sitting room where her husband sat in an armchair with his walking stick resting between his knees. She brought it over to him.

'What do you think we should do with this?'

'It's a Nobel peace prize certificate in amazingly good condition. We must return it to the owner, who I fear may be dead, or failing that to his family.'

Although he now required a strong walking stick to support his left hip. Manfred was preparing to return to teaching at the beginning of the academic year. He glanced down at the fine parchment he was still holding in his left hand and heard the front door of the apartment closing announcing Clotilde's return home from university. Fräulein Müller always knew that it was Clotilde before she even heard her voice. Within moments she was nestling against her legs and purring loudly.

'Father, I've made an exciting decision at the campus today.' Her enthusiasm tailed off a little when she saw what her father was holding in his hand. 'Oh dear, the certificate of the Nobel laureate.'

'Fräulein Müller brought it to us. Of course we'll now try and return it to the family but I'm amazed that it's in such fine condition; not a sign of dirt or a tear. Someone has looked after it very well.'

'Mother did ask that it should be put in a place where no one could find it.' Clotilde smiled and give her father a kiss on the cheek. 'Fräulein Müller has been looking after it in her basket.'

'Didn't you think that we should give it back to its owner?'

'Well it wasn't coming to any harm and not causing any trouble.'

'Perhaps your beloved lady pussycat has made a decision for us.' Manfred paused for a moment. 'And on the same day as you've come to another important decision.' He took her hand. 'What has been happening in your university world today?'

Suzanne and Margit came into the room. Clotilde's elder sister spoke for them both. 'We could not avoid overhearing your conversation.'

The language student turned and smiled at the rest of her family. 'I've put my name down for a skiing trip at the beginning of March. I was going to add yours Margit but I felt that I should ask you first.'

'Sweet as ever, Clotilde! I should love to come skiing with you; I will certainly come and see you off on your journey but I've promised Mother and Father to keep up my translation work with the Americans until Father returns to teaching in October.'

Meanwhile in the Zimmerman household Kurt sat down with Maximillian, Marlena and Romhilde for their evening meal.

'That is a delicious smell coming out of the kitchen, Mother,' said Marlena. The daughter of the house had managed her diabetes brilliantly throughout the hazards, food shortages and lack of medical care during the war years; she was now a beautiful young woman of whom her parents were justly proud.

'I've to thank you, my dear. Your expedition to the shops in the American Sector was a great success. I'm sure that you enjoyed shopping without a ration book.' Mitzi served the steaming hot bratwurst made from finely chopped beef.

'I've signed up for me and Marlena to go on a skiing trip at the beginning of March,' Kurt said. He was now a happy confident student studying economics and he felt that he was in the department that best suited his temperament and abilities.

'How wonderful! Thank you for thinking of me.'

'Where will you go for the snow and the slopes, Kurt?' Maximillian was genuinely interested; it reminded him of his younger days when he had a passion for athletics and gymnastics.

'We haven't been given the details yet but I think we shall be travelling by bus to the Alps on the border with Austria.'

'That will be a long tiring bus ride.' Mitzi looked over at Marlena. 'Do you think you will be all right, my dear?'

'Of course I will, Mother. I can't wait for March.'

'I hope you're both going to take up the sport.' Their father smiled at his son and daughter. 'I will buy you some skis tomorrow.'

'How wonderful!' Marlena noticed the huge wink that came from Romhilde and felt certain that she would play a part in the purchase. 'Thank you, Father, and thank *you*, Grandmamma.'

'We expect a full report when you return. Take care while you're away; both of you are Germany's future.' Romhilde spoke with matriarchal authority.

On the afternoon of March 3rd, 1950, students began to assemble in front of the main announcement board of the Freie Universität Berlin. Among the first to arrive was the very attractive twenty-one-year-old Clotilde Schultz with a fair complexion and her long light-brown hair neatly plaited and tied with bright red ribbons. Gradually the other members of the party arrived including an earnest-looking young lady with long dark hair parted at one side, wearing a dark-green woollen cardigan and brown corduroy trousers.

'I'm Greta Khunsberg and I'm the leader and organizer of this group.' She produced a clipboard from a battered sheet-music case that she then tucked underneath her arm. 'I will first of all check your names, then it will be time for questions.'

The group of excited skiers drew closer to their leader. At precisely six o'clock a very elegant young man joined them; he wore reddish-brown flannel trousers and a tweed jacket with a salt-and-pepper pattern, had wavy fair hair and was smoking a pipe that he appeared to have omitted to light but it still gave a wonderful intellectual gravitas to his persona.

Clotilde took in all this at a glance. 'He's mine!' she said under her breath.

It was a group of twenty including Greta that were finally registered and paid up for the trip. 'Now I urge you to get home and have an early night because we're being picked up by the bus with its trailer outside the Berlin Zoo at six o'clock tomorrow morning.'

'What is the name of the ski resort where we shall be staying?' A tall slim dark-haired young man, wearing an old army greatcoat with all the military insignia removed. 'My name is Klaus Schweitzer by the way.' He seemed to Clotilde to be rather sad for someone about to go on holiday.

'We're driving to the Alpine resort of Balderschwang; it's in the Oberstaufen region on the border with Austria.' Greta opened up a map and pointed it out.

'I'm sorry to leave it so late but will skis be available?' Clotilde asked. She was very uncertain about this new world that she was entering.

'Absolutely no problem at all; most people are hiring them. The ski instructors are very reliable and will ensure that you get a good-fitting pair.' She turned to leave. 'I will see you all in the morning outside the Zoo.'

Clotilde followed her out and saw no sign of that lovely young man.

The following day Margit went with Clotilde to the Zoo. Clotilde was wearing a thick red home-knitted sweater and a rucksack on her back but still shivered a little in the early-morning cold. The bus had already arrived and some of her fellow students were on board; Greta saw her from the door of the bus and beckoned her to join them.

Clotilde gave her sister a hug and a kiss, followed by a 'thank you'.

Inside the bus Klaus Schweitzer came and sat beside Clotilde. The student of English and French Philology turned to the window and gave a final wave to Margit as she walked towards the S-Bahn station. She anxiously consulted her watch; at two minutes before six o'clock Kurt strode confidently towards the bus carrying skis; he was followed onto the bus by two other young women. Her heart skipped a beat.

'Just in time!' Greta smiled, shutting the door behind them. She gave the driver a tap on the shoulder for the vehicle to start its long journey.

Clotilde eagerly leaned forward to hear what the fair wavy-haired young man was saying to the group leader; the noise of the engine made hearing what was said extremely difficult.

'This is my sister Marlena' was easy to hear but what followed was drowned out by the motor; she could see the family likeness with the sister but the other young woman she thought looked different ... ugly! They took their seats on the opposite side of the bus a little further back from Clotilde and she was disappointed to see Marlena's brother sit next to the ugly one behind his sister.

He leaned forward. 'Are you all right, Marlena?'

'Yes thank you, Kurt.' She turned and gave her brother a reassuring grin. 'I'm going to have five lumps of sugar for breakfast.'

At least Clotilde knew his name now. She let it roll off her tongue and liked the experience: 'Good morning, Kurt ... I hope you slept well, Kurt ... Yes I would be very pleased to accompany you to the university ball, Kurt.' She could not resist murmuring these phrases and trusted the engine noise of the bus prevented her from being heard. She was forced to stop her excursions into fantasy when the bus came to a halt in Potsdam to pick up two other members of the ski party. They took their places in the trailer.

'This is our last stop before we have a break at the Helmstedt crossing point from the Russian Zone into the British Zone in about three hours.' Greta looked around the passengers. 'Are there any questions before I ask the driver to get us on our way?'

Kurt's sister Marlena put her hand in the air. 'May I have a private word with you?'

'Of course!' Greta stepped off the bus.

'How can I help you, Marlena?' They quickly and quietly discussed insulin injections and the need for privacy. 'No problem! How many injections will you need during the journey?'

'I think it will only be once and that should be in about twenty hours.'

'That will be fine. If we're really in difficulty finding a suitable stopping point you can come down to the front of the bus with me; we'll have curtains on three sides and I will stand between you and the driver, which will give you complete privacy.'

'Thank you so much, Greta.' A much happier Marlena returned to her seat, gave a cheerful nod in Kurt's direction and took her seat.

Greta shut the door and the bus moved off along the still-darkened road west through Potsdam before heading towards the crossing point, notorious for its lengthy delays while passports were collected, checked, stamped and returned. Most of the passengers were catching up with their disturbed night's sleep.

Clotilde stole a backward glance at Kurt and was pleased to see the ugly one resting her head against the window with her mouth open but her eyes closed. However, Kurt was awake and looking in her direction. He gave up the struggle to keep his eyes open, joining the others in their slumbers, and didn't notice Clotilde blushing a little before she finally rested her head against the backrest of her seat and happily dozed off.

It was daylight when most of the ski party opened their eyes to find that they were coming to a halt beside a single-storey wooden building with a platform separating it from the bus. Pacing alongside and peering in through its windows were Russian soldiers wearing grey–green long woollen coats, fur hats with a red star on the front and holding the leash of German shepherd dogs with one hand and an automatic rifle slung over the opposite shoulder; some of them were women.

Clotilde's neighbour Klaus turned to her. 'I hope you've had a refreshing sleep?'

The young man sounded genuinely concerned for her welfare. She felt that she could not let the attraction that she had for Kurt cause her to be rude to this courteous young man. 'I did, thank you!' Clotilde found it difficult to take her eyes off the Russians on the other side of the glass in the bus window.

'Where do you live?' she asked politely.

'In Dahlem with my aunt. My parents were killed in the '43 air raids.' He grimaced. 'I survived but had nowhere to go. My aunt took me in and has been wonderful ever since then.'

A burly Russian soldier clambered onto the vehicle and Greta spoke to him and then addressed the passengers. 'Everybody has to hand over their passports to this military man; he will take them into that building and return them when they have been examined for stamping.' The Russian said some more to Greta. 'I've to tell you all that no one should try to leave the bus until it's passed into the British Zone.' There were murmurs of disapproval but no one was openly hostile.

The Russian left the bus carrying the pile of documents. 'Please don't be alarmed; the passports will be returned, although we'll have to wait a few minutes.'

'I hope they don't get lost. It was such a complicated process getting mine from the authorities in the first place. I dread what it will be like if it gets mislaid.' Marlena's forehead was creased by a frown and most of her companions' eyes were focused on the shed-like structure outside.

Twenty minutes later a woman Russian soldier emerged from the building holding some of the documents but clearly a few had been left behind. She handed them to the party's leader and left without uttering a word. Greta distributed the passports that had been returned to their owners and then put her right forefinger up to her lips. The quiet in the vehicle began to feel oppressive. The door of the building opened to allow an elderly man carrying a bucket and broom to come out; there was a collective sigh in the bus as the door was closed behind him but almost immediately it opened again and the original soldier came out carrying the remainder of the passports which he handed into Greta, who had opened the door, and then he waved the driver to carry on.

'I apologize for the delay and the charade. There was never anything wrong with your documentation; nevertheless they persist in playing these mind games. If we had protested the bus would have been emptied and searched together with all the passengers.' She shrugged her shoulders. 'It's happened many times ... Now we're about to enter the British zone.'

They barely slowed as the barrier was raised by a red-capped military policeman and they drove on one hundred metres to a wood-and-glass canteen where the driver stopped the vehicle.

Greta stood up again. 'You can buy snacks here and there are toilet facilities.'

The ski party took advantage of the border café and half an hour later the bus set off north-west towards Hannover. Klaus was more cheerful after the crossing.

'Reconstruction is proceeding at a much faster pace in this zone; the road is good and we're making progress now.'

Clotilde, who was having another little excursion into fantasyland with Kurt, came back to reality. 'Oh I think you're quite right; we'll be passing Hannover soon – we might catch a glimpse of the new Deutsche Industrie-Messe – the German Industrial Fair – on the edge of the city.'

Two hours later the bus changed direction, turning south-west, and after a further fifty kilometres they came across a bend to the left in the road and a variety of vehicles drawn to a halt on the right-hand side. There were lorries, vans, buses and a few cars being escorted by British soldiers towards the River Weser, which could be seen in the distance.

The bus slowed, then stopped and Greta opened the front door and spoke to one of the escorts. 'I'm afraid we shall all have to get out of the bus to cross the river. The bridge that was blown up at the end of the war has still not been replaced; the temporary pontoon bridge will only allow the bus to cross if it's empty.'

The occupants of the bus followed Greta onto the grass verge. The vehicles in front passed onto the temporary bridge, while their passengers followed on foot. When it came to the turn of the ski party to cross they followed at fifty metres behind the bus but could still feel the bridge moving beneath them. Clotilde didn't like the sensation and spread her arms to aid her balance, From behind her there came a voice:

'You look like a beautiful flower in full bloom.' She didn't dare to turn around for fear of overbalancing into the water but she knew who the owner of the voice was.

'Hello, Kurt.'

'Hello, Clotilde.' He was still behind her. 'I can save you if you lose your balance.'

'How nice … How did you know my name?'

'I looked at Greta's list and then worked it out for myself, Fräulein Schultz.'

By this time the bus had reached the road on the other side of the River Weser. 'I think that when we get back on board I would like to sit next to you please.'

'I already have someone sitting next to me.' Clotilde smiled sweetly at this confident young man.

'That is not a problem, Clotilde. My sister Marlena has already asked him to sit next to her on the other side of the aisle.' He grinned broadly. 'Let's get back on the bus.'

They joined the others, eager to find the seat back on the vehicle and found that Klaus had accepted Marlena's invitation and looked much more cheerful sitting next to her. Kurt introduced himself to Klaus and sat down next to Clotilde and much to his surprise he found himself lost for words. It was the girl whom he had gone to great lengths to get close to who saved the situation.

'What are you studying at university?'

'I started by doing a year studying law but for some reason I wasn't entirely comfortable with the subject and changed to economics and I'm finding it suits me very well. I wonder if I can guess what you're studying, Clotilde?'

'You could not possibly know.' She looked at him and raised her eyebrows. 'Well?'

'I think you're studying English and French philology.'

Clotilde was amazed but didn't let her face betray her surprise. 'Quite right!'

The bus was now making good progress south-west along a resurfaced road.

'Where are we heading for now, Kurt?'

'Frankfurt, though it will be three or four hours before we arrive there.

366

During that time the pair remained deep in quiet conversation. The hours passed quickly for these two young people and in due course the vehicle arrived in the great German city which was rapidly being restored after devastating war damage; all the passengers were relieved to get out and stretch their legs. Half an hour later, refreshed and more comfortable the students returned to their seats; Marlena had remained on board to attend to medical matters together with Greta. Klaus brought them brown bread sandwiches with sauerkraut filling which he handed to the girls on his return. When all the passengers were settled they went on their way again, south through the American Zone towards Stuttgart. There were further delays for river crossings.

At Stuttgart the bus parked near an all-night café but before the students were able to stretch their legs Greta put her hand up to stop them. 'I'm afraid that we're going to have to leave our trailer here in this car park; the roads from here to our destination are too narrow and bendy, so we'll have to make room when you come back for our luggage and skis.' She grinned as the announcement was greeted with good natured comments.

Kurt secretly welcomed the turn of events as it brought him very close to Clotilde. 'I hope you're not feeling crushed?' he enquired.

'Yes but in the nicest possible way.'

It was midday as the vehicle wound its way into the ancient city of Ulm on the left bank of the River Danube in Baden-Württemberg; it had been badly damaged by air raids in 1944 and was now largely rebuilt in a more modern fashion. Only the cathedral seemed to be a reminder of earlier times. The ski party alighted from the bus once again. Clotilde took Kurt's arm and pointed to the cathedral spire. 'That's the tallest spire in the world.'

'I'm impressed!' Kurt was thrilled by her touch. 'I must try and match you.'

'You don't have to.'

'It's male pride.' They both laughed. 'All right then, what can you offer me?'

'Did you know that Albert Einstein, the great physicist, was born here in Ulm?'

Clotilde was amazed. This young economics student was surprising her. 'Now it's my turn to be impressed.' She took his arm. 'Let's join the others for a cup of coffee.'

Everyone squeezed back onto the bus, which then passed through Sontofen just after nightfall in the foothills of the Alps and finally came to a halt in the snow-covered mountains at eleven o'clock in the evening. The party took their skis, rucksacks and other luggage; followed Greta one hundred metres further up the mountain to a large house, and the whole ski party trooped inside.

Greta embraced a fair-haired lady wearing a pale-blue apron over a black wool dress and turned to face the weary group of students. 'Welcome to the ski resort of Balder-schwang and this is the lady of the house, Frau Bertina Schröder.

'I'm pleased to see you all. I'm sure you're very tired after such a long journey; Greta has a list of your room numbers and through there in the dining room is some freshly made hot chocolate.' She pointed through a large open door.

Peaceful refreshing sleep came easily to everyone that night, although Clotilde did spend a little time saying 'thank you' under her breath; the quiet breathing from the opposite side confirmed that she had not disturbed her room-mate.

The following morning after a sumptuous breakfast the enthusiastic students set about their activities on a beautiful sunny day, Kurt assisted Clotilde on that occasion; on subsequent days they were to be seen gliding happily down the slopes together. Many couples teamed up as an item during the holiday. Their colleagues noted this and gave them famous names from history or literature; it wasn't long before Herr Zimmermann and Fräulein Schultz became known as Tristan and Isolde – the Cornish prince and Irish princess whose romance was the basis of Wagner's opera.

The holiday was a wonderful contrast to the conditions that most of the students had experienced over the past decade. It was this thought together with Kurt that occupied the front of Clotilde's mind as she sped down the slope with the wind in her hair and the sun shining on the white, white snow.

# Epilogue

The 1935 Nobel Peace Prize was awarded to the journalist Carl von Ossietzky while he was an inmate in a concentration camp near Oldenburg suffering from severe tuberculosis. He wasn't released to collect the award in Oslo but transferred to a hospital in Berlin-Charlottenburg under Gestapo supervision. He died on the May 4th, 1938. The whereabouts of his Nobel diploma are unknown but a statue of him is to be found in the Pankow, Berlin.

Harald Quandt was the son of Magda Goebbels and her first husband, the industrialist Günther Quandt, who went to live with her after she married the propaganda minister; he did require extra tuition to pass his school examination in 1940 which enabled him to train as a pilot in the Luftwaffe. He was captured in Italy in 1944, becoming a prisoner of war and released in 1947. He was therefore not present in the bunker when his stepbrother and sisters were murdered by their parents, who then committed suicide. He subsequently took over his father's engineering company and died in an air crash in Italy in 1967.

General Kurt Meyer was captured in Normandy in 1944 after distinguished war service marred by his sanctioning of the shooting of Canadian prisoners of war. He was tried for war crimes and served nine years in prison; he died in 1961 after prolonged ill health partly as a result of his numerous war injuries.

The White Rose movement of University students in Munich was led by the enormously courageous Sophie Scholl, her brother Hans, and Christoph Probst who advocated non-violent resistance to Nazi oppression and tyranny by circulating anonymous leaflets. They were arrested, tried for treason and sentenced to be guillotined on the same day but not before their sixth pamphlet had been smuggled out of Germany and taken to England via Scandinavia. It was then reproduced by the millions and dropped all over Germany by the RAF. A black granite memorial to those students, their colleagues and an inspirational professor can be seen in the Hofgarten in Munich.

The notorious, ranting, sadistic judge Roland Freisler who had dealt out the summary justice to the White Rose students was killed during a massive bombing raid by the USAF on Berlin while he was in the People's Court on February 3rd, 1945.

Berlin hospital records show that between 93,000 and 130,000 women of all ages were raped during the Russian occupation of the city; the real figure was probably greater. There has been a great deal of speculation about the motivations behind this terrible phenomenon, but they were probably complex. The German military resistance at Breslau was fierce and there were heavy casualties: 170,000 civilians, 7,000 Russian troops and 6,000 German soldiers were killed before the city capitulated to the Soviets on May 6th, 1945. Stalin then moved the German–Polish border 150 kilometres to the west and the city became the Polish Wrocław.

William Joyce, alias Lord Haw Haw, was hanged as a traitor in Wandsworth Prison in London on January 3rd, 1946; Dr Reginald Glanvill who anaesthetized Joyce for removal of a bullet from his buttock returned to general practice in Putney in south-west London. In 1949 the first

371

post-war twenty-four-hour motor car race took place in Le Mans, France; it was won by Selsdon and Chinetti in a Ferrari.

In 1951 Clotilde spent three months at Nottingham University on an exchange visit, and during that time Günther S., who had been helped to leave Germany by her father in 1936, came to see her and gave her £3, which was a substantial help and she felt as though she was in heaven.

The final group of German prisoners of war returned from Russia in 1956; countless thousands didn't come back and the fate of many them remains unknown. In 1957 Manfred's non-functional troublesome left kidney was removed and he lived until the age of ninety-three.

In due course Kurt and Clotilde were married. Their first child, a daughter, was born in the Gertrauden Kranken-haus: this was the same hospital in which Clotilde's mother, Suzanne, underwent her operation that had cost one bottle of Benedictine liqueur.

In the course of his banking career Kurt had occasion to visit the Bank Deutscher Länder which he had first seen from the balcony of the American Embassy on the opposite side of the Pariser Platz as he stood beside his father during the State visit of Mussolini in September 1937.